Steppes
to the
Cross

Steppes
to the
Cross

Donna M. Young

Published by Donna M. Young
P O Box 76, Lawton, IA 51030
dmywriting@wiatel.net

Author photo by Elizabeth Rose Kahl

Book Cover and Layout by Christina Hicks Creative
christinahickscreative@gmail.com

Published in the United States of America
ISBN: 978-1-947143-16-6
Fiction / Christian General
Fiction / Historical

www.donnamyoungwriting.com

Refer to page 559 for a Glossary of Hebrew and Yiddish Words and Terms throughout the book's text.

PRELUDE

Though the nation of Israel has carried the Biblical moniker of "God's Chosen People", since their inception in Genesis 32:28, through the name given by God to the patriarch Jacob. That God given name has not always been popular with other nations. Much to the contrary. Whether it be from distain for anyone who would have the audacity to call themselves "Chosen". Or, perhaps, sheer envy for all that the Jewish nation has accomplished since their establishment; even in the midst of persecutions unimaginable; we may never know. But we do know that other nations and peoples have attempted to wipe them permanently from the face of earth since their origin.

In Genesis 15:17-21 we see that the land in which Israel abides was a gift from God to Abraham as a covenant for the future of the nation,

"When the sun had gone down and it was dark, behold, a smoking fire pot and a flaming torch passed between these pieces. On that day the Lord made a covenant with Abram,

saying, "To your offspring I give this land, from the river of Egypt to the great river, the river Euphrates, the land of the Kenites, the Kenizzites, the Kadmonites, the Hittites, the Perizzites, the Rephaim, the Amorites, the Canaanites, the Girgashites and the Jebusites."

According to the Bible, Israel's character as the chosen people is unending and unconditional as it says in Deuteronomy 14:2,

> *"For you are a holy people to YHWH your God, and God has chosen you to be his treasured people from all the nations that are on the face of the earth."*

From Egypt's pharaoh, who refused to obey God's commands through Moses to, "Let My People Go"; to Ancient Greece and Rome; Christian and Muslim anti-Semitism in antiquity and the particular hardships of the middle ages; to Catherine the Great of Russia declaring Jews to be less than, and therefore not eligible to be Russian citizens. So much so that she banished an entire people group to the "Pale of Settlement". To those who murdered in Jewish pogroms, and Hitler's Third Reich. It seems there have always been those who would choose to obliterate the Jewish people and believe they were doing a just and enduring service to the rest of the world.

Now, here we are today and it seems anti-Semitism still rears its ugly head.

I believe what those who hate the Jewish nation fail to realize, is that when God told Israel they were chosen, He did not stop there, or with them.

Our creator came to earth through His birth to a young virgin, grew up in human flesh, and then gave His life for us on the cross of Calvary. When He rose from the grave, and overcame death, He gave every single person on earth the same opportunity to be His "chosen". All nations and all peoples, Jew and gentile alike can come to Him, repent of their sin, and believe in Him as Savior. When you do, you will forever be changed. And you will forever be His chosen ones.

Romans 10:9 "Because, if you confess with your mouth that Jesus is Lord and believe in your heart that God raised him from the dead, you will be saved."

"And I will appoint a place for my people Israel and will plant them, so that they may dwell in their own place and be disturbed no more. And violent men will afflict them no more, as formerly, from the time that I appointed judges over my people Israel. And I will give you rest from all your enemies. Moreover, the Lord declares to you that the Lord will make you a house." 2 Samuel 7:10-11

"You will bring them in and plant them on Your own mountain, the place, O Lord, which You have made for Your abode, the sanctuary, O Lord, which Your hands have established. The Lord will reign forever and ever." Exodus 15:17-18

CHAPTER 1

Distant sounds of rumbling thunder caused Batya to burrow more deeply beneath her eiderdown. Extremely dry weather these past weeks made their meager crops; wheat, kasha, sunflower, beets and hay, most desperate for moisture. She was sure rain would please Saba and Papa. So, in spite of her desperate fear of storms, she smiled sleepily under her covers. Farming was certainly far from an easy life in the Pale. Nevertheless it was their life, together, and the only life she'd ever known.

Batya's large family lived in the constant shadow of lack, entirely dependent upon the whims of Mother Nature, but growing up poor had its advantages too. Through hard times and plenty of adversity they'd become a family of fiercely hard workers, not dependent on the hand of any other.

Imaginative traders, and creators of invention due to necessity, they were graced with the humble motivation to do whatever menial task it took to put food on their large table. They ensured by their willing hearts and tireless efforts that they'd always manage to get by somehow.

By combining the magic of Bubbe's vast culinary knowledge and Mama's innate ability to pinch a penny in the kitchen, they never went hungry.

Many tasty and satisfying meals were produced on the ancient, scarred wood stove. Wonderful Blini (buckwheat pancakes), Pierogi (light pillows of potato dough filled with goat cheese and served with sour cream), Knishes (Potato and buckwheat pies), and Boranki, which was Freida's favorite, (sour cream dough cakes with poppy seeds).

Hot soups made with beet and root vegetables of all sorts, lentil, bean and chicken with thick noodles or plump dumplings were also a staple. Dishes that filled the rustic kitchen with mouth watering aromas were the magnificent result of their hours spent laboring over the old, iron pots.

Cucumber pickles, gefilte fish, chopped liver, cheese curds, and Batya's absolute favorite of all, noodle kugel. Drizzled with honey and topped with freshly picked, by her own hands, gooseberries and raspberries rounded out their usual daily fare.

That amazing kitchen, meager in furnishings as it was, would always be the little girl's favorite place in the world. And Bubbe, her very favorite person with which to share her limited free time. That is, once her many daily chores were done.

Rough plank floors aside, the cozy warmth of that place coupled with the smell of scrumptious suppers simmering on the stove and the fragrance of freshly baked rye bread fresh from the oven, was a comfort to her soul. More than that, she learned so much of life in that old kitchen.

Batya never grew tired of watching her grandmother knead dough on the worn butcher block in the center of the room. Her spotted, gnarled and wrinkled hands were amazingly strong. At the mere sound of bread being started, as if she could sense it from any location on the farm, Batya ran to the kitchen, mounted her small, rickety stool and closed her eyes. Taking in the rhythmic thump whack, thump whack, thump whack of dough rolling and hitting the table as yeast was "properly" activated, she smiled.

The year was 1905. At only five years old Batya was

becoming a pretty proficient bread maker herself. Poised on her special seat she patiently waited for an invitation to help.

Baking was one of her favorites. Though the things she learned from Bubbe weren't all about cooking. A wealth of available knowledge simmered beneath the old woman's piercing gaze, just waiting for the proper moment to leap out and inform, or enlighten.

Bubbe's age clouded eyes had seen much in their time on this earth. The old grey head surrounded in dancing wisps of hair, escaped from the confines of the scarf she wore to contain them, held more wisdom than, well, anyone Batya had ever known.

And the twinkle in her eye? Well, that twinkle reminded the young girl that there was joy in even the most menial of tasks. Bubbe had a saying for every situation known to man and she wasn't afraid to use them. One of Batya's favorites was, "It's as appropriate as a pig." Batya never fully understood that one, but it always made her laugh.

Their wide-ranging work load, which lasted each day from before sunrise until long after the men were settled in their chairs at night, was lightened by their special time together. Bubbe, Mama, Freida and herself. And now that she was learning to help, and could officially count herself among 'the women', she was proud as could be to occupy a place in the kitchen. Because, while they labored, they shared so much more than work; laughter, stories, and the kind of love that can only blossom through mutual affection and genuine respect.

Though the men tended the main crops, the women had more to do than simply care for the house and various indoor chores, as if that were not enough. They managed the family's chickens, goats, sheep, honey bees and a very large fruit and vegetable garden. This included preserving and canning everything in sight, as soon as it was deemed ready for harvest by Bubbe's watchful eye. Vegetables, fruits, jams, preserves and even dried meats were put up in the summer and fall, for future use in the hard winter months.

Batya couldn't remember a single time in her life when she'd ever seen either her grandmother's, or her mother's, hands idle. Even in the late evening, as the men relaxed to ready for work the next day, the women were always busy darning socks, knitting, or mending by lamp light.

When the girls traveled into town to sell vegetables,

pulling their small, wooden cart behind them, they also took along homemade cheese curds and butter; honey, complete with the delicate honeycombs nestled inside the sticky golden syrup; and fresh milk for purchase. Since Mama and Bubbe had all they could do to keep their large family fed three times a day, the laundry scrubbed and the house in order, much of the outside work fell to Batya and Freida. So, little Batya followed her older sister like a shadow, copying and learning.

Batya had to admit that while flashes of lightning, and thunder booming loudly over her head, had always scared her right down to the tips of her toes, she didn't dare confess her fear to anyone for the teasing which would ultimately ensue from her slew of intrepid brothers.

She never wanted to appear weak to those strong, daring young men, as she looked up to every one of them with admiration. In her eyes they were extremely brave, chasing off foxes and wolves from the hen house, fishing in the fast moving river, and never crying or complaining when they were sick or injured. However, at only five years old, there were still plenty of things that caused her own young heart to skip a beat.

Lightning and thunder were high on that list, followed closely by falling into the deep, swift river flowing not far from their prairie home, bee stings, bites from the nanny goats during milking, and being pecked by their largest and most vicious hen while in the process of collecting eggs. Her small hands were often swollen and covered in bites and deep bloody marks from these daily tasks. Nevertheless, she would never have thought to complain, as that was just the way of it for a farm girl.

Batya shared an exceptionally small room with her sister, Freida, in the family's ancient clapboard farmhouse. The room, before her birth, was a back porch. This was enclosed five years ago, in order to serve in its present capacity. Containing a hand crafted wooden bed frame, overlaid with a firm plank, a straw tick, and warm, handmade eiderdown, there was barely room in the tiny space to move about in order to dress. A covered basket for clothing occupied one corner of the room and contained their carefully folded and covered Shabbat attire; and, after a weekly wash, their every day work clothes as well.

The only extravagance in their tiny space was an intricately carved antique mirror hanging on a faded, plank wall. Papa traded for it with a bag of beets and another of potatoes only last year, when many in the area were in dire circumstances, as a special Hanukkah gift for his girls. They knew the price was dear and they treasured the thought. Batya could often be seen examining herself in the depths of the hazy old glass, wondering why she was the only member of her family with blue eyes and hair the color of wheat ready for harvest.

Freida, who had also been awakened by the mounting noise of the coming storm, rose to peer out the window in the rear of the small dwelling. As the din of thunder drew nearer; oddly thus far, without a single flash of lightning; she became more confused.

With the small window open a bit, one would expect to see the muslin curtain rustling in a soft summer breeze. But the night was still as death and the window coverings hung motionless.

By then, Batya, who had pulled her covers down just enough to peek out and see what her sister had been up to since she'd climbed out of bed, noticed a faint red glow reflecting off the window's wavy glass pane. She rose to stand by the older girl and reached out to place her small hand in her sister's larger one.

A faint odor began to permeate the air, and it made her nose wrinkle in aversion. Then she recognized the stench. It was the smell of burning. At that moment she saw it. Way out, toward the Shtetl that bordered the eastern edge of her family's farmland, the world seemed to be on fire.

Looking up she watched her sister's face and a reflection of the flickering flames dancing in her ever widening, brown eyes. In only seconds she witnessed an expression of wonder, turn quickly to bewilderment and then to raw terror, as Freida suddenly realized what was taking place.

"Get dressed, Batya, quickly."

"But why, Freida? It's still dark outside."

"Don't argue. Quickly, do as I say. I must wake the others."

Batya didn't argue further. Freida, who was ten years her senior and the oldest sibling, carried almost as much authority in her world as Saba, Bubbe, Papa and Mama. She dressed in a flash and rushed to join her family.

Freida pounded on her parent's bedroom door, and found them already awake, dressed and about to rouse the rest of the children. They needn't have bothered. The escalating ruckus had already woken the rest of the clan. Her brothers; Aleksander, fourteen; Bohdan, thirteen; Borysko, nine; and Fadeyka, seven; were dressed and assembled, ready to follow Papa and Saba outside. "No, Papa, please, not the little ones."

"Mama, we are not the little ones," Borysko pouted, "and we want to help Papa and Saba."

"No, boys, your Mama is right. Stay here and protect the girls. Aleksander and Bohdan, you come with me and Saba."

"I don't need protecting, Mama. I don't."

"Batya, hush now my little ketsele. Let the men handle this."

"But Bubbe."

"You heard me. Now hush I tell you. Listen to your Papa and Mama."

"Yes Bubbe."

The men ventured outside and immediately heard the faint sounds of screaming far off in the distance. Watching as the fire seemed to grow larger by the minute, Saba and Papa began giving orders.

With the men outside; concentrating on moving

their few sheep, goats and chickens to safer ground; the women began gathering a few kitchen staples together in muslin bags, while Batya, framed by the open door, stood transfixed in the red glow of Voronko in flames.

The sound of rumbling came closer, but still there was no lightning and not even the slightest hint of rain.

"Freida take the little ones to the privy."

"Oh Mama, must we?"

"Yes my dear. Go. And, if things get out of hand, you know what you must do. Protect the little ones. They are our future. We love you all."

"Do as your mother says, Freida."

"Yes Papa."

"Now, all of you. Listen to your sister. If anything happens to us, you will do as Freida tells you. Do you understand me?"

"Yes Papa."

Freida led Batya, Borysko and Fadeyka to the privy, where they would wait until danger passed.

Seconds later horsemen emerged headlong from the darkness, into the family's formerly quiet barnyard. Appearing like the hounds of hell; torches held high, crazy, demonic looks of hatred on their faces; they shouted, over and over, "Kill the Jews". Freida suddenly realized it wasn't thunder they'd been hearing all along, but the pounding of horse's hooves on hard dry ground. She felt suddenly cold, empty and very vulnerable, fearing for her parents, grandparents and brothers who were exposed and helpless out in the night. Batya tried to pull away from her sister's iron grasp, but Freida held her tight.

From cracks in the privy door they saw dozens of wild eyed black horses, glowing with greasy sweat, snorting through flared nostrils and pawing the hardened dirt of the yard.

The men they carried; who were breathing hard from the exertion of swinging shashkas; were altogether splattered with the gore of their innocent victims. Their eyes crazed with the unmistakable look of unadulterated blood lust, they resembled the demons Batya had seen in her story books. Batya sunk back into her sister's arms, and began to weep quietly.

The riders, who she would later learn were Terek Cossacks, wore; grey-brown, long, open fronted Cherkesska coats and light blue beshmets (waistcoats), with white gymnasterkas (blouses), now splattered with the blood of many. Grey trousers, tall fleece hats, black boots polished to a shine; and scabbards hanging by each man's side; completed their imposing uniforms.

Saba and Papa stood, feet planted firmly on the hard packed ground of their land, in front of Bubbe and Mama; faces stern; with Aleksander and Bohdan off to one side. The men held pitchforks, the tools of their trade and the closest thing they had to a weapon of any sort.

The soldiers, whose horses were still skittish after the pounding ride, were suddenly slowed to a halt. They seemed amused by the show of strength from these peasant farmers and laughed among themselves.

For a few agonizing moments they teased and toyed with the impudent Jews who had the blatant audacity to stand up to them in their; what must certainly have felt like; justified rage. Poking and prodding them with their blades. After all, these were nothing more than filthy Jews. Filthy Jews who stood in their way at that.

Cossacks surrounded the small group, looking down from their perches atop mighty steeds and began mocking and thrusting their torches closer and closer to the frightened family's faces.

Freida had all she could do to contain her two small brothers at this point, who strained to leap from the privy to fight the Cossacks. And she was forced to put her hand, hard, over Batya's mouth, to keep her from screaming when one of the riders suddenly held his torch to Saba's clothing and set him afire.

They watched helplessly as their grandfather flailed wildly around the barnyard, never making a sound. He finally dropped to the earth, with an audible thud, still burning. Shock sent violent shudders through Batya's tiny body, as the smell of burning hair and flesh seeped in through cracks in the door. She could also feel, through her sister's firm hold, those same brutal jolts of shock attacking Freida. And for a moment, when her sister's grip loosened, she thought her older sister might faint and give them all away.

Bubbe and Mama began to wail, and Papa lunged at his father's attacker with his pitchfork, as the women tried in vain to extinguish the flames consuming their beloved. The two older boys broke ranks and ran, screaming, at the horses. They were cut down in their tracks. First Aleksander, split open from head to midsection, standing in shock, watching his own entrails fall to the ground as he died to the ear piercing shrieks of his mother. Then Bohdan, relieved of his head, to the horrified and helpless wailing of his father.

One soldier, who appeared to be the leader of this blood thirsty group, gave the order to tie Papa to a post. He fought his assailants with all his strength, knowing full well what was likely to be their next vile move. There he remained, shouting and cursing their God, as the Cossacks took turns raping and sodomizing Bubbe and Mama. When they were done, the soldiers thrust the broken and weeping women through with their swords, and, in what appeared to be almost an afterthought, set Papa ablaze.

Freida, holding the three children, was sobbing quietly when she suddenly noticed one of the soldiers walking toward the privy where they hid. She quickly, and quietly, lowered the children down the hole into the mess beneath and then followed without a second's hesitation. The man opened the door, relieved himself unknowingly onto the frightened children beneath, and slammed the door shut. The murderous horde moved on. Riding off in triumphant victory, to whoops and shouts of malevolent joy, to see where else they might seek to destroy innocent lives. But not before setting the family's buildings and fields on fire.

Freida, and the children, stayed put until she was reasonably sure the danger had passed. Once it was safe, she climbed back up through the privy's seat and pulled each of the three younger ones out of the stinking muck.

Numbed by fear and stunned by emotional anguish, the children sat on the hard packed earth of their former barnyard and watched as everything they'd ever known burned to the ground. The cloying smell of burned flesh and singed hair hung heavy in the air, but the bodies of those they loved were mostly unrecognizable now.

Freida shook her head slowly, trying to wrap her mind around what had just happened. Dumbfounded, she wasn't sure where to turn. Yes, Papa and Mama had trained her to care for the younger ones. However, no one had ever seen this coming. How would she feed them? Where would they sleep?

Borysko suddenly rose and lunged at Freida. Shrieking, he began pummeling her with his small fists. "Why wouldn't you let me help them? I don't understand. Why wouldn't you let me help? I might have saved them. Now they are dead. I hate you." Falling back to the ground he lay in a small heap sobbing until his breath came in small hiccups.

Freida lifted him into her arms and held him tight. "Borysko, If you had left us you would be dead too. I was doing what Papa and Mama told me to do. I was protecting their little ones."

"I'm not a little one! And, I don't care. I wish I was dead. Look at them. All murdered. For what? Why? What made those men come out here to kill us?"

"You heard the men yelling, little brother. They were shouting, 'Kill the Jews'. That's why. They came to kill the Jews. That's what they were doing earlier in Voronkov, and in Kiev days before that. I heard about Kiev when I went to town to shop for Mama. I tried to tell Mama and Papa about the killing, but they simply told me that we had nowhere else to go and would have to take things as they came. You may as well learn the truth now little brother. Christians hate Jews, and Christians kill Jews. It is just the way of things."

"But why, Freida? I don't understand why they hate Jews? And, what are we supposed to do now? I just wish you would have let me protect my family. Even if I was killed, what would it have mattered? At least I would be with Papa and Mama. Tell me, Freida, what will we do now? How will we survive without them?"

"Stop it. What would Saba and Papa say if they could hear you right now? One minute you tell me you are not one of the little ones and the next you are whining like a helpless baby. We are here together, the four of us. We have all lost our Saba and Bubbe, our Papa and Mama, and two of our brothers. We are all wondering what we will do now. And we are all sad. Now we must try to find a safe place. And, we must try to make our family proud with everything we do going forward. They have taught us how to survive. We have done that all our lives in this god forsaken place, with no help from anyone. They sacrificed themselves to keep us safe, so that our family would go on. So, we must go on, for them. And, as for you, you will now protect your family, Borysko, you and Fadeyka, or what is left of us anyway. You will make your Saba and your Papa proud."

That night, caked in human waste, hungry and exhausted, the four huddled together near the burned out barn and shared a fitful sleep filled with flashes of demons from hell. Batya woke several times in the night shaking, screaming and clutching at thin air. Freida soothed her as best she could. They awakened sore and tired, but they would do what they had to do, as their family had always done. They would survive.

Before they left the property they scratched out burial plots from the hard packed earth and conducted a Levaya of sorts. Burying the ones they loved as best they could. Each of them threw three shovels of dirt onto every one of the six graves. Freida tried to pray, but anger and grief closed her mind and her throat, causing words of comfort to escape her. There would be no Sitting Shiva for their family. No friends and relatives to drop by. No black clad mourners noshing on gifts of food to words of comfort and condolence.

They searched for anything they might salvage to take along. Digging through piles of burned rubble they found a few small coins, a knife, the family's menorah, and a couple of clay jars that made it through the devastation, somehow, without breaking. The fire had done its ravenous job in the dry tinderbox and almost all was gone. What they had left was "bubkes", as Saba would have said. The hay fields were gone as well, but, not all the sunflowers were sacrificed, so they proceeded to salvage as many of the ripened seed heads as they could carry and there was kasha too, so that could be harvested before they left.

Fadeyka found some beets and some potatoes that weren't too badly trampled and ran excitedly to tell his sister of his discovery. Meanwhile, as they worked to collect the produce, one of the goats found her way back to them.

Borysko wove a leash and tied it around the neck of the nanny. Then, fashioning produce bags by weaving stipa together; the grass whose magnificent plumes dominate the Plaines from midsummer until fall; they filled the sacks with sunflower seeds, kasha, small, tender beets and potatoes.

Batya even managed to save some carrots, turnips and a little cabbage, that survived horses hooves, from the garden in back. Freida was feeling just a bit more hopeful about being able to care for the little ones, with their bags of hard won bounty. So they made their way slowly to the Dneiper River, schlepping their heavy packs behind them.

Once at the river, they stripped to their underwear and submerged in the brisk, rapidly flowing water. Allowing the current to help them remove layers of crusted waste from their bodies. Freida used fine sand to scrub the scalps of the little ones, as they fussed and complained, and then attended to herself. She didn't know if she could ever rid her nostrils of the smells from the previous night. The overwhelming odor of burning flesh and hair, coupled with the pungent aroma of human excrement was overpowering. She almost drowned herself trying to cleanse the nauseating smell from her nose, as she simultaneously found herself racked with sobs that threatened to undo her. With great difficulty she calmed herself and made her way back up to the children. Even in a state of total exhaustion, she would show them strength such as parents would expect of her, so that the children would not fear.

Next, she scrubbed their clothes on rocks by the edge of the river, taking out her frustration and hatred on the innocent clothing, until every bit of the horrid stench was removed from the fabric. They had no other garments to wear, so they dressed in their wet clothes and allowed the fabric to dry as they walked in the warmth of the afternoon sun. Feeling a little closer to human, now that the contents of the privy was removed, they made their way to town.

Voronkov was just left of the Dneiper River, so when they had sufficiently dried they made their way into the

Shtetl. The sights and smells that assailed them as they entered the village were reminiscent of their own experience from the previous night. Many of the buildings around them still smoldered, and bodies of the dead lay everywhere. Some beheaded, some torn to pieces, some burned, all hideously maimed and similarly murdered. Batya clung tightly to Freida, as the boys tried to look brave leading their goat and dragging their sacks of produce. They came across a woman, holding a baby who had been torn in two. Her apron was wrapped loosely around the poor child's dead, mangled body, as if she were trying somehow to put him back together. She rocked and hummed to the lifeless child. They walked on.

A small group, following the tradition of 'tzedakah' had set up a medical station, of sorts, and lines of people waited to be treated. Some with bad burns, others even more serious, with missing digits or limbs, and still others whose eyes were simply vacant after the horrors they'd witnessed the previous night. All moaning, wailing and crying, begging for help. Another line offered a simple meal of beet soup and bread to anyone who could find a vessel to fill. Freida stood in line and took bread as the volunteers filled her two jars.

The foursome would find a place to sit and eat before going on. Looking around at the broken and ravaged people, the destruction, the loss, she couldn't help but shake her head and wonder. How could human beings be so terrible to one another. Freida would never understand this herself, so it would be impossible for her to try and explain it to the little ones.

Freida knew she must come up with a plan soon. The growing season was essentially over. It would begin to get cold all too soon. And, as hot as it was on the Steppes in summer, it was equally, bitterly cold in the winter.

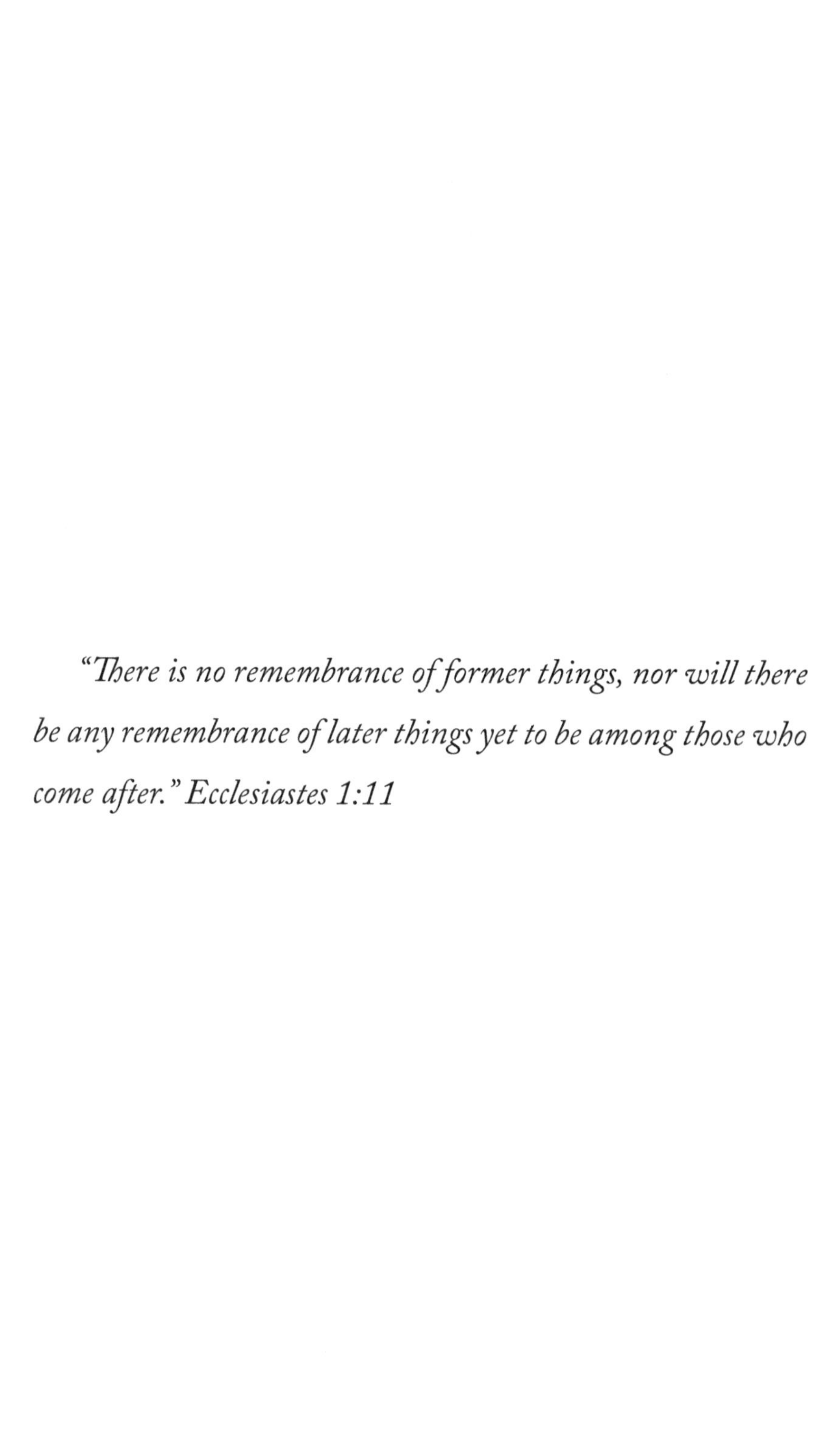

"There is no remembrance of former things, nor will there be any remembrance of later things yet to be among those who come after." Ecclesiastes 1:11

CHAPTER 2

Making her way through rubble and smoldering debris Freida, leading her charges, was able to locate the nearest merchant group with which to trade the supplies they'd managed to salvage. The small town square held lines of hungry, hurting people looking for a little food, some help, anything to relieve the horror of the past twenty four hours.

She wanted desperately to leave, to escape. Not just to leave town, but to leave the Pale. But where? Yes, she knew the Jews of this land were permanently confined to the Pale of Settlement, and she knew it was against the law to move from this appointed place. But she didn't care. She just didn't care anymore. Who were these authorities who had decided they were god over the whole of Judaism and it's people? Why should she listen to them?

It was only a matter of time before the Cossacks returned, wasn't it? Perhaps, next time, somebody even worse would wake them in the dark of night. Their attackers were Christians after all. Let's face the truth, they would never be happy until every living Jew was dead. She would find a place. A place where they could live in freedom, away from all those who would do them harm. She knew her parents would have disagreed, even argued with her. Family, tradition, their god and so on. They believed Christianity, just like Judaism, was an honorable religion, though it wasn't theirs. But she was tired of counting on an angry god who didn't seem to care at all about her family. And she refused to be a sitting duck any longer, not with so much humanity crammed into such a small place.

As Saba would have said, "Packed in tighter than herring in a barrel". The sound of his voice rang out so loud in her head, she had to smile as tears of grief overtook her. Remembering his body thrashing about and burning in the darkness of their farmyard caused her to shake her head again trying to dispel the image forever engraved into her psyche.

After Kiev was so brutally attacked; and before the attacks on Voronkov, or their own farm; she'd talked to some young people on her recent shopping trip into town. Young people who were angry about the intensifying and ongoing pogroms taking place around the country. Pogroms which were obviously organized, or at the very least condoned, by local authorities after the Tsar's Manifesto of October 17, 1905 was published. How could they ever be safe here, or frankly anywhere, again?

Most of all, how could she keep the little ones safe, as she'd faithfully promised her parents she would do, as long as those who hated them roamed free?

She found some sources who might be helpful. Old acquaintances of her grandfather, who had items to trade and sell. There would always be those who would profit from the hardships of others. Something she'd realized at a tender age. So, even though there were currently social welfare groups all around the small town, trying to ease the suffering of others. She knew it was only a matter of time before the vultures came out of hiding.

"So, you have something to trade, young lady?"

"Yes, we've put together quite a bit of produce. I think it should be worth a great deal. Especially after most of the crops in the area were burned and so many supplies lost in town."

"Well, you let me be the judge of that, hmmm? I know your grandfather, don't I?"

"Yes, you do. But, my grandparents and parents were

murdered last night, at our farm, along with two of my brothers. I'm sure it was the same Cossacks who rode through here."

"I'm sorry to hear it. Your grandfather was a Mensch. He was always kvelling on about his grandchildren. Every one of you gave him many reasons for shepping nachas. Do you have Mishpocha in the region?"

"No, we had only each other here. My mother's sister is still alive. In Warsaw, Poland I think. I believe she works for important people there. But I don't know exactly where and I wouldn't have a clue as to how to find her, now that my mother is gone. I will have to make a plan. That is all there is too it and that is all I can do."

"Now, you know I would never tell a soul. Nevertheless, aren't you afraid the authorities will discover if you've left? They consider it a very grave offense, worthy of death, to leave the Pale you know."

"I am aware. But how would the authorities ever find that out, unless you told them? I have not mentioned my desire to leave this place to anyone but you. So, if you aren't going to tell a soul, then I guess we will be fine. Besides, I can't leave right away. We will have to figure something out. I need to come up with money, supplies and a working plan before I can take off across the Steppe with three small children. Now, what can you give me for this produce? We will keep some for ourselves, and also some to share, but I can trade or sell half, for a fair price if you're offering one."

"What has the world come to when the eggs think they are smarter than the chickens?"

"My grandfather taught me well, Sir."

"It seems he did young lady. But remember, in bad times even a penny is money."

"Yes Sir. My Mama would certainly agree with you."

"Young woman?"

"Yes Sir?"

"I want you to remember that gentiles have been trying to wipe us off the face of the planet since Pharaoh stood toe to toe with Moses. The only true safety is in numbers. For the sake of your little ones, you might want to reconsider your position, at least until they are a little older."

"Yes Sir. I promise. I will do that. I only want them to be safe."

When their business was concluded, Freida felt she'd not been cheated too badly. They were still in possession of half their goods, and she'd bargained for a nice bit of coin, in exchange for the other half of the seeds, kasha, beets and potatoes. She would be able to rent a small room in town, if they could find someone who was willing to let them in amidst all the death and destruction. She had much to think about. Perhaps the old man was right. A young woman and three small children. What chance did they stand against all those who would rather see them dead? Maybe she would stay until the children were a little older.

"Freida, did we get a good trade?"

"Yes Borysko, I believe we did just fine. Saba would be proud."

"Good. Then we are proud of you as well. And, we still have some food and the Nanny goat too."

"Thank you young man. However, I believe Saba would have said of that man, "If his word were a bridge, I'd be afraid to cross it.""

"Ay, and, Bubbe would have said, with that stern look she did so well, "He should drink too much castor oil." They all laughed together, and walked on as they talked.

"Yes, Batya, I believe she would have done so. I miss them so much. Yet I feel as though they are still right here with us, don't you?"

"I think so too. I feel I can still hear all their voices, as I walk. Saba, Bubbe, Papa and Mama, instructing me, telling me what to do, and telling me that they are proud of us."

"Yes Fadeyka, so can I, as if they live right here in my head."

Voronko was resilient, just as its people were resilient. In only a few short weeks they'd repaired, or torn down, many of the damaged buildings on their main street, depending on the degree of mending needed. The dead were buried, the wounded bandaged, and the hungry fed. These were a people of tzedakah, and, if they could help it, no one wandered the streets hungry or hurt.

Freida secured residence for herself and her three siblings in a room above the town's bakery. The smells emanating from the kitchens below were mind bogglingly lovely, and they woke each day with smiles on their faces when the owners began baking dozens of beautiful rye loaves to sell.

Freida struck a deal with the bakery's owners. Room

rental, and two loaves of rye bread each morning, in exchange for a thorough cleaning of the bakery's kitchen every night after closing hours. She was also allowed to keep their nanny outside in the small back yard, where she made sure the goat was fed and watered. Each morning and night Batya milked the goat. They drank some of the milk, and made cheese to eat and sell with the rest. Their coins were lasting much longer this way, and Freida was pleased with the choice she'd made to stay and make a life here, at least for now.

Mornings sent a smiling Batya scampering down the stairs to the establishment below, to pick up their loaves of warm, rye bread to eat with their cheese curds and sunflower seeds.

Freida secured employment as a seamstress with the town's only tailor. Sensible people, in hard times, usually mended versus purchasing new. So there always seemed to be plenty to do. For now just mending and alterations, but with a promise of more work and better pay in the future she was hopeful she would be able to put more away for their future move.

Thankful her Mama and Bubbe had taught her so well, she sewed each stitch thinking of them and the wonderful hours they'd spent sharing and laughing, with small Batya at their feet. She was able to bring Batya along to the tailor shop where the younger girl was summarily put to work sorting buttons and such. The little one was paid a pittance a week for her trouble. Freida allowed the girl to spend her meager wages on sweets for her brothers and herself and smiled when the small girl looked so proud of being able to contribute in some way.

The boys; Borysko and Fadeyka; began attending Yeshiva, as soon as it was up and running following that awful, bloody night. Through daily shiurim (lectures and classes), as well as chavrutas (study pairs), they would learn the Talmud and the Torah. When they reached the age of thirteen, they would each become a Bar Mitzvah (a young man responsible to follow the commandments), as their brothers Aleksander and Bohdan had also done at their age. Just last year Bohdan had finished his studies and proudly became a bar mitzvah.

The celebration was grand, with roast lamb, roasted vegetables, blini and boranki.

Aleksander, the year before that, made this step into manhood as well, with much commemoration. Their parents and grandparents were so proud. Saba and Papa kvelling all over town to anyone who would listen.

Freida wondered, who would be there for these two young boys when the time came? She was hardly a good substitute for the men in their life, no matter how hard she tried to be so. Tthinking such things always made her sad.

Her own studies had taken place at home, under the watchful eye of her grandmother, since women were not allowed to attend Yeshiva. That was fine with her. Her instruction had included things the boys would never know, including the needle arts that were currently keeping her employed and she became a bat mitzvah at twelve. Her family celebration was not nearly as grand as that of the boys, but that was okay too. She knew her family was poor. She also knew they were proud of her many accomplishments.

Now, though, she just wasn't sure she believed any of it. This God, Jehovah. Who was He anyway? If He was so great, why did He let His people suffer so? If this was all the more that He cared, she could ignore Him just the same way He seemed to discount her struggles.

However, she wouldn't refuse the little ones their Jewish heritage. She was well aware that would have angered her family. So, each day, Borysko and Fadeyka donned their yarmulkes, picked up their satchels, and headed out the door for the local synagogue in order to learn the Law from Rabbi Zimmels. Leaving Freida and Batya to earn the wages and keep the home fires burning, just as it had always been.

With Hanukkah quickly approaching Freida worked especially hard to put a bit of money away, in order to purchase a few small trinkets for the children. They weren't expecting anything, as they were all very much aware of the family's ongoing situation. However, that made the idea even more appealing to her. They'd all been through so much, and, true to form, they'd not complained about their circumstances a single bit.

Unwrapping the family's salvaged menorah was a singularly solemn moment, and the act brought tears to every eye in the room. This would be their first such celebration without Saba, Bubbe, Papa, Mama, Aleksander and Bohdan and the weight of their grief was heavy indeed.

For the beginning of their 'Festival of Lights' celebration, as Freida lit the Shamash, she recited the blessings for the first night of traditional candle lighting. The first of the three prayers made young Batya's throat fill with tears, as she remembered Saba and Papa reciting this exact same blessing on the previous and every other year of her life. She coughed and closed her eyes tight as she tried hard not to cry. *"Ba-ruch A-tah Ado-nai E-lo-he-nu Me-lech ha-olam a-sher ki-de-sha-nu be-mitz-vo-tav ve-tzi-va-nu le-had-lik ner Cha-nu-kah." Translated:* "Blessed are You, Lord our God, King of the universe, who has sanctified us with His commandments, and commanded us to kindle the Chanukah light." This first blessing would be recited on every night of the eight day celebration.

Freida then handed the Shamash to Borysko, who looked surprised, though deeply honored. He stood, lit the first candle on the far left of the menorah, blew out the Shamash, replaced it on the stand and sat back down on the floor.

The second blessing, which would be recited after the first, for each consecutive night of the celebration, went: *"Ba-ruch A-tah Ado-nai E-lo-he-nu Me-lech Ha-olam she-a-sa ni-sim la-avo-te-nu ba-ya-mim ha-hem bi-zman ha-zeh." Translated:* "Blessed are You, Lord our God, King of the universe, who performed miracles for our forefathers in those days, at this time."

And the third blessing: *"Ba-ruch A-tah Ado-nai E-lo-he-nu Me-lech Ha-olam she-heche-ya-nu ve-ki-yi-ma-nu ve-higi-a-nu liz-man ha-zeh." Translated:* "Blessed are You, Lord our God, King of the universe, who has granted us life, sustained us, and enabled us to reach this occasion." Which would be recited only on the first night of celebration.

Once the candles were lit, and the blessings performed, the prayer, "Haneirot Halalu" was recited by the whole family: *Ha-nei-rot ha-lo-lu o-nu mad-li-kin Al ha-te-shu-ot ve-al ha-ni-sim ve-al ha-nif-la-ot, She-a-see-ta la-avo-tei-nu ba-ya-mim ha-heim biz-man ha-zeh, Al ye-dei ko-ha-ne-cha ha-ke-do-shim, Ve-chol she-mo-nat ye-mei cha-nu-kah ha-nei-rot ha-la-lu ko-desh hem, Ve-ein la-nu re-shut le-hish-ta-meish ba-hen, E-lo lir-o-tan bil-vad, ke-dei le-ho-dot u-le-ha-leil le-shim-cha ha-ga-dol Al ni-se-cha ve-al nif-le-o-te-cha ve-al ye-shu-o-te-cha.*

Translation: "We kindle these lights [to commemorate] the saving acts, miracles and wonders which You have performed for our forefathers, in those days at this time, through Your holy priests. Throughout the eight days of Chanukah, these lights are sacred, and we are not permitted to make use of them, but only to look at them, in order to offer thanks and praise to Your great Name for Your miracles, for Your wonders and for Your salvations."

Lastly, with tears glistening on her face, Freida began to sing the first and last verses of the Ma'oz Tzur. Halfway through the first verse, the children joined in. When they were done, they sat in silence as the profound power of the moment hung in the air around them.

The candles would be allowed to burn for thirty minutes before being extinguished to await the second of the eight nights of celebration. During that thirty minutes Freida pulled out the tiny trinkets she'd wrapped for the children. She'd purchased gifts for every one of the eight nights and couldn't wait to see the surprise on their faces when they received the small tokens each night.

On this first night of gifts Freida was treated to squeals of delight from Batya and Fadeyka (who proceeded to look embarrassed at his openly gleeful, and less than manly, display), and a hearty, "Thank you", from Borysko. They played with their dreydals for a full hour before Freida made them clean up their new toys and prepare for bed. The boys would have the full eight days off from lessons, however, not without a list of chores to attend to. But Freida was all too aware she and Batya would be back at work before dawn.

Word did not reach Voronkov, until the evening of January 23rd, about the shocking events of Bloody Sunday. The girls heard women whispering in the tailor shop on the 24th and wondered what all the secrecy was about.

Freida was perfectly aware that the people of the Pale were not the only forgotten and needy ones, in these god forsaken lands. She'd spoken with enough others from the village and those travelers passing through, to know that life for working class people and peasants all over the country was tremendously difficult and getting worse by the day. They worked for very little pay, often went without food and were exposed to dangerous working conditions in thankless jobs. Worse yet, the aristocrat class looked at the peasants of the land like slaves, giving them very few rights under the law and treating them like mere animals. In this regard Jews had much in common with those poor unfortunate wretches.

Another thing they had in common was their love for

their Tsar and his family. However misguided that love might be. Common citizens believed that Nicholas was a man of the people and truly cared about his subjects. The same could not be said about the general population's feelings for the government of the land. People generally placed the blame for their circumstances on the ruling government and assumed all their problems were due to a blatant disregard of their Tsar's wishes.

On January 22nd, 1905, a large number of workers marched to the Tsar's palace in order to present a petition for better working conditions. They were fired upon by soldiers and many people were killed or injured. Before Bloody Sunday most peasants and working class revered the Tsar believing he was on their side. However, after the shootings, the Tsar was perceived as an enemy of the working class.

From here, the seeds of revolution were planted, and they began to grow rapidly. Word spread throughout all of Russia's lands, of the brave Bolsheviks, who sought fairness for all.

Freida wasn't sure what to think when she heard the dreadful news. Her grandparents and parents had always been loyal to the royal family and believed the Tsar to be a man who cared about the common people. Though they knew the Tsar lived well, and they had always been poor, they knew their monarch had his country's best interests at heart. It was hard to learn the truth and she wondered how her family would have taken this news.

These reports were most disquieting and folks in Voronkov would continue to walk on egg shells for some time to come. No one in the village could have imagined how circumstances would unfold.

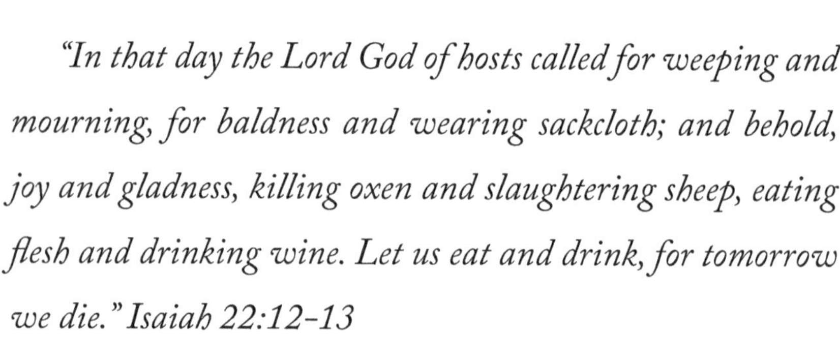

"In that day the Lord God of hosts called for weeping and mourning, for baldness and wearing sackcloth; and behold, joy and gladness, killing oxen and slaughtering sheep, eating flesh and drinking wine. Let us eat and drink, for tomorrow we die." Isaiah 22:12–13

CHAPTER 3

Seven years passed since Voronkov burned. Seven years since Bloody Sunday and the disquieting of the masses began. Seven years since the thoughts of revolution began growing in the minds of Russia's despondent hordes. Seven years of the tides of rebellion mounting throughout the land. Seven years since Batya's family had buried their grandparents, their parents and two of their own brothers. Seven years.

Freida and Batya worked tirelessly at the small tailor shop, year after year, making their employer famous far and wide for the beautiful work coming out of his establishment. Freida also took care of the books, and, though she received several increases in pay over the years for her excellent work, it was not nearly the reward the business' owner gained by having her in his employ. Batya had taken her place beside her sister. Though not yet quite as accomplished a seamstress as Freida, she could easily hold her own against any professional tailor.

Batya's studies, at her sister's feet, entailed much. And, even included those religious lessons that their mother and grandmother had instilled. Freida was sure they would have wanted it so. And, she knew that Bubbe and Mama would be proud of their littlest one. Batya would become a Bat Mitzvah this year. She was pretty and bright, as well as kind and industrious. She also had a love for God that her older sister simply could not understand, after surviving so many tragedies in their lives.

Borysko and Fadeyka had grown into strong young men of sixteen and fourteen, and were employed by the shtetl's lone smithy. The blacksmith there taught them to fashion everything from a horse shoe, to an intricate menorah. They also continued on with their studies a couple of evenings a week, and were considered quite learned for their ages. Respected in the community they contributed from their pay to the temple and to the family's savings each and every week. Saba and Papa would have looked upon them with great pride, carrying on the family's name in such a hard working and honorable way.

The oldest of the two boys was known around town as a very pious and rigid young man. And though he was good to his own family, he believed each one in the community should carry his own weight. He followed God's commandments with great fervor. However, he frowned on tzedakah, except in the most extreme cases and thought it a generally overused practice. He still held much bitterness toward those Cossacks who'd stormed onto his home and killed his loved ones. That bitterness and un-forgiveness took root in his soul, without any way to escape, turning him into an angry young man with a very hard heart.

Fadeyka's shtick was a bit more complicated. He tended to be soft hearted and compassionate to a fault. Helping everyone who needed assistance, even those who had clearly gotten themselves into bad situations all on their own. Though he'd studied with the same Rabbi as his older brother and had become a Bar Mitzvah at thirteen, he just didn't believe in his heart, all the god stuff, to the same degree as his older sibling. In that way, he and Freida were very much alike.

Deep in his heart he felt that if this, here on this planet, was all there was to one's existence, he should try to fill it with as much love and as much fun as he possibly could while still here on earth. After all, who knew what the hereafter held? Would he ever see his lost loved ones again? He didn't know. He guessed he hadn't seen anything in his years of yeshiva to prove otherwise. He wouldn't disrespect his brother by pushing the issue, but he wouldn't compromise his own heart either.

Freida, who had been actively pursued by several eligible men after the death of their parents chose instead to continue on the familiar path of caring for her younger siblings, instead of resorting to marriage. The last thing she needed was another human being to do for now, or for that matter, ever.

Since she was a mature woman of twenty two, it seemed her peers had mostly paired up and married off anyway, leaving her with very little choice in the available suitor department for their immediate region. With the negligible choices presented to her, she decided she'd much rather continue on a single's course unless, or until, some dashing stranger should happen to cross her path.

Freida was always a hard worker, just like everyone in her family, and could take care of herself. And unlike some cultures, or times in history, where it was frowned upon for married women to work outside the home; women who lived in shtetls in the Pale of Settlement were expected to help care for their families in whatever capacity was necessary at all times. Culture often tended to be a bit more lenient in situations of extreme poverty.

It was into this time and place that Borysko's letter of conscription arrived. He was ordered to report to St. Petersburg in two months, over eight hundred miles away, to serve in the Tsar's army.

Freida and Batya were in a state of panic. They'd heard tales of service in Nicolas II's army, from those who'd been forced into enlistment in the past. Men sent into battle without shoes, proper weapons, or food. The Emperor's armies were vast, but poorly outfitted and terribly underfunded. Considering the Tsar's particular hatred of the Jewish people, recruits from the Pale were especially mistreated.

"I think we should run away. There are places we could go where I'm sure they would never find us."

"I won't run, Batya. I'm not a coward."

"Borysko, we would never paint you as a coward and Batya didn't mean that. We simply know that the Tsar hates Jews, something our parents did not yet know before they died. He sends them into battle with no supplies and no armaments. Why should you fight for a man who has proven so often that he hates our people?"

"Like it or not, Freida, Nicolas is our Tsar too. If I ran, I would be marked a traitor and would spend the rest of my life in hiding, or executed for desertion. Not to mention the things they could do to my family. I would never subject any of you to that kind of danger. No, I will do what I must. If that means I must fight, then I will fight."

"Then we are coming too. We will move to St. Petersburg, so we can at least be close enough to help you if the need arises."

"You can't do that. If it is discovered that you've left the Pale, they may hunt you down."

"Well, just as you will do what you must. I will do the same. St. Petersburg, just like Moscow, allows some Jews to live within its borders, as long as they can show they have a high degree of talent in the trades. Batya and I are the best seamstresses in the country. They won't turn us away. And, Fadeyka is talented in metallurgy and the art of blacksmithing. I'm sure he will find employment quickly."

"I know better than to argue with you, Freida. But, I will ask that you don't tell anyone where you are going. And that we leave right away, without fanfare, to keep the talk in the shtetl at a minimum."

"Who would we tell, brother. Let us pack up as quickly as possible. We've saved quite a tidy sum in the past seven years. It should be sufficient to transport us and set us up in a small business of our own. With plenty to see to your military needs. I won't have you ill prepared should you be sent into battle, Borysko."

"Thank you, sister. We will need to use a portion of that money to hire a wagon for the journey. We will never make over eight hundred miles in the time necessary without some sort of help."

"You're right. Now, let's prepare ourselves. We mustn't forget anything necessary. We won't have occasion to make our way back to retrieve items we've forgotten."

"I'm frightened, Freida. If the Tsar hates Jews so much, and we are even closer to him there, than we are now, won't that put us in more danger?"

"We've already been through our share of danger, Batya. We will not be afraid. We will face, head on, anything that they throw at us. Understand that it will be different living in St. Petersburg, but it won't be impossible. We mustn't speak Yiddish anymore, unless we are behind closed doors. Our mama loshon is greatly frowned upon in and around non-Jewish settlements, and we don't want to draw attention to our situation any more than we have to. If we are careful, we can live in a large city without creating problems for ourselves. But, we must be diligent."

"Can't we at least say goodbye to the Rabbi, Freida? Surely he would never report us."

"I would hope he wouldn't, Borysko, but what if there are others around?"

"Please, sister, it would mean a great deal to me."

"Fine, we will pack first. Then we will say our farewells to the Rabbi, once we can see that the Temple is empty, and before we head out on the road. We will walk the first leg of the trip, and find transport when we reach Kiev."

"That is a very long walk, Freida. Do you think Batya can manage such a long walk, especially in the cold?"

"Don't speak of me as if I am not standing right next to you, Fadeyka. I suspect you are more concerned for yourself than you are for me. I am perfectly capable of taking care of myself and I am not a baby you know."

"Okay, now, no arguing. If we are to go, we must go tonight, so let us pack and prepare for this long journey. I will gather some food. We will take the nanny, at least until we reach Kiev. I'm sure we can find a family to take her there. Pack only clothing that will blend in with that which is worn in a larger city. I have sewn each of you some serviceable pieces that are also very much in style. And, I know they are not worn out, since I never see any of you wearing them."

"Do you blame us, Freida? Our friends make fun and call us dandies. Besides, they aren't very practical for everyday."

"Well, perhaps it is good you haven't worn them out. Then you will all look presentable when we arrive in St. Petersburg. We are more likely to fit in and be accepted by those people of means living in the city, if we look the part. For most of the trip we will dress in our everyday clothing, and you each have two changes. When we are close to the city we will put on clean garments. We should be able to pass easily as merchants or artisans, which is truly exactly what we are."

After an hour of packing and preparing, Freida left a note for their landlord. "Please accept our apologies for this hasty departure. There has been a grave emergency in our family, and we must take care of the situation promptly. We will most likely be gone for quite some time, so we certainly don't expect you to keep the apartment open for us. We are most grateful for all you have done for our family. Sincerely, Freida."

The group took their bags and went quietly into the night. Standing outside the synagogue, they waited until they were sure the Rabbi was alone. Goodbyes, prayers and blessings were said, but as they left the temple they heard, "Gay ga zinta hate" (Go in good health), from their good friend.

There wasn't much they would miss about this god forsaken place, but the Rabbi had been like a father to the two boys since they'd lost their own Papa and Saba. Freida knew it was hard for them to say farewell. She was grateful for the influence the man had been in their lives. And, though her views were much different from his concerning his God, she sincerely wished him well. They left to the sounds of a small village locking down tight for the night and the plaintive bleating of their nanny goat as she was led into the darkness. They would follow the river, which would lead them directly to Kiev. There they would find someone willing to transport them on to St. Petersburg.

As they walked Freida looked up at the cloudless sky, and an abundance of stars there, and felt as though her parents and grandparents watched them as they went. The sweet fragrance of late crops and grasses along with the smell of farm animals filled the Autumn breeze that wafted through the air. Suddenly she knew her heart was at peace with the decision to go, no matter the consequences of her decision. She also knew they would never see Voronkov again.

They slipped into Kiev, quietly, in the pitch black of a moonless night. Just the same way they'd left Voronkov. Their trip, so far, mostly uneventful. Following the river as they'd planned, they ate twice a day and slept each night near a fire of gathered sticks and moss. Thankfully they brought their warmest, winter outerwear and plenty of blankets because it was very cold on the Steppes in November. However, none the worse for wear, as they were a pretty hardy bunch living successfully off the land their whole lives, they arrived at their destination remarkably unscathed.

Borysko and Fadeyka were forced to remove their yarmulkes, so as not to draw attention to themselves throughout the arduous, though sparsely populated journey. They actually looked like any ordinary wretched, menial workers when they entered the town. Not at all like the displaced Jews they actually were. There would already be enough obstacles along the way, without having to explain why they'd left the Pale without permission. Borysko said he felt naked without his head covering, but Fadeyka felt no such discomfort and decided he might make this a permanent transition.

Making a few discrete inquiries of those on the side streets when they arrived in the city, they were directed to an old, untidy man named Igor with a scraggly beard, very few teeth, a stained eye patch, a good horse and a cart.

Automobiles; though they were most certainly a reality, a Russo-Balt car placed 9th in the 1912 Monte Carlo Rally after all; were not common place in this part of the world as of yet. Unreliable, at best, they were susceptible to weather and common upsets that might occur on the road. Freida and her family needed transportation they could count on to get them to their destination on time.

Arrangements were made to travel the following day. Igor directed them to a small inn where they could spend the night, owned by his equally unkempt relative. He'd agreed to take them on to St. Petersburg, for a costly but fair sum, at first light.

The inn was not much more than clapboard siding and

stained cots, but, it served as a roof over their heads. It was good to sleep inside for a change. Much more than that, the price was right considering the large sum they must dole out to Igor for transportation.

Days of cold weather, rationed food, and many miles of grueling travel had been extremely taxing on their strength and they still had far to go to reach St. Petersburg. So, rest would be important. They were all anxious to get on the road and first light was a most welcome sight.

Borysko and Fadeyka loaded bags and parcels onto the old man's ancient wagon and they all piled in. Freida, wrapped in her warmest winter gear, hands buried deep in her fur muff, rode up front on the worn plank seat with the one eyed driver. Meanwhile the other three settled in the bed of the cart, under blankets and straw, in order to stay warm on the long ride.

Igor spent much of his time glancing sideways at the attractive, young woman, licking his lips, and attempting to make small talk. His tedious, odiferous self, blood shot eyes and all; with his constant scratching and coughing; made her shudder. But, she was aware they needed him, much more than he needed them, so she quietly endured his attention and tried to be as polite as possible under the circumstances.

As long as the four of them slept together in the wagon, under the oiled canvas, while the old man made up his bed in a small tent on the ground she was safe enough from any unwanted advances. So, she would simply endure.

This would be a long trip, especially in the cold. Covering about fifteen to twenty miles a day, they would be on the road with Igor for more than a month and a half. They would arrive in St. Petersburg around the end of February, hopefully, just as winter weather was beginning to break. Travel on their trip would prove to be harrowing at times. Two broken wheels, a few frightening snow storms that caused them to seek shelter in small towns along the way, and even an attempted highway robbery, plagued them. But, they forged on, and were grateful though surprised when Igor unexpectedly pulled an Arisaka, Type 30, bolt-action service rifle from under the driver's seat of his wagon, to scare off the outlaws.

Forced to exchange horses along the way, when theirs stepped in a hole and came up lame, their driver was devastated. Igor was loath to leave his well trained, beautiful draft horse behind with the friendly farmer who gave them a loaner to finish out the trip. The new equine recruit proved not nearly so disciplined as her previous counterpart, and made the rest of the journey much more surprising for all of them with her unexpected antics and misbehavior.

Igor expected to be fed and reimbursed for expenses along their journey, in addition to the agreed upon fee. Though costly, that seemed fair considering the more than three months of his time he would spend ferrying them to St. Petersburg and making his way back. But the trip was taking a bigger dent out of their cash reserves than Freida would have liked.

However, they were seeing more of the world than they'd ever thought possible, coming from their humble beginnings. Days and days of beautiful scenery and on the roadway even an automobile, which was especially exciting for the boys.

When all was taken into account, even with his lack of cleanliness and rude behaviors, Igor proved himself to be an excellent guide, protector and friend.

"Thus says the Lord, your redeemer, the Holy One of Israel;"I am the Lord your God, who teaches you to profit, who leads you in the way you should go." Isaiah 48:17

CHAPTER 4

As the weary little, rag tag group crested the last hill standing between them and their destination; distance and barriers suddenly dropped away and laid St. Petersburg out before them in all its magnificent glory. They sat amazed, gazing at the enormity of it all. Framed in first morning light, the palace and surrounding churches glowing with thousands of pounds of pure gold adorning their edifices, the sight was almost impossible to believe for these un-traveled youngsters. Obviously, none of the four had ever seen a city so large, or so staggeringly opulent.

Igor had made this trip many times over the years and seemed unaffected by the glorious view. But the others agreed there was simply too much to take in all at once. Their driver took them to a sector of the city in which they might easily secure a temporary room while they got situated. There would be so much to do for these unseasoned newcomers.

It turned out to be harder to take their leave of the foul smelling one eyed man than Freida thought it would be.

He'd gotten them to their destination in one piece and for the agreed upon sum no less. Having to admit to herself that the old man had grown on her over the past almost seven weeks, she shook his hand and leaned in to give him a quick hug. However, Igor pulled her close, and gave her a big wet smooch on the cheek. She quickly pushed back against his chest to release his hold. "Igor, you are incorrigible!"

"Yes, young lady, I am! Nothing new there. You all take care of yourselves. And remember, not everyone is as trustworthy as good old Igor, so watch out what kind of characters you let into your lives."

"We will, Igor. You have been a true friend. And we will never forget you." The old man came away with a huge grin on his furry mug, waving as he went off the way from which they'd all just come.

Beautiful St. Petersburg, situated on the Neva River, at the head of the Gulf of Finland on the Baltic Sea, was founded by Tsar Peter the Great in 1703. The city was Russia's political capital and was considered her cultural capital as well. Tsar Nicholas II's family made their home here. And, for the foreseeable future, it would be their home too.

Frightened, but deeply exhilarated, was probably the most apt description of how Freida felt in this new and exciting place. They would not claim their Jewish heritage here and she was sorry if that caused Saba and Bubbe to roll over in their graves, but it was for the safety of the children. True, Borysko must soon report for duty in the Tsar's army. Likely at that time, his heritage would be revealed. But for the rest of them, trying to make a living in the city, it would be imperative that they keep their lineage a secret.

The story the family agreed to use was that their tradesman father died on a trip to Europe and left his business to his heirs to carry on in his stead. Soon Freida, Fadeyka and Batya had rented a small shop space and opened a business of their own, where the girls were using their sewing skills to impress the well dressed ladies of the city, and Fadeyka was implementing his unique metal working abilities in the back rooms, to draw in the men.

The shop came equipped with a small second floor apartment, much grander than any place they'd ever lived before, and at the same time, if truth be told, quite hey-mish. The tiny kitchen sported an actual ice box, where food could be stored and kept cold, simply by purchasing blocks of ice from a gentleman who daily drove a wagon through the streets shouting, "Ice, get your ice here."

Blocks of ice, cut from the frozen river in winter, wrapped in burlap, packed all around with straw and stored in large underground ice houses, were brought out to be loaded on his cart each day for distribution. If you bought ice from this man, you could also chip off pieces from your block to add to your glass for a cold beverage. Ingenious!

For the first time in their lives, they also had running water. Indoors! It was only cold water, which meant they had to heat it on the stove for washing dishes and bath-ing, but it certainly seemed a luxury compared to hauling it in from the river as they'd done on the farm, or an out-side pump, as was their custom while living in Voronkov.

Most marvelous of all was the water closet! Some-thing they'd not had the pleasure of experiencing in all the years of their lives. A clever invention that allowed one to take care of their business in the privacy of a small room; similar to a privy, but not a privy; and flush it away.

No chamber pots, no running out in the cold to use the outhouse. What a joy!

"So, where does it go?"

"I'm not sure, Batya. I believe the landlady said it was called a sewage system."

"Well, whatever it is, I love it. No more emptying chamber pots for me."

"I agree, sister. I can't believe we've lived our entire lives before, not knowing what a water closet was. I shall never be without one again!"

"Me either. And, I love the ice box. Especially the ice chips in my water. If only Mama and Papa could see."

"Yes, wouldn't Bubbe be surprised to see water coming from a pipe inside the house? Think of how much easier these things would have made Bubbe and Mama's lives on the farm."

"Oh, Freida, I miss them so much. Especially when I lay in bed at night, wanting to tell them all the marvelous things we've seen and the troubles of the day. It makes my heart hurt terribly sometimes."

"I know, Batya. I miss them too. I think about how important their faith was to them. It defined who they were. I know they would be sad to see us ignoring that faith now. I hope they understand why we must have the rules we follow now."

"Oh, don't worry about that, Freida. I have not abandoned my faith. I pray for us all every day. I know that Borysko does as well. He made me promise that I would never forget. We are just very careful to pray, only when no one else is around."

"Good, Batya. You must do what you know in your heart to be true. Just be very careful not to be seen, or heard, by anyone."

"Yes, Freida. I will be watchful."

They were very careful not to speak Yiddish either, or refer to customs and traditions which would mark them as Jews. And the neighbors all seemed to be sufficiently fooled by their story, or perhaps they just didn't care much and thought it best to mind their own affairs.

Freida noticed that the people here were all so busy, they didn't seem to have quite as much time on their hands as the gossipy women in Voronkov, to be involved in everyone else's personal business. That was just fine with her. It made life easier when she didn't have to explain herself.

Borysko reported for duty, without his yarmulke, on the appointed day and proceeded to train for military combat. If his superiors knew of his Jewish heritage, they gave no indication. Freida made sure he was outfitted with sturdy boots and all the proper gear, which was much more than most of the other new recruits possessed. Sadly, the Tsar could press these young men into service, but was not obligated to supply them with the necessary supplies and equipment for the battles ahead. So, if their families could afford to meet their needs, this practice was encouraged. If the family was poor and could not supply their needs, they simply went without.

Russian people were becoming more disillusioned with their ruler by the day. Agitators walked the streets distributing flyers and leaflets, drawing many newcomers to their cause. Sentiments were growing stronger against the Tsar and toward the entire Romanov family as more young men went to their deaths in the ranks of the Emperor's army. Underfed, under equipped and underfunded, soldiers suffered while the Romanovs lived in the lap of luxury, snug in the Winter Palace.

As the popularity of the Bolsheviks was bolstered by turbulent times, the name, Vladimir Lenin, was becoming more well known and ever more popular among the masses.

It didn't take long before the ladies of St. Petersburg discovered the talents of Freida and her sister, Batya. In no time at all women, most of them wealthy, were calling for fittings in the shop and at their homes. Freida and Batya traveled to many a prominent household to measure and fit for upcoming balls and other extravagant affairs.

By 1912 the silhouette of ladies dresses had simplified and became somewhat columnar. With a new, long, corset design which gave the body an upright posture. The basic silhouette was straight, with a slightly raised waistline, smooth fit over the hips and full length skirt without a great deal of fullness. Sleeves were fairly fitted with no gathers at the top. Skirts could have peplums or shaped overskirts and they might be split or shaped to reveal pleated or decorated gathered underskirts.

Evening dresses were usually made of fine silks, with open necklines and short sleeves, which could be cut in one with the body of the dress. Fabrics were satin, brocade, lace, chiffon and intricately embroidered silks. Many fabrics could be layered to create a rich effect without a lot of bulk. Closures were usually hidden under the various layers. The bodice lining was structured, closely fitted to the figure and boned. The typical day dress usually had long sleeves, fitted nicely to the arm. For day wear one-piece dresses in silk or cotton (lingerie dresses with lots of lace trim), blouses and skirts, jackets with matching jumpers or skirts were all popular.

Being the excellent seamstresses they were, during an age when fashion was at its height before WW 1 would put a damper on the fashion world for a time, they were hugely successful. Their prices were fair for their wealthy paying customers, but also very fair for the hard working girls who frequented their shop, and their personal coffers grew enormously.

In time they were called to the Winter Palace, to fit Empress Alexandra and her daughters. "What are we going to do, Freida?"

"We will go of course."

"But, what if they discover who we are? You know that the royal family hates Jews, Freida. What if they somehow detect a difference? The Tsar will kill us for daring to come so close to his family."

"Oh, Batya. Stop being fearful! We have been able to keep our secrets for well over a year and a half now. What makes you think the Empress will magically know what no one else in the world knows? This is an opportunity for our names to be so famous that business will flow freely through our doors."

"Freida, we've lived here for less than two years, and we can't keep up with the work load now. Women are waiting weeks and weeks for a dress as it is. We have more money than we will ever know what to do with. Why should we take that kind of chance?"

"Batya, I don't think we can say no to the Empress. People are imprisoned for things like that. Besides, is there ever enough money? We shall never be poor again little sister. Not if I can help it. You are worrying about nothing."

"Fine, Freida, I will go. But, I don't have to like it. If we are caught and tortured, I will remind you of whose idea this was."

The 'Winter Palace' was more opulent than anything either of the girls had ever seen. Even though they were taken through the servant's entrance, Freida was terrified to touch a single thing. When they were ushered into the Tsarina's dressing rooms, they both forgot how to breathe. First they measured Alexandra, and then each of her daughters: Olga, Tatiana, Maria, and Anastasia. They were treated kindly, if a bit coolly.

Anastasia smiled shyly at Batya as the girls took measurements and wrote them down. She was only a year younger than Batya that year. Short and a bit plump, the Tsar's youngest daughter had blond hair and blue eyes similar to those of Batya, with a bright and clever look that practically bordered on the edge of evil. She was forever in trouble with her parents and the palace staff, who called her "shvibzik", the Russian word for imp.

Freida and Batya spent hours with the royal women, going over patterns, fabrics, and designs to implement for upcoming holidays and events. Batya guessed that if she were ever asked, she would have to say that her favorite of the royal women was Anastasia, imp or not. She was the only one of the Imperial Highnesses who treated her as a regular person, instead of a mere servant.

Batya and Anastasia became more friendly as the girls ventured back for fittings and further orders. Batya discovered that, though the Tsar and Tsarina lived in opulence beyond belief, their children lived much more simply than one might imagine. They slept on camp cots without pillows when they were in good health; took cold baths in the morning; and had to clean their own rooms. All the girls were taught to mend their own clothing, in case of emergencies, and tend to their own needs. It seemed they weren't as spoiled as some thought.

Anastasia told Batya that when she was ten years old she rolled a rock into a snowball and threw it at her older sister, Tatiana. she was punished severely for that. She also climbed trees, tripped servants and pulled naughty pranks on family and staff alike. However, as she'd grown older, her father helped her mend her ways and these days she led a much more discrete life. Yes, Batya liked the youngest Romanov girl the best.

"Wouldn't it be just awful to live in that enormous palace and sleep on a camp cot?"

"What are you talking about, Batya?"

"The Tsar's children sleep on camp cots, without pillows for that matter, while their parents live in more luxury than most people can even imagine."

"Who told you that, Batya?"

"Anastasia and I were talking. She is actually very nice."

"Don't let the Empress find out you know so much.

She might not be very happy that you know their family secrets, Batya. You haven't been sharing ours, have you?"

"No, Freida. Of course not. And, I would never tell on Anastasia either. She would be in a great deal of trouble with her parents for talking to an outsider about what goes on in the palace. I just found it interesting and a bit disturbing as well that the parents treat their children so, when they live a life of such great ease. Our parents and grandparents sacrificed every day to make sure we had what we needed. Even going so far as to do without to make sure we had treats for holidays and birthdays. Even eventually, sacrificing themselves to keep us safe."

"Well, perhaps the Tsar and Tsarina don't want their children to grow up spoiled, surrounded by so much sumptuousness. Their children certainly don't seem to be lacking any important need met. We are making some lovely gowns for the girls, are we not?"

"Yes, I suppose so."

"Hey, Freida, Batya, were you two at the palace again?"

"Yes, Fadeyka. All day as a matter of fact. We didn't see you last night, because you came in so late. Who were you with this time?"

"I've made some new friends. I'll be going to another

meeting tonight."

"I don't want you getting mixed up with any of those revolutionaries, Fadeyka. You promised me that you would not get into trouble and that is not likely if you're in league with the Bolsheviks."

"Don't worry, Freida. I'll not endanger the family. These are good men. I'll be in earlier tonight."

"See that you are little brother. You haven't even had your sixteenth birthday and you're out carousing until all hours. What would Mama and Papa say?"

"Well, there's no carousing going on, just meetings. So, I think they would be fine with me making friends. And, I will be sixteen soon. Old enough to be conscripted into the Tsar's army, the same as Borysko, so I'm anxious to discover what other options I might have."

"Options? I won't have you signing up for any other options without running them past me first. Do you understand?"

"Yes, Freida. Though, once I'm sixteen I will be making my own choices and won't need permission from you or any other. Back home, I would have been making decisions at thirteen. I know what I'm doing and I will do what I must for that which is on my heart."

"Please, Fadeyka. Just don't do anything rash. Promise me."

"Yes, Freida. I promise not to do anything without thinking it through."

"What about the shop? How are things going for you?"

"I have more orders than I can fill in a lifetime. Just like you ladies with your sewing, I have become the place to go for the best in metal work."

"I'm glad, little brother. Saba, Bubbe, Mama and Papa would be so proud of you. But, this is a dangerous time in which to be a Jew. Be careful to remember that."

"I will, sister."

"Do you think he's involved with the Bolsheviks, Freida?"

"Yes, Batya, I do. But he will be sixteen soon, and in this culture he can make up his own mind at that age. I don't want to alienate him. I can only hope he doesn't do anything that will risk his life."

"I will pray for him, Freida. You should pray too."

"Thank you, Batya."

Fadeyka had indeed been meeting with a group of Bolsheviks. Followers of Vladimir Lenin, Joseph Stalin and Leon Trotsky, who believed that the Russian government should be a Marxist (communist) one. A government without the hindrance of religion, or a belief in God. Many young men, who were discouraged and without any spiritual foundation, would join the ranks, as the army grew and thrived in the shadows of the palace square. Though they were not yet ready to make their move, the waves of dissidence were growing stronger.

"For thus says the Lord: "Even the captives of the mighty shall be taken, and the prey of the tyrant be rescued, for I will contend with those who contend with you, and I will save your children." Isaiah 49:25

CHAPTER 5

reida and Batya went to bed exhausted. Another long day's work had lasted well into the night and they were still not caught up with the piles of dresses yet to finish. Summer heat had been oppressive all month, with no signs of letting up. The windows of their second floor apartment were thrown open wide to catch any possible hint of breeze. With sweat soaking through her muslin shift to her coverlet, as she tossed and turned in her bed, Freida finally fell asleep to the hushed and repetitive sounds of their equally worn out back street neighbors. The girls woke suddenly, terrified, very early the next morning, to the frenzied shouts of a young boy hawking newspapers.

Germany had declared war on Russia as they slept. It was August 1st, 1914. Germany, along with Austria-Hungary and Italy formed what the world had dubbed the Triple Alliance. Though, secretly, Italy had decided to wait and see in what direction the conflict would unfold; before officially declaring their allegiance to any side; Austria-Hungary and Germany were mobilizing troops to invade. Soon others would join the conflict including the great Ottoman Empire.

Not to be outdone, France and Great Britain joined with Russia, in an association which was labeled the Triple Entente, promising assistance if either of the other two were attacked by the Triple Alliance. Later, Belgium and then Italy, along with other European neighbors, joined members of the Entente.

The Great War had begun.

Running as fast as their legs would carry them, the girls made their way to the army depot where Borysko was currently stationed. A seasoned soldier now, though still not battle tested, of over two years. They arrived on base as Borysko was actively readying for deployment into Germany. The girls were forced to push past station guards and other soldier's family members to reach their brother. Borysko's face told a story his mouth wouldn't ever think to utter in front of his equally terrified comrades.

He was petrified, but resolved and honor bound to fight for the Tsar and his country. It seemed the commanders had done their job and the young man they'd known was now replaced by a warrior. Freida and Batya, frantic and horrified, watched as their beloved brother joined rows of other battle programmed soldiers. Some with the gear necessary for their upcoming ordeal, such as Borysko and some without even shoes on their feet, readying to march off to combat.

Fadeyka wasn't yet home from previous night's activities when they ran out of the shop, no doubt off with his rabble rousing friends again and not even present to convey proper goodbyes to his brother. A decision Freida hoped he wouldn't come later to regret.

The girls held tightly to their, visibly uncomfortable, brother for as long as his commanding officer would allow. Then they watched as, stone faced and bare headed, he marched off to war with his Mosin's rifle hanging from his shoulder. Freida and Batya, dazed by the suddenness of the morning's events, walked home stunned. Tears of fear and anguish streaming down their faces. Dismayed at what the future might hold for their brother and for what remained of their little family, they walked silently hand in hand.

That afternoon, Fadeyka barged in through the shop's

door, laughing and carrying on with a friend. Freida and Batya sat upstairs, consoling one another after the morning's goings on. The mere sound of his brazen merriment caused Freida to feel an immediate sense of disproportionate rage.

"Is that you, Fadeyka?"

"Yes Freida, I've brought a friend for supper, if that's okay?"

Freida was infuriated. Not only had the incorrigible scamp not been present to say farewell to his brother, but he then deemed it appropriate to cause her additional work to top it off? Well, she would give him a piece of her mind! She proceeded downstairs at full speed.

"Fadeyka, I can't imagine for a moment why you would think it acceptable to bring a guest home when we are grieving the departure of your brother off to war! I am shocked..."

Her last word stuck firmly in her throat as she lit on the bottom step; looked up into the most gorgeous, piercing, ice blue eyes she'd ever seen; and fell headlong into the arms of their unexpected guest. Tall, with blond wavy hair, his slightly mischievous smile revealed a deep dimple on the left cheek of his ridiculously handsome face. He was obviously much older than Fadeyka, more her own age of twenty four or so. Clearly amused at her impromptu rant and ungracious ballet into his arms, he was doing his best to stifle a laugh.

So shocked at the presence of this attractive stranger in her shop, it took her a moment to realize he still held her firmly in his grasp. "Oh my, I'm so sorry sir. I'm not usually so clumsy. Forgive me."

Freida righted herself and blushed a deep red, as her mind lingered on the feel of the strong arms holding her only seconds ago. Straightening her skirts and looking down at the floor, she tried to regain composure. "Oh, don't be sorry on my account, Miss. I will be here to catch you any time you please."

She looked up at his laughing tone, thinking he might be making fun of her plight, but saw only kindness in his face. "Thank you. I would never intentionally put you out Sir. I thank you for your chivalrous actions. I'm sorry, but we haven't been properly introduced, so I don't even know by what name to call you."

"Demyan, Miss. My name is Demyan."

"Oh, Yes, these are my sisters, Demyan, Freida and Batya. They run the dress shop on the front of our store.

My metal shop is in the back. I can show it to you now if you like."

"Perhaps later my friend. I am much more interested in getting to know your lovely sister, I mean sisters, a little better. I am very pleased to meet you Freida and Batya."

"I'm so sorry I was rude upon your arrival. I haven't yet started to prepare our evening meal, but I can throw together a little something now, if you would like to stay and share it with us."

"I would be most pleased, Miss. Is there anything I can do to help?"

Freida blushed again. "Yes, you may call me Freida. And I am pleased to meet you too, Demyan."

Fadeyka and Batya looked at each other sideways and tried not to laugh. Neither of them had ever seen their sister so obviously smitten with anyone. To the two of them; who knew this serious, organized, humorless young woman better than anyone; it was indeed an odd thing to witness.

According to an aggressive military strategy known as the Schlieffen Plan (named for its mastermind, German Field Marshal Alfred von Schlieffen), Germany began fighting World War I on two fronts, invading France through neutral Belgium in the west and confronting Russia in the east.

On August 4, 1914, German troops crossed the border into Belgium. In the first battle of World War I, the Germans assaulted the heavily fortified city of Liege, using the most powerful weapons in their arsenal—enormous siege cannons—to capture the city by August 15. The Germans left death and destruction in their wake as they advanced through Belgium toward France, shooting civilians and even executing a Belgian priest they had accused of inciting civilian resistance.

From August 26th - 30th the battle of Tannenberg was fought between Russia and Germany. That clash on the Eastern front, during the first month of the war, resulted in the almost complete destruction of the Russian Second Army and the suicide of its commanding general, Alexander Samsonov. A series of follow up battles, including the first battle of Masurian Lakes destroyed most of the First Army as well and kept the Russians off balance until the spring of 1915.

Borysko and his comrades, those that survived the first battle, were reeling physically and mentally from devastating losses. Their medic was hit early on in that first conflict, by rapid machine gun fire, when well camouflaged German machine gun nests mowed down oncoming troops like a scythe through wheat. Without a medic, many men who might have otherwise survived, didn't have a chance.

Rag tag groups of wounded, vacant eyed men were moved from one point of combat to another, without regard for their injuries or mental state. Relocated first to Belgium, and later to France through rain and increasingly cold weather, as fall and later winter descended upon them, Borysko's battalion was exposed to trench warfare at its worst. In the trenches, which were initially designed to help guard against machine gun fire and artillery attack from the air; the narrow, long ditches often gave troops additional time to don gas masks when German divisions began employing chemical weapons such as chlorine gas and mustard gas against their enemies. A definite advantage.

Borysko and many of his comrades, at least those who survived the relentless attacks, would carry scars from the blistering mustard gas for the rest of their lives. However, other dangerous health issues also ran rampant in the trenches, and many thousands would succumb to these.

With soldiers fighting in close proximity, usually in extremely unsanitary conditions, infectious diseases such as dysentery, cholera and typhoid fever were common and spread all too rapidly among the troops.

Borysko was suffering greatly, after discovering first hand that trench foot is the very devil itself. Rotting tissue had taken over large areas of both his feet, so he was struggling simply to walk. He was considered one of the healthy ones. He'd been taught the dangers of trench foot in basic training, a condition sometimes requiring amputation if not treated immediately. However, in filthy ditches filled with rain water, mud and human waste his options were somewhat limited, so his socks and boots were always soaked.

Men were effectively trapped in those interminable trenches for long periods of time, under nearly constant bombardment. Due to these circumstances many soldiers also suffered from "shell shock". One of Borysko's trench mates, a friend he'd known for his entire term of enlistment, finally reached his limit. He used his own bayonet. Falling on it, at just the right angle to achieve his sad purpose just the night before, ended his suffering.

In the First Battle of the Marne, September 6-9, 1914, allied forces confronted the invading Germany army, which had by then penetrated deep into northeastern France, within thirty miles of Paris. Allied troops checked the German advance and mounted a successful counterattack, driving the Germans back to north of the Aisne River. This defeat meant the end of German plans for a quick victory in France. Both sides dug into trenches and the Western Front became the setting for a war of attrition that would last more than three hellish years.

Ever the innovators, Germans used hand held flame throwers on February 26th, 1915 at Malancourt, near Verdun. The results were horrendous. Trenches filled with screaming burning men. Borysko was haunted by memories of a distant barnyard and the burning bodies of loved ones. He didn't think the smell of burning flesh and singed hair in his nostrils would leave him ever again. Over the course of the war Germany utilized over three thousand 'Flammanwerfer' troops to set their enemies afire. And those few foe who escaped death by burning in those evil attacks, lived with catastrophic disfigurement.

Borysko found himself thinking of home often. Not home in St. Petersburg, for that was never home to him, but home in the little clapboard farmhouse of his childhood. Where the golden feather grass grew tall as a man and his mother's smile woke him every morning. He found himself crying almost constantly, and would have been embarrassed, except for the fact that he was not the only one suffering from a home sickness so deep it seemed to encompass every ounce of his soul.

Demyan was dear to her, and she could tell he felt the same way, but life is not always so simple as it seems. She'd known him for three years now, but their relationship had not progressed to marriage. She imagined their deepest beliefs were simply too opposite to ever merge and they were each too stubborn to surrender their personal opinions.

She assumed she loved him, though she'd never loved a man before Demyan, so she could not be sure. The look in his eyes sent her the same message, or so she thought. But in the past year she'd felt a bit betrayed. During one of their many long talks, talks that lasted far into the night, she discovered he was a member of the Bolshevik resistance. The group that followed Lenin, Stalin and Trotsky.

This was a piece of information he'd not shared with her before. To keep her safe, he posited. She was deeply disturbed by the news, much to her own amazement.

She'd always thought him a simple printer and understood her brother to be only his friend and occasional assistant. However, she discovered Demyan had acted as sponsor for her brother, who ultimately joined that resistance group as well. Now, she felt a fool. How could she not have seen the evidence of their involvement in that rapidly growing movement?

Freida was conflicted. Demyan was handsome and obviously interested, but his personal beliefs were thousands of miles separated from her own. She and Fadeyka had always held similar feelings about the Jewish religion they'd grown up with. A feeling that perhaps there was a God, but that He might not be terribly interested in what was going on in their family. After all, their parents and grandparents had been avid followers of Judaism and firm believers in Jehovah God, but were brutally murdered on their own farm. They, Freida and Fadeyka, on the other hand, had pretty much deserted their religion over the years and yet were quite successful in their business ventures and even life in general. Was there any advantage to following their god?

Just take the example of Borysko. Deeply religious, yet off fighting a war for a Tsar who could care less if he lived or died.

Batya still prayed, every day, but Freida couldn't remember the last time she'd done the same. At least until things changed when her brother went off to war three years ago.

Now, she and her younger sister prayed for Borysko daily. She would never have thought to skip that practice, as even the ritual itself gave her comfort regarding Fadeyka's safety. Had she slowly come back to faith? Perhaps or perhaps not. But she knew, at least, that she wasn't ready to declare to the world there was no God. Of that much she was certain.

Demyan, on the other hand, held the same beliefs as his illustrious leader, Lenin, who espoused ideas completely foreign to her. He supposed there was no God at all. Perhaps she was just getting too old, at twenty-seven, to make a change so drastic to her upbringing. Or, maybe, she was more deeply connected to the God of the universe than she'd ever realized. Whatever the reason, she didn't believe they could be compatible on that basis alone.

Freida and Batya had also become very close to the women of the royal family, after five years of measurements and stunning dresses.

Even throughout the war years when the rest of the country went without, the Romanov ladies were still beautifully adorned and the dress shop continued to thrive, so they spent time together weekly.

The Romanovs were Christians. Freida was fully aware that if her Jewish heritage were ever to be discovered, they would be pariahs to the Romanovs who despised Jews. But for now, they were still friends. She was sure, though, that Lenin's ideologies were not highly regarded in those royal circles, for more reasons than one. Solely for the sake of her dear friends, she secretly hoped that nothing would ever come of the rumors of revolution.

Demyan and her brother nagged at her continually to cut ties with the royal family. She argued that the business they did with the royals and their wealthy friends provided a good living for the whole family. But he warned that someday, possibly sooner that they realized, a revolution would put her on the wrong side of history, where she and Batya would find themselves in danger they could not avoid.

In early 1917 a large group of workers decided to strike. It was finally time to demand what they should have been given freely; decent working conditions, better pay, and safety. During the strike, many of the workers got together and began discussing politics. Angry that so many of their young men had died in the Tsar's wars (nearly two million dead and five million wounded) the people blamed the Tsar for every ill to befall their country. The group quickly grew, became a mob, and riots broke out.

The Tsar ordered his army to suppress the riot, but many of the soldiers refused to fire on the Russian people. Very soon the whole affair turned into outright mutiny against the Tsar.

With his army turned against him, Nicholas II was forced to give up his throne and a new government took over as the royal family was summarily imprisoned in Alexander Palace to await their fate.

Over the next few months two political parties ruled Russia: the Petrograd Soviet (representing the workers and soldiers), and the Provisional Government (the traditional government without the input of the Tsar). Buried within the Petrograd Soviet was the revolutionary group we know as the Bolsheviks. Lenin believed the new Russian government should be a Marxist (communist) government. In October of 1917, Lenin took full control of the government in what would later be called the Bolshevik Revolution. Russia was now the first true communist country in the world.

After the revolution, Russia exited World War 1 by signing the Treaty of Brest-Litovsk with Germany. The new communist government in Russia took control of all industry and moved the Russian economy from a rural to an industrial one. Seizing farmland from rightful landholders, they distributed it among the peasants. Many of whom had never done a day's farm work in their lives. This further added to a situation which would later lead to desperate need across the nation. Religion was banned from most aspects of society, and ownership of Bibles became instantly taboo.

Those who were, or ever had been, friends with the elite and royal began to hide their former relationships. Expecting, and rightly so, stern retribution from this new government for those frivolous former dealings. People were watching all around them. And, those people were likely to report anyone who seemed overly sympathetic to the Romanovs and others in the previous government. Freida; who had recently been corresponding with their mother's sister, Fern, outside of Warsaw, and Batya; closed their shop and decided to lay low until conditions were more favorable.

The Tsar's army was on its way home. The biggest difference between present time and their departure three years ago, lay in the fact that these men were no longer members of the Tsar's army. Today there was no Tsar's army, but simply a communist army of the people. Intermingled with shocking physical and emotional injuries were the confused feelings of torn loyalties, anger over so much devastating loss for no good or apparent reason and a strange sense of abandonment.

The ladies awaited the return of their brother with great joy, but also extreme trepidation. Who would it be that might return to them. After so much shock and suffering, would Borysko be the same man who'd gone off to war three years ago?

When he arrived at the depot, Borysko was almost unrecognizable. At only nineteen years of age his hair had turned from dark auburn to shocking white. Walking with a cane and a noticeable limp, his feet appeared to be of little to no use to him. Blister scars and deep emotional shock, had changed his face so entirely, his sisters almost walked right past him. He was unbelievably thin and had the worn down, beaten up, look of an old man who'd seen far too much tragedy in his life.

When the girls finally recognized and ran to, Borysko, he took a step back from their eager advance. Even when he finally allowed their physical contact, Freida noticed that he shook from deep within, as if from a bone chilling cold that would never be warmed.

They gathered his things and headed back to their small apartment above the shop. While they walked, arms supporting their brother, Freida and Batya couldn't help but notice the trail of tears trickling down his scarred face, and soon their own cheeks were wet as well.

Arriving home seemed to settle him a bit, but as they sat him down and proceeded to remove his boots his anxiety rose again. Freida calmed him but noticed a smell so foul, it gagged her, as she carefully peeled the socks from his feet. She was appalled at what she saw. In some places the flesh was clearly dead and stunk like rotting meat. In other places the outer skin was completely absent, revealing bits of inner muscle laced with deep, oozing, puss pockets. She didn't know where to begin, so she sat back on her heels and began to sob. Borysko reached out softly to stroke her hair.

"Batya, please go and get the doctor. Tell him we need him right away."

"Yes Freida. I'll go right now."

"Oh, my dear brother. I can't even imagine how you have walked at all. If I had known your feet were so badly damaged, we would have hired a wagon to carry you. How could this happen? And, why has no one done anything to help you?"

"When we were called to return home, there were very few of our original battalion left alive. Our medic was one of the first killed, in the initial month of our deployment. We have had essentially no medical help since then. It has been difficult, but some of us have managed to survive. It is indeed hard to walk, but there are whole parts of my feet that I cannot feel anymore. So, it isn't quite as painful as it looks. Please don't fret sister."

"Did they tell you why you were returning home?"

"Yes, we were told that there was an uprising, a people's revolution and that a new government now rules. We were told the Tsar and his family have been arrested. Freida, I and many of my comrades are still loyal to the Tsar. We just didn't know what to do."

"Don't let anyone hear you say that, Borysko. Especially your brother and his friend, Demyan. They are loyal to the Bolsheviks, and are completely brainwashed, along with much of St. Petersburg. Batya and I have walked on eggshells since finding out that your brother is part of the new revolution. We are not sure how far his loyalties run, but we believe he would report us if he discovered our contrary feelings. We were not so poorly off as many other workers and didn't share the deep disenchantment that seemed to engulf them. Our own shop has been very successful. We weren't in favor of the revolution or the new communist government. Besides, we've made friends with the Romanov women designing and sewing dresses for them over the years. Especially young Anastasia."

"Many of my comrades spoke of the revolution as we walked home. I couldn't help but feel like a traitor even as I listened. I know the Tsar and his family have had a good life, even when ours was poor. I also know the Romanovs hate Jews. But he is still my Tsar. Besides, this new government doesn't believe in God. How can I back a government that doesn't believe in God?"

"I'm not telling you where to direct your loyalties, nor am I telling you to back a government that doesn't believe in God, brother. I'm simply telling you to be careful of what you say and to whom you say it."

"I will, Freida. But I don't know how I can stay here now. We are Jews and just as hated by this new regime, or perhaps even more so, as we were by the Tsar's government. With a brother who knows that we are not atheists, our secrets might be too many to hide."

"I know, Borysko. Batya and I have saved a tidy sum from the success of our dress business. We have also been laying low, so I'm sure there would be very few who might notice our absence. I have been corresponding with our mother's sister, Fern, who lives outside of Warsaw. She told me that the Pale has been eradicated since the end of the war. No one would question our right to travel now, even if they discovered our Jewish heritage. She has invited us to come and join her in her home."

"No matter where we go sister, there will be those

who wish to destroy us. The Bolsheviks are no friend to Jews, not any more than the Tsar's government was. As we walked home, I heard men bragging that revolutionaries killed over two hundred thousand Jewish civilians in the border areas, while the war was coming to an end. For no other reason than that they were Jews. A small piece of me wanted to tell them I am a Jew. The man who saved your life, all your lives, on the battlefield is a Jew. The Tsar's government at least tolerated our presence for the most part, as long as we kept our place in the Pale. I know that's a terrible way to live, but at least we knew where we stood. I wanted to come home to you sister, so that you would not spend your lives wondering what happened to me. I know that the infection in my feet is too severe to heal without removing my legs. If I allow that, what use would I be to you or anyone else?"

"Borysko, please don't talk that way. We love you. We will figure everything out and all will be well. I told you that Batya and I have done well in our business, and we have put away a large sum that should see us through. When we move, we will simply use our talents in our new location, perhaps open a little shop. Aunt Fern is very excited for us to come. She is getting old and never had children of her own, so we could be of great help to her also. We are just happy to have you back home dear brother. Until you are fit to travel, we will just lay low and not bring attention to ourselves."

"I don't want to be a burden to you sister. I am quite serious about that. I'm afraid I might even be a danger to you. It is very hard for me to act like I agree with these atheist Bolsheviks, and if I say the wrong thing..."

"Batya and I have not told a soul that we are Jews, for that very reason. And, though Fadeyka is one with the revolution, I'm sure he has kept our secret as well. He could not reveal our story without uncovering his own. Here comes Batya with the doctor. Just be still Borysko. Let us see what we are dealing with now."

When the doctor arrived and entered the room, he took one look at Borysko's feet and his face told them all they needed to know. He examined the soldier and asked if he could speak to Freida outside.

"Doctor, whatever you have to say to my sister, you can certainly say to me. I am a grown man and capable of making decisions concerning my own health."

"I'm sorry young man. There is much damage. Extensive enough that I don't believe we would have any chance of saving your feet. The infection has advanced to at least the knee on your left leg, and perhaps further on your right. If we don't amputate, the infection will travel on to your heart and kill you, probably within the week. I will give you a bit of time to talk, but we will need to know how you wish to proceed very quickly if we are to save your life."

"Freida, I want you to let me go. I've already told you that I don't want to come back here and be a burden to you and Batya. I won't have it."

"Borysko, I won't let you talk that way! You are not a burden to us. We love you...... Doctor, please make whatever arrangements you need to make for the surgery. I will not have my brother go off to fight in this ridiculous war, to come home alive, and then to die in his own home!"

Batya was crying by this time. "I won't hear of it either, brother. I might be younger than you, but I will fight for your life. Do you hear me? We have waited much too long for you to come home, to have you die in your own bed."

"Alright, doctor, do what you must. Batya, please stop crying. I think it is a mistake Freida, but if I can't get you to listen to reason, then I will do what has to be done."

Surgery was scheduled for the very next morning, so Freida made a nice supper of roasted lamb with vegetables, and the three of them prayed together and ate their meal quietly. Borysko on his bed, and the ladies on a small table pulled up close to their brother. After their meal they talked for hours of old times with the family on the farm and then they prayed some more. They remembered their parents and their grandparents and shed a few tears for those they'd loved and lost. The girls sat with Borysko until he was fast asleep, then they retired to their own bedroom.

"The dogs have a mighty appetite; they never have enough." Isaiah 56:11

"The righteous man perishes, and no one lays it to heart; devout men are taken away, while no one understands." Isaiah 57:1

CHAPTER 6

"Nooooooooooooooo, Freida, come quickly, please. Help me."

Freida woke with a start, to the sound of Batya's mournful cries. Grabbing her housecoat, she pulled it on as she ran in the direction of her sister's pleas. "Oh, Borysko, no. Oh my dear brother." She dropped to the floor beside Batya, who was holding their brother's head in her lap. From the looks of it, he'd kept his knife from the lovely lamb supper she prepared the night before and slit his own throat, from ear to ear, as he lay in bed. So, that was what he meant when he said, "I will do what has to be done".

Perhaps he regretted his decision to end his own life, soon after he'd made the choice, and decided to seek help. This might explain his presence on the floor and the amount of blood everywhere. If only one of them had heard him, before it was too late.

The entire area, bed, floor, and rug were soaked in the young man's blood. And now, his little sister was covered too. Sobbing and rocking, as she stroked Fadeyka's head, she was inconsolable. Freida tried to comfort the younger girl, but Batya pulled away and would have none of it.

Freida called for the doctor and the police. As they took her brother's body away, she held her young sister. For now, all she could do was close his bedroom door. There was just too much blood, too much loss.

Why? Why would he have chosen to end his life in so gruesome a manner, knowing that his younger sister might be the one to find him? They would never know. Obviously, he was dead serious about not wanting to be a burden, no matter what she said to the contrary. Her heart was broken.

Fadeyka arrived home with Demyan not far behind the departure of the police. "What's going on? I saw an ambulance and police cars."

"Your brother, Borysko, came home little brother. Didn't you hear that the troops had returned?"

"He did? No, I've been in meetings with the group. Where is he?"

"He's gone, Fadeyka."

"Gone? He didn't even want to stay around long enough to say hello to his little brother?"

"He killed himself last night, Fadeyka. He slit his own

throat. Somehow he thought he should do this terrible thing, so he wouldn't be a burden to us. And now he's gone, just like everyone else we've ever loved." Fadeyka sat down, hard, on the nearest chair.

"Freida, I'm so sorry."

"It doesn't matter, Demyan. You wouldn't have liked my brother. He believed in God and was very loyal to the Tsar."

"Oh, I didn't know. What about you, Freida?"

"What do you mean, 'what about me?'"

"Are you also loyal to the Tsar?"

"I don't feel like talking to you right now, Demyan."

"I'll just take Demyan into the other room. We have some matters to discuss."

"I can't believe you are going to sit here, in this house, and talk about your stupid Bolshevik revolution when I just told you that your brother is dead! No. You know what? I don't care what you do, Fadeyka. Please just go away and leave me alone."

Fadeyka went into his room and Demyan followed, wearing a suspicious expression as he looked back over his shoulder at Freida. Perhaps the men believed they would have privacy with the door closed. But, Freida and

Batya could hear every word the men said as they sat at the kitchen table holding hands. Freida wouldn't have cared about their conversation, at all, except the very first thing Demyan said caught her attention. "So, the plans are made."

"He's really going to do it then? Is it necessary to kill them? Wouldn't it be just as effective to keep them imprisoned?"

"Are you starting to go soft?"

"No, no, I'll do whatever I must, but the children. I mean, if it comes right down to it, I can see Nicholas and maybe even Alexandra, but the children?"

"Listen, Fadeyka, Lenin and Stalin want to be sure the whole Romanov line is wiped out, so this kind of loyalty to royalty can never happen again."

"So, where are we supposed to go to do this thing? Are the royals still being held at Alexander Palace?"

"No, they've been moved to Ipatiev House in Yekaterinburg."

"I understand. When will it happen?"

"Lenin says Wednesday the 17th of July. He thinks fewer people will notice if it is carried out in the middle of the week. He doesn't want to create any martyrs. Now, that leaves less than a month for us to get everything there and set up before the day. He also doesn't want people to believe the new government had anything to do with the assassination of the Tsar, so all preparations must be done ahead of time. It must be made to look as if a mob of the people of the revolution did this. And that Nicholas was the only one executed. Not his family."

"Okay, then we'd better get a few things arranged. That doesn't give us a lot of time. I will call around and see if we can rent transportation. A wagon would work if we will be taking supplies."

"Good idea. And, Fadeyka....."

"Yeah, Demyan?"

"Can your sister be trusted? Is she loyal to the Tsar? Do you think she will be causing us any trouble?"

"No, no, don't worry about Freida. She's just upset about our brother. You know how women are, don't you? No, I will talk to her. She'll be fine."

"Okay, see that you do. We'd better start getting some things going, or we'll never be ready in time. I'll see you later."

As Demyan left the bedroom and walked past the girls who were sitting at the kitchen table, they kept their heads down as if they were still crying. Then when Fadeyka entered the kitchen, they acted as if he wasn't there at all. They wouldn't let on that they'd heard the entire conversation in all its sordid detail. But what could they do about it now?

"I have to go downtown for a while, and when I get back I'm going to pack. I have some business out of town that will take some time."

"So, you aren't even going to stay for your brother's levaya?"

"Freida, this is urgent business and can't wait."

"More urgent than your family? Never mind brother. You do what you must. Batya and I will take care of affairs here, as usual. So, where are you off to?"

"I can't talk about it. I would tell you if I could, but I can't. Okay, I'll see you later. Perhaps we can have supper together before I go?"

"Certainly, Fadeyka. Supper it is. Do you have any requests?"

"No, I'm sure anything you make will be great."

Freida had all she could do to control her anger, responding with as real a smile as she could muster, as her brother gathered a few things and left the apartment.

"Freida, what are we going to do? We can't let them kill Anastasia."

"Batya, for now we must act as though we didn't hear a thing. They can't know we overheard their plan. Do you understand? Not only would they be forced to kill us, but the assassination of our friends would still proceed as usual. No, we must keep this information to ourselves and assume there is no one we can trust. We will arrange transportation to the Ipatiev House in Yekaterinburg, then we will have a private burial for Borysko before we leave. When we arrive at our destination, we will have devised a plan and we will do what we must. Are we in agreement?"

"Yes Freida. I think that is a very good idea. As soon as Fadeyka leaves we should pack, don't you think? We will hide our money at the bottom of our case, in an item that would not raise suspicion, should we be stopped for any reason."

"Yes, Batya. That is very good. We will do exactly that. After we have done what we can for the Romanovs, we will go on to Warsaw. Fadeyka will be free to pursue his life with the revolutionaries if he wishes, but we will help Aunt Fern for as many years as she might need us. It will be nice to be with family again, don't you agree?"

"But, won't you miss, Fadeyka, Freida? Even a little?"

"Yes, Batya, but I will miss the boy he was, not the man we see today. A man who thinks little of honorable things and believes it okay to murder someone, just because of their politics, their religion, or who they are. That is no different than the Bolsheviks murdering Jews just for being Jews. No, I will miss the silly, loving, freckle faced, little boy I once knew. I will bury him in my mind when we bury his brother. It will be only you and I now, Batya. I know it will be hard, but can you handle it?"

"Freida, you have always been here for me. As long as you and I are together, I will be fine. With God watching over us, I know that everything will be okay."

Blue skies and soft breezes made for a beautiful day, when they walked their brother to his final resting place. They didn't cry. They'd already done plenty of that. Packed and ready to go, so they could leave on the 10:00 am train right after the levaya, they held hands and looked at each other with the conviction of those on a mission. They were set on doing all they could to save the Romanovs.

They'd let their shop and apartment go back to the landlord, knowing when Fadeyka returned home in a couple months from his terrible, murderous mission, he would be forced to find another place to live. Perhaps he could room with his dear friend, Demyan. That would suit them both.

The girls rented storage for his tools and equipment, emptied his shop, and left a note with the landlord as to where he could find his belongings. Of course, they hoped he would be returning as an enormous failure and be forced to leave his beloved cause, but that would be entirely up to him.

Walking the main streets to the local rail yard, the ladies could already see plenty of evidence of the evil effects wrought by the new communist government. There were hungry and homeless people everywhere. Many were elderly, but there seemed to be an inordinate number of small children running the streets as well. Angry Bolshevik appointed guards were summarily beating the destitute to get them off of the public byways. After all, Lenin and Stalin would be coming through the city later that day and they certainly wouldn't want the leaders of their movement to see the negative results of their 'people's revolution'.

Sadly, in years to come, the people of Russia would come to regret putting their trust in the false purveyors of a so-called united USSR. Under Stalin's rule around twenty million would lose their lives to labor camps, forced collectivization, famine and executions. So much for the Bolshevik's utopian vision.

The trip from St. Petersburg to Yekaterinburg would take two days by train, but that should put them well ahead of Fadeyka and Demyan who were traveling by wagon. It would certainly be great to know exactly what their plan was, but for now they knew they would just have to play it by ear when they arrived.

Views from their train car window were beautiful and, under normal conditions, could be considered quite re-laxing. However, the girls found relaxing quite impossi-ble when they were on a mission to save the royal family. Freida didn't know how they would proceed, but she was ready to lay down her life to save her friends if it came to that.

In Yekaterinburg Freida and Batya rented a room and

used their best acting skills to act as if they were tourists when speaking to the hotel's owner. Suspicious looks abounded, when they asked directions to Ipatiev House, so they requested directions to several other locations as well. Then, off they went in search of the house where they knew their dear friends were being held.

Stopping for a bite to eat, half way through the day, Freida and Batya put their heads together and began hatching a plan. All too aware the date for the pre-arranged assassination was July 17th, now they had to figure out how to get into that house to set the prisoners free before that date arrived.

Asking around led them to some facts that might be useful. The house had belonged to a merchant named Nicolai Ipatiev. However, after the revolution the government requisitioned the home, removing the owner and confiscating his property, as usually happens during initial takeover in socialist and communist regimes. Now it was being used to secretly house the Romanovs until their upcoming death sentences were carried out.

Their presence in the house was a well known fact around the town, but most didn't care. It was still early enough in the years after the uprising that many people believed all the lies the Bolsheviks were feeding the Russian people. Especially the enormous lie that the downfall of the royals and others with wealth would lead to unlimited prosperity for the masses. Sadly, they would realize soon enough the opposite is true.

Freida and Batya would have to make their way inside the home in order to get the lay of the land and plot their rescue, but how? Freida decided a bold approach would be best, as they didn't have many days head start on the men. The following day the girls marched right up to the front door and knocked. A guard answered and gave a sly smile to the two lovely and well-dressed young women standing outside.

Freida and Batya planned their conversation to confuse the guards. "Good afternoon sir. We are looking for our cousin Nicolai. Can you tell us where we might find him?"

"Your cousin no longer lives here. This house has been appropriated by the people's government, miss."

"I told you sister. I didn't think he was here anymore. He didn't answer any of my letters."

"Well, what are we to do now? We have come all the way from St. Petersburg to see our cousin, and now we don't even know where he is. Is there someone in charge that we might talk to, who may know where our cousin has gone?" Now crying.

"I'm not sure miss. Please stop crying. Why don't you come in. I'll get my captain. He might know where Mr. Ipatiev has gone." Once inside the doors, and with the guard headed upstairs, the girls looked around quickly to see if there was any evidence of where the Romanovs were being held. After a cursory search they heard boots on the stairs and speedily resumed their places by the front door.

"May I help you?"

"Yes sir. We hoped you might know the whereabouts of the man who was owner of this house before the government requisitioned the property. You see, he is our cousin, and we were supposed to be coming here to stay with him after our parents were killed in an accident."

"Miss, I'm afraid your cousin has been executed for crimes against the people's state. If you are relatives of his, you should probably be brought in for questioning as well."

"Sir, I assure you that we have done nothing wrong. We arrived here just yesterday from St. Petersburg. Would you like to see our train tickets? We only rested a bit and then proceeded to discover where our cousin's, or excuse me, the government's house, was located." Now, both of the girls began to cry again, loudly.

"Here, here, Miss. I believe that if you just go along on your way, we can forget your small indiscretion in coming here at all. Do you have someplace to stay, or do we need to call for someone to escort you to suitable accommodations?"

"No sir, we can find our way from here. Thank you so much for your help."

Clear of the house, Batya began excitedly to tell Freida what she'd found. "I think I know where they are being held. There was a door that I'm sure led down to a basement. There was a bucket and some other things there that made me think the guards use them to go downstairs and empty chamber pots and such. If we can just get past the guard in front and get to that inside door."

"I can't let you go back into that house, Batya. This will be something I do myself."

"No, Freida. How will you know where the door is? No, I will come with you, and that is all there is to it!"

"Batya, I made a promise to our parents all those years

ago, to keep you children safe, and so far, you are the only one I haven't completely failed. I won't let you go with me. You will not change my mind on this. Tell me where the door is and I will do my best to free our friends. But if I fail, you must go on to Warsaw to be with Aunt Fern. You will care for her and she will care for you. There is plenty of money in our suitcase to take care of your needs for a very long time indeed."

"I won't allow it, Freida. You sound as though you've already given up. I will go with you. It will be safer if we both go. We can watch out for each other, just as it's always been."

"We'll talk about it later little sister. I'm tired and I think we should go to bed. We'll have clearer heads in the morning. Then we will decide what we must do."

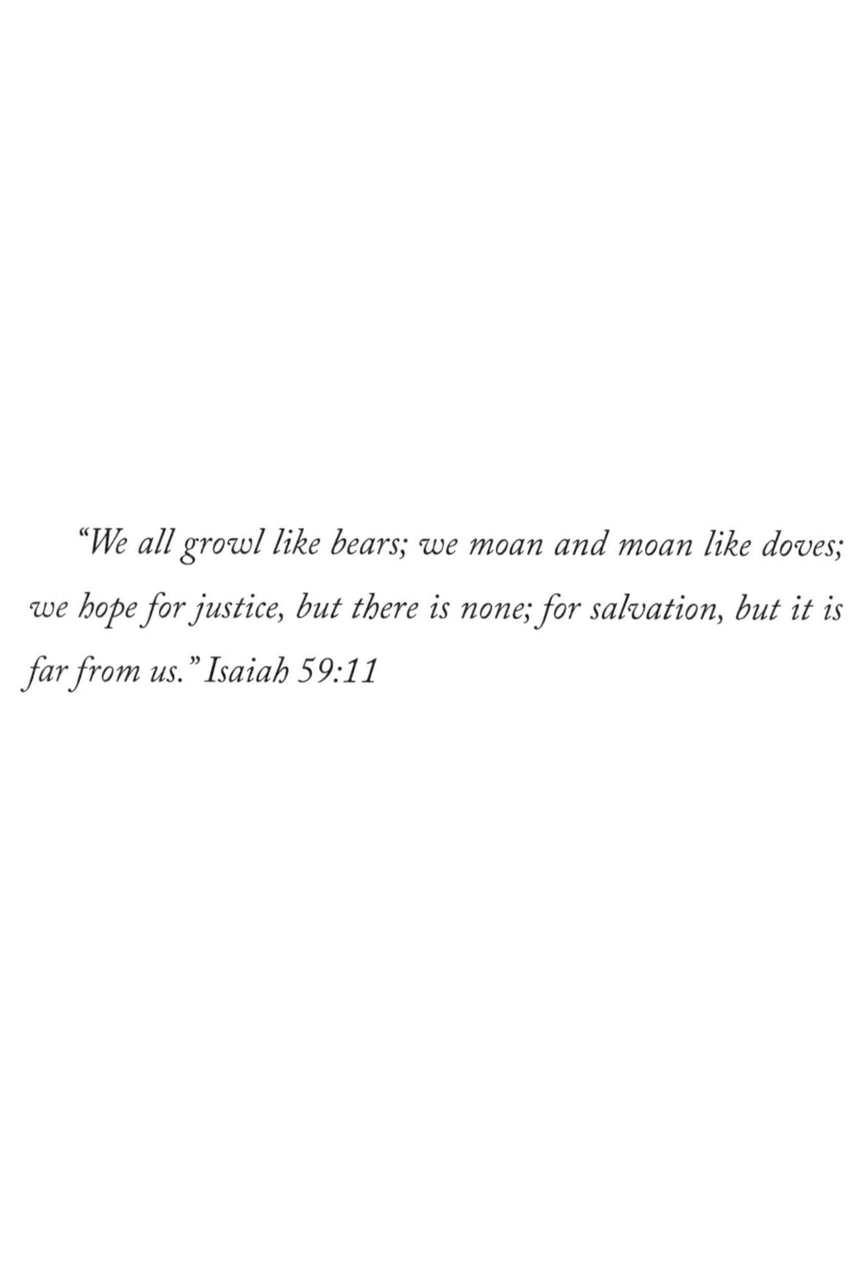

"We all growl like bears; we moan and moan like doves; we hope for justice, but there is none; for salvation, but it is far from us." Isaiah 59:11

CHAPTER 7

When Freida awoke early the following morning, to the sound of birds chirping and a sweet breeze blowing the curtains in their hotel room window, she noticed immediately that Batya was not in her bed.

Looking around she found that Batya's clothing was also gone, and there was a note on the desk. "Freida, I couldn't let you do this thing alone. Especially when I was the one who said that we couldn't let them kill Anastasia. How would I ever live with myself if something happened to you my dear sister. I promise that I will be careful. I have taken a small amount of money from the case, in hopes that I might find and purchase a gun from someone on the back streets. I don't want you to worry about me. If something should happen, you go on to Warsaw and live with Aunt Fern. I'm sure you will be a much better helper to her than I could ever be anyway. I love you sister. Batya."

In a panic, Freida pulled on her clothes and flew out the door. The morning was lovely, but her mind was focused on one purpose only. She hollered for a cab. A cart and driver pulled up in front of the hotel and she jumped aboard, giving the driver the address in mid leap.

Perhaps, if Batya was looking to purchase a gun before attempting to rescue their friends, she might arrive on location before her sister. Urging the driver to move swiftly she gained the address and didn't see any sign that her sister was, or had been, there. Breathing a sigh of relief, she paid the driver and sent him on his way. Then she positioned herself across the street, beside a building where she had a clear view of the front of the house.

She'd been there only a few minutes when she heard the distinct sound of gunshots. She ran forward, trying to determine whether or not the shots were coming from the house. Hearing shouting, she realized the ruckus was going on at the rear of the building. Dashing off the curb and across the street, she made her way around to the back of the house, only to see her sister engaged in battle with the same guard from the day before.

She ran to her sister's side, just in time to intercept a bullet meant for Batya; and just as her sister's bullet entered the head of the guard.

Toppling to the ground, she heard Batya's agonized

cries as she fell. Then, her little sister was hovering over her, crying and asking what she could do. "Batya, there is nothing you can do now. You must go. Now that they know someone is trying to rescue the family, they will never be accessible to us again. Go, shayna maidel. You must get to Aunt Fern. Go to the train depot and purchase a ticket, or we will both be lost. Please." Blood gushed from Freida's wound, and she gasped painfully for each successive breath.

"Oh, Freida, look what I've done. My impulsive actions have only hurt you my sister. You are my angel. The only family I have left. How could I have been so foolish? Please, what can I do to help?"

"There is nothing to be done now little sister, not now. I'm not angry with you for trying to help our friends. No, it was a brave thing you did. But you must go. I can tell that I haven't much time left, and you cannot let them catch you. I hear others coming from the house who will find you soon if you don't leave."

"I can't just leave you. How can I just leave you, Freida?"

"You can and you will, Zeiskeit. Who will care for Aunt Fern if you are captured or killed? I love you, Ketsele. Go now and live for our grandparents, for our parents, our brothers and for me. Go."

Leaning over to kiss Freida's forehead, tears dripping from her eyes, Batya whispered into her sister's ear, "I will never forget you, Freida. Thank you for loving me and protecting me. I will see you in my dreams sweet sister. Goodbye meyn lib."

Just as the Captain and his man burst through the back door, to see the dead guard laying on the steps, Batya was rounding the corner of the house and heading for the street. The men saw Freida lying on the grass, with a handgun nearby and assumed she was the only assailant, so no one gave chase after young Batya.

Making haste through the streets, flagging down a cab and hurrying back to the hotel, Batya collapsed on the bed in a sobbing heap. "Oh, Freida, what have I done? What have I done? How will I live without you? I wish it was me lying dead in the grass. You never did anything evil in your life. You did naught but love us." She lay on the bed weeping, until she was all cried out.

After calming down she realized there was nothing she could do for her sister now. There was also nothing she could do for the Romanovs. So, there was nothing else she could do in Yekaterinburg.

Knowing Freida would want her to go on to Warsaw, she packed up her things; checking to be sure the money was still secure in the bottom of her case; and headed for the train depot.

Freida, left for dead, wasn't dead at all. The captain's man carried her into the house. The captain didn't want the furniture bloodied, so she was carried to the storage room and dumped unceremoniously on the floor to be interrogated. "Who sent you here?"

"No one, Sir. I came on my own."

"Aren't you the girl who came here yesterday looking for her cousin?"

"Yes sir, I am."

"There was another girl with you. Where is she?"

"I don't know sir. She didn't know I was coming here. She wasn't part of this."

"What exactly was, 'this'?"

"I was trying to save my friends from assassination."

"Assassination? Who told you they would be killed?"

"I overheard men talking. These are people I care

about. I couldn't just stand by and do nothing."

"Do you think these royals would have done the same for you? They think of no one but themselves. Why would you risk your life for them?"

"As I said, they are my friends."

"How are they your friends young woman? How do you know them?"

"I'm their seamstress. I make their dresses. I feel that we have become very close in these five years. Especially the girls and I, and I couldn't just sit by after overhearing this conversation concerning their soon demise."

"Well, young woman, I can promise they don't feel the same about you. I am very sorry that you would risk your life for these people. To them you are but vapor in the wind. However, if you insist they are such great friends, I will allow you to be put to death at the same time they are killed, if you think you can make it that long. After all, you are bleeding quite profusely and I will not be calling a doctor. I'm sure they will be excited to have so great a friend sharing their prison in these last days."

Thrown over the guard's shoulder and carried to the basement door, Freida was tossed unceremoniously down the stairs. At the bottom, a bruised and crumpled heap, she moaned and tried to move. It was useless. Blood still flowed freely from her bullet wound and she was becoming weaker by the minute. Her head ached as if she'd been kicked by a mule. She opened her eyes and tried to focus. Then she saw the royal family looking down at her. Familiar faces. First, the face of Anastasia, then each of the other children, one by one, before finally Tsar Nicholas and Empress Alexandra stood gazing down at her. They helped her to one of the pallets on the floor, slowly, leaving a trail of blood all the way to her destination.

"Who is this woman?"

"Nicky, this is our dress maker."

"What is she doing here?"

"I assure you I don't know."

"I came to rescue you, Your Highness."

"It appears you have failed."

"Yes sir. It appears I have."

"Miss Freida, I can't believe you're here. How did you come all this way? What do you mean you came to rescue us?"

"Yes, Empress. My sister and I came by train, after we overheard plans to execute you and your family on July 17th. We couldn't just stand by and do nothing as someone was about to hurt our friends."

"So, they really are going to go through with it after all. Where is your sister now?"

"I sent her on ahead. It seemed too dangerous a task, and I didn't want her injured. She believed me to be dying when she left for the train depot."

"Well, you appear to be correct in that it was a dangerous task. We've been led to believe all along that the people of Russia hate us and want to see us gone."

"That's not true your highness. There are still those who are loyal to the crown. They are just unorganized and underfunded. I don't know if they would have been able to wage much of an offensive, so, here I am."

"Yes, here you are. Thank you, Freida. It means a lot that you would care enough to risk your life for us."

"You're welcome, Anastasia. Batya has left and will be moving on to live with an Aunt in Warsaw, but she wanted you to know she cares and wishes you all the best."

"You're hurt and bleeding. What can we do to help?"

"There really isn't much you can do. The men upstairs told me they won't be calling a doctor. I think I've probably lost too much blood already."

"We could try putting bandages over the wound, but

we have no clean cloth."

"Mother, we can rip lengths of cloth from our petticoats. That could serve as bandages."

"Yes girls, that would be good." Each of the girls contributed a length of relatively clean cloth, and the wound was dressed."

The family let her rest on the pallet, as they contemplated their soon coming fate.

Batya purchased her ticket to Warsaw, feeling as though she was leaving part of herself behind. She would never know that her sister had survived the bullet meant for her, only to meet her sad fate along with the royal family.

Fadeyka and Demyan arrived a few days later, to join the Bolshevik secret police in setting up the ruse that would trick the nation's people into believing 'the people's army' had killed the Tsar. Fadeyka didn't know his older sister was in the basement along with those who would soon die.

On the night the military contingent entered the house, to complete the task assigned to them, they first had to take some steps to make it look as though the guards had been overcome, though, in reality, those very same soldiers helped with the necessary effects. Yakov Yurovsky, a revolutionary who led the Bolshevik's secret police led the men down the basement stairs and told Nicholas he was about to be executed.

"What? What?" the Tsar exclaimed, trying in vain to shield his wife. But it was too late.

Even with an entire contingent of soldiers, the murder of the imperial family was no simple affair. It took multiple attempts and more than twenty minutes to kill every family member. Yakov Yurovsky and his men used the butts of their guns, bayonets, knives and brute force to finish off the Romanov children and their servants. When Fadeyka saw that his sister was one of the prisoners in that basement he cried out for the men to spare her life, throwing his body over hers. Demyan, annoyed that Fadeyka seemed to be shirking his duty and showing weakness once again, shot and killed the young man along with the rest. The brother and sister died, tragically, in each other's arms.

On July 17th, 1918, Tsar Nicolas II, Empress Alexandra, their daughters, Olga, Tatiana, Maria, and Anastasia, and their son Alexi, were all brutally murdered by the Bolsheviks.

Then it was time to cover up the murders. Chaos ensued as Yurovsky and his men drove the bodies into the forest, stripped them down, and confiscated their jewelry and the jewels that were hidden in their clothing. As they did so, they covered them in acid and buried them. But the grave, located in a mine, was too shallow, and when the men tried to collapse the mine with grenades it failed. Instead, they disinterred the bodies as they frantically searched for another grave site.

Finally, they dug another shallow grave, and, after abusing the corpses even more, buried all but two of the family members, Maria and Alexei, who were later burned. The remnants of their bodies were buried in another, separate grave nearby.

A few days later the Bolsheviks announced the Tsar's murder to the world and the party used the elimination of their biggest enemy to consolidate their political power. Newspapers and party communications played up Nicholas' perceived weakness and denounced his monarchy as evil.

"Nicholas Romanov was essentially a pitiful figure," *Pravda*, the official party newspaper, declared after the murders. The editorial called the Tsar "the personification of the barbarian landowner, of this ignoramus, dimwit, and bloodthirsty savage." The people of Russia had no use for monarchy any more, it continued. "Russian workers and peasants have only one desire: to drive a good aspen-wood stake into this grave cursed by the people."

The official party line was that the Tsar's wife and family were being cared for in an undisclosed location, but rumors began to swirl about what had happened to Alexandra and her children. Meanwhile, Bolsheviks went on a murder spree, killing every Romanov family member and associate they could get their hands on. Twenty-seven others were slaughtered in the next eighty-four days. Only a few of their remains were ever recovered; the rest were dumped in mass graves or burned beyond recognition. The Romanov line was extinguished.

"Oh Lord our God, You answered them; You were a for-giving God to them, but an avenger of their wrongdoings."
Psalm 99:8

CHAPTER 8

World War 1 was finally winding down in Europe, and America's huddled masses were exhausted, though heartily relieved that their boys were coming home. Anthony Shepherd had served his country proudly, on the European front, as an Army chaplain in the Lord's service. He'd been abroad for two years, while his wife, Margret, carried on at home with the farm and their four children in Nebraska.

Wounded in service, he'd been sent home minus his left leg, but otherwise surprisingly intact for all the horrors he'd encountered in battle. He loved the Lord Jesus and he loved his country. No sacrifice would have been too much, in his estimation, for the land he treasured.

His congregation welcomed him home heartily. He would have some adjustments to make in running the church. But the biggest changes would come in doing chores around the farm. The children would be a big help with much of that, just as they had been for their mother while he was gone. Soon things were settling back into a sense of normalcy and time marched on.

Margret was on her way back from the outhouse when the worst of her contractions began. As she came through the door she called. "Anthony, could you come down her please?"

"Yes, my dear, I'm coming." When he arrived at the foot of the stairs he knew, by the look on her face, it was time.

With four older children, they both knew the drill. Dad's job would be to get the kids loaded into the wagon and over to Aunt Doris' house. If for no other reason than to keep them out of the way until the blessed event occurred.

The kids, two boys and two girls ages nine to thirteen, weren't naive. They'd lived on a farm their entire lives. All around them God's hand and the unique ebb and flow of nature taught the lessons of life, death and the miraculous beginnings of every living thing. They dressed quickly, grabbed biscuits from the basket on the stove in the kitchen and piled into the wagon for the ride to their Aunt Doris and Uncle Dick's farm a couple miles down the road, where they would wait to hear of the birth.

Anthony's instructions included dropping the four kids off, then swinging into town to pick up Doc before heading back home. At his current rate of travel, he should be able to get back to the farm within the hour. Fully aware Margret had been down this road before, he was also sensitive to the fact that no one knew what complications might arise now that she was getting older, so he didn't want to leave her on her own for very long.

He arrived in Springfield promptly and headed straight to the doctor's office on Main St., his crutch thumping loudly on the wooden plank sidewalk. He knocked on the clinic door, Doc saw him, grabbed his bag and they hurriedly made their way to the wagon for the short journey back out to the farm. "How are you, Pastor? I see you aren't using your prosthetic leg. Has it been bothering you?"

"Oh, you know, just the usual. I guess I'm doing okay, Doc. It just rubs the skin raw. Sometimes it's just easier to grab the crutch. But we've got bigger fish to fry, Doc. I'm just a little worried about Margret. This one has been giving her some real problems. I hope we didn't get ourselves in deeper than we could handle this time around. We should have known this might happen with us being older now."

"I think she'll be fine, Anthony. As long as all goes well during the birth, a child later in life can be a real blessing. You folks will have one to take care of you when all the others take off to make a life of their own. We'll all work together on this one and she'll be fine. You just wait and see. Now don't you worry, okay?"

"Okay, Doc. I'll try not to worry. And, I know what you mean. Margret and I married pretty late, because we were both taking care of elderly parents. I sure wouldn't want to be that kind of burden to my child."

"Well, then you'll just have to stay healthy, won't you?"

"I guess I will, Doc."

Once there they checked on Margret, who appeared to be quite advanced in her labor, with beads of sweat collecting on her face and running in rivulets down her neck. "I'm so glad you made it Doc. I was getting pretty sure I'd be delivering this one by myself."

"Don't be silly, Margret. I've delivered every one of your young uns, and I'm not about to break tradition now. Anthony, head out to the kitchen. Boil some water and get me some towels, as many as you can find."

"Right away, Doc."

It was a difficult labor. Doc was truly beginning to worry, as his patient's physical strength started wearing out. He knew if things went on much longer, he might lose Margret. So, he enlisted Anthony and they began to pray. Doc also began to prepare for a cesarean section, offering some last-minute hope if things didn't resolve quickly. Anthony held Margret's hand and tears filled his eyes as he watched her losing her battle to exhaustion.

Suddenly, as if lifted up on angels' wings, Margret seemed to fill with a new strength. She resumed her practiced breathing and bore down hard. With one last push their son was born, Jeffrey Adam Shepherd. Their eyes met and locked. There was something very special about this one. Mother and child were doing fine, and all was great with the world.

The three adults took a moment again to pray together and finished cleaning up mother and baby. Then the doctor, smiling and rolling down his sleeves, headed out to the kitchen to find a cup of coffee and one of Margret's famous biscuits waiting for him on the stove.

Stepping off the train at the Warsaw depot, Batya felt

at least a million miles from anything she deemed formerly recognizable. Warsaw was a bustling city, just like St. Petersburg. The similarities ended there. Landmarks, local culture and the people were completely strange and unfamiliar. She hadn't felt so alone since leaving her poor dead sister's body bleeding in the grass at Ipatiev House. Managing to contact her aunt by telegram, from the information found in her sister's belongings, had been a feat in itself. She was expecting someone to meet her at the depot, though she hadn't a clue who to search for in the glut of humanity pressing in around her.

Then, in the crowd, an extremely handsome young man wearing the garb of a chauffeur, holding a sign with her name emblazoned upon it, attracted her attention. He smiled when their eyes met, and the kindness she saw there made her feel instantly better. She returned a shy smile of her own and attempted to move toward him. Attempted being the operative word.

At eighteen years old, Batya had grown up to be a very lovely young woman. Her wide brimmed traveling hat sat upon perfectly quaffed, golden blond hair fashioned in the latest style. Eyes as blue as newly laid robin's eggs, and a perfect, peaches and cream complexion were set off by a smart, blue and white pin stripped day dress, fashionably cinched in at her tiny waist. Just under five feet tall, she was a little bit of a thing.

She'd always been told she was very strong for a girl and could hold her own when it came to physical activities of practically any sort. So, she was surprised at the effort it was currently taking to hold her place in the crush of bodies surrounding her.

Batya hadn't ever really been a tom boy, but she'd not been a vain girly girl either, certainly not after growing up with brothers around for most of her life. However, though she wasn't full of herself, she'd not failed to notice men's heads turning as she walked in public places. She never let the attention of men go to her head though. She was much too bright and focused for that.

The young man holding the sign walked toward her through the crowded depot, as she tried, without much success, not to be swept away by the flood of bodies exiting the train. She was beginning to feel a bit panicked, as the wave of people pulled her along, until she saw and grabbed a pole, wrapping her arms around the stationary object and holding on for dear life.

She heard the laughter of a strong baritone voice, as

the tide of humankind thinned and abated. A bit red faced over her situation, Batya turned toward the young man. As he drew closer, she noticed his slightly mischievous, smiling eyes, which were a particularly beautiful shade of green, looking down upon her in a kindly way. He removed his cap and gave her a sharp bow, revealing wavy, chestnut brown hair. And, upon his rising, she noted he possessed the most adorable set of matching dimples when he grinned. "I'm so glad I've found you, Batya! Are you okay? I thought I would lose you there for a while. Your Aunt Fern would have had me skinned alive if I came back without you!"

"I'm confused. I was led to believe, by my sister Freida, that our Aunt Fern was housekeeper for a wealthy family in Warsaw. Are you their chauffer?"

"Actually, I was. But, I have stayed on for your aunt entirely by choice. The couple, Mr. and Mrs. Wójcik, grew quite elderly while your aunt was in their employ. First the gentleman passed away, and then about a year ago the lady followed. They loved your aunt. She'd always taken such good care of them. And, because they had no children, they left their house and a goodly amount of money to your aunt, to care for her in her old age."

"But she is Jewish. Did they know this?"

"Yes, they did. When they brought her into the household, she was alone and incredibly grateful. She was with them for many years, and they have looked after her and cared for her, as she was taking care of them."

"So, how, again, did you become her chauffer?"

"Oh, that. Well, I was already the Wójcik's chauffer, and I always liked your aunt, so it was only natural that I should stay. There have been many changes in this past year. I wouldn't have wanted her to be alone. It isn't particularly safe for Jews to walk the streets since the war. And, as you know, she is quite fragile now. The Blue Army is still a presence in Warsaw, so I also act as her personal bodyguard when she must leave the house for appointments and the like."

"I don't know if you are aware, but I don't really know my aunt. She was corresponding with my sister, Freida, before her death. We were planning to come here together. Now, sadly, it's only me."

"She will still be happy to see you. I try to keep her company, but I'm sure she will benefit from having a female companion. The two of you will get along quite famously, I'm sure."

"So, how does she manage to not be harassed? Do the authorities know she is a Jew?"

"They do. The Wójciks, who were the people she worked for, were very respected in Warsaw. This is a very different sort of place compared to many parts of Europe. He was a Polish merchant of excellent repute and taking in a young Jewish girl as servant isn't as frowned upon as it would have been in many other places in the world. Jews have never been quite so ostracized here. And, now that the Pale has been disbanded, Poland is accepting many Jews from there and from other countries across Europe. Your aunt is well liked in the community, and, I might add, anxious to see her long lost niece. Enough questions for now, Batya. I'm sure your aunt will have much to tell you."

"I have two more questions for you, before I will move a step further."

"Okay, go ahead. But only two."

"First, what is your name? We have not been introduced."

"That, I am sure is my mistake. My name is Jakub. Jakub Nowak. And your second question?"

"My second question might not be any of my business."

"Go ahead, ask."

"Are you Jewish, Jakub?"

"Yes, I am, Batya, and very proud of my Jewish heritage. This is part of the reason the Wójciks took me in. Just as they took your aunt in. I was only eight years old when my entire family was killed in a very bloody pogrom. These kind people cared for me and treated me as if I was part of their own family. Your Aunt Fern and I became quite close over the years. And, we have remained like family, even after the passing of our employers."

"You might know, Jakub, that most of my family was also killed in a pogrom outside of Voronkov."

"I do know that, Batya. Your sister and your aunt exchanged quite a lot of information in their letters during these past months. I am very sorry for your loss."

"And I yours."

"Alright now, that was two questions. We should go. Your aunt will wonder where we've gotten off to."

Jakub walked Batya to the shiny automobile that would be their mode of transportation back to the house and opened the door for her. The car was lovely. Bright yellow, with black wheels, a matching black top and leather seats. Batya had never ridden in an automobile and found herself experiencing equal parts trepidation and excitement at the prospect. "Jakub, would you mind if I rode up front with you?"

"That hardly seems proper, Miss Batya. What will people think?"

"As you come to know me, Jakub. You will find that I care very little about what people think. I would much rather ride up front, so that we might continue our conversation. It would make me feel more comfortable."

"Then, I would be greatly honored. As you wish, Miss Batya. I think you will find that you are a great deal like your aunt Fern." Jakub chuckled and walked to the front passenger door to help her in.

"Good, then I believe we shall get along quite well."

Within moments Batya felt as though she'd known Jakub her whole life. They shared more about their histories, beliefs, hopes and dreams. Suddenly she felt a little embarrassed at the amount of information she'd shared with this handsome, yet charming, stranger. Knowing, all the while, that it was most certainly not socially acceptable behavior.

Realizing she'd been gushing like a schoolgirl with

a crush she blushed and decided, reluctantly, to conduct herself in a more lady like manner for the rest of their trip.

When their conversation slowed, Batya found herself self-consciously looking straight ahead at the buildings visible through her window, so as not to look too terribly interested in the dashing young chauffer seated next to her. Jakub glanced over, wondering what had silenced his passenger, and smiled when he noticed her blushing cheeks.

As she sat rigid, in the front seat, she thought. Freida had always been the business head in Voronkov and then later in St. Petersburg as well. Taking care of all the accounting duties and receiving dress orders from customers. But Batya had watched carefully over the years and was confident she could make a go of it here in Warsaw, opening a small dress shop of her own. Tides had changed since the war ended and folks weren't afraid to spend a little money again. She would use that to her advantage.

Batya would use a tiny portion of the money buried in the bottom of her case to rent a space and buy the supplies she needed to start her own dress shop. Her skills with a needle and thread had improved with practice and easily matched those of her sister, perhaps even surpassing Freida's talent. Her work would soon catch the eye of discerning clientele, as it had in Voronkov and St. Petersburg. She knew she could make her sister proud, she was sure of it.

"Ahhhh, Batya, zeiskeit, such a shayna punim. Your sister told me so much about you meyn lib, but not what a shayna maidel you are. I am so happy to meet you. I hope you will find my home as heymish as your own, and be velkhed here."

"Aunt Fern, I am so happy to meet you. Thank you for allowing me to come. I am grateful and will try to be as little a burden as possible on you and your household."

"Derfele, you could never be a burden to me. I thought I would never again lay eyes on mishpocha. I am dankbar you have come. Here, sit beside me. I wish to hear all about your journey."

The old woman and the young woman sat for the next few hours talking about many things. "I am so glad you have come to stay with me, Batya. I have been so long without the companionship of a woman. Jakub is kind and tries very hard, but there are simply things that a man doesn't understand."

"From our conversation, on the journey here, it sounds as if Jakub loves you very much and has a great deal of respect for you."

"As I have for him. Jakub and I have been through many things together in these thirteen years since he came to live with us. He is a fine young man."

So, that answered one of many questions Batya had about the handsome young man. She knew, from their conversation earlier that he was eight years old when he came to stay so, added to the thirteen years supplied by her aunt, she gathered that he was twenty one. Three years. That was not so great an age difference, was it?

"How did you come to work for this family, Aunt Fern? Mother never talked about that, or of pretty much anything concerning her family and her years growing up."

"She wouldn't have. You see, we had a very troubled childhood. Our eltern died when we were klein, and a distant cousin of our Papa's took us in. She sold me into servitude at the first opportunity she had. Your Mama and I lost touch and were never reunited again before she died. I miss her, my sweet, sweet sister. Our relative was an angry woman and beat us often. I would imagine that situation became worse for your mother once I was gone."

"I never knew. No wonder family was so important to her. Her last words to my sister, Freida, were to say how much we were loved. Telling her to protect us and she did. With her very life. I will always be grateful for that sacrifice. However, I will spend the rest of my life missing her. She was dear to me."

"I always wanted a family, but I wasn't blessed in that way. Jakub is very much like a son to me, but I never had a daughter. I am so happy you are here ketsele. We will help each other and this coming together will make both of our lives better."

"Aunt Fern I have saved some money and I plan to open a dress shop here in Warsaw. I will need to locate a suitable storefront, and clients, but I am an accomplished seamstress and I know I can be very successful now that the war is over."

"Well then, we will put out the word that you are looking for a suitable place and Jakub can drive you if you need to be out and about. With the war over there has been some harassment of Jewish people in the area by the Blue army. I wouldn't want you to be accosted. You will be safe with Jakub."

"Thank you, Aunt. That will help a great deal. If you would be more comfortable I will only go to the shop during certain hours of the day, to take orders and do fittings. I can do most of my sewing here. This way we will have more time together."

"I would like that very much meyn lib. I believe we will get along famously. I am so sorry about Freida, I'm sure you miss her, as I will miss my own sister for the rest of my life, but to have you here is a bigger blessing than anything I could have hoped for."

"I agree, Aunt Fern. I am also blessed and grateful indeed."

"Blessed is the man who trusts in the Lord, whose trust is the Lord." Jeremiah 17:7

CHAPTER 9

The years with aunt Fern were wonderful. Batya's shop thrived and became the talk of the town. Everyone in Warsaw,, and for many miles around knew of the little blond, Jewess dress maker. Other things flourished as well. Jakub and Batya became great friends. Talking and going for walks on the grounds. Then, with Fern's permission, Jakub asked Batya if he might call on her as more than a friend. She was beyond thrilled, as she'd loved him from the first moment she'd looked into his gorgeous green eyes.

Batya and Jakub would never have done anything to shame Aunt Fern, or to create a situation that might sully their reputations in proper society, so their time together was always handled appropriately. However, it didn't stop them from stealing furtive glances and dreaming of a future that held more than secretive looks and heated dreams.

Soon they were walking together, each day, as far as the city's main park. This was the park which was positioned directly in the middle of Warsaw. The one with lovely tree lined paths and a beautiful carousel that ran all day and played melodies guaranteed to remain in your head whether you wanted them to or not.

After three years of proper courtship they were walking in their park, on a particularly beautiful day. Jakub stopped and held out his hand. Batya placed her small hand in his larger one and followed where he led. He took her to the carousel and helped her mount the circular deck. Once aboard he placed his hands firmly around her tiny waist and lifted her onto the back of a gilded steed. Looking deeply into her eyes, he reached into his vest pocket and pulled out the most beautiful ring she had ever seen. She looked up at him with tears shining in her eyes and began nodding before he asked her to be his bride.

Aunt Fern was likely more excited than the future bride and groom, practically floating through the house with joy over the prospect of the upcoming nuptials. After all, she would have the opportunity to help plan a wedding. She couldn't have been more thrilled. Not having children of her own this was more than she'd ever dreamed and an honor she truly thought she'd never have the opportunity to share.

Batya designed and created her own wedding dress of satin and lace. Form fitting the garment to her petite and shapely form, as was the prevailing 1920s trend, without presenting a look too revealing proved difficult.

In the end, she achieved a finished item that was both fashionable and tasteful. The skirt, long and narrow, being dictated by the day's current styles. Her veil short, coming only to her shoulders, fulfilling both tradition and style. Bead work on the bodice was the single most time intensive and creative feature of the dress, but the finished result was absolutely dazzling to behold.

Jakub didn't have any living relatives and Aunt Fern was Batya's only family, so the old dame and several good friends would be doing some substantial substituting during the wedding ceremony, filling the void in those pieces of the ritual traditionally left only for family members. Fern was inviting absolutely everyone who was anyone in the community and couldn't wait for the blessed day.

Though the kabbalat panim and the nissuin would be held in their back yard and would be officiated by their synagogue's rabbi, the reception would be celebrated in the house. Aunt Fern was deliriously happy planning every detail of supper and the festivities. Of a certainty the meal would be kosher, and would include mevushal wine, challah bread, succulent roast chicken, roasted potatoes, and an assortment of delicious roast vegetables. Dessert would, of course, be a traditional wedding cake.

The day of their wedding dawned bright and clear. Jakub and Batya would fast before the ceremony, as was custom. Truth be told, Batya couldn't have eaten a thing for the nerves which were causing her stomach to twitch and leap about. She wasn't sure how she would make it through the long day.

She wasn't anxious about the man she was marrying, no, her feelings for Jakub were the one thing she was more sure of than anything else in her life. But, the idea of being paraded in front of scores of people, many of whom she didn't know, had her almost ready to faint. She'd not wanted to rein in her aunt too much, knowing how important the day was to her. Although she feared the excitement had gotten a bit away from the old dear.

Jakub couldn't wait to see his beloved. And though he too was fasting, he wasn't nearly as nervous as his soon to be bride and felt as though he could have eaten a whole chicken.

He'd known since the first day he saw Batya at the train station that she was the only woman in the world for him. Over these past three years, he'd grown to love her more each day until his heart was fairly bursting at the idea of finally having her as his bride.

Her beauty was eclipsed only by her humble grace, kindness and sweet spirit. He knew that their lives together would face challenges. Nevertheless, to approach those challenges arm in arm with the most beautiful, clever, talented and charming woman in the world could only be joy unspeakable.

Jakub and Batya approached the area where the kabbalat panim would be held and the tena'im would be read, though, without living parents theirs represented ritual more than practical application and was part of the day merely for the sake of tradition.

They greeted their guests together, which was breaking from custom a bit, but made the couple a smidgen more comfortable in the midst of a crowd of Aunt Fern's friends and elite members of the community.

Then, Jakub performed the traditional bedeken, lowering the veil over his beloved's face. Where, as their loving gaze met, Batya could see unshed tears of joy in her darling's eyes. Her heart felt ready to burst, as she knew without question this was the most precious and wonderful day of her life.

Their katubah, or marriage contract, which had been signed before the ceremony by two witnesses, was read aloud by the rabbi. Then two of Jakub's friends helped the 'chatan' don his kittel, lit their candles and walked him to their chuppah. The chuppah, made of four posts and a roof, signified the home they would build together. Batya thought it extra special indeed, because Jakub's friends had covered the roof of the chuppah with their tallits, to express to the betrothed that their combined prayers would forever follow the new couple into their fresh married life.

Next, Aunt Fern and one of Batya's friends lit their candles and walked the 'kallah' down the aisle, to the chuppah, to meet her groom. As their wedding guests watched the fair-haired young woman walk gracefully and steadily down the aisle, they could be heard exclaiming over her extraordinary beauty.

Batya circled Jakub seven times, indicating the new family circle they were creating on this day. Rabbi took the wine filled kiddush, reciting a betrothal blessing from the Talmud, while holding the cup out for the couple to taste of the wine. Jakub fished the ring he intended for his bride from his pocket, while softly reciting these words as their witnesses watched, "Behold, you are consecrated to me with this ring according to the law of Moses and Israel".

Batya then presented her groom with two gifts. First, a ring, while speaking these words from the Song of Songs, which were also inscribed within the ring; "Ani l'dodi, ve dodi li" (I am my beloved's and my beloved is mine)" and then a pendant, made of silver and inscribed with the Ten Commandments. He would wear them both every day.

What followed was the splendor of the sheva b'rachot. The custom of offering seven blessings for the couple over a cup of wine. Several of their dearest friends offered blessings and prayers for the pair, including blessings of joy, celebration, love, companionship, rejoicing and health. Then it was Aunt Fern's turn to bless them. Being the only family either of them could claim, her blessing would be most special.

"My dear ones. I want you to know that you could not be more dear to me, had I given birth to you myself. These past three years getting to know you, my darling niece, Batya, have been the happiest of my life. You are a special young woman indeed, certainly blessed by God. And, Jakub. You have been like a son to me, the child I never had. I love you both to the depths of my heart and soul. I hope for you, eternal health, the joy of lifelong companionship, celebration and rejoicing and, last but certainly not least, lots of children for me to spoil. May your lives be filled with laughter and love. God bless you on this day and always!"

Taking the wine glass wrapped in cloth, the rabbi placed it on the ground before the groom. Jakub stepped down hard and a loud pop could be heard resonating throughout the assembly. "Mazel Tov", shouted the crowd. The newlyweds linked arms and made their way to a special room set aside and decorated for their yichud.

"Are you okay?"

"I think so. I was certainly terrified to be in front of all those people."

"Even I was a little uncomfortable. I think your aunt Fern invited most of Warsaw. There are some very prominent and influential people out there."

"It certainly seemed so. Well, we have only to make it through the rest of the day. I'm sure I can do it with you by my side."

"Yes, my lovely wife. I love the sound of that! My lovely wife. I wanted to tell you that I almost forgot who I was when I saw you walking toward me in that amazing dress. You are indeed a vision to behold."

"Thank you, husband. You are very handsome also. You have always been handsome. I have thought that since the first day I saw you. Do you remember the day we met at the train depot?"

"Thank you meyn lib. How could I ever forget the best day of my life? Though today has now officially become the best and happiest day of my life and I know it will only get better when everyone has gone. Shall we join our guests to eat and dance?"

Batya's face bloomed crimson, as she smiled and leaned over to kiss her husband before they walked out from the yichud room to thunderous applause.

Rejoining their assembly for the festivities, Jakub and Batya made their way to the head table. Jakub took a loaf of covered and blessed challah bread and broke it. Then he and Batya passed out small pieces of the ceremonial bread to each of their guests. Once ritual was satisfied, they ate. The roast chicken and vegetables were a huge success and much appreciated after their time of fasting. They spent more time gazing into each other's eyes than paying attention to their guests, but no one seemed to mind.

Once the meal was cleared away and furniture moved, the music and dancing began. Laughter and revelry ensued as wine was drunk and the "Horah" was danced until wee hours of the morning. After the last reluctant guest was ushered out the door, Aunt Fern, Jakub and Batya dropped into the nearest chairs to praise one another for the success of the day. "Thank you, Aunt Fern. This day couldn't have been more perfect and we have you to thank for all of it."

"No, my dears, not at all. I thank you for allowing me to be a part of your special day. I will remember the honor of being a small portion of this happiness for as long as I live. Now, you two head upstairs where you belong. Go on now. This is your wedding night!"

Again, Batya's face turned bright red at the obvious insinuation. Then Jakub swept her into his arms and carried her swiftly up the stairs, over the threshold of their bedroom, and into a night of marital bliss neither of them would ever forget.

Next morning the couple wore a shared glow that was unmistakable. Aunt Fern was never married and had never experienced the cause of that glow. However, due to their obvious joy and many shared glances and smiles, she was sure theirs was a union that would be happy for many years to come.

"I waited patiently for the Lord, He inclined to me and heard my cry. He drew me up from the pit of destruction, out of the miry bog, and set my feet upon a rock, making my steps secure. He put a new song in my mouth, a song of praise to our God. Many will see and fear, and put their trust in the Lord." Psalm 40:1–3

CHAPTER 10

Jakub and Batya worked hard every day, spent time with Aunt Fern in the evenings, then retired to their bedroom to share expressions of their ever-deepening love. Before long Batya was with child. They couldn't have been more overjoyed. While Aunt Fern was over the moon making plans and decorating a room for the new addition to their little family.

In between beautiful dresses for the area's ladies to wear for their elegant affairs, Batya sewed tiny items of clothing for the little one who would be joining them soon. Often finding herself wishing her own mother and sister Freida were still alive to share in her joy, she dreamed of reunions with her family and the delight they would have experienced over the news of a coming child.

Months and months of dreadful morning sickness, combined with long hours at the shop, were beginning to wear on her and Jakub became insistent that she tell her clients she would be taking some time off. "I just have a few more dresses to complete my love. You are right to insist that I take some time off. However, these are dresses for some very important women in the city and I promised them for an upcoming event long before I even knew we were expecting a child. I have no recourse. I must finish them before closing the shop. I won't take any new clients, but I have to finish these. Do you understand?"

"Of course I understand, Batya. I'm just concerned for you. I have never seen you looking so tired. We have our baby to think of. I only want you and the child to be safe. Now, you must promise me that you will not take any new business. I want you to rest before the baby comes."

"I promise meyn lib. Just these three dresses, then I am done. You go help Aunt Fern. I'll be fine here. You can come back to pick me up later."

Suddenly and without warning, she knew there was something utterly, terribly wrong. She tried to make her way to the phone in order to reach out for help. But Batya couldn't hold onto consciousness long enough to make that call. Clinging to her extended abdomen and the precious child she knew abided there, she dropped to the floor of her shop. Disjointed memories danced in her head. Recollections of days on the farm, her Mama and Papa and her sweet Bubbe, then nothing.

When Jakub arrived to retrieve her he didn't understand why the lights had not yet been turned on though it was already long since dark outside. Entering the shop he anxiously walked toward the work area in back and almost tripped over his unconscious wife. Quickly finding and lighting a lamp, he set it down to assess Batya's condition. Shocked by the amount of blood he found on the floor and on his wife's clothing, he called for an ambulance.

Batya awoke the following day in an unfamiliar room with her husband and aunt beside her bed. She was immediately distraught. "Our child?" Jakub, with tears in his eyes, only shook his head. She tried to rise.

"No, meyn lib, you must rest. The doctors have told us that you could have died with the loss of so much blood. They were barely able to save your life."

"But our beibi, Jakub. What have I done? If only I had listened. I wish they had not saved my life. Please God, what have I done?" Jakub wrapped his arms around her and held her as she sobbed for what seemed like hours over the loss of their precious, unborn child.

When her doctor deemed it safe she returned home. Aunt Fern had intentionally closed the door to the nursery and hidden away all reminders of the tiny, lost infant. Their joy had so swiftly become sorrow and though Aunt Fern and Jakub were also sad, they were much more concerned over the degree of distress displayed by Batya. They decided to take shifts by her side, so she would never be alone.

For weeks Batya wandered the house pale faced and vacant eyed, until one day she turned to her husband and asked, "Where is our child, Jakub?"

Confused by her question Jakub answered, "Batya, meyn lib, you know what has happened, don't you? Do you not remember?"

"No, husband, I know that our beibi has died, over my own foolish desire to do more work. To be more successful in the eyes of the city. I am asking if you know where our child is now."

"I'm not sure what you mean, Batya?"

"Jakub, I want to know where my beibi is right now. For someone as devout as you, husband, that should not be so difficult a question."

"I heard conversation. How are you feeling my

zeiskeit?"

"I am better, Aunt Fern. Perhaps you can answer my question, since I seem to have stumped my husband. I merely asked where my child is now."

"Meyn lib, we have taken care of all that. The child has been buried, as is custom. You were in such a state that we didn't concern you with that matter."

"No, Aunt Fern. I'm not asking about the child's physical remains. I'm asking you where the part of my beibi that would have been her joy, her character, her personality, her spirit, has gone."

"Well, as Jews we are taught that the righteous will live again and will one day inhabit the world to come. You know this, do you not?"

"But what is 'the world to come', and what must we do to be righteous? How can we know that we have done more good than evil and who is it exactly that makes that determination Aunt Fern? In this case we are talking about a tiny, tiny child. One who never had a chance to do good or evil. Who makes the decisions about those souls?"

"Mcyn lib, please, settle down. You are supposed to be resting. Don't do this to yourself darling. You will do further harm."

"Jakub, I need to know. Are we serving a God who rips a wanted child from its mother's womb and sends it to Sheol, or a loving God who cherishes this child as we would have gladly done if given the chance? Who is this Yahweh we strive to serve?"

"That is a question I cannot answer, Batya. We can certainly ask the rabbi when we see him next Shabbat."

"You don't think it strange that we three, who faithfully read our Tanakh. And have done so our entire lives, I might add, have no answers for these questions? How is this so hard a matter to uncover? Unless of course there is no answer. And if there is no answer, then perhaps there is no Yahweh? Can you assure me that there is a god, or a 'world to come'? Is my child with this Yahweh, or simply disintegrating somewhere in the cold, hard ground? I need to know!"

"Oh, Batya. You are distraught. Please, come and rest now. We can talk more later."

"No Jakub, I will not rest. Not when I do not know where my child resides."

Life on the farm was great. Lots of hard work, but

the air was fresh and crisp, with acres and acres of land to wander and explore. There was plenty to eat, which was always a very important factor in the life of a swiftly growing lad. Five year old Jeffrey, tow headed and freckle faced, with deep brown eyes and a quick smile, adored his dad and vowed to be just like him when he grew up. Oh, not a farmer, though he loved helping his father with farm chores; anything to be nearer to the man he respected above all others; but a preacher, sharing the Word of God with all those lost and hurting.

Dad was one of Springfield's two preachers. But, in a town of less than seven hundred; many of them, as his mother vehemently described them, 'soulless heathens'; and two churches, there was often not enough in the offering basket to pay the church's bills, much less make ends meet at home. So, the working farm was their life's blood, and they praised God for it every day.

Jeffrey loved working the soil and helping his mom till, plant, weed and harvest the large vegetable garden behind the house on their property, along with his many other chores. He also loved the animals. Their milk cow, with her soft nose and big brown eyes, the baby miniature goats that followed him around like small bleating puppies when he was in the barnyard, and his big dog, Duke. He was less fond of the chickens who pecked his hands, until they bled, as he attempted to collect their eggs. These days, he tried to stay completely clear of the pig pen after falling into the sty one rainy day and being nearly trampled to death by the huge frightened animals.

His favorite place to play when he wasn't busy with chores, was down by the small stream on their property, beneath the shade of the trees. He loved hunting and fishing with his father, to provide food for their family. And he could spend hours catching tadpoles in the mossy shallows. Of course, on hot days, you could catch him swimming in that part of the creek where the water rounded the bend swiftly enough to make a deep depression in the smooth, sandy bottom. Deep enough to dive into from the branches of trees above, he often pretended to be Tarzan of the jungle, as he swung wildly over the water and let go to plunge into the cool depths.

Jeffrey missed his older brother Dan, eighteen now, who came home for visits only on holidays. He worked for a large contractor in Omaha six days a week. The twenty-two plus miles, round trip, was difficult to manage for a young man who didn't have reliable transportation. Dan, of all his siblings, was the only one who had suffered his little brother to tag along behind him his whole life, pestering and peppering him with question after question about the farm, the animals and life in general.

Jeffrey had been to Omaha only once in his life. He'd gone there with his family, to see his brother graduate from business college before he began his job. The drive took almost two hours in the family wagon, but he saw much along the way and felt very well travelled once he arrived back home.

He would make that trip again the following spring in 1924, at six years old. When people from all around the tri state area came to witness the renaming of Fort Crook, to Offutt Field, in honor of World War 1 pilot and Omaha native 1st Lieutenant Jarvis Offutt who died during the great war.

Young Jeffrey dearly loved their church and unlike many young boys throughout the ages, he loved school too. Especially learning to read and write. At only five years old, mostly due to his expressed desire to be a minister like his daddy, he received his very own Bible. It was a birthday present. The best present he'd ever received in his life. The feel of the tissue thin folio between his fingers, the beautiful maps and lettering and the smell of new ink on printed page was nothing short of a miracle to him. As odd as it might sound, he slept with that Bible right next to him, every night for many years.

Soon, through the authentic and precious scriptures contained in his Bible, he discovered how much God loved him and quickly trusted Jesus as His own Lord and Savior. Spending more time in the Word each day, he grew wise beyond his years.

Studying scripture improved his reading skills, but more than that, reading the Bible served to make him sensible. A trait not often found in one so young. His intelligence was so lauded in the area that adults consulted him, daily, for answers to many difficult questions and were amazed at the prudent answers they received.

He grew to adore the Lord Jesus more each day and wanted everyone he met to know of the Lord's love for them too, sharing the Gospel everywhere he went. Though he wasn't perfect, by any means, his mom and dad often said he was one of the nicest people they knew, even if he was their own son.

The loss of their first child had changed her. Batya didn't smile anymore and though she still adored her husband, she couldn't look at him without feeling she'd failed him miserably. He tried over and over to reassure her that his love was without condition. But it wasn't until more than a year after the loss of their first baby, when she discovered she was again with child, that a small spark of life once again filled her lovely blue eyes. This time she would be careful. This time she would put her child before her business and her success as a dress maker. Once again Aunt Fern, older, but still plenty spry, began to prepare for the arrival of a tiny bundle of joy.

When the day came and Batya's labor began, she was filled with fear. Would this child be born well and whole? She no longer believed she could trust God for good results. Would her lack of belief cause Him to curse her and worse, her baby?

Labor was long and excruciating, as she was such a tiny thing, but she stayed strong. The doctor, who'd been there for her after the loss of her first child, was filled with words of encouragement. Aunt Fern held her hand

and supported her every moment of the way. After hours of hard work and with Jakub pacing the outer room with tears streaming down his worried face, the baby came.

Jakub heard a small cry. Then the cry grew and became a howl. He smiled and made his way to Batya's side. Sarah, the name they'd agreed upon if the child was a girl, had come forth with gusto to meet the world.

Watching the babe sleep became Batya's favorite thing to do. The child was beautiful, with her mother's golden curls and her father's stunning green eyes. She had tiny dimples on her chubby cheeks and perfect pink, bow shaped lips. If Jakub was ever looking for his wife and couldn't find her right away, he knew right where to go. Then, when he found her beside the crib, they'd hold hands and watch their little miracle together.

Aunt Fern was in heaven after becoming a great aunt. Often found spoiling her grand niece in the front parlor, she had a continuous smile on her face these days. "She is just perfect, meyn lib. How have we become so blessed?"

"I think we deserve it, do we not? After the tragedy we survived, it is only fitting that we should have this lovely babe, isn't it?"

"Ah, Batya, we should be grateful for this tiny miracle and thank God for His goodness. Please do not tempt fate."

"Yes, I suppose we should be grateful to Him. For your sake and Jakub's, I have begun again to pray. I would not want to gain God's wrath for not giving Him credit for our good fortune. Heaven forbid, I would never want to tempt fate. Therefore, I will certainly praise God for this child."

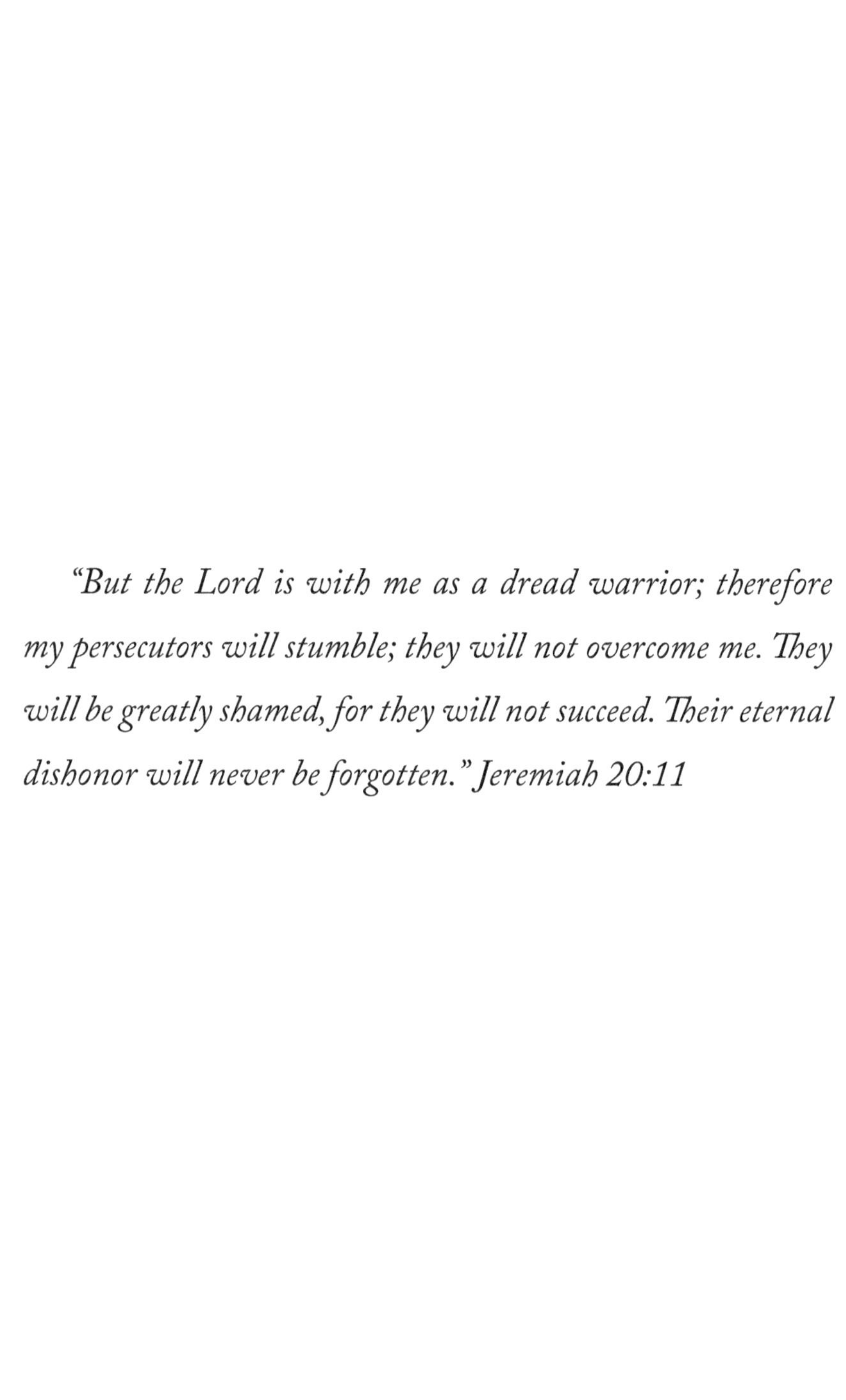

"But the Lord is with me as a dread warrior; therefore my persecutors will stumble; they will not overcome me. They will be greatly shamed, for they will not succeed. Their eternal dishonor will never be forgotten." Jeremiah 20:11

CHAPTER 11

Eleven years old, when the stock market crash of twenty-nine launched the nation into a downward spiral that would last ten long years. Jeffrey didn't feel the hard sting of deprivation that so much of the country experienced. Being a farm boy meant there was always enough to eat and plenty of wood for the fire. So, he concentrated on his studies and his chores, cushioned from the worst of those first brutal days of the Great Depression. It wasn't until he began to notice the effect of complete lack on his neighbors in town that his eyes were opened and his heart yearned for a way to help.

Father and Mother were growing older. Their other four children had all left the nest long ago. The girls married and the boys off in search of independence and fortune in the waning economy. So, it was left to him to see that his parents were safe and cared for. He didn't mind. He adored them both. They had always been good parents to him and they loved the Lord. Now it was his turn to show them the honor they deserved. However, this meant that the bulk of the work in caring for the church and farm fell to him.

Their church became a place of sanctuary for many who had lost everything in this difficult time. By 1931, when Jeff was all of thirteen, the country was in especially dire straits. At this time his efforts were most sorely needed, and greatly appreciated in the community.

Jeff, at the very top of his class, found time not only to study and do all the daily chores required on their farm, but to minister in many ways to those in town who found themselves without resources. He'd revamped the family vegetable garden to include more rows of life sustaining fresh produce and he held an open food pantry every Saturday at the church to distribute provisions to those in need. Countless families in town depended on the bounty donated by Jeff from the Shepherd's garden.

He learned to can fruits and vegetables with his mother, picking up recipes and techniques along the way, all in preparing for a time when she might no longer be there to help him. He also explored ways to dry various meats and fish gathered from his fishing and hunting forays with his dad. Cheese was his latest conquest. Now that his siblings had left home, they found there was just too much milk for the three of them to consume. So, cheeses were something else he could share with their neighbors. Some of these staples would sustain his family through the winter, and some would go to the food pantry to help others. He'd become very well known around town, and many thought him nothing short of a saint, even at his tender age. He didn't let that go to his head, however. He knew God and God alone blessed them and their farm, solely to be a blessing to others in these desperate times.

"Hello ketsele. How was your day at school?"

"It was okay, Mama. Do we have any of those biscuits left over from supper last night?"

"We might. I don't know what your father packed himself for lunch at the factory today. We can check when we arrive home, okay? Didn't you eat your lunch?"

"Yes Mama, I ate my lunch. I'm just especially hungry today. Perhaps it's because of the cold. Teacher let us play in the snow today and I had a wonderful snowball fight with some of the girls. It was great and our side won!"

"Did you wear your gloves and hat meyn lib?"

"Yes Mother. Of course I did. Teacher won't let us go out if we don't."

"Did you learn anything interesting today?"

"I guess so. We did arithmetic and reading. We also learned that Germany elected a new chancellor. I think teacher said his name was Adolf Hitler. She said he promised more jobs and better wages for the German people, so that is a good thing I suppose."

"Good. I hope he follows through with his promises. We haven't had much luck with our own President Moscicki keeping his."

"Well, I guess I don't even know what any of it has to do with us, Mother. Germany is very far away, isn't it?"

"Not so far as you might think meyn lib."

Sarah wrinkled her nose in that adorable way she had when she was finished with a conversation. Batya looked over at her daughter as they walked. How could it possibly have been ten years since her birth? Ten years! Sarah had been an exceptionally beautiful baby and she was a striking young girl. Her golden curls bounced as she walked, and her green eyes sparkled when she grew excited. She was a slight thing, like her mother, but scrappy and stubborn, taking after her mother in that regard as well. She was also her father's princess and the apple of his eye.

Childbirth had been particularly difficult on Batya, and God had not chosen to bless the couple with more children. But if they could only have one, Sarah would absolutely have been the chosen one.

The house seemed quieter these days. Aunt Fern had been gone for a year now and they all missed her. In times past she would have been near the door to greet them after their walk from school. With a big smile, a plate of warm cookies and a pitcher of cold milk. She was always such a welcome sight and now there was a loss, an emptiness that was hard to explain. She had left them the house and a bit of money, which made their lives much easier, but Jakub and Batya put that away. They would encourage their daughter to go on to university and the money they saved would see her through.

For now, Batya still used her talents to design and make dresses. Her flair for fashion continued to be in high demand in the city and beyond. However, she worked only partial days now, in order to walk her daughter to and from school. Jakub had been hired on at the local factory after Aunt Fern's passing. There was no need for him to hang around the house, now that the old dear no longer needed his help. He decided he would put away the money he earned for their future retirement, or perhaps even some traveling, once Sarah was off to higher learning.

"I miss Aunt Fern, Mama."

"I do too zeiskeit. She was always here for us. She loved you very much you know."

"Yes Mother. I know, and I loved her as well. I've been thinking a lot. Where do you suppose she is Mama? I mean, now that she isn't here, is she anywhere at all?"

"I'm sure she resides in 'the world to come' derfele. And if we obey God's commandments, so that we too may become righteous, then we shall see her when we pass on into the next life."

"But I am not always righteous, Mama. I break the rules sometimes, don't you? If those are the laws, and we are not following them, how can we expect to go to a place that rewards righteousness? How then can we know for sure where we will be when we die?"

"Enough of this, Sarah. Here we are safe at home. Let's see if we can find some of those biscuits you wanted, okay?"

"Don't be angry with me, Mama. I just didn't know. Is it so bad to want to know the truth?"

Sarah was asking the same questions she herself had asked when first her family, then her sister and later her child died. Questions for which she still didn't have any answers. Where was Aunt Fern? Where was her own mother, her father, her child and the rest of her family? Oh, she'd gone back to the synagogue, and continued to pray, in order to sooth her husband and aunt, but her questions still burned even when she prayed.

The thing is, for all these years she'd felt as if she was praying to nothing but thin air. There had to be a God, though, didn't there? They lived in a glorious world, filled with so much beauty and so many wondrous things. Certainly, there was a creator.

What about her husband and daughter? Surely only a brilliant God could have created these two blessings who filled her life with such joy. However, there was also much ugliness, death, pain and greed. How could she explain the dichotomy to her inquisitive daughter when she didn't understand it herself? Surely there had to be a way to know.

She supposed the only way to know for sure would be to talk to God. But how could she contact Him? Where was this Yahweh, somewhere in the midst of the universe? If He did indeed exist, why could she not reach Him? And worse, what if they tried to reach Him, but He just didn't want to be reached? She needed answers, so she could pass those answers on.

"Batya, are you here?"

"Yes Jakub. I'll be right down. What's going on meyn lib?"

"Some new Jewish families have moved to the area. They've come from Germany and the men have been hired on at the factory."

"That's nice, Jakub. Isn't it?"

"Sure, it's great. However, I've been talking to them and the reasons they came to Poland are causing me great concern. I was thinking that perhaps we should be thinking of moving on to someplace a bit safer."

"Moving? Leaving our home? This is the only place Sarah has ever lived. Why would we give up everything we know to move to a strange place? Tell me what these people are saying, Jakub."

"Well, they are saying that this chancellor Hitler is far different than they had believed him to be when he was first elected."

"Aren't they all? Politicians, they're all a bunch of liars and windbags, aren't they?"

"No, this is different. Soon after he was selected chancellor, he began instituting new policies that isolated German Jews and subjected them to severe persecution. They eventually grew accustomed to that, as Jews have been forced to do throughout history, but it has gotten worse as Hitler's Nazi Party continues to espouse extreme German nationalism and anti-Semitism."

"Well, it's not as if we have ever lived in places where Jews were not discriminated against, Jakub. This world is what it is, and sometimes people simply need to adjust to survive. Those who stay in Germany certainly must do that."

"That isn't the half of it, Batya. Hitler commanded that all Jewish businesses be boycotted and all Jews barred from civil-service posts. Then, all of the writings of Jewish and other "un-German" authors were burned in a communal ceremony at Berlin's Opera House."

"What? Now, that's horrible! Burning books?"

"Yes. Now, this year, German businesses have announced that they will no longer offer services to Jews.

And, from what the men at work were saying, Hitler even passed new legislation, named the 'Nuremberg Laws'. These laws decree that only Aryans can be full German citizens. It is now illegal for Aryans and Jews to marry. I just think it might be safer for Sarah's future if we were to live somewhere else. This Hitler sounds less like a politician and more like a maniac. If his policies continue down this path, what other insane laws might he create?"

"You are right, Jakub. All of this is terrible. But, that is German law, not Polish law. We have been safe here. Sarah is only twelve years old. I don't want to take her from her friends and turn her life upside down."

"That is exactly my point meyn lib. She is only twelve years old. Better to give her a new life now, when she is still young enough to start over and make new friends. I have heard some very good things about America. Every person there is allowed to follow their own dreams and to prosper. They are even more accepting of Jews than those here in Poland. I believe this is something we should seriously consider meyn lib."

"I don't know, Jakub. I would hate to leave all we know behind. All that Aunt Fern has left us, our memories, everything that our daughter knows, my clients, our life and friends. Please, I don't think I want to talk about this anymore today. This is becoming quite upsetting."

Jakub tried again later to talk about a move, but Batya shut him down. All the while anti-Semitism grew and tolerance of Jews waned. Europe boiled and Germany was quite literally about to explode.

It was a bitterly cold morning in November of 1937, when Margret and Jeff laid Anthony to rest. They chose to bury him under his favorite tree, on a small hill near the stream where he loved to fish with his son. Fall's colors were fading and leaves fell like soft rain from the branches above on the bleak morning of his graveside service.

Jeff fashioned a simple cross to adorn his dad's grave and carved his name, along with his date of birth and that of his death, into the wood. He added "Beloved husband and father", which made his mother happy, because, she said, he was indeed much beloved.

As they prayed together alone on the hill, but for a few dear friends from the church, Jeff remembered aloud what a great example his father had always been to him.

A man filled with love for God and his fellow man. Always ready to sacrifice for others, to do without in order that his children might have, to work hard even when his age and health would dictate that he do otherwise. Yes, he had been a great husband, a great father, a loyal soldier, a humble preacher and in Jeffrey's eyes a very great man indeed.

He was a simple man, who loved the Lord, loved his country and his family; and whose memory would remain with those who loved him still.

The world was still very much in turmoil and none of Anthony's other children made the trip back for their father's funeral. Jeff was sure his father would have been saddened by that, but he also would have understood. He'd always been an understanding sort, who would happily give you the shirt off his back; and for anyone who asked him, the benefit of the doubt as well.

This past eight seasons had been hard on the country he loved and especially hard on the people of his congregation. He'd been struggling with his health for a considerable number of years. The great war had taken its toll and farm life was a difficult one, especially for a man who'd been broken so badly in battle. Finally, the last bout of pneumonia was more than his worn-out body could endure.

Margret was devastated. They'd been married for over fifty years, even after wedding so late in life. Thankfully she wasn't left alone, but had her dear son to look after her. She lasted only six months without her sweet Anthony. One more Thanksgiving. One more Christmas. And one more spring planting.

Jeff laid his mom to rest beside his dad, her beloved Anthony, in the soft brown soil she loved so much. The earth was bursting with new life in the spring of 1938. Birds chirped and trilled in the branches, on the fresh, crisp morning of that solemn day.

Jeffrey fashioned another cross to match the one he carved for his father. On it he inscribed, "Beloved wife and mother. Rest well Mom. Save me a place at the table."

He would miss his mom very much, just as he missed his dad. But he never once felt alone. He didn't have time for loneliness. He knew Jesus was by his side and they had much to accomplish together.

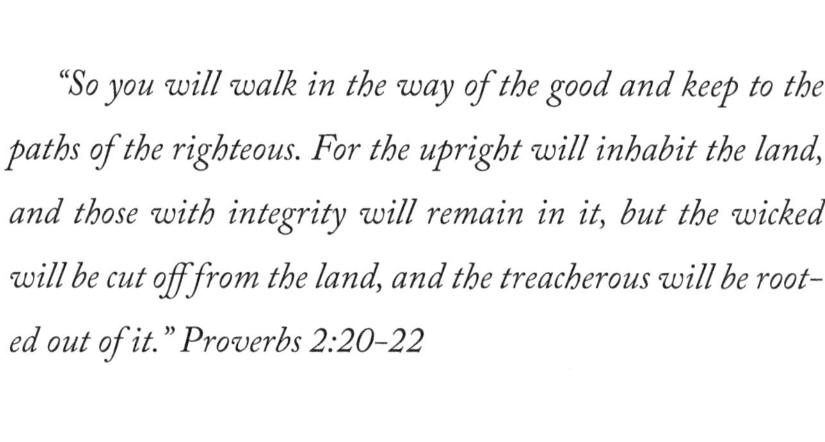

"So you will walk in the way of the good and keep to the paths of the righteous. For the upright will inhabit the land, and those with integrity will remain in it, but the wicked will be cut off from the land, and the treacherous will be rooted out of it." Proverbs 2:20–22

CHAPTER 12

Herschel Grynszpan was angry, so angry he couldn't think straight. It was early in the fall of 1938 and he'd just discovered that the Nazis had exiled his parents to Poland from Hanover Germany. Hanover was where he'd been born and where his family lived for many years. Herschel was living in France at the time, and with travel for Jews severely restricted, felt helpless to aid his parents against further threats by the Nazis.

Herschel quickly plotted and carried out a plan for retaliation. On November 7th, 1938 the young man shot Ernst vom Rath, a German diplomat, who was visiting in Paris. Rath died two days later from his wounds, and Hitler attended his funeral. Hitler's Nazi minister for public enlightenment and propaganda, Joseph Goebbels, immediately seized on the assassination to rile Hitler's supporters into an anti-Semitic frenzy.

Beginning on the night of November 9th, and throughout November 10th, 1938, in an incident known as "Kristallnacht" Nazi mobs in Germany torched, vandalized and destroyed thousands of synagogues, Jewish homes, schools, businesses, hospitals and cemeteries; murdering nearly a hundred Jews. Nazi officials ordered German police and firefighters to stand down as the violence raged and buildings burned, although firefighters were allowed to extinguish fires that threatened Aryan-owned property.

In the immediate aftermath of Kristallnacht, the streets of Jewish communities were littered with broken glass from the vandalized buildings, giving rise to the name 'Night of Broken Glass'. Nazis, inflicting an additional slap in the face to the area's Jewish population, held the German-Jewish community responsible for the damage and imposed a collective fine of $400 million. A fine impossible to pay considering the destruction of so many Jewish businesses and property.

More than thirty thousand Jewish men were arrested and sent to the Dachau, Buchenwald, and Sachsenhausen concentration camps in Germany. Camps that were specifically constructed to hold Jews, political prisoners, and other perceived enemies of the Nazi state.

Kristallnacht was a wakeup call to European Jews, many of whom began to plan an escape from their native land. However, though Roosevelt condemned this Nazi violence in the strongest of terms, the U.S. refused to ease immigration restrictions it had in place preventing masses of German Jews from seeking safety in America. Instead, many Jews left Germany for Poland, which up to now had been kinder and more accepting of them.

The Night of Broken Glass marked a turning point toward even more violent and repressive treatment of Jews by the Nazis. By the end of 1938, Jews were prohibited from schools and most public places in Germany and conditions only worsened from there. Step by step the march toward Hitler's "Final Solution" drew nearer.

Most young men of nineteen would have been completely overwhelmed by the responsibilities leveled on Jeffrey, but he had those responsibilities well in hand. Since the death of his father over a year ago he'd been preaching in their church on Sundays and caring for the people of their congregation every day of the week, in addition to managing and working their family farm and all that this entailed. He'd graduated high school at the top of his class, but university was out of the question for now. After all, who would care for his flock?

He'd developed new and modern ways to get more crops out of less acreage and bred quite a variety of poultry and other animals for meat to feed to those in need throughout his district. Highly respected by everyone in his community, he felt as if he was truly fulfilling the purpose for which he'd been called by God.

Jeff studied his Bible daily and though he was not seminary trained, he could have outmatched any university educated preacher in knowledge of God's Word if the need arose. The people of Springfield were blessed to have him and they knew it.

He was tall at six feet four and due to his busy and laborious life style, lithe, muscular and strong. His hair had turned from blond to a light chestnut brown over the years, but he still sported a light sprinkling of freckles across his nose, softening his chiseled features to go with his kind, deep brown eyes. Young women in town vied for his attention. But as busy as he was, Jeff didn't have time for any of that nonsense. He knew when the right girl came along, God would let him know. So far, no one matched the desires of his heart. He didn't want to be alone for the rest of his life, but for now he was content to work and wait on God's timing.

"Jakub, did you pick up the cake?"

"Yes, meyn lib. The Kowalski's asked me to thank you for the order. They haven't had a real cake order at the bakery in a while. Where is Sarah?"

"She's at Gretchen's house. The girls know to keep her busy until we can set up for the party. I can't believe our baby is sixteen years old!" She walked into the kitchen as her husband was carefully setting the neatly boxed birthday cake on the butcher block table.

"Well, I can't believe her mother is old enough to have a sixteen year old daughter. You are as beautiful today as you were the day you stepped off that train." Jakub grabbed her around the waist and planted a big kiss on her eagerly waiting mouth.

Giggling, Batya kissed him back, hard. Giving him a look that promised better things later, she smacked him on the bottom and pulled away. "Come on meyn lib, we have much to do and little time in which to do it. Help me get the dining room set up. I've made all of Sarah's favorites and decorated with fresh flowers."

"She is very lucky to have such a thoughtful mother. Where did you get the extra ration stamps? And, for goodness sake, where did you ever find fresh flowers that we could afford?"

"I've been saving and the flowers I picked myself, though please promise not to tell our neighbors. I scavenged them from various gardens on my walk home. Our daughter having a summer birthday means no school, so her friends can attend without difficulty and I don't have to pay for decorations. We can count ourselves lucky. It has gotten harder and harder to make ends meet these days as you well know. Women just don't buy dresses and go to fancy events as much as they used to. No one can afford to be extravagant when things are so tough."

"With more than 20% unemployment, we are very fortunate that the factory hasn't closed and I still have a job. It can't go on like this forever. But, I understand things are hard all over Europe and even in America. We are blessed to have a roof over our heads and food in our bellies. It is much more than many have."

"You're right Jakub. To me the most important thing is that we are all together. I don't know if things would have been better if we'd moved to America four years ago as you wanted, but we are making the best of it now, are we not? Our beautiful daughter is doing well, here, with her friends and family. I couldn't ask for more than that."

Just then, the house became filled with the laughter of six teen aged girls, as Sarah and her friends burst through the kitchen door with Gretchen apologizing, "Sorry, Mr. and Mrs. Nowak. I tried to keep her away longer, but I'm sure she figured out you two were planning something special!"

"That's fine, Gretchen. Everything is about ready anyway."

"Oh Mama, my goodness. You've made all my favorites: gefilte fish, chicken soup and noodle kugel. Oh, and look, what is that? A cake? Let me see, please?"

Batya laughing, "Shame on you young lady! This was all supposed to be a surprise. No! You will not see your cake until it is time to blow out the candles! Now scoot out into the dining room before I give you a swat. We will be out in a minute."

"Oh Mama, everything is beautiful! Thank you, thank you Mama and Papa. You are the best parents ever!"

It was Saturday and, as usual, Jeff was hauling a wagon of fresh produce, eggs, cheese and dried meats to the church for his weekly open food bank. Many would come from all around the area to avail themselves of the provisions so lovingly supplied by this generous young man.

In the past few years of the Great Depression he'd given thousands of pounds of food to members of his congregation and others in the region. He didn't consider himself anything special. He knew absolutely that it was God providing the blessing. It felt good to give and he knew that in doing this small thing he was doing the Lord's work. But, lately, he felt a subtle shift in the universe. He knew deep in his spirit a change was coming soon.

When the wagon was finally empty and the last armload of groceries disappeared down the street, he stopped long enough to check the church, making sure everything was set up for tomorrow's services.

Done, he sat wearily, but contentedly, in the front pew. His long legs stretched out before him and his arms hooked over the back of the wooden seat. Looking lovingly at the cross above the pulpit, he felt tears of gratitude sting his eyes. "Lord, I know all things are in Your hands and I trust You with everything in my life. Help me to know that I am in Your will. I feel as if there will soon be a shift in world events. Use me Lord, in whatever way will bring You the most glory. I am Yours sweet Jesus." When he was finished with his prayer he felt a peace and knew, deep in his heart, that God would soon be using him in ways he currently couldn't imagine.

September 1st, 1939. Just weeks after Sarah's sixteenth birthday party. Nazi Germany's air and land forces invaded Poland. Adolf Hitler, seeking to regain lost territory and ultimately rule all of Europe, crossed that line. World War II had begun.

The German invasion of Poland was a primer on how Hitler would wage war. What would commonly be referred to as the "blitzkrieg" strategy. Characterized by extensive bombing early on to destroy the enemy's air capacity, railroads, communication lines and munitions dumps. Followed by a massive land invasion with overwhelming numbers of troops, tanks, and artillery. They would overwhelm their opponent and gain an advantage before their rival ever knew what hit them.

Once the German forces plowed their way through, devastating a large swath of territory, infantry moved in, picking off any remaining resistance.

After Hitler had a base of operations within the country, he immediately began setting up "security" forces to annihilate all enemies of his Nazi ideology, whether racial, religious, or political. Concentration camps for slave laborers and the extermination of civilians went hand in hand with German rule of a conquered nation. For example, within one day of the German invasion of Poland, Hitler was already setting up SS "Death's Head" regiments to terrorize and control the populace.

The Polish army made several drastic strategic miscalculations early on. Although One million strong, the Polish forces were severely under-equipped and attempted to take the Germans head-on with horsed cavaliers in a forward concentration, rather than falling back to more natural defensive positions.

The outmoded thinking of the Polish commanders coupled with the antiquated state of its military and equipment was simply no match for the overwhelming and modern mechanized German forces. Of course, any hope the Poles might have had of a Soviet counter-response was dashed with the signing of the Ribbentrop-Molotov Nonaggression Pact. In other words, there would be no help from the East.

By September 27th, Warsaw surrendered to their German aggressors. October brought occupation, wherein many grand houses were seized for government use. Jakub and Batya were forced to pack up and leave the home Aunt Fern had so lovingly left them upon her death.

"The Germans don't yet know that we are Jews, Batya. Please stop, don't make a scene. Since our house is not in an area widely populated by Jews, they are only taking it because it will make a great command center for their officers."

"They have no right! This is our property. My aunt gave us this house."

"Meyn lib, they do not care, I assure you they are not overly concerned for our rights. Please, if you continue on in this way and someone hears, they will arrest us. And then they will discover who we are. It is a well known fact that Hitler is no friend to Jews. We must try to stay out of the line of fire, if only for Sarah's sake."

"You're right, of course, Jakub. I should have listened to you four years ago meyn lib. You were right and I was wrong then as well. What are we going to do? Where shall we go?"

"I have some friends who live near the factory. Their houses are not the sort that will be desirable for any kind of government takeover. I doubt any high official would lower themselves to even enter the neighborhood in which they stand. Let me ask around."

"And, I will approach some of my clients. Perhaps one of them will open her heart in our time of need?"

It turned out that one of Batya's wealthy clients, whose house had not been confiscated by the Nazis, offered them a couple of rooms until they could make other arrangements. They left most of their belongings behind. There simply wasn't room to store them. Taking only clothing, jewelry and a few personal effects, they left the only real home Jakub and Sarah had ever known.

"Mama, Papa, it's terrible."

"What has happened zeiskeit?"

"Oh Mama, Gretchen's father has been arrested."

"Oh Sarah. I'm so sorry. Whatever for?"

"The Nazis stormed into his newspaper office and destroyed everything. They took him and two other men away. Gretchen doesn't know where, but someone told her that they are taking all the Jews they arrest to their labor camps. She thinks it might be Dachau."

"Meyn lib. I am so sorry for your friend. Now, more than ever, I wish I had listened to your father four years ago. Perhaps we would have been somewhere safer by now."

"Batya, don't do that to yourself. I was only guessing. There is no way anyone could have known for sure what would transpire in the future. I love you and I don't blame you for the things that are happening now."

"I love you, Jakub. Thank you for your kindness, but I don't deserve it. I should have heeded your words. Now, we will have to reap the harvest of my foolishness."

Jakub and Batya didn't know that those, for the most part, who had chosen to emigrate to America were no better off than they. Seeing the writing on the wall, so to speak, many families made the difficult decision to seek asylum in other lands.

Their voyage was joyous, as they knew they were escaping the iron grip of the Third Reich. However, the United States, along with virtually every other country with a sea port, was turning Jews away. On May 13th, 1939 the SS St Louis left Germany with over nine hundred Jews on board, ready to leave their homeland behind and embrace a new land and a better future.

Sailing across the Atlantic they arrived outside the port of Havana, Cuba on May 27th and were refused entry. Based solely upon their status as Jews. They made their way to the coast of Florida and were again refused entry, once more due to their Jewish heritage. Urgent communications were relayed to President Roosevelt requesting asylum, which were summarily dismissed and the ship was sent back on its way.

The trip back across the Atlantic was far less joyous. Faces of the passengers were shadowed with the grayish hue of doom. One desperate passenger, so distraught over his future prospects, slit his own wrists and threw himself overboard to escape his fate at the hands of the Nazis.

The captain, frantically contacting Europe's many nations finally arranged for his passengers to be taken into Belgium, France, Holland and the United Kingdom.

Those passenger's freedoms, though, would last only

as long as it took the Nazis to march into those formerly free lands. Ultimately, more than two hundred and fifty of that ship's passengers would die at the hands of the Third Reich, and many more would suffer miserably in various concentration camps until the liberation to come.

In late 1939 the first of many anti-Jewish decrees was issued forcing Jews to wear a white armband with a blue Star of David emblazoned upon it for easy identification by patrolling German soldiers. This began a series of events whereby Jewish citizens were singled out and preyed upon by German forces. Subjected to firing from their jobs and harassment of all sorts, in addition to economic prejudices, life became more difficult by the day for Jewish inhabitants. However difficult this seemed, it was only the beginning.

"Take care lest you forget the Lord your God by not keeping His commandments and His rules and His statutes, which I command you today, lest, when you have eaten and are full and have built good houses and live in them, and when your herds and flocks multiply and your silver and gold is multiplied and all that you have is multiplied then your heart be lifted up, and you forget the Lord your God, who brought you out of the land of Egypt, out of the house of slavery, who led you through the great and terrifying wilderness, with its fiery serpents and scorpions and thirsty ground where there was no water, who brought you water out of the flinty rock, who fed you in the wilderness with manna that your fathers did not know, that He might humble you and test you, to do you good in the end. Beware lest you say in your heart, 'My power and the might of my hand have gotten me this wealth.'" Deuteronomy 8:11–17

CHAPTER 13

O ctober 2nd, 1940. Pressured by Hitler's Nazi party, Ludwig Fischer, Governor of the Warsaw district in the occupied general government of Poland signed an order to officially create a Jewish district. A Judenrat (Jewish Counsel) was established under the leadership of Adam Czerniakow, and in mid-October 1940 the establishment of a ghetto was announced.

Rushing home from work, Jakub burst through the door. "Batya, he finally gave in to the Nazis."

"Who, meyn lib? Who gave in to the Nazis?"

"Governor Fischer, that's who. He signed an order today. A new Jewish district is being created and we will have to move again. All Jews are to be relocated by November 15th."

"But, how can they do that, Jakub? Will they allow us to leave the area instead? Surely they can't force us to stay in Poland if we wish to travel to other, friendlier parts of Europe? We are not even native to Warsaw."

"That is exactly what they are doing, Batya. And no,

we are not permitted to leave. Actually, once we are confined to the new district, I believe it will be as if we never existed to the rest of the world at all."

"Oh, meyn lib, I'm so sorry, and I'm so sorry for our poor dear Sarah. I should have listened to you when you wanted to leave Poland five years ago. If I had, we wouldn't be in this predicament now. Please forgive me, Jakub."

"No, no, Batya. You were thinking of what might be best for our daughter. It wasn't a selfish thing. You don't need to continue asking for my forgiveness. No one could have predicted the spiteful nature of this man Hitler, who hates Jews and has decided he wants to rule the world."

"It doesn't matter that I was thinking of Sarah, Jakub. Now she is a young lady of seventeen, and my actions have put her in a place of much more danger than ever before. A place where she is at the mercy of this crazy man."

"It will be okay, Batya. We just have to make sure we stay together, meyn lib. As long as we are together, we can face anything. We will keep each other strong."

"Yes, Jakub. You're right. That's the most important thing. We must stay together and strengthen one another. But, we must also tell Sarah what has happened, so she will be prepared. We can do it together, shall we?"

Batya's client, who had unselfishly provided shelter for their family during the past terrifying year, held her and cried on the day Batya's family was transferred to the new Jewish district. "You know I would let you stay with me as long as you need to, Batya. I am so sorry this is happening to you and your beautiful family. Tell me, please, dear friend. What else can I do to help you?"

"You've done more than I could ever have expected already. More than anyone would ever expect. We thank you for your kindness my dear friend. But, I can't let you put yourself in further danger by going against this new order signed by the governor. It's being enforced by Hitler's 'Death squads' as we speak. Jakub, Sarah and I will still be together. That is the most important thing. So, we will keep each other strong and somehow we'll figure a way out of this mess. I'm sure people will see the insanity of this move and someone will step up to help. They must."

"God bless you and your little family, Batya. We will keep you in our prayers."

On November 15th the remainder of Warsaw's Jewish population walked through the entrance of what would ultimately be branded, 'The Warsaw Ghetto', and the gates were summarily locked and sealed.

Surrounded by walls they were forced to build with their own worn and blistered hands, under strict and extremely violent, constant guard, the Jews of Poland were effectively cut off from the rest of the world. The appalling conditions of their new living arrangements were clearly not suitable for any human being, but Hitler and his kind would ultimately surmise that it was more than they deserved. After all, they were only Jews.

The density of humanity in the ghetto was such; with numbers at its population height over 450,000; that a ridiculous 146,000 human beings were crammed into every square kilometer of space. This meant an average of eight to ten souls per small room. More than 85,000 of this number were children under the age of fourteen. Circumstances were horrendous and unsanitary, leading to constant, and drastic, repercussions.

Residents were allowed only the most basic clothing, personal effects and bedding, so the resulting conditions created a poverty so extreme that one would never surmise that many of these people had come previously from moderate or well to do circumstances. In this severe state of affairs, the population of the ghetto oscillated continually between life and death. The new Nazi government provided only minimal food to the ghetto residents, so malnourishment, resulting in starvation, was an issue right from the very beginning of their forced incarceration.

With precious few jobs available in the ghetto, most were unemployed. And those situations attainable to Jews offered very little by way of compensation, but Jakub managed to land one of the positions, such as it was.

Most would not envy his work, as it consisted of collecting bodies of the deceased for cremation in the pits outside the Ghetto.

Sadly, from almost the beginning of their Ghetto confinement, there was no shortage of work for Jakub's small crew, and the piles of decaying corpses needing attention stacked up in the streets. Starvation, cold, close living conditions and lack of medical care resulted in the rampant spread of several contagious diseases plaguing the ghetto's inhabitants, and the numbers of dead grew daily.

However, with residents added every day, from the

Jews and Gypsies captured throughout Poland, their numbers and crowded conditions only increased. Even the unspeakable number of deaths did nothing to diminish their growing overcrowding issues.

Batya and Sarah helped their neighbors in any way they could throughout the district. Considering the shortages they too faced, all help was a sacrifice. But they gave happily to lessen the suffering of others.

However, the ridding of filth, which was the most unchecked culprit, was difficult if not impossible to achieve in such overcrowded conditions with so little by way of cleaning supplies. Lately, with lice infestations rampant amongst the population, waves of typhus ravaged the settlement. More and more each day they were seeing symptoms of the disease: high fevers, headaches, chills, vomiting, stupor and a spotted rash. First, mostly the elderly, the starving, and small children. Then, later on, less likely victims.

Jakub and the other two strong men that made up his work crew, who were labeled 'the grim reapers', daily stacked corpses on a cart to be wheeled to a communal ditch outside the Ghetto's gates. There they would be dumped and burned along with their infected clothing and bedding.

His work put him in grave danger of contracting disease, or being a carrier, and taking it home to his family. But more than that, the pall it placed over his daily mental well being was enormous. He could feel the depression, which began as an occasional dark mood and grew into periods of lying in bed at night trying to hide bouts of uncontrollable tears from his concerned wife, became overwhelming.

Batya, who originally came from a family of traders and barterers, learning at the feet of her Saba, her Papa and her sister Freida, was more practiced at the art of survival in difficult environments than her beloved Jakub. Much of what she did to survive in her new surroundings would have been considered highly illegal by the Germans, however, she was quite good at coming up with little bits of traded this and that to feed her family and friends. It appeared, from all obtainable evidence, that those who were active in these small illegal acts were actually the ones most likely to survive in the atmosphere of the ghetto and beyond.

Other survivors included those of unquenchable hope: the artists, musicians and godly intellectuals. Optimists who seemed spurred on by a desire to create, in the midst of disaster, a culture that could not be snuffed out by the Nazi scourge.

Sarah, who was not as devastated by their current predicament as her parents supposed she might have been, started engaging socially with a small group of artists. These individuals, who continued their creative endeavors as an expression of the destruction that was visited on their world, became her constant companions.

In the process of seeking comrades and purpose among her new friends Sarah discovered a fresh talent of her own. Her ability to draw and paint the truth surrounding her was nothing short of astounding. The realism of her work was mind boggling and surprised even her.

Henryka Lazowertowna, a talented writer whose poetry touched all who read it, became one of her best friends. One piece, especially, reached Sarah with its depth of authenticity. It was entitled "Little Smuggler", a piece about the thousands of small children who smuggled food into the Ghetto several times a day from the Aryan side of the wall, at constant risk for their own lives. Part of it went like this:

Past rubble, fence, barbed wire,

Past soldiers guarding the Wall,

Starving but still defiant,

I softly steal past them all.

This collection of talented youth in the ghetto helped to start some of the numerous underground libraries ultimately flourishing in their new world. Other Ghetto residents even managed to develop a world class symphony orchestra in the midst of their immediate horror.

Smuggled books and music provided a much-needed escape from the harsh reality surrounding them and also helped to remind them of their previous life. One of culture, beauty and knowledge.

On those occasions when Jakub and Batya couldn't find their daughter, which were many, it was all but assured she was with her new found friends of the "Oneg Shabbat" Archive.

However, in searching out other avenues for her artistic pursuits she also joined another group of which she was sure her parents would not approve. This faction would remain a secret for the time being, but would affect her life in ways no other single thing ever could.

Sarah had quickly become an independent young

woman of strong principals right before their eyes. Her parents were more proud than ever of the young woman she'd become in these less than perfect conditions. Nevertheless, they were terrified that her defiant new nature, the rebel in her heart, would get her into trouble with German officials looking for any excuse to come down hard on Jews with ideas or opinions of their own.

On the 7th of December 1941, while German armies were freezing outside Moscow, Japan suddenly and without provocation pushed the United States into the middle of the struggle by attacking the American naval base at Pearl Harbor, Hawaii. Four days later Hitler, true to his arrogant nature, declared war on the United States. President Roosevelt called on Congress for immediate and massive expansion of the armed forces. However, twenty years of neglect and indifference toward the country's military readiness could not be overcome in a few days.

A nationwide call went out for soldiers and chaplains to do their duty and serve their country. Offutt Air Field was putting together groups of Army Air Corp troops to train for overseas deployment as the fighting in Europe and the Pacific escalated. It was decided that a duly trained chaplain would accompany and look after the spiritual needs of each new squadron which the military put in place.

Jeffrey Shepherd reported for duty in December of 1941, after the Japanese attack on Pearl Harbor and was immediately appointed to the rank of Captain. At the age of twenty-three he'd already been pastor of his father's church for almost ten years. Now, the congregation would be left in the capable hands of a group of elders who would look after the people, the Shepherd farm and the community, continuing the feeding program he'd started as a boy.

Sent immediately to Fort Monroe in Virginia for chaplaincy training, Captain Shepherd would ultimately return to Offutt for formal assignment.

Jeffrey had known for some time that God would be using him in new and different ways, but never guessed at the time it would be in a war zone. However, he was not afraid. Far from it. He knew Jesus watched over him and kept him safe. He trusted the Lord with every fiber of his being and every part of his life and welcomed the challenge.

After assignment and introduction to his new squadron and commanding officer, he looked around at the faces before him. Those young men so eager to serve their country. But in those enthusiastic faces he also saw boys who were clearly terrified of what the future might hold. He thought it such a strange feeling to know that the spiritual well being of so many men; most just kids in their teens; would be in his hands. However, he also knew how important it was to be sure each of those brave young men knew the Gospel message.

He was all too aware he was God's tool in the process. If these young men perished in battle without knowledge of the one true Savior, he would have failed miserably at his job and he absolutely could not let that happen.

Helpless, as American garrisons in the Pacific fell to Japanese in the spring of 1942. Military leaders in Washington worked feverishly to create a headquarters that would be able to direct a distant war effort and turn the fledgling ground and air units into practical, balanced fighting forces. In early 1942 the Joint Chiefs of Staff surfaced as a committee of the nation's military leaders to advise President Roosevelt and to coordinate strategy with the British.

In March the War Department General Staff was reorganized and the Army divided into three major commands: the Air Forces, Ground Forces, and Service Forces. Thirty-seven Army divisions were in some state of training, but only one was fully trained, equipped, and deployable by January 1942. Army planners of the time estimated that victory would require an Army of nearly nine million men, organized into two hundred and fifteen combat divisions, estimates that proved accurate regarding overall manpower; but much too ambitious for the ninety divisions that were eventually established and supported on far-flung battlefields.

The first U.S. troops arrived in the British Isles in January 1942. Nearly a year passed, as they prepared, before they went into action against the Axis. Meanwhile, air power provided virtually the only means for the Allies to strike at Germany. The Royal Air Force began its air offensive against Germany in May 1942, and, ironically, on July 4th the first American crews participated in air raids against the Continent.

Forced to be flexible in his duties, as he didn't know

from day to day where he might be needed, Captain Shepherd prayed in abundance and trusted the Lord. Knowing he could be summoned at any time, in the field or on the base, he tried to be prepared for anything.

Chaplains were thoroughly combat trained, and often found themselves in grave situations. However, Jeffrey grew up hunting with his dad and was handy with all manner of firearms, so he was confident in his ability to handle most circumstances.

Armed with a M1903 Springfield in one hand and a well-worn Bible in the other, he often found himself escaping impossible situations. Covered by the Hand of God while on the battlefield, dutifully attending to his men.

Life in the Warsaw Ghetto was rife with peril of all sorts, as was proved abundantly every day. "Jakub, I'm so glad you're home safe. When I heard that more men were shot today trying to escape, I was terrified."

"Batya, I would never leave without you. How could you even think I would meyn lib?"

"I didn't think you would leave without me, Jakub.

But I'm aware you've been helping others to escape, and I'm afraid that if you were ever discovered..."

"Oh Batya, I didn't know you had found out about that. I'm so sorry. I would never put you and Sarah at risk that way. That's why I didn't tell you. I figured if I didn't tell you, then you could honestly say you didn't know about any of it if you were asked."

"Just by being involved, Jakub, you put us all at risk. But I am not angry about that. We are all at risk daily, simply because we are enemies of the Nazis. I do my share of illegal bits and pieces to help our family and the community as well. However, I have had several women ask me about getting out of the Ghetto, and I have had to tell them that I don't know what they are talking about. Just today on the footbridge going back to the small Ghetto, Hilda Fitz approached me about arranging escape for her oldest son, so I knew that the message was getting out there whether you wanted it to or not. You need to be more careful meyn lib. How exactly do you manage it, getting these people out?"

"The cart. We just place dead bodies over those we are hiding. When we dump the cart into the ditch outside the Ghetto, they are on their own from there. They know they have to make their way out before nightfall, when the ditch is set afire for that particular day's disposal."

"They don't mind being buried under all those bodies covered with contamination and disease?"

"They are desperate people meyn lib. Willing to take a risk of possible death, versus what they consider to be an absolute death sentence by remaining in the Ghetto. I have heard talk about Hitler closing the ghettos down for good and shipping all of us that remain alive to Nazi concentration and death camps. Many would rather die than risk going through that. I've often thought about a way to get all of us out before that happens, but I haven't been able to devise a plan yet that would free us all."

"Well, be sure to let me know when you do meyn lib. Sarah and I will surely go with you." Batya said laughing. "I assure you I have no fondness for this place. And, now that Sarah is nineteen years old, I'm sure she would be open to some thrilling new travel adventures."

Jakub watched his wife's animated face change and glow as she spoke. One of the many things he'd always loved about her and still did. When she laughed her eyes still twinkled in that familiar way that made him warm all over. And though her forty-two years had not been easy ones, he soundly affirmed, at least in his own mind, that she was still the most stunning beauty he'd ever known in his lifetime.

It was true, she'd grown a bit thinner during their forced incarceration, but her shapely form still radiated a time defying confidence and grace when she walked. And her eyes, yes, her eyes, the pure unadulterated blueness of them continued to captivate him. He couldn't imagine his life without this firecracker of a woman. Which was exactly why he had not availed himself of the many opportunities he'd had to escape on his own. No, he would never leave his wife and daughter behind. They were the two greatest loves of his life.

Sarah, at nineteen, was ravishing. Her golden hair was radiant in the sunlight. And her bright green eyes, so like her dad's and so out of the ordinary in the large Jewish settlement, caught everyone who met her off guard. Tiny, but mighty, she had a confidence in her step that belied her hard and gritty circumstances. Bright and talented, she was also opinionated and stubborn, much like both her parents. But her smile was the most disarming of her features. When she graced you with a smile that traveled clear to the visible love in the depths of her eyes, complete with dimples in both cheeks, you would not soon forget it.

Though she knew it would behoove her to keep her opinions to herself, after so much time in the Ghetto, she simply had to be heard. Papa and Mama constantly asked her to stay out of the line of fire, but it was not in her nature to remain quiet when she saw someone being treated badly. Especially when those being treated badly were her own people. No, she would never stand by and see another hurt when she could do something to help.

"But Joseph said to them, "Do not fear, for am I in the place of God? As for you, you meant evil against me, but God meant it for good, to bring it about that many people should be kept alive, as they are today." Genesis 50:19–20

CHAPTER 14

Around a hundred thousand residents of the Warsaw Ghetto had already died of various contagious diseases and starvation before the mass deportations began in the summer of 1942.

Earlier that same year, during the Wannsee Conference near Berlin, Hitler's Final Solution was set in motion. It was a secret plan devised by the General Government to mass-murder all Jewish inhabitants. Techniques used to deceive victims and ensure a smooth transition to the gas chambers, were based upon experience gained at the Chełmno extermination camp. The ghettoized Jews were rounded up, street by street, under the guise of "resettlement" and marched to the holding area. From there, they were sent aboard Holocaust trains to Treblinka, built in a forest 80 kilometers northeast of Warsaw.

The operation was headed up by the German Resettlement Commissioner, SS-Sturmbannführer Hermann Höfle, on behalf of Sammern-Frankenegg. Upon learning of the plan, Adam Czerniakow, leader of the Jewish Judenrat Council, the same man who had helped to imprison his fellow Jews in that awful place, saw what his compliance with Nazi rule had produced and promptly committed suicide.

He was replaced by Marc Lichtenbaum, who was then tasked with managing roundups with the aid of Jewish Ghetto Police. No one was informed about the real state of affairs.

Treblinka I was largely a forced labor camp, whose prisoners worked in the gravel pits, and irrigation areas; or in the forest, cutting wood to fuel the cremation pits. From 1941 to 1944 more than half of its 20,000 inmates died of summary executions, starvation, disease and mistreatment.

Extermination of Jews by means of poisonous gases was carried out at Treblinka II under the support of Operation Reinhard, which also included Bełżec, Majdanek, and Sobibór death camps. About three hundred thousand Warsaw Ghetto inmates were sent to Treblinka during the 'Grossaktion Warschau', and tragically murdered there between Tisha B'Av (July 23) and Yom Kippur (September 21) of 1942.

For eight weeks, the deportations of Jews from Warsaw to Treblinka continued on a daily basis via two shuttle trains: each transport carrying four to seven thousand terrified people, crammed together like sardines in a tin and crying out in desperation for water. One hundred people to a cattle truck, they were packed together so tightly they could barely breathe, couldn't raise their arms above their heads and were ultimately covered in their own waste and vomit by trip's end.

The first trains each day rolled into the camp early in the morning. Many times after an overnight wait at a lay-over yard; still jammed together in transports in the sweltering heat and prisoners with no food or water. The second trains arrived in the scorching heat of mid-afternoon.

Often, upon opening the doors, piles of corpses had to be removed before those still alive could be herded off the transports. Dr Janusz Korczak, a famed educator, went to Treblinka with his orphanage children in August 1942. He was offered a chance to escape by a group of Polish friends, but he chose instead to share the fate of his life's work, the children he loved. His decision became the death of him.

New arrivals were sent immediately to the 'Sonderkommando'. A group of Jewish men who were not killed immediately upon arrival in the death camp, but set aside to be utilized as slave labor.

Sonderkommando were a quickly trained squad that grudgingly managed the arrival platform; where their morbid work was to relieve new prisoners of all clothing and any personal effects such as wedding bands, jewelry and the like, readying them for the gas chambers. Most, if asked, would say they would rather have been marched to their own death by gas than to do this awful job. Yet, they were not given a choice.

If truth be told, usually when chosen for this despicable task and after some quick thought, the human desire to survive persuaded them to quiet their useless protests, lest they be immediately grouped in with the next to be tormented and brutally murdered. Deviously used by the Germans against their own, they were looked down upon by some and envied by others for their luck.

From the arrival platform the naked and terrified captives were sent directly on, herded like cattle, to the gas chambers and their horrifying deaths.

Victims were suffocated to death in batches of two hundred at a time with the use of monoxide gas. As dead bodies were emptied from the chamber, they were further debased by being relieved of any gold teeth. Other valuable, though odd, items such as: tattoos, birth marks, or anything which might be considered worthy to decorate some Reich officer's new wallet, were carved off the recently deceased to be used later as a grisly keepsake. In September 1942, new gas chambers were built, which could murder as many as three thousand people in just two hours.

Civilians were forbidden to approach the camp area. In the last two horrific weeks of 'Grossaktion Warschau' ending on September 21, 1942, some forty eight thousand Warsaw Jews are deported to their deaths in Treblinka ll.

The last transport with twenty-two hundred victims from the Polish capital included the very same Jewish police officers and their families who'd been involved in helping with deportations. Snatching from them any hope that having worked together with the Nazis to destroy their fellow Jews would gain them an advantage in the eyes of Hitler and his ilk.

In October 1942 the Jewish Combat Organization (ŻOB) was formed and tasked with opposing further deportations of their Jewish brothers and sisters. It was led by twenty-four year old Mordechai Anielewicz.

Meanwhile, between October 1942 and March 1943, Treblinka received transports of almost twenty thousand foreign Jews and Gypsies, slated for extermination, from the German Protectorate of Bohemia and Moravia via Theresienstadt and from Bulgarian-occupied Thrace, Macedonia, and Pirot following an agreement with the Nazi-allied Bulgarian government.

By the end of 1942, it was clear to everyone that the deportations from Warsaw and other Ghettos, feigned to be relocations, were actually to their deaths. The underground activity of Ghetto resistors in the group 'Oyneg Shabbos' increased after learning that the transports for "resettlement" led to the mass killings, and finally, preparation for the long awaited rebellion began in earnest.

In late 1942, Polish resistance officer Jan Karski reported urgently to Western governments on the untenable situation occurring in the Warsaw Ghetto, and on the extermination camps being used to murder his fellow Jews, to no avail. It seemed, just as Jakub had predicted at the outset of this latest atrocity, that the Jewish people had simply ceased to exist to the rest of the world.

Many of those remaining Jews decided to take matters into their own hands, no matter the consequences, to resist further deportations by any means necessary. And they began to smuggle in weapons, ammunition and supplies, made available by Aryan sympathizers. Among those eager and resilient resistance soldiers were Jakub, Batya and Sarah Nowak. Jakub's job and access to the Ghetto's gates, was a perfect cover.

On January 18, 1943, after almost four months of resistance activities putting a stop to deportations, and copious amounts of flak from Nazi higher ups, the Germans suddenly entered the Warsaw Ghetto intent upon further roundups of candidates to board the death camp transports.

Within hours, some six hundred Jews were shot and five thousand others removed from their residences. The Germans expected no resistance, but they were in for a very big surprise. The action was brought to a halt by hundreds of insurgents armed with handguns and Molotov cocktails. These fighters, without regard for their own lives, mounted tanks and threw explosives inside, destroying several of the enemy's rolling fortresses. The Nazis were not amused.

Preparations to resist had been going on secretly since the previous autumn and proved at least moderately successful. The first instance of Jewish armed struggle in Warsaw had begun. Underground fighters from ŻOB (*Żydowska Organizacja Bojowa*: Jewish Combat Organization) and ŻZW (*Żydowski Związek Wojskowy*: Jewish Military Union) achieved considerable victory initially, taking control of the Ghetto. They then barricaded themselves in the bunkers and built dozens of fighting posts, stopping the removals of their brethren. Taking further bold steps, a number of non-Jewish collaborators were also executed by the rebels for their traitorous acts.

An offensive against the Ghetto underground, launched by Von Sammern-Frankenegg, was unsuccessful. He was then relieved of duty by Heinrich Himmler on April 17, 1943 and court-martialed for his failure to achieve the goals set down by the 'Reich'.

Jakub and his troops were ready to die for the cause, but, like any loving husband and father, he wanted to keep Batya and Sarah protected and safe. They, on the other hand, were as committed to the battle as he was and wouldn't stand for being put to the side. Armed with weapons and explosives the family was posted very near the wall which was breached by the approaching Nazi troops.

The final battle of the Warsaw Ghetto started on the eve of Passover, April 19, 1943, when a Nazi force consisting of several thousand troops entered the Ghetto with tanks and machine guns. After initial setbacks, two thousand Waffen-SS soldiers under the field command of Jürgen Stroop systematically burned and blew up Ghetto buildings, block by block, rounding up anybody they could capture, and murdering any who resisted. Herding people that remained into the streets, where women were raped and mutilated and multitudes of people were tortured and burned by blood thirsty soldiers, the Jews were sitting ducks.

Jakub managed to shield his women from the marauding soldiers by burying them quickly under loose rubble near the breached wall.

Before placing the last stone loosely and strategically, to give them an easy exit later, he gazed into Batya's eyes. Mouthing the words, "Until we meet again, meyn lib", he ran to divert attention from his loved ones, as far as he could remove himself from their position.

Gunfire erupted again all around him. He shot back with his final bullets, and threw his last Molotov cocktail, hitting the advancing Panzer positioned before him. As flames burst forth, a volley of machine gun fire showered his position. He was knocked backward by the shot that hit his chest. As his mind went suddenly black, he fell limp into a pile of brick and rubbish.

Significant resistance in the Ghetto ended on April 28th, and the Nazi operation officially halted on the 16th of May 1943 as Germans destroyed the Great Synagogue on Tłomackie street in Warsaw. An act which proclaimed the final containment of the Ghetto uprising. General Jürgen Stroop, the commander of the S.S. unit engaged in the suppression of the uprising, presided over the demolition. Stroop added the following caption to a photo album documenting the repression of the Warsaw Ghetto uprising, during April and May 1943: "There is no longer a Jewish quarter in Warsaw."

According to the official report, at least fifty six thousand and sixty five people were killed on the spot or deported to German Nazi concentration and death camps (Treblinka, Poniatowa, Majdanek, Trawniki). The site of the Ghetto became the Warsaw concentration camp.

Captain Shepherd was deeply respected by the men in his squadron. They knew without question they could count on him in all circumstances. That he was not afraid to be right in the thick of combat with them. He'd held many a dying young man in his arms on the field of battle as they took their last breath, always with Jeff's fervent prayers ringing in their ears when they passed into eternity.

He'd led many to the Lord. Most off the battlefield, but some as they lay failing in his arms. He'd heard it said that 'there are no atheists in fox holes' and in the midst of the horrors of war, he was pretty sure that was a true statement.

Every one of his men, at his urging, had written a letter home. These were to be delivered, 'in case'. They'd all compiled a last will and testament at his insistence, to include with that letter. He'd performed way too many funerals, back home, for members who had not sufficiently prepared for the inevitable. Leaving grieving families to wonder what they should do next. Sadly, in the chaos of war, he'd had to mail some of those letters. He always included a letter of his own, telling the family how brave their young soldier was when it counted most.

At night, as he lay in the dark with tears streaming down his face wondering if this war would ever end, he prayed for the wisdom to do what the Father would have him do in every situation. He knew that not all those in his charge had been reached, no matter how hard he tried. And that some who were reached, later and much to his sadness, turned their backs on the only One who could save them. It tore his heart apart to know that any on his watch were lost. But he would not lose faith, no matter the struggle. For now he would do the only thing he could do, he would stand firm and fight.

As clean up and demolition of the Ghetto began, Batya and Sarah were discovered; covered in concrete dust and shaking with fright under rubble near the breached outer wall. The officer in charge who first saw the beautiful, flaxen haired women was captivated. Men later would comment that he seemed as enthralled with his find, as if he'd discovered mystical unicorns under that pile of rock.

He wondered, at first, if these lovely creatures were

in fact even Jews, due to their fair complexions and light eyes. Then, he decided he didn't care if they were Jews or not. He made an executive decision not to put them on the last available transports to Treblinka. But, instead to take them with him to his next posting. Wilhelm Eduard Weiter would become the eighth commandant of the famed Dachau concentration camp.

Batya didn't want to leave the Ghetto without her beloved Jakub, but Sarah convinced her that if it were meant to be, they would see her father again. Little did they know that Jakub had been shot by the advancing troops after he'd hid his wife and daughter under the rubble of the wall.

Some would later remember the day that all the Warsaw Ghetto burned. Billowing clouds of grey and black smoke from that infamous fire filled the clear blue Sunday sky, in the hours after their peaceful and uneventful services in the churches of Warsaw.

Civilians outside the walls, just a short distance away at one of the city's famed parks, would comment off handedly, "Jews are frying", as their own children rode the same beautifully gilded, musical carousel where a young Jewish man proposed to his beloved so many years ago.

Captain Shepherd lay in the dark watching evidence of fighting in the distant night sky. If he hadn't known differently, he might have thought the folks in some far-away town were having a fireworks display. After all, that's what folks at home did on the 4th of July.

He wondered how his church back in Springfield was doing. In his imagination, he could feel the ground of his beloved farm beneath his bare feet and smell the heavenly scent of good black earth as it clumped together, moist and magical in his hands. There was no other smell in the whole world quite like it. Then he imagined chickens clucking and goats nudging him along the path to his house. The memory made him smile.

The sight and smell of vegetables, fresh and abundant, filling his wagon. And the joy he experienced as he shared the bounty with those he loved. He would have given just about anything to close his eyes and wake up there now.

Smiling again as his imagination caught a whiff of freshly extinguished candles at the end of Sunday services, he felt a tear escape the corner of his eye and trace its way through the stubble on his face. He'd always loved that smell, ever since he was a tiny child. And the view of the cross hanging above the pulpit, as he leaned against the back of the pew in the front row of his small church. How long ago that last day seemed as he looked back now. He would survive this war. Of that he was certain, as God had showed him glimpses of the future. But there had been so much loss, so much death. And there was no sign, not that he could see, of an end to the horrors of the Nazi Reich.

"Behold, I send an angel before you to guard you on the way and to bring you to the place that I have prepared." Exodus 23:20

CHAPTER 15

Jakub; waking in the dark and immediately terrified to his core; tried without much success to make out his surroundings. Crammed into what he could only assume was a prisoner transport, with ninety-nine other wretched souls, he couldn't move a muscle.

Smells of vomit, sweat, urine, feces and death permeated the space, consequently invading every pore of his being. His chest hurt as if he'd been kicked by an angry mule. He was unaware at the time, but his pendant; the one Batya had given him on their wedding day; saved his life. A bullet had struck him, hitting the keepsake and knocking him backward into a pile of rubbish. Unconscious and supposed dead upon first inspection, by the guards surveying the carnage. He lay for untold hours, covered in the blood of others, narrowly escaping a bayonet to the heart.

Later, when guards more thoroughly swept the area to gather remaining prisoners for transfer to Treblinka, he was discovered moaning softly in the pile of rubble and loaded immediately in with other captives for the harrowing trip to death's door.

A few questions, answered by those captives closest to his painful position on the cattle car, told him all he needed to know. He prayed Batya and Sarah had escaped their hiding place before discovery by the soldiers, but didn't know for certain if that was the case. Could they possibly be crammed in this transport with him? He called out their names but got no response. Tears of frustration and loss trickled from his eyes.

Breathing was almost impossible due to the lack of space and his still painful chest, but the biggest single issue was thirst. People around him cried out for the lack of water. And though his heart broke for their circumstances, especially for the old and the very young, he couldn't do a thing to help them.

His transport did contain a few women and children, but, from the sounds of the wailing and prayers around him it seemed most were men. He supposed they were what remained of the bulk of freedom fighters left in the Ghetto at the end of the unsuccessful uprising. A lot of good it had done, this attempt at freedom. Now, for all he knew, his wife and daughter were gone forever because of his failed shot at liberty.

Arrival at Treblinka was just as frightening as he'd supposed it would be. Doors of their transport were shoved open and a number of dead bodies fell to the ground between the railroad car and the platform. Quickly hauled away, they would be stripped and searched later.

Others who'd died en route, but who managed to stay upright by the sheer pressing in of humanity around them, were dragged off and thrown into a heap to be dealt with once the live prisoners had been processed.

Most of the living were shoved and prodded into a line, going toward yet another platform. However, Jakub and several other men who looked to be stronger than some of the rest, were singled out and grouped together to stand on the adjacent platform awaiting orders.

Jakub, whether he liked it or not, was abruptly drafted into the Sonderkommando. He had no choice in the matter. Neither did any of those selected with him for this terrible task. If they didn't do as they were commanded by the guards they would be tortured and killed on the spot, so that others might take their place.

The small, select group of men were swiftly trained to do the revolting work set before them. Informed as to which valuables went in what containers and where to stack additional personal items removed from new prisoners; as those poor souls were unceremoniously paraded naked and afraid to the gas chambers; the forced labor carried on. Mindlessly performing their duty as they'd been instructed to do, it felt as if time stood still. Hours later the darkness came and yet they toiled on until all the transports for that day were emptied.

Jakub found that day after day the only way he could do this unimaginable thing he was forced to do, was to turn off the aching of his heart and refuse to look into the eyes of those precious people. These were his people. Many of whom he knew by face and some he recognized even by name. Most of those poor ravaged souls didn't understand, clear up until death overtook them in the gas chamber, what was happening.

For those who caught on more quickly and began to make a fuss, guards ended them quickly with a bullet, or the rapid thrust of a bayonet.

During the daytime hours; standing in the heat of the summer sun; Jakub was stone faced and unreachable, performing his work. His mind raced as he took in every detail of his surroundings, biding his time, until he could figure out a way to escape. At night he prayed, sobbing quietly into his sleeve, reliving each excruciating moment on the platforms. He hoped that if his beloved Batya and Sarah were captured, they would necessarily have to go directly past him. If that happened, he would figure out a way to save them, or die trying. At least then, he figured, they could all perish together.

Captain Shepherd was just a man, not unlike any other man in military service. At least that was how he viewed himself. However, to his soldiers, the young men he loved and cared for, he was more. Like a brother to some, and even a respected and honored father to others, he was absolutely a spiritual guide to all. He bore his responsibility with strength and humility. Deeply saddened by the loss of even one soul to the darkness he never gave up or gave in to the temptation, which overtakes so many, to keep his beliefs to himself.

Known to most everyone in his orbit as 'The Shepherd', he leaned on the actual Shepherd, Jesus, in all things. And he never let the nickname go to his head. He was just grateful to be used by God in this awful place and during this perilous time. Glad to be a light in that seemingly endless darkness of the Nazi shadow.

Jakub dreaded his unthinkable situation more each day, mounting the platform to help strip and humiliate his fellow Jews. But the whole ordeal became even more torturous and maddening after the arrival of a new guard who, through his rampant cruelty, quickly earned the nickname, "Ivan the Terrible". He arrived in camp with an arrogant swagger and took up residence on the platform nearest the Sonderkommando.

"Ivan" was actually John Demjanjuk. A Ukrainian. Like many Ukrainians, Demjanjuk was glad to help the Nazis massacre Jews. In 1942, he volunteered to be a 'wachmann', a member of the extermination crews the Nazis set up all over Poland and in the Soviet Union. He was sent for extensive training to the Trawniki concentration camp, where he took an oath of loyalty to the SS and received its official tattoo.

Like the other 'wachmanner' trained at Trawniki, Demjanjuk mastered every stage of the extermination process, from rounding up Jews in ghettoes to pumping carbon monoxide into the death camp's gas chambers.

Watching this Nazi animal work haunted Jakub in ways he wouldn't forget until his dying day. The man was brutal and vicious in so many absolutely unnecessary and heinous ways. Using means that went far and above the Third Reich's mandate to extinguish the Jews.

From repeatedly stabbing prisoners as he gleefully shoved them into gas chambers, to cutting off women's breasts and brutally slicing them between the legs when they walked past him frightened as wild deer. He often used a saber to lop off the ears or noses of those marching to their deaths, laughing all the while in the way of a madman, as blood of his victims spouted forth making platforms slick. Even going to the extreme of impaling innocent babies who were held in their mother's arms, as they waited in line to be gassed to death.

It amused him to see the mother's horror and grief over the loss of her child, mere moments before her own awful demise. The sense of power he felt, reigning over the life and death of these prisoners, was like a narcotic to this sick, deranged man.

Once, he ordered a prisoner to lie down on the loading platform. Then, taking a tool used for drilling wood, used it to drill holes through the man's buttocks. That prisoner's cries resonated in Jakub's ears until he thought he would go mad.

'Ivan's' brutality grew as he discovered new ways to torture his victims. Lashing people with a whip or beating them in the head with wooden posts as they walked past his station, so that now they staggered to their deaths. His face: often contorted in an insane and joyful smile, as he tormented those weaker than he; caused Jakub to long for a day when he might exact revenge for all those wounded souls.

Jakub knew he would never forget the screams of his fellow humans at the hands of this demon. More than once, he was sorely tempted to grab the wachmann and beat him to death, even if it meant his own instant demise. The one and only thing that kept him from doing so was knowing that his wife and daughter might make their way to his platform at any time. If he died trying to save all these doomed prisoners now, he wouldn't be here to free Batya and Sarah when the time came; as his attack would certainly end in his death.

Sadly, he also knew if he managed to kill 'Ivan' there would be another just like him to quickly take his place. The world seemed filled with men who found pleasure in killing random, innocent Jews these days.

What Jakub couldn't possibly know is that his beautiful wife and daughter would never enter the gates of Treblinka, as they were presently residing with the 8th commandant of Dachau many miles away.

Batya and Sarah didn't know what to make of their current situation, or their present captor. Commandant Weiter had actually been most kind to them. He preferred to live in accommodations off site from Dachau with his very authoritarian wife. She did not take kindly to his idea of bringing the two lovely Jewish women with him when they left Warsaw, and her attitude was apparent in the way she treated them.

Jealousy was more than likely the motivating factor, as she was a particularly unattractive woman. However, the ladies were fine with whatever chores she threw at them, as the living conditions in Weiter's household were far superior to those of the Ghetto and surely better than those in Dachau.

Batya and Sarah were made to clean house, do laundry and cook. They slept together on a single camp cot in a small back room. One that reminded Batya of the room she'd shared with her sister Freida, when she was a little girl a very long time ago. But it was far and away more comfortable than the filth of their previous situation in the Ghetto. Considering their status as prisoners, they were convinced this place was superior to Dachau and they were otherwise happy and healthy.

Weiter's wife witnessed the way her husband looked at the women and she would not let down her guard for a moment, for fear that he might avail himself of forbidden pleasures. That was fine with Batya and Sarah. They wanted nothing to do with the odd, little man who constantly followed them with his bloodshot eyes and strange, wistful look throughout the working of their daily chores.

Weiter spent many years as a book salesman before the war. Quiet, and a bit meek, he was a born 'desk man' and a half hearted Nazi at best. He spent very little time at the concentration camp with which he was charged, preferring to handle administrative concerns in his office away from the camp in the comfort of his own home.

The camp deteriorated further during his time of appointment there, but that wasn't entirely his fault, as the site had begun to receive more inmates during the steady advances of Soviet troops and the closing of other facilities. Due to this, and his infrequent and less than thorough inspections, atrocities abounded at the hands of over-zealous guards in the infamous Dachau.

Batya and Sarah knew they were extremely blessed, but Batya never stopped believing that Jakub might also still be alive out there too, somewhere, in the middle of all this chaos. She prayed for her husband many times a day. And, in the evenings, after all the work was done and the house had settled for the night, the women held hands and talked about Jakub and their life in Warsaw before the war and their subsequent years in the Ghetto.

"Mama, do you really think Papa is still alive?"

"Yes, Meyn lib, I do. I believe I would know in my heart if he was no longer here."

"But the machine gun fire and explosions, after he hid us near the wall. How could he have survived that?"

"Don't underestimate your father, Sarah. He is a strong man and he has a strong faith. Stronger than mine."

"I have always thought you were the one with a strong faith, Mama. Why do you say that your faith is not strong?"

"I had always believed my faith to be strong in my youth. I was brought up in a good family, by good Jewish people. However, when I saw most of my family killed, I think it damaged that young faith a bit. Then when my baby died, well, it was difficult for me to believe in a God who would take a child from the womb of parents who wanted him so desperately. At that point I was pretty sure God didn't care about me very much at all."

"But you pray, Mama. And you keep all of the holidays and celebrations of our people. Why do you do that if you don't believe?"

"I think your father was very sad when I became distant and I do love him so much. It was important to him for our family to remain in faith, no matter what tragedies befell our household. For instance, he wanted you to be raised in such a way that you would always be faithful to Jehovah and to your Jewish faith. I began again to pray and observe our holy days when I knew it was important to him and continued when I realized how important it was for you to have a sound foundation. I guess there was always some part of me, though, that felt there was something missing. I don't know. Perhaps I don't explain myself well. Do you understand what I'm saying?"

"I do Mama. I've wanted to share this with you for a long time, but I didn't want to upset you. I thought being Jewish was important to you, so I kept this secret to myself. To answer your question, yes, I have always felt that something was missing from my relationship with God. I've been searching for answers for a long time."

"Tell me Sarah. What is it that you thought would upset me so much?"

"When I was regularly seeing my new friends in the Ghetto some of us were going to meetings."

"What kind of meetings?"

"This is where it gets a little complicated. We were meeting to discuss Jesus. One of my friends had a Bible. We were studying the New Testament. Did you know, Mama, in the Christian Bible they use most of the same scriptures for their Old Testament scriptures as we have in our Tanakh?"

"No, I suppose I really don't know very much about the Christian Bible, or the Christian faith, Sarah."

"Oh, Mama, the New Testament is truly amazing. It tells all about the life of Jesus. The way He healed people and helped so many along the way during His ministry on earth. The brave way He stood up to the Pharisees and the way they turned Him over to the Romans. It describes the sacrifices He made for all of us. The way they beat and scourged Him, hung Him on a cross and killed Him. But, it also tells about when He rose again, triumphant over death, and made salvation available for everyone who believes in Him. Did you know that He actually had disciples who believed in Him and the ministry of His Truth so much that they died for their faith in Christ? Martyred for their faith, Mama. Can you imagine? It is truly remarkable."

"That sounds like something I would like to know more about. You know I have heard of the Bible, but I have never held one in my own hands."

"I don't have a Bible either, Mama, but perhaps Mrs. Weiter would let us use hers? I saw one on a pedestal in the library. I want you to know that I've already asked Jesus to come into my heart and forgive me of my sins. I am a Christian now, Mama."

"I don't know how your father will feel about that, Sarah. He is very proud of our Jewish heritage, but I am happy for you. It seems you are very content in your decision. And that is certainly much more than I can claim."

"I am, Mama. I was always pretty happy. You and

Papa saw to that, even when times were tough. But I am filled with a joy now that I can't quite explain. I know I have a purpose and that's something I never felt before. I am certain that I'm supposed to share my Lord Jesus with the world."

"Well, you're off to a good start, meyn lib. You have shared Jesus with your mother. Now we will have to see about getting a Bible, so you may also teach me what I am missing."

Overhearing conversations between Weiter and his wife, over the next weeks, and then with officers who came to him for daily orders, the ladies gathered that the Soviets were advancing further and gaining ground every day. They also understood that American soldiers were involved in the fighting now and their actions were driving the Nazis further afield. They began to wonder if there might be an end to this madness somewhere in the near future after all.

When Mrs. Weiter discovered the sewing prowess of her servants, their new mistress allowed the girls to create a couple of new dresses for her and then, with a lesser quality of fabric, to sew simple dresses for themselves. Though they knew it was more to keep up appearances for the frequent guests who paraded through the house to see the commandant, Batya and Sarah were grateful for the kindness. However, the new dresses made the ladies even more appealing in appearance. Now the commandant's eyes were further glued to their shapely forms, as they went about their daily duties. It would only be a matter of time, they thought, before the commandant's wife grew impatient with her husband's wandering eye and sent them off to less than desirable circumstances.

Due to this, Batya felt compelled to boldly ask her mistress if they might use her Bible. Mrs. Weiter seemed shocked at first, after all they were only Jews, but then in a moment of generosity she agreed to let the ladies use her Bible in the evenings. Thinking that would keep them in the back of the house and out of her husband's line of sight.

It was clear to see that the Commandant was terrified of his dominating wife. So, as much as possible for everyone's sake, they stayed out of sight and hopefully out of mind, studying the Word together in the privacy of their bedroom.

The overwhelming heat of August 1943 hit Treblinka's population like a suffocating wall. Jakub and his fellow Sonderkommando had been standing on the arrival platforms of the death camp for months, watching the brutal atrocities committed against their people as they were marched to their deaths. They had simply come to the last of their tolerance for the Nazi monsters and their cruel hirelings.

Jakub wanted to ring Ivan's neck, more than once, but held himself back over and over again for the sake of saving his wife and daughter should they happen to come this way. However, after time it became apparent that his family was most likcly dead. He decided now was the best time to act. His brother prisoners agreed with him that something had to be done. They couldn't continue any longer to act as slave labor for the Nazi regime. Some things, including their own lives, didn't seem to be worth the toll this work was taking on their collective mental state.

During his time as Sonderkommando, on the arrival platform in Treblinka ll, he'd made friends with some of the men assigned to perform the same tasks he was given. Ludwig, Shlomo, Herman and Samuel, were all decent men who wanted to live as much as anyone else. But they felt in their hearts, just as he did, that they had to do something to stop the madness of the Nazi regime. Even if it meant sacrificing their own lives.

Nights became a time for planning. Laying in their bunks, close together for fear of being overheard by guards or prisoners looking to gain favor with those same guards, they plotted their escape.

With no weapons, wooden slats, pried loose and secretly stolen from beneath sleeping pallets, then split and sharpened to a point, would be the best they could do. These knives, of sorts, were a perfect size to fit under their shirts, tucked in the waistbands of their pants.

The Sonderkommando were better fed than the rest of the camp's prisoners, which wasn't saying much. However, those few extra morsels of food probably kept them alive. Nevertheless, they were still, each and every one, thinner by a dozen pounds or more since their 'relocation' to the death camp months earlier. So, due to their somewhat weakened state, conviction of cause would necessarily have to be the main propellant in the aggression to come.

Whether they prevailed, or their attempt proved to be disastrous, every man involved was willing to lay down his life taking out as many of the cruel Treblinka guards as possible to risk escape for themselves and others.

Once outside the camp they would quickly seek help for those still imprisoned inside. Certainly, the world would not be so uncaring as to allow the travesty, which was Treblinka ll, to go unchecked. When they knew what was actually going on inside its gates, rational heads would prevail. The men were sure of it.

These men; due to the mode of arrival to their new situation; didn't realize the camp was located deep in the forest and unknown by many. They were also unaware that, frankly, the rest of the world was mostly deaf and blind by choice.

That morning's combat had been especially costly. Captain Shepherd stood outside his tent, on guard, with his use-worn Bible in hand. Tears shone in his war weary eyes, then ran down sunburned cheeks, as he thought of the three young men who'd sacrificed their lives in the bloody battle that very day.

In the distance he could see that the mêlée still raged into the night. But his own exhausted guys were attempting to grab a couple hours of well deserved rest, away from the conflict, as he stood watch.

He'd chosen to take first watch and intended to post a double, if he could get away with it, to give the guys a break. Mostly so he could be alone to pray. "Lord, I trust You. I know that You want only good for those who follow You. Keep Your mighty hand on these brave young men. Thank you that those who came home to You today have trusted You for salvation and that they have now found eternal rest and peace in Your loving presence. Please give me the words to say to their soon grieving families. And Lord, if it is your will, please stop this mad man who seeks to rule the world, so we can all go home at last. Thank you, Father. Amen"

Jeff couldn't know then that the war would rage on for almost two more years. Throughout it all he would remain faithful to His God and to the soldiers in his charge. And, though young men would come and go, some in body bags, others missing limbs or the sanity they had held dear when they arrived in this madhouse, he stayed to support and love them through it all.

"There is none like You, O Lord: You are great, and Your name is great in might. Who would not fear You, O King of the nations? For this is Your due: for among all the wise ones of the nations and in all their kingdoms there is none like You." Jeremiah 10:6–7

CHAPTER 16

August heat, combined with rampant nerves over the upcoming action, kept most of the men up throughout the night. Today was the day. Jakub and the others planned to wait until half the camp's guards broke for lunch. Attack would likely be more successful when the mid-day temperatures would be a distraction and afternoon activities would be in full swing. Their plan was to kill those five wachmann guards closest to them, take their rifles, then get rid of as many additional Nazis as they were able before making their way to the front gates and into the forest beyond.

Once there they would press on to the nearest town and seek help. Sure there would be Polish people in the village willing to help them find a way out of their terrible situation, they were willing to bet their lives on the chance they were taking.

Captain Shepherd readied the men for battle with a prayer. He patted each man on the shoulder as they filed past and then continued his prayers for each one as he did. The battle that day would be especially brutal, with much loss of life, but they achieved the next hill and the one after that. Hitler's greed and desire for power had killed so many. His hatred of anyone he considered to be beneath him, Jews, Gypsies, mentally challenged and those with physical handicaps, murdered many more. What could finally rid the world of this maniac?

Enemy combatants had set up on the other side of the field in the thick of the tree line. From where the Captain and his men stood it looked as though their foe was prepared and ready to do battle.

Jeffrey shook his head and wondered exactly what it was, millennia ago, that caused people to start running across fields shooting and stabbing one another? What is it that brought us to this place where we are ready to face death? For what? Why is humanity filled with so much hatred for others, especially anyone a little different from ourselves, that we feel it impossible to live on the planet together? And, why does it seem that everything is run by individuals whose egos become so inflated they will never be satisfied until they rule the world? It is a sad state of affairs and surely not the way God intended.

The German's Blitzkrieg method of attack had evolved somewhat over the course of the war. Moving in quickly with tanks, air strikes and mobile forces usually made for a quick victory, with less loss of men and equipment, for their side, than conventional warfare. However, they hadn't counted on the heart of those American soldiers. That heart along with their adeptness at Guerilla warfare and close quarters combat would make a difference that the German forces hadn't anticipated. These young men had been taught to use their rifles, but they were also proficient with knife, bayonet and unconventional weapons. Once they got close to their enemies, nothing could stop them.

He would be right out there with the men, as per usual, offering comfort and his own rifle when the need arose. Often it was his own quickly deployed bullet that ended the brutal Nazi attack on one of his boys. His prayers were constant throughout the battle and continued long after. Today would be no different. He was tired, but he knew his men were tired too.

Batya and Sarah were overhearing more reports

from messengers who came to share information with the commandant. The allied forces gained more ground and German military units were forced to give up many of the towns they'd fought hard to capture before the Americans became involved. The women were shocked at some of the details they gleaned from secret conversations not meant for their ears.

Now, the Nazis didn't want to surrender anything to their foe, so when they left a town, or village, to the allied advance, they first set every building in that town ablaze. It was not uncommon for them to kill every farm animal they found, set all crops on fire and level towns and villages to the ground. All in an effort to leave the area and those now occupying it with no resources whatsoever.

With a new surge of hope, the women began to believe they just might get out of this impossible situation alive. Perhaps things were coming around for Jakub too. Did this mean there was a way that he might come back to them after all?

Sarah and her mom read Mrs. Weiter's Bible every night and Batya, for the first time in her life, was beginning to feel another kind of hope. The more she heard and read about this man Jesus, the more she wanted to know. She was falling in love with the Lord. Realizing at last that He really was the Messiah, the Son of God, the Savior that her people still waited for so patiently. He'd been here all the time and they'd missed Him. How could she not have seen? Well, she'd simply been taught differently, that was all there was to that. Now she knew the Truth and the Truth was about to set her free.

One evening after an especially impactful Bible study with her daughter, in the quiet of a summer night, Batya confessed her sin to the Lord and asked Him to come to live in her heart. Sarah held her and they cried together for a long time. She felt the weight of the world and her own transgressions fall away and she knew she would never be the same again.

Batya believed to the depths of her soul that her husband was out there somewhere. That he wasn't dead, but merely lost for now and she couldn't wait to share Jesus with the man she loved when at last she found him again.

Jakub and his friends, Ludwik, Shlomo, Herman and Samuel, stood on the arrival platform and assumed their duties, just as they had every other day for months. Aware that it was imperative they look as normal as possible so as not to attract attention. They were waiting for the afternoon transport. When it arrived the activity of newly arriving prisoners and the absence of several guards due to scheduled lunch breaks would coincide to make perfect conditions for an attack.

They all wanted to take "Ivan" out of the picture, but he was one of the stronger guards, and their chances of escape would effectually plummet if they had to match physical strength with the likes of him. They intended on taking as many of the new prisoners out of the gates with them as they could manage. So, that strategy would require making their move before those folks could be loaded into awaiting gas chambers. This also meant some of those prisoners would be running naked out in the elements. However, the men believed since it was summer, it was better to be freed naked than to be dead.

Jakub's gut was churning and rivulets of sweat began accumulating, to run down his back and soak into the waistband of his pants. He thought he might vomit, but knew that would draw lots of unwanted attention, so he took a few deep breaths and focused on the next step. Many lives were hanging in the balance and he didn't want to mess this up like he believed he'd done during the resistance movement in the Ghetto.

The unforgivable way he'd put his loved ones in danger. He would never forgive himself for that. If only he knew whether or not Batya and Sarah were still alive. That alone would make it all worthwhile. He would give anything, including his life, for the sake of the ones he loved.

The men waited a long, excruciating ten minutes after Ivan and the other guards left their posts for lunch, to give them enough time to make it all the way to the mess hall to fill their trays. Then looking around, Jakub gave his men the 'go' sign and they attacked. Grabbing guards, in unison, silently from behind they employed their improvised weapons to cut the throats of all five guards remaining on the arrival platform.

To say the guards were surprised would be an understatement of epic proportions. One guard staggered forward and looked down, puzzled as to why the front of his uniform was covered in blood, before he collapsed in a heap. Another grabbed his throat, and began spinning in circles, as if that would stop the blood spurting from his arteries. Still another fell to his knees gurgling, reaching out as if to elicit help from the very one who had just cut his throat. The other two fell immediately, as the damage to their throats was so severe. In only a couple of moments all five lay lifeless in puddles of their own blood.

Once the guards closest to them were dispatched, the men confiscated their weapons and ammunition for the next step in the plan.

Prisoners standing on the platforms watched. No one screamed or made a scene. It was surreal, almost as if they'd been a part of the plan all along and knew exactly what to do. But it wasn't that. No, they were tired and weak and weren't about to expend the last of their strength to help the very men who had just been herding them like cattle to their deaths.

Jakub spoke up, "Run. Quietly. Go now, through the forest to the nearest town. Make yourselves known. Get help for those who can't run. We will clear the way." Then he and his men made their way to the entrance of the camp, killing more guards along the way and making quick work of the unsuspecting gate guards. They were soon successfully through the entrance of the camp. However, now the guards who'd been on lunch break during the attack were alerted and grabbed their weapons to give chase.

Two hundred prisoners were on the run. That was how many were able to escape due to the bravery of Jakub and his men. Some of the escaped were clothed and some were naked, to sprint frantically through the surrounding forest. Jakub and his men stayed together, taking cover on and off throughout the woods and shooting back at the men giving chase whenever the opportunity arose.

Treblinka's guards were better equipped. Compared to the prisoners, especially those who had escaped without clothing and shoes on their feet, they were more than a match. Successfully shooting many of them as they made their mad dash to liberty. Jakub's gut twisted each time he heard the crack of a weapon firing and the cry of one who'd been hit. The only consolation was that if they had to die, at least they died reaching for freedom and not in the cement bunker of a gas chamber.

Two hundred prisoners escaped Treblinka death camp that day. One hundred were killed in the subsequent chase through the forest. A hundred made it deeper into the woods. Some would later succumb to hunger and the elements, but they died free from that horrid place. Some, including Jakub and his four men, would go on.

Jakub and his men, along with a number of survivors of the camp revolt hid in the forest beyond Treblinka ll until things seemed to calm down from the day. Surviving on berries, mushrooms and wild onions for a few days didn't seem as bad as one might think after the previous starvation conditions under the Nazis. However, this couldn't go on forever.

As suspected, Treblinka communicated with the nearest town and police there were on the lookout for escapees from the "criminal labor camp" in their nearby woods. When four of the prisoners traveling with Jakub decided to go against the group's better judgment and made their way into town to seek help, they were summarily arrested and returned to guards who were sent from the camp to collect them. They would be immediately tortured and killed upon arrival back in camp, for all to see, as a warning to others with similar intentions.

The rest of the refugees were made suddenly aware that the world was not the slightest bit interested in their plight. They would have no heroic rescue, no respite from the dangers of the chase. They were on their own and would necessarily have to figure out the rest of this journey using only their wits.

Jakub didn't like the idea of stealing, as he'd tried very hard to be a righteous man in his lifetime. Nevertheless, after killing so many guards in their recent escape, he decided this sin was far less damning than some of his previous transgressions. The group waited in a nearby tree line until dark and then crept quietly into the inhospitable town to take items off various clothes lines. Along the way they found some fruit and vegetables in root cellars, eggs in chicken coops and oats in barns that would further sustain them along the way. Now that they were appropriately dressed and supplied, their trek would be less complicated.

This band of scraggly looking escaped prisoners, all with prices on their heads, were looking for escape from the land where they were born and bred, the only land that had ever been home to any of them. They were searching for a place where they could be free. They planned to make their way to the nearest port city and work for passage on a ship bound for the United States of America.

Captain Shepherd was sad, and weary to the bone. Writing letters again. This time it was one to the parents and another to the fiancée of a young man he'd grown very close to since they were deployed.

John MacDonald was due to be married upon return home to Nebraska in less than two months. They had a lot in common, including the fact that they'd both grown up on farms in that great state. The other men teased John, calling him 'Farmer John', and 'Old MacDonald', though he wasn't a bit older than any of the rest of them. He took it all in stride. He was a kind and gentle young man, with a quick smile, who loved the Lord and would have made an excellent husband and father if he'd been given the chance. Jeffrey was having a tough time with this one.

John often spoke of his parents, who sounded a lot like Jeffrey's own folks. Listening to the young man go on felt almost like being home for a visit back when his mom and dad were still alive. Those stories always put a smile on the tired chaplain's face.

When John spoke of his future wife he got a dreamy

look in his eyes and a wistful tone in his voice, that made the Captain wish he had that kind of love in his own life. Someone to fight for. A good reason to continue getting up in the morning. Oh, his relationship with Jesus was still strong and always would be, but the human side of him longed for moral support from a special person in his own life.

When he finished the letters Captain Shepherd placed John's dog tags in the envelope along with the two folded pieces of paper. He had closed each letter with the assurance, to John's loved ones, that John knew the Lord well and that he was walking with Jesus in glory.

Jeffrey wasn't sure how much more death he could take. But, he couldn't bring himself to leave. He had no one at home waiting for him and so many of these young men still did. Yet, through it all, they toiled on. How could he go, knowing that they needed his council and compassion? No, he would stay, as long as it took for this madman, Hitler, to be brought to justice.

Jakub and the other escapees were making their way to Gdansk, three hundred and forty kilometers North

West of Warsaw. They would have a journey of well over four hundred kilometers from their present location to make that port town. This would include a wide swing around the city of Warsaw, which they were pretty confident was still in the hands of German forces.

Traveling by night, knowing the Nazis were still looking for them and holing up in bombed out farms and deserted towns by day. They ate what they could find and washed up when they found water in a place that afforded any privacy at all. Jakub and the other four armed men provided security for the rag tag group of refugees and took turns posting watch in the daytime while the others slept.

Much of the itinerant group spent an inordinate amount of time grousing and complaining about almost everything. Food, weather, travel time and anything else they could point to, to lay blame for their plight on the five men who, with God's help, had freed them from their prison.

Jakub wondered if this must be the way Moses felt wandering in the desert for forty years with the people of Israel, as they complained every day of their circumstances. There were times he considered leaving while they were sleeping, to find help on his own, which would certainly have been easier than being responsible for this ungrateful lot. But he didn't leave. Something, deep inside, convicted him of his accountability to God for his fellow human beings and he soldiered on.

Along the way they lost members of their group. So many had been at the end of their strength, even when they'd escaped the death camp, that Jakub wondered how they'd made it this far. Each time they lost one of their own, the congregation murmured and grumbled. Each time, they tried to lay the blame on Jakub. Until one day when, in a fit of indignation, Ludwik spoke out. "Do you know where you would all be if not for this man? You were standing in a line to be gassed in the chambers at Treblinka, do you remember this? This man, with the help of God, has saved your lives. Now, if you no longer want to travel with us, the choice is yours. Leave, you ungrateful lot. We will not force you to remain with us. But, if you choose to stay, I will hear no more of your constant complaining, do you hear me? No more of it at all! You are worse than the Israelites who were freed from Egypt and had to continue wandering around the mountain for forty years due to their ingratitude. Decide what you will do now. This night you may go or stay." None left.

Gdansk being a port town, and due to its regional importance, still had a Nazi presence. However, due to the push by allied forces, that presence was minimal and would fall away to almost nothing within the next couple of months. Jakub and his band of expatriates, a group of less than thirty now, were able to lay low and stay out of sight for the most part. When German troops marched out of town for the last time they tried setting buildings afire, but the town's citizens quickly doused the flames and saved almost all of the structures. Jakub and his crew were a great help in salvaging the community that day and were swiftly welcomed into society there.

Jakub and the men who traveled with him applied for and secured positions on the docks of the sea port. From here they would work to earn their way on ships bound for their new promised land.

An estimated nine hundred thousand Jews were slaughtered in the gas chambers of Treblinka ll between July of 1942 and October of 1943, the deadliest phase of Hitler's 'Final Solution', a death rate second only to that of Auschwitz.

Gassing operations at Treblinka ll ended in October 1943 following that revolt by the Sonderkommando in early August. A number of guards were killed, and around a hundred prisoners were never accounted for. It would amount to very bad PR once those prisoners began to show up on the world stage. The camp was dismantled ahead of the Soviet advance. A farmhouse for an appointed watchman was built on the site and the ground quickly ploughed over in an attempt to hide the evidence of genocide that had occurred in that dreadful place.

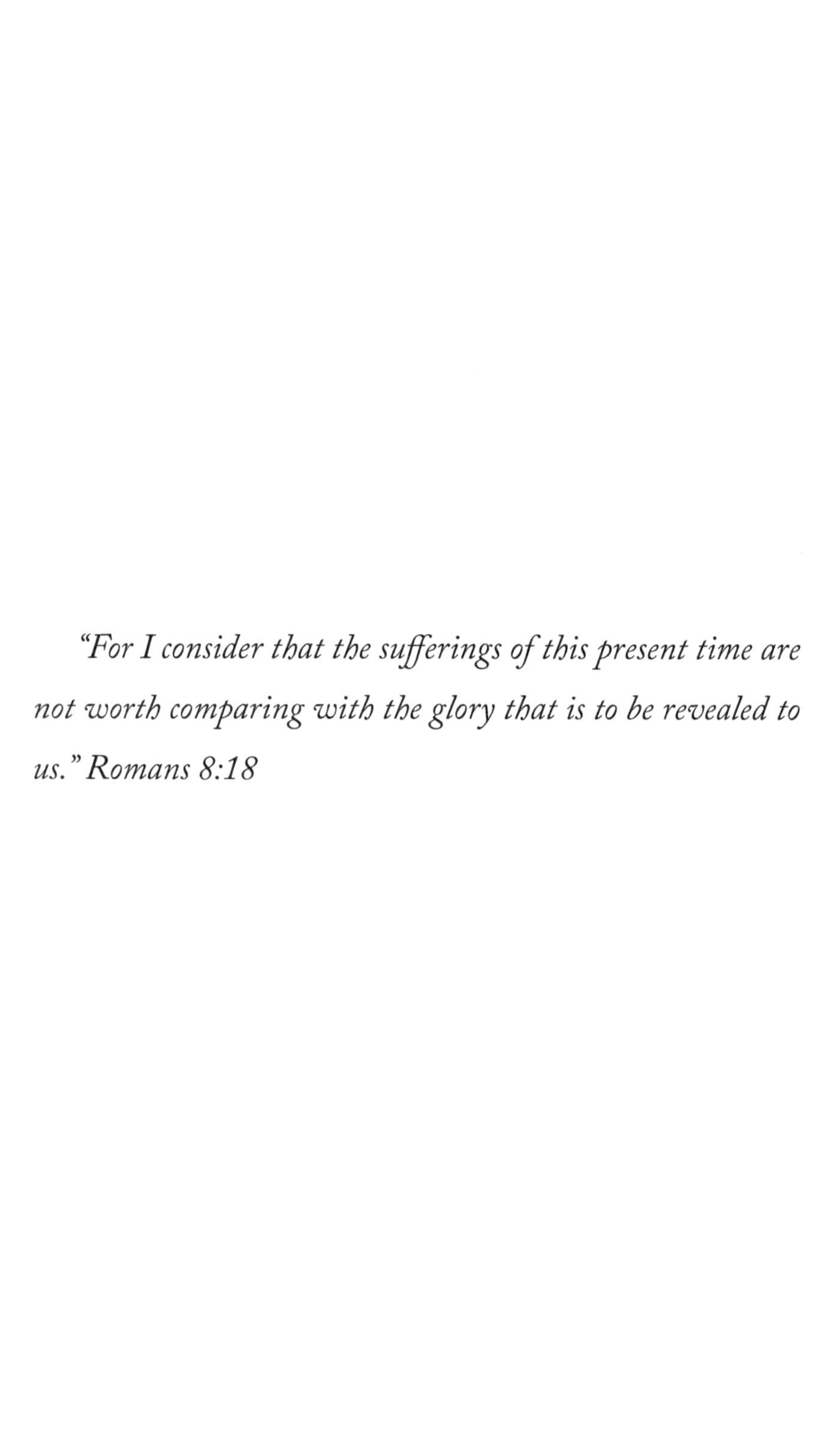

"For I consider that the sufferings of this present time are not worth comparing with the glory that is to be revealed to us." Romans 8:18

CHAPTER 17

Batya and Sarah awoke to a house shaken by news of a new allied advance. Mrs. Weiter was packing to leave and required the help of the ladies to prepare for travel. She would be making her way to safer regions, while the Commandant wrapped things up in Dachau. "I'm very sorry I can no longer protect you, Batya and Sarah. You will be going with my husband to the camp. I have no way to take you with me and there is no other option. You are Christians now and God will protect you in that place, I am quite sure of it."

"We understand, Mrs. Weiter. We wish you God speed. Thank you for your kindness where we are concerned. We know we have received only good at your hand and you will be in our prayers for safe travels."

Though they chose not to show it, the news came as a shock to the women, who knew they would be at the mercy of Commandant Weiter and the guards at Dachau. They helped where they could to set Mrs. Weiter's house aright, saw her on her way and then sat down to pray together.

The commandant was an emotional mess. He was

giving up his house to avoid the advancing troops. As a result, he would now be forced to live at the camp. That was the last thing in the world he wanted. Truth be told, he'd been dependent upon his wife to handle all of his affairs since the day they'd married and he didn't know what he would do without her guidance. The ladies felt almost sorry for the man. He'd been mostly kind to them, even if it was only because he thought of them as some kind of prize possessions, like exotic birds or fish in a glass bowl.

Once at the camp the women were assigned sleeping quarters near the medical buildings. They would attend to the commandant in the evenings, but would effectively live among the other prisoners for purposes of sleeping and meals. They would also be lent out to other officers on site for duties and chores not yet explained to them. This was a worrisome thing.

At this point the only thing keeping them calm was their faith that the Lord would remain their protector. They reasoned that at least they had been assigned to the same barracks which was some comfort.

In no time at all they were put to work. Most of the Nazi officers found the women to be a unique pair. Beautiful and intelligent. Though they would never have admitted that directly to the ladies. After all, this would allow the prisoners a sense of worthiness not generally given out indiscriminately to mere Jewish dogs.

Actually, most of the doctors in camp doubted the two ladies were of Jewish descent at all, due to their coloring and features. Except, as in most things, they were wrong. Several of those doctors were actually scheming to get the girls away from the watchful eye of the commandant, for other nefarious reasons. There were a number of rather dangerous experiments for which the butchers thought the ladies would be perfect candidates.

Pressed immediately into service as medical scribes, they were promptly assigned to Dr. Sigmund Rascher. Doctor Rascher reported directly to Reishsfuhrer-SS Heinrich Himmler, who would go down in history as one of the most cruel and pitiless men in the Third Reich. He was known widely for using prisoners as lab rats in experiments that would ultimately kill, maim, and disfigure almost everyone he touched. Now that he had control of these two lovely women, he would keep his eyes open for an experiment of especially wide-ranging potential. It would be no use to waste such perfect specimens on anything that wouldn't gain him much acclaim in history's prominent medical circles.

Batya and Sarah were horrified by the things they saw. They prayed every day for the poor souls used in these atrocious experiments. One of the first they witnessed took men dressed in uniforms similar to those worn by Nazi pilots and submerged them in freezing water. Some up to their heads and others completely sunken beneath the icy depths. This was in an attempt to discover a way to keep actual German pilots, whose planes were shot down over water, from freezing to death in those circumstances.

As the prisoners were lowered into the icy depths, within glass front tanks, the women watched their expressions go from fear, to panic, to helplessness and finally resignation as the icy water overtook them. Over a hundred men died in this particular test.

Other experiments exposed prisoners to infectious diseases and left them to suffer and die, without medical help, in order to watch the progression of the illness from its inception to its dreadful end. This horror was in an effort to discover some way to help their own soldiers and citizens in case of epidemic.

In one test where twelve hundred were exposed to malaria, over six hundred died and many others were left with lifelong effects of the disease. Other tests included exposure to typhus, tuberculosis, typhoid fever, yellow fever, and infectious hepatitis. Watching these people suffer, day by day, through the glass panels of their observation deck was excruciating torture for the tender-hearted women.

Those prisoners, exposed to chemical burns from mustard gas, were the worst. Their agony was palpable, and the women cried as they took their required notes. If there had been a way to save those injured souls Batya and Sarah would have taken it, but they were heavily guarded and locked safely in their glass front observation booth without a way to provide aid of any sort. More than once Batya wished God would strike her blind, rather than be forced to witness one more moment of the suffering of their people at the hands of these madmen.

Back in the barracks they were shunned by their peers. People who didn't understand why they got, as was perceived, favored treatment. They had only God and each other to lean on. However, that proved in the end to be enough for them. In the evenings they were ordered to the commandant's chambers to take care of his needs. So far he was still only looking, but their fear was that he would become bolder over time as his wife was absent. They prayed that the advancing allied forces would be quick to come for them.

Captain Shepherd felt his prayers were being answered. By all accounts the allied forces were successfully pushing the Nazis further afield. They were winning, but there was that age old question, at what cost?

Jeffrey received a letter from home, written by an older church member, telling him of his favorite brother's death by influenza. He hadn't seen his brother in many years, and the news was almost surreal. He'd not really thought of his siblings for a long time and felt a little guilty for not being more affected than he was. However, he knew his brother was saved. He would see him again in the hereafter.

His true purpose, as he saw it, was to see the Gospel shared with those who God had set before him. He would push on, until every person God set before him had heard 'The Good News'.

Grunting as he picked up and carried a large crate of goods to the proper pallet, Jakub strained to stack the items and then stretched his back as he stood for a moment to inspect the integrity of his effort. Work on the docks was tough and some of the refugees had a difficult time keeping up. But Jakub and his friends were right at home with hard work. They were steadily making progress toward the goal they'd set. Weekly pay was adding up and they had already filled out paperwork necessary to sail to America, where they could apply for citizenship and make a new life. This wasn't an easy process, as America was still severely limiting its allowance of Jewish immigrants.

"Hey, Jakub."

"What's going on, Herman?"

"Are we done after this shipment, or do we have another load coming in?"

"I think this is it. It's almost dark anyway, and the boss doesn't want us trying to unload in the dark after that fellow on the other team dropped a crate on his leg. Why? Do you have somewhere to be? Another date with the teacher perhaps?"

"Another date? This is his fifth date with Emma. I think he's going to pop the question any day now. Aren't you, Herman?"

"Knock it off, Samuel. I don't know where this is going yet. I haven't even told her I'm a Jew."

"You haven't told her you're Jewish? Are you ashamed of your heritage?"

"Hey, both of you. Stop the arguing. We aren't being paid to stand around and yammer. Samuel, it's up to Herman when he tells this girl his business. Nevertheless, Herman, if I were you, I wouldn't keep secrets from this young lady forever, especially if you're really interested in her."

"Yeah, I guess you're right. It just seems like the world isn't too keen on Jews these days, and I didn't want to stir up any trouble. What if she says something to her parents and her father doesn't like me? That would be one way to get rid of the guy that's dating your daughter, wouldn't it? Just turn him over to the SS and be done."

"Very good point. You're right. It might be better to keep that information to yourself until you figure out how serious the relationship has gotten."

"Isn't that sad?"

"Isn't what sad?"

"Isn't it sad that the world hates us so much that we have to worry about what we say to someone, even if that someone is a person we really care about?"

"Yes, Herman. That is very sad. Now let's finish up. I'm hungry and I want to get some rest. Tomorrow is payday and we are getting very close to our goal."

Jakub wished he could share this time, unchained and unfettered, with his beloved Batya, but she was certainly gone after all this time and he would have to go on to make a life without her. The idea of sailing without his family filled him with great sadness and pain. Though, he found the prospect of adventures in a new country that did not have a Hitler in its midst very exciting indeed.

the thought of a place where he could work hard and see rewards for his labor and diligence. His heart broke all over again for his daughter, poor Sarah, who never really had a chance at life. He would have given any-thing to hold his loved ones again and to see his daughter bloom and prosper in the new land.

The third Reich didn't have much of a presence in the port region anymore, now that allied forces had advanced yet again. But when those distinctive Nazi helmets and uniforms were spotted in the crowd at the loading docks, non Jews working with the men in Jakub's crew quickly warned them and hid the refugees under barrels and tarps until the soldiers had gone their way. Jakub and his men were grateful for their new friends and worked all the harder to repay them, making the dock run smoother and the work load go easier for everyone.

Winter was rough that year, taking ten more of the escaped prisoners who traveled with Jakub. Simply too weak, after all they'd been through, to survive the hardships of freezing temperatures no matter how well Jakub and his men provided and cared for them. The original group of almost a hundred was down now to less than twenty souls.

By summer of 1944 Jakub and the men had saved enough money for passage to America for those who remained and wanted to travel with them across the ocean. They booked passage and boarded the ship, taking their meager possessions with them, on a journey that would provide a new home, a life of opportunity and a freedom they'd never really known.

Batya and Sarah settled into a workable routine. They despised their work as medical transcribers for the evil Nazi doctors, as they were forced to witness the heinous torture of helpless human beings every single day. However, they weren't in a position to argue with their jailers. So, they did as they were told, making mental notes of everything they saw along the way should the opportunity ever arise to give testimony for the atrocities they'd seen.

Evenings in the commandant's quarters were less objectionable. It appeared that his roving eye didn't amount to much more than that. He never did try to touch either of the women, so his wife needn't have worried the way she did after all.

They did his cooking, cleaning and laundry, all while he tracked them from chore to chore with his characteristic eerie gaze. They could live with that too. Mrs. Weiter had even sent an old Bible along for the ladies to study. It seemed she really did have a heart.

They weren't allowed to take the Bible, or any personal belongings, into their barracks. They did manage to sneak a little food back to some of the more seriously suffering among their barrack mates, and that act of kindness was earning them some respect. They'd learned quite a bit of German reading Mrs. Weiter's Bible and even some English by listening to some of the intercepted communications relayed from allied forces. So, they were much more aware of what was going on around them than their jailers knew.

After doing their chores, Batya and Sarah would read for a while before going back over to the barracks at night. Then they would disperse the rescued bits of food to those who needed it most.

The ladies were learning more about the Savior and His disciples. The more they discovered, the more they adored Him and wanted to be like Him. Batya's heart ached to share the Gospel with Jakub, but where was he?

Four weeks at sea seemed like more than an eternity. Packed away like sardines in the bowels of the ship, most of the refugees were so seasick they prayed daily for death to take them. Jakub, Herman and Samuel, the only ones who didn't seem affected by the constant pitching and rolling of the ship, were trying to aid and comfort their fellow travelers in any way they could.

The lower decks, 'steerage', reeked of vomit and human waste, and the three men had all they could do to hold their breath while continually going up and down, emptying buckets over the ship's railings. Trying to keep everyone hydrated was another obstacle, everything that went down came right back up. Caring for their group and mopping the wood plank floors was a nasty and thankless, full time job that would give them nightmares in future when they were once again on dry land.

Sailing into New York harbor on a warm, clear June day, Jakub stood on the sun-drenched deck of their ship with tears of joy streaming from his eyes. He took in the majesty of the great Lady Liberty which had been standing tall on Ellis Island since 1886. Her copper exterior, whose patina had taken on an oxidized coat of green, was both ancient looking and reassuring in the light of a new day.

One of the sailors shared that to the top of her gargantuan torch measured over three hundred feet. Jakub would later learn that on a bronze plaque mounted inside the lower level of her pedestal were the words penned by a famed Jewish poet, Emma Lazarus. Those words read:

Not like the brazen giant of Greek fame,
With conquering limbs astride from land to land;
Here at our sea-washed, sunset gates shall stand
A mighty woman with a torch, whose flame
Is the imprisoned lightning, and her name
Mother of Exiles. From her beacon-hand
Glows world-wide welcome; her mild eyes command
The air-bridged harbor that twin cities frame.

"Keep, ancient lands, your storied pomp!" cries she
With silent lips. "Give me your tired, your poor,
Your huddled masses yearning to breathe free,
The wretched refuse of your teeming shore.
Send these, the homeless, tempest-tost to me,
I lift my lamp beside the golden door!"

At the end of their long voyage to freedom and after the loss of three more precious souls along the journey, a mere sixteen of the almost one hundred escapees from Treblinka ll were ready to walk down the gang plank to touch the soil of their new home. However, entry into the great United States of America was not quite so simple.

A heath officer boarded the ship to check for any

possible contagious illness or disease that might keep someone from disembarking. Several were held back and would wait on the ship for further examination. This process would take several days. Jakub and the others were anxious to see their new home and the wait seemed interminable.

Healthy first and second-class passengers were allowed to leave the ship and head straight into the country on their first day in port, skipping the long registry lines on the island.

Once the steerage passengers finally filed off the ship, they headed up a long staircase to the second floor of the registry offices in the magnificent, great hall. Doctors stood at the top of the stairs looking down to keep their eyes open for anyone having difficulty managing the assent. This would give them a bird's eye view of possible health problems among the poor refugees.

Inside the registry office each passenger was subjected to a short medical examination. If trained personnel saw something that might require further attention, that individual would go to a holding area on the island to be more thoroughly examined by a senior doctor. This procedure of quarantine in the island's holding area could take as little as a few hours, or as long as several months.

Once cleared by a medical exam, the immigrant would go on to another line to be scrutinized for possible legal issues. Each passenger was asked twenty-nine questions pertaining to the information available in the ship's registry log; name, profession, area traveling from, area traveling to, etc. If any of their answers did not match what was on record, they were removed to another holding area.

At the end of all examinations they were processed through and given entry documents, usually with their name misspelled, from which they could later go on to take the steps of becoming a citizen. Jakub Nowak was now officially Jacob Novak.

Several passengers from steerage were further detained for medical issues; but all of Jacob's group, having passed their exams, were allowed entrance into the country.

Now the real challenge would begin. Jacob needed a job, and he wanted to learn more English to better communicate with the people of his wonderful new country. All the men from Treblinka ll would remain close throughout their lives, but this was the place and time where they each needed to start being responsible for their own futures.

Jacob boldly walked into the office of a nearby construction site, something he would never have dared to do back home and was hired on the spot. With some of his remaining money he rented a room in the nearby boarding house. He would be fed three meals a day and share the bathroom down the hall with five other men, all hard-working immigrants, just like him.

His room, containing only the barest of furnishings; a bed with clean bedding, which would be diligently changed once a week by the woman who ran the establishment; wood floors; a small table, chair and lamp; a radiator for heat, controlled by the very frugal owner of the house; and a radio, complete with instructions to keep unnecessary noise to a minimum; was so much more than anything he'd had for such a long time, it seemed to him more like a palace than a mere boarding house.

He was grateful to be in a place where he had, not only a roof over his head and three meals a day, but a good job so soon after arriving. He would save his money and perhaps he could start a business in time. Several ideas came to him. He was experienced at providing transportation, and he'd worked on the docks for months. Maybe providing a service to transport goods? After all, people did say this was the land of opportunity. Jacob only wished his beloved Batya could be here with him in this magical place, to see the wonderful prospects open to them.

"Deliver me, O Lord, from evil men; preserve me from violent men, who plan evil things in their heart and stir up wars continually. Psalm 140:1-2

CHAPTER 18

Unusually cold, especially for the middle of April, the women made their way to the medical experimentation building wrapped in the scratchy, worn blankets from their sleeping cots. The threadbare fabric against their shoulders did little to relieve the morning chill, but was better than nothing at all. Spirits low, regarding what they knew lay before them, the ladies marched off to another day of forced horror.

Batya was surprised to see; as they rushed past the iron gates of Dachau and the two armed guards posted there; that swaths of tulips and daffodils had sprung up in surrounding fields seemingly overnight. Bravely pushing their colorful heads through the thin layer of new snow covering the ground, it seemed no one had told them the world as they knew it was falling apart and no longer fit for something so beautiful. The sight slowed her down and then stopped her in her tracks, causing her to feel just the tiniest glimmer of hope for the future as a slight smile curved her lips. That is until a guard pointed his rifle directly at her and told her to, "Beeilen Sie sich. Weitergehen." (Hurry it up. Move along).

Noticing a flurry of activity at the commandant's chambers, her smile faded and was replaced by a look of concern. Batya and Sarah slowed down further, trying to listen in and make sense of the commotion. It seemed the commandant was packing up to leave. They altered their path to put themselves nearer his quarters. He walked outside and their eyes met, causing him to avert his gaze and quickly turn away.

"Commandant. Commandant, are you leaving?"

"Get back. Get along to your assignments girls. Leave the commandant alone."

"No, no, guard, go ahead and let them through. Go on about your business. They will be fine here with me."

"Are we to be going with you commandant?"

"No, ladies. I will not be taking you with me this time. You will remain here under the supervision of the medical staff at the camp."

"But commandant, you can't."

"No, there is no more to be said about it. Decisions have been made and I am to go on to my next assignment immediately. There will be no more provision made for the two of you."

In reality Weiter was nothing more than a crafty coward who was actively making good his own escape. The allies were closing in from all sides and he didn't want to be caught at Dachau when they arrived.

It was widely known in the camp that Himmler had issued Weiter with an order Codenamed "Volkenbrand". To liquidate all Dachau inmates, preventing them from falling into Allied hands. And further, that Weiter had refused to comply with this order. He just wasn't as cold blooded a killer as so many of his Nazi peers proved to be. So, while Himmler was attending a meeting at headquarters, Weiter would manage to pack up and slither away into the countryside, leaving the girls and all his other prisoners, to deal with the whims of the camp's less than compassionate guards.

"Now, ladies, go on to your work assignment, before you cause trouble for yourselves."

"Yes, Commandant. We will do as you say. However, in future, if we die at the hands of these monsters remember that you could have done something to prevent this."

"Go girls. Now I tell you."

The women walked away slowly. Batya put her right

arm around her daughter's shoulders and gave her a scrunch. "I don't want you to worry, Sarah. I believe that God has plans for us and those plans don't have anything to do with dying here in a Nazi concentration camp."

"I'm not worried Mama. I know God will protect us. I also believe that He intends for me to share the Gospel with many people. I've told you as much many times. Therefore, I cannot die here in this place."

"Yes, my beautiful Sarah. You are correct. You have told me this before. So, we will simply wait on the Lord to rescue us from this situation, as He has so many times in the past. After all, He is good, is He not?"

"Yes Mama, He is good. Now, we'd better get over to the medical building quickly, or they will surely send someone looking for us."

With their protector gone, things were about to get a whole lot worse for Batya and Sarah.

Jacob was more proud of this particular purchase than he would have ever thought possible and was mentally patting himself on the back. It represented much hard work, lots of saving, and a freedom he'd never even dared believe for at any previous time in his life. He'd put away every cent of the money he had earned until he could afford a truck for the hauling and ground shipment of goods.

His 1945 Ford, V8, had an oversized bed for transporting cargo, and a fully equipped dark green cab, with a roomy interior large enough for two men and their belongings.

The name of Jacob's trucking firm, B, S & J Hauling, was an idea he'd come up with to honor his wife and daughter. He intended to start serving customers locally at first, but would branch out across the country in time. He'd heard there was a great deal of profit to be made in the transporting of goods around the nation, at least for men who weren't afraid of the hard work and long hours involved in building that kind of business.

During his time in America he'd studied for and achieved citizenship through learning the laws of the land and passing a grueling test administered by the department of naturalization. He'd also worked very hard learning and then further improving his English. At his citizenship ceremony he answered questions and repeated an oath, which read: "I hereby declare, on oath, that I absolutely and entirely renounce and abjure all allegiance and fidelity to any foreign prince, potentate, state, or sovereignty, of whom or which I have heretofore been a subject or citizen; that I will support and defend the Constitution and laws of the United States of America against all enemies, foreign and domestic; that I will bear true faith and allegiance to the same; that I will bear arms on behalf of the United States when required by the law; that I will perform noncombatant service in the Armed Forces of the United States when required by the law; that I will perform work of national importance under civilian direction when required by the law; and that I take this obligation freely, without any mental reservation or purpose of evasion; so help me God."

He was saddened, as he had repeated those words, that his loved ones could not be there to hear them, and a feeling of emptiness seemed to eat away at his gut. However, he was glad so many of his fellow 'new citizens' were surrounded by their proud friends and family, believing in his heart that somewhere his beloved Batya was watching.

This was a noteworthy day for B, S & J, as Jacob already had his first commercial customer and his first commercial order. He would be driving a load of goods to New Jersey today and picking up another load to transport back to New York. The combined time to load, drive, unload, reload, drive and unload would take the entire day, but he had hired some reliable help. His friend Samuel was his second; and having cut his teeth on the same busy docks as Jacob, he knew Samuel was almost as strong as he was himself. So, the work should go pretty smoothly.

Driving over the George Washington Bridge into New Jersey, in his brand spanking new truck, was amazing. The winter had been colder and wetter than usual, according to locals, and the Hudson river below the bridge was running fast and high. This gave occupants rolling across the bridge a surreal feeling. Jacob felt like he was floating on top of the world.

Filled with a great sense of accomplishment in the long-fought battle to become a business owner, in his newly adopted country, Jacob could not contain his joy. Samuel slapped him on the arm and grinned as they crossed into New Jersey to deliver and retrieve cargo for the first time. "Here we go, Jacob! Can you believe this? This is the first day of your brand-new business. This is great!"

"Thanks, Samuel. For coming on board, I mean. I have a lot of confidence that this is going to be a very successful undertaking and I am proud to have you as my second."

"Hey, my friend, I am grateful that you offered it to me. Prospects were slim and you likely saved me and my family. Thank you. You know that isn't the first time you've saved me."

"Aw, come on Samuel. I think we make a good team and I am glad to have you."

Within just a few short months his profits provided Jacob enough capital to buy two more trucks. He hired Herman to drive his second truck, with Shlomo as his second; and Ludwik to drive the third truck, hiring a new friend, Klaus, as second for that crew.

Herman and Ludwik were both tireless go getters. Having proved their industrious nature on the docks and Jacob rewarded them by paying in bonuses for completed jobs rather than a mere hourly wage. Soon B, S & J was known far and wide as the most dependable, reliable and hard-working hauling and transport firm on the East coast. In no time at all they were adding more and larger trucks and were branching out across the country, just as Jacob had dreamed of doing all along.

The tide had turned. German forces were retreating rapidly, as allied forces locked in win after win on the European front. In some cases, Nazi officers were so desperate to prevail that they were willing to subject their own troops to impossible odds and more than impossible situations. More than once Captain Shepherd found himself ministering to broken German soldiers left dying, by their own military divisions, on the blood soaked battlefield.

He'd learned enough German by this time to converse with these terrified soldiers facing death so far from their loved ones. He also learned these soldiers were not so different from his own young charges. Simply men willing to die for a cause they had been led to believe, long ago, was an honorable one. Most of them figured out, by the end of the war, that Hitler was insane. But it was too late to do much about things that had already passed. Loads of these young men would have gladly gone back and done things differently now, but obviously that was impossible.

He led many of these young German boys to Jesus and His divine saving grace on those blood-soaked fields. At first some of his own men wondered why he bothered, after all they were only krauts. They weren't even worth saving, were they? Until they realized that his humanity and his devotion to Christ would not allow him to do anything less than share the Gospel with every creature.

As American soldiers liberated town after town throughout the German countryside, local people cheered for the troops. For the first time, in a long time, Jeffrey knew why they'd come to this place and he was glad for every life and every soul that had been saved along the way. He was beginning to see the devastating results of Hitler's Third Reich, even on the people it was supposed to be freeing and helping. These people had been sucked into the vortex of Adolf Hitler's lies and promises. Only to discover that Satan cannot deliver good things, just as a rotten tree cannot produce good fruit. Only the Lord Jesus can bring about good results.

It'd been almost a year since bombing raids conducted by the RAF began on Munich, destroying around 50% of the city. Which succeeded in limiting the production of necessary parts needed for various German aircraft. However, infantry had not yet been heavily deployed into the area, not until now. American soldiers would remedy that situation post haste.

Over the past couple of weeks, the situation for Batya and Sarah had grown exponentially worse. Without the protection of their sponsor, they were at the mercy of those low-ranking officers left behind to manage the camp. One, especially, had grown rather fond of Sarah and was making his interest known with unwanted and uncalled-for advances.

Living day to day in the barracks with other prisoners and not able to escape to the commandant's quarters for better food and warmer conditions, left the ladies in a declining state of health.

Most of the medical experiments going on in the large buildings on site had ceased, due to the rapid advancement of allied forces and the obviously related sudden disappearance of most of the camp's high-ranking officials. This was a wonderful turn of events for the camp's prisoners, bringing glimmers of hope all around.

Because of the quick departures of those high-ranking officers it became apparent in this ongoing and deteriorating situation that the rats weren't willing to go down with this sinking ship.

Batya and Sarah prayed before retiring for the night. As they lay in bed, they discussed some Bible verses they'd read and memorized, the last time they had access to Mrs. Weiter's Bible.

"I think Philippians 4:13 is one of my very favorites. "I can do all things through Christ who strengthens me." It makes me feel quite powerful!

"I agree that is a great scripture, Sarah. There are so many wonderful words in the Bible. One of my favorites is just a few verses further in Philippians. 4:19 says, "And my God will supply every need of yours according to His riches in glory in Christ Jesus." That gives me so much hope and comfort. I know He is with us and that He won't let us languish here for long."

"I believe that as well, Mama. Good night and

sleep well."

Thankful that they'd memorized so many of the verses they read, they knew that even when all material possessions were stripped from them no one could steal their precious thoughts and memories, those most important things that were written on their hearts.

As they settled on their bunks for the night, the young officer who'd been bothering Sarah suddenly burst into the women's barracks. The ladies sat up and several women in the room cried out in fear. The whole space suddenly reeked of alcohol and rancid sweat.

The intoxicated officer lunged at Sarah, grabbing at her clothing and ripping the front of her shift open. The sight of exposed flesh seemed to propel him into a further frenzy, sending him bug-eyed and drooling, grabbing and groping at his prey. Batya leapt up to defend her daughter. Sarah was pinned down now, helplessly splayed out under the drunken man and struggling to get away. Batya lifted her mattress and grabbed a wooden slat from under her bunk, swinging it, she hit the soldier square in the back of the head. The man went suddenly limp, and dropped to the floor, unmoving.

Everything had happened so quickly. The women

looked at one another with expressions of horror, as a growing pool of blood collected around the young officer's head. What were they to do? Just then a guard who'd been in the vicinity when he heard women screaming threw the door open and saw the body of his comrade laying on the floor in a pool of his own blood. He yelled for back up and all hell broke loose. Guards grabbed all the women from their beds and dragged them outside. "It was me." Batya screamed.

"Please, it was me. These other women are innocent. I did it."

Sarah shouted, "He was attacking me. My mother was only protecting me. He was drunk. He was all over me, trying to rape me. Please stop." But the guards didn't stop. They tied the hands and feet of every one of the women from that barrack, and began to beat them mercilessly. Then they attached each bound prisoner, in a standing position, to a pole in Dachau's center courtyard. All the while kicking and whipping them at will. The night was bitterly cold, and the women were wearing only shifts. No shoes, no blankets, no other protection from the cold. Some of the ladies were already weak and vulnerable and Batya knew they wouldn't last long in the frigid night air.

"Please, I beg of you. I am the one you want. I killed him. He was attacking my daughter and I killed him. Please let these other women go back inside where it is a little warmer."

"You are all prisoners of the Third Reich. As prisoners of the Reich, your judgment will come from headquarters. Now, shut up. One of the guards is making a call now to determine your fate."

One of the older women, nothing but skin and bones, was shaking so badly from the chilly night that Batya thought she might pass out. Then thought that actually might be the best solution to keep her comfortable. Feeling terrible that these women were all suffering for something she'd done completely by accident, she began to apologize to everyone. The guard came back out and whispered something into the officer's ear.

"We have just received a judgment from headquarters. It has been decided that since there were no credible witnesses to what happened in the barracks, you are all found guilty of murder. Tomorrow you will be executed by firing squad."

"No, no, what do you mean no one saw what happened? I told you I did it. You can't do this. They are all innocent. I am the guilty one. Take me. Let them go, please. My Lord, please, listen to me."

"I told you to shut up woman! Now, shut up!" The officer slapped Batya, hard, and Sarah yelled out.

"You monster. Leave her alone. Leave my mother alone." The officer approached Sarah and punched her, first in the stomach and then in the face. When she cried out, he smiled a huge, satisfied, arrogant smile, punching and kicking her again.

When Batya saw her daughter being beaten, she quickly shut up, for the sake of Sarah. Squeezing her eyes shut tears began to roll down her cheeks, but not for herself. The tears were for her daughter and for the rest of the women caught up in this mess. She began again to pray for a way out.

B, S & J was getting so much new work Jacob was forced to hire an office manager to field calls and schedule deliveries. He could have done that bit himself, but he wasn't a desk man, never had been. He loved being free to drive the country, seeing all the new and wonderful places available to a United States citizen. Donald

Maassen, the company's new office manager, was a whiz with numbers and an absolute godsend. He kept everyone on track, including the boss.

Jacob's trucks were all outfitted with brand new CB radios, which were great for local communication. However, the firm was taking jobs as far out as California now, and they had recently landed a couple of new, very lucrative, government contracts. They would be hauling various pieces of military equipment to bases around the country. For those trips the drivers had to call in from pay phones when they stopped for meals and gasoline.

Jacob was required to pass some heavy scrutiny to be considered for those government contracts and was proud that he'd passed muster with flying colors. He usually spent so much time working that he'd never bothered to move from the boarding house. There was no need. The place had everything he required. A bed, a radio, a place to clean up and hot meals when he was in town. What else could he want? Well, that is, besides his family.

He was taking off in the morning to deliver military goods to Offutt Air Force Base in Nebraska. He'd never been to Offutt before, but would begin to make many trips there due to his new military contracts. "The wife made some cookies for the trip.”

“That’s great, Samuel. You’ve got yourself a real peach in that one.”

“I know. I never thought I’d be able to love again after, well, you know.”

“Yeah, I do know. Does your wife mind that I’m taking you on longer and longer hauls these days?”

“No. She knows the paycheck is great and she wants to have a family before we get too old. I’m not sure about that part yet. Not after Anna and the baby. You know how that feels.”

“Samuel, Anna would understand. I don’t think she would expect you to be alone for the rest of your life.”

“I know. I don’t feel as though she would be angry about Elle. I just don’t really feel ready for a baby myself. Not with someone besides Anna. How about you, boss? Have you met anyone you would feel comfortable with yet?”

“You know I’m married to my job, Sam. And, I know I’m not ready for anything like that. Batya was special. I doubt I would ever find anyone else who could touch me the way she did. I still hear her laugh sometimes. When I turn around and she’s not there, my heart stops beating for a few seconds, waiting to hear her voice again."

"I know, Jacob. The way you talk about her is as if she were an angel. But, if you change your mind, Elle has a sister. She's a nice young girl. You might really like her."

"Well, I don't know what a nice young girl would want with an old dog like me, but I'll keep that in mind."

Allied forces were marching on Munich in the morning. There was little if any resistance remaining from Nazi forces in the area. It seemed almost as if the Germans, for all intents and purposes, had vanished off the face of the earth. That is, until they heard an explosion off in the distance and the night sky lit up like fourth of July fireworks reflecting off a layer of newly fallen spring snow.

Shepherd could see his breath. Small white puffs, hanging in the still, cold air and it reminded him of long nights back on the farm. Like the night his cow, Clara, gave birth to twins. It was a sad night. They tried, but couldn't save her. Clara was like a pet to him, a great big slobbery, half ton pet. One he'd known his whole life.

There were three calves to start, which was rare. One was born breach and just plain old got tangled up inside her mama. They almost lost all the babies but managed to save two of the three. He bottle fed the two calves for six months, until they could eat forages and grains on their own. Those nights in the barn were chilly ones. A man finds out a lot about who he is, when another living being depends on him for everything.

It was April 1945, and from the looks of the quiet German countryside the war was finally winding down. He updated his look out replacement, wrapped his coat tighter against the chill of the night and crawled into his tent.

"Ladies, stay awake. Don't nap. The cold will take you in your sleep. Are you alright over there, Sarah?"

"I'm okay, Mama. My face hurts. I think he may have broken my nose. I tasted quite a bit of blood. But, other than that, I think I'm fine. Just cold and tired."

"Try to stay awake, Sarah. I'm right here meyn lib. Ladies, please, fight the urge to give into the cold. Stay with me."

"Batya, what difference could it possibly make at this point? The Nazis are set on killing us tomorrow if the temperatures don't take us tonight. I would rather die in my sleep, than at the end of a Nazi rifle, wouldn't you?"

"I have no intention of dying by either, Greta. God will make a way. He will save us. I feel it in my bones."

"The only thing I feel in my bones is cold. Look at poor Verta, she's shivering so badly she will never make it through the night."

"Please, ladies, I beg of you, don't give up. Let me tell you something. A secret I have been keeping. My daughter and I are Christians now. We have been reading the Christian Bible and have come to trust in the Lord Jesus. I have never been so filled with joy and happiness at any time in my life before. I have faith that the Lord hears our cries and I believe with all my heart that God will save us today. We must live, so we can share salvation through Christ with all the world."

"Batya, your parents would be ashamed of you. Why do you talk like this on the eve of our execution? If this Jesus, this Messiah, is real, then why are you tied to a stake in the middle of a Nazi concentration camp like a common farm animal? Tell me that."

"I don't know all of the answers yet, Greta. But I know that our Lord is faithful, and I know He loves you. Will you let me pray with you? Will you believe?"

"Pray if you must, Batya. But don't include me in your insanity."

"Then we will pray for you, Greta. God loves you and He wants you to know that He is all you need."

"Batya, will you pray for me to your Jesus?"

"Yes Verta. But, better yet. Will you pray with us?" At that moment Batya and Sarah prayed for all the women in the courtyard. But they prayed a special prayer with Verta. The elderly woman trusted Jesus for salvation and turned her life over to the King of the universe. When they were done her countenance had changed. She stopped shivering, her fear was replaced by a peace she didn't really understand and an unexplained calm surrounded her, as she stood bound to a wooden pole right in the middle of a Nazi death camp.

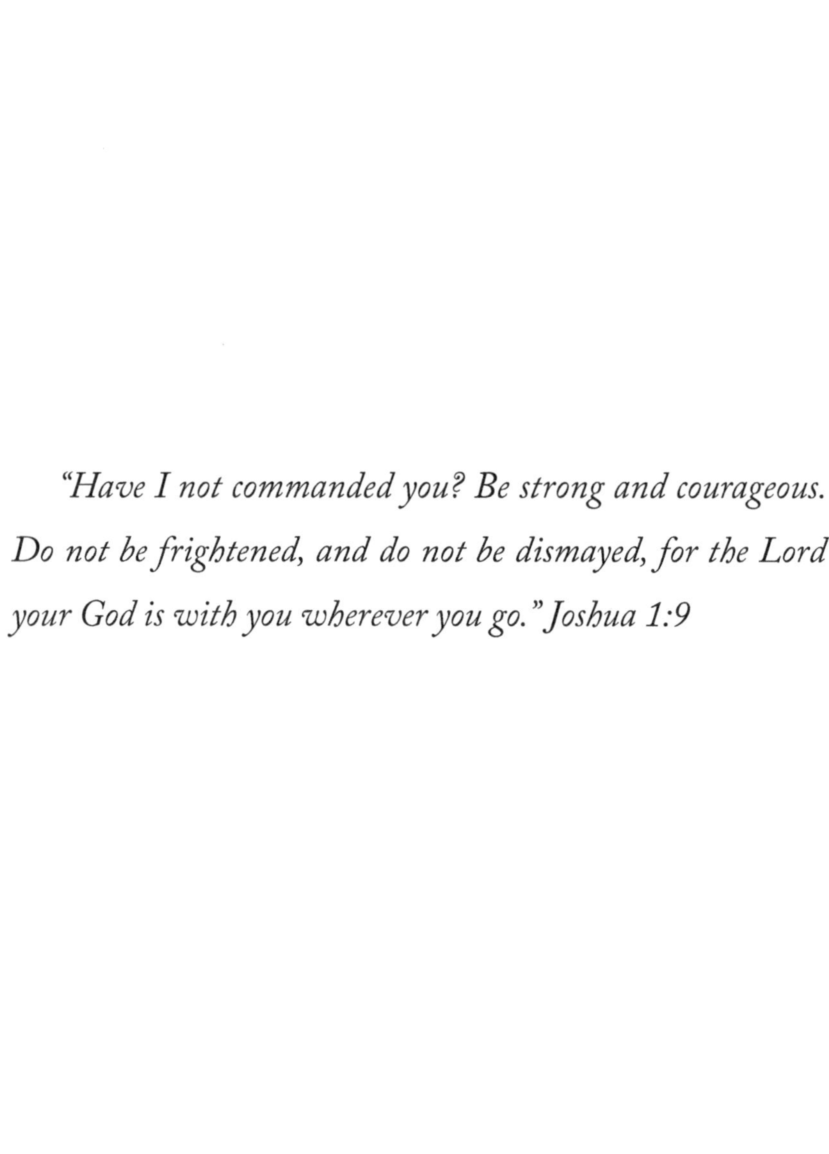

"Have I not commanded you? Be strong and courageous. Do not be frightened, and do not be dismayed, for the Lord your God is with you wherever you go." *Joshua 1:9*

CHAPTER 19

Jacob woke with a sense of hope unlike anything he'd felt for some time. He didn't know why, though it was actually quite an odd and unfamiliar feeling. He had seen something in his dream that gladdened his heart but couldn't for the life of him remember now what it was. Even with rain pouring down in sheets onto the busy New York streets, he saw only rainbows and couldn't stop smiling.

The business was doing wonderfully well, but that was nothing new. It had been hugely successful on a very consistent basis for many months now. So, what was different about this day? All he knew was that he felt a joy that tingled from the soles of his feet clear up to his scalp. When he met Samuel at the truck they loaded up and headed out on the road. "Why are you so happy today, Jacob?"

"Is there something wrong with being happy?"

"Of course there's nothing wrong with being happy. I'm just not used to seeing YOU happy, that's all. You are usually all business, all the time."

"Oh, that's not true. I'm a happy person, Samuel."

"No, actually you're not, Jacob. My Elle can barely stand to be around you anymore. She calls you Mr. Grumpy pants behind your back. She doesn't even bring up introducing you to her sister anymore, because she wants her sister to be happily married to a nice man."

"Oh, really?"

"Yes, really. So, tell me, why all the smiles today?"

"I don't know. I just feel that something great will be happening soon, Samuel. Now, let's get this load delivered."

Captain Shepherd and his men, part of the 42nd infantry division. Along with the 45th infantry division and the 20th armored division of the United States Army, were piled into troop transport trucks, forming part of a convoy heading out from Munich. The green canvas top of their transport cracked and snapped in the wind, but at the very least it was keeping most of the rather persistent rain off the exhausted men inside. Wrapping up the city had not been as difficult as they'd thought it would be, thankfully, with the Nazi presence down to a minimum in the region. But this had been a very long war and if truth be told, the soldiers were more than ready to be on their way home. The whole area was beginning to resemble a ghost town, albeit with demolished buildings and huge bomb craters dotting the ravaged landscape.

The troops were driving out to the countryside to check out a facility thirty minutes North West of the city. Much of the country had recently been liberated from Nazi control and whole families stood alongside the road to cheer the soldiers on. The soldiers were feeling great about their welcome from the locals; so, Shepherd and the others were handing out chocolate bars, and other packets of food and hygiene items to smiling, grateful people in the crowd.

At one point on the journey, Jeffrey looked up and saw swaths of tulips and daffodils in the fields alternating between areas of devastation. Red and yellow flowers dancing in the rain without a care in the world and he smiled. Those spring rains had managed to bring forth life even in the midst of the chaos and death of the Nazi regime. It reminded him again that God was still in control even in the madness of mankind's wars.

However, the rain also made travel a huge mess. Many

of these country roads were little more than dirt and gravel paths, which had quickly turned to mire when the clouds opened up a couple of days ago, adding melting snow to the mix. When the transports got bogged down for what seemed like the hundredth time during their trip, the men piled out and eager citizens ran forward to help push trucks out of the mud.

Batya and Sarah looked around in confusion. When morning dawned, they expected to see men with rifles lining up to execute them where they stood, still tied to posts in the center courtyard of Dachau concentration camp. Instead, when the sound of birds woke them from an exhausted stupor, they still stood alone. No one, including men in uniforms, was milling about with guns or otherwise. Slowly, prisoners were sticking their shorn, scabby heads out of barracks doors. They were in the same state of confusion over a sudden lack of camp guards.

Most of the bound and brutalized women had miraculously withstood the night's cold. Except, it seemed, for poor Verta. From the looks of what remained of her earthly form, she had passed peacefully into glory sometime in the night and was surely, at this very moment, dancing with Jesus on streets of gold. It was hard to shed a tear for her, as she was the only one among them who was surely free.

"Hello? Is anyone there?"

There was no answer. "Please, can someone help us?"

Batya and Sarah didn't know it at the time, but camp guards had gotten word, several days ago, that American troops were on their way to Dachau and they'd decided they didn't want to be anywhere near the camp when those soldiers arrived.

Receiving orders from headquarters, German guards had quietly gathered seven thousand of the camp's prisoners together and on the 26th of April headed out on what would later be dubbed the "Death March to Tegernsee", a Nazi base farther to the south. They had planned several more of these marches, in an effort to keep their war prisoners out of the hands of allied forces. However, time was not on their side and the initial group of seven thousand was all they managed to steal away for 'relocation'.

On that forced march prisoners suffered from exposure and beatings. The weather was cold, and they were starving and exhausted. The Germans were not sympathetic and shot anyone who could not keep up.

Consequently, on April 28th, when the few guards who remained in camp heard the Americans were almost upon them they didn't waste any time at all collecting a few belongings and sneaking off into the dark of the night like the cowards they were.

Dachau's other prisoners, peeking from behind door posts, were just too frightened to help the suffering women in the courtyard. Thinking perhaps this was some kind of cruel test, that perhaps the guards might be hiding and watching to see if they would defy orders to leave the guilty women to die. Therefore, they made no attempt to give aid. Leaving them tied to their posts in the cold, stinging rain.

Batya was concerned about Sarah. The guard had punched her hard and though the rain had washed away most of the blood, it hadn't done anything to heal the wounds. She could see in her daughter's eyes and hear in her voice, the amount of pain she was suffering, though the girl would never have admitted as much. As the day wore on, Sarah appeared to be losing her battle to stay conscious and her mom continued to talk to her, trying to keep her from falling asleep. "Sarah, meyn lib, please don't drift off. Stay awake. You cannot let the cold take you. You have a purpose, remember? You must share the Gospel with the world."

"Yes Mama. I am still here. I have not left you. He is coming to save us."

"Yes zeiskeit, I know He will save us. We must have faith."

"No Mama, I mean the man. He is coming to save us. He will be here soon. The Lord is sending him to me."

"Sarah, what man? What do you mean? Meyn lib? Sarah?" Batya could no longer get a response from her daughter. She had passed out from the pain and cold temperatures. Batya began to pray, as hot tears mingled with cold rain. "Lord God, I trust You. I know that You are our protector and our provider; our source and our joy; our salvation and our peace. I don't know what Sarah was saying. I don't know if she is hallucinating Lord. Did she have a word from You? A vision perhaps? Whatever it might be Lord, let help come quickly. I don't know how much longer she can survive like this. Thank you, Lord Jesus."

April 29th, 1945. On the ground and from a distance Dachau was fairly non descript. However, as they drew nearer a smell, most foul, filled the air and the troops discovered more than thirty railroad cars filled with the dead bodies of Jews, mostly in an advanced state of decomposition. Rats, carrion birds and vermin of all types skittered and swooped in and out of the cars, hoping for a stolen, grisly morsel.

Upon closer inspection the road to the Dachau prison compound gatehouse was paved with brick, leading to iron gates inside an arched brick entry. The brick and mortar gatehouse was rather substantial and could even be described as stately. A narrow-gauge railroad track ended a few feet from that gated entry. The iron gate within the gatehouse, created by a prisoner named Karl Roder, held the slogan 'ARBEIT MACHT FREI' (Work Brings Freedom). The phrase was coined by propaganda minister Josef Goebbels, in a misguided effort to convince the public that Nazi concentration camps were merely work camps for the political rehabilitation of communists, social democrats and anarchists.

The bulk of the enormous camp consisted of buildings used to house SS officers who were trained on the premises; barracks, mess and medical facilities; other buildings set aside for medical experimentation on unfortunate prisoners and the usual administration offices one would expect for an operation of that size. One rectangular shaped piece of property within the camp was set aside to house prisoners and contained literally dozens upon dozens of long, squat buildings, row upon ugly row.

When American soldiers arrived at the gates and entered, they were horrified by what they found. Prisoners began to emerge from barracks and other buildings, drawn by the noise of so many incoming troops. As he looked around, Captain Shepherd couldn't imagine how most of these people were still alive. Their heads were shorn; most wore rags that had once been some sort of uniform perhaps; and their faces, their bodies, were nothing more than paper thin, grey skin stretched tightly over bones. Many were covered by open sores, scabs and rashes, some had been rendered blind due to malnutrition. Still others were missing fingers or toes due to frostbite resulting from exposure to the harsh winter that had just passed. Their sunken, haunted eyes and skittish movements caused them to look for all the world like frightened animals emerging from their burrows.

Shepherd saw a group of women tied to poles in the middle of the main courtyard and went quickly to investigate. "What is this? Someone come and help me cut them down." He sliced through the thick rope binding one of the prisoners and she opened her eyes, for just seconds, as she fell limp into his arms. His breath caught in his throat. Her green eyes were so disarming he almost dropped her on the muddy ground but managed to hold tight to her slight frame even in his shock. He removed his jacket, wrapped her inside its woolen warmth, and carried her to safety. She was so small in his arms. This caused him to want to protect her even more. He pulled her tightly, but ever so gently to his chest, in an effort to warm her.

"Wiedzialem, ze po mnie przyjedziesz. Chwalcie Jezusa." The beautiful young woman whispered.

"What did she say? Does anyone speak Polish?"

"Yes Captain. She said, 'I knew you would come for me. Praise Jesus.'"

He looked about at the decimated human beings crowding around his soldiers and the sight filled his eyes with unshed tears. He wanted to cry, but instead he would try to help as many as he could. He placed the woman, wrapped in his coat and a blanket he'd snagged from one of his men, inside one of the transports and went to cut the bonds of the other prisoners. One of the other women, speaking in bits of Polish, German, and broken English, with what sounded like a faint Russian or Ukrainian accent, was desperately trying to find out where her daughter was. She was also a very beautiful woman and he quickly put two and two together. He led her to where the younger woman lay, and she fell on her daughter sobbing.

A search of the encampment uncovered atrocities unlike anything these men had ever seen. Fully functional gas chambers, made to look like large shower facilities, where prisoners were led to their deaths thinking they were being sent in to wash up. Those chambers, with large back doors, led to ditches in which the bodies of the dead were discarded. And those ditches, piled high with the skeleton like remains of the poor souls who were now nothing more than food for the rats, crows and ravens who feasted on their withered flesh.

The camp had been dreadfully overcrowded due to the constant influx of prisoners from other camps ahead of the allied advance, and a wave of typhus had swept through the encampment killing many more over the past weeks. Their bodies lay discarded in decaying, pest covered, piles around the camp.

Soldiers discovered the medical experimentation buildings loaded with diseased, dead and rotting corpses surrounded by thick black clouds of buzzing flies. The experimentation facilities had been closed for weeks at this point and the smells encountered upon entering were enough to send grown men running to lose their breakfast on the ground.

Additionally, there were various areas in camp where extensive blood evidence of mass torture and executions, was apparent. The Captain's heart ached for the pain and suffering of this evil place and he knew all too well this was not the only one of its kind. Satan had indeed used Hitler and his ilk to perpetrate genocide on the Jewish people of these lands.

He was further angered when he discovered that the camp seemed to be very well supplied. For it was as plain to see as the nose on your face that the prisoners here were starved. A mess tent abounding with provisions for the guards and officers stood mere yards from where other humans were dying of hunger. Sleeping quarters for Nazi officers, fit for kings, stood directly across camp from the mean, barren hovels used for their prisoners. He found it beyond rational thought that any human could do these things to another living being, no matter their religious or political beliefs. He was dumbfounded.

There were over thirty thousand souls crammed behind the gates of Dachau when Americans liberated the camp. Most of them looked for all the world like the walking dead.

U.S. troops rounded up all the supplies in the mess tent and various storehouses and fed those prisoners, handing out blankets, slippers and clothing, before arranging transportation for them that would whisk them away to better circumstances.

But where would that be? These people had nowhere to go. Their homes, towns and villages had been destroyed by the very Nazis who slaughtered six million of their brothers and sisters, mothers and fathers, husbands, wives and children. For survivors, the prospect of rebuilding their lives was daunting. Tens and tens of thousands of Holocaust survivors would spend much of the rest of their lives in displaced persons camps with little to nothing, simply attempting to exist.

Possibilities for emigration were few it seemed. Just as in the time before and during the war when Jews were persecuted unto death, no one on the planet wanted to take on the burden of the Jewish problem. The so-called civilized world, including the church, had simply turned a blind eye. And even America's record for offering asylum to Jews, up to this point, was pathetic at best.

Captain Shepherd searched all around the camp for the young green-eyed woman and came upon her receiving help from one of his medical team. She was currently still unconscious. Her mother, who sat beside her stroking her hand and weeping quietly explained that a guard had beat her daughter and that the Captain had rescued them just in time, because they were due to be executed by firing squad that very day. "Thank you so much Captain......."

"Captain Shepherd, but please, call me Jeffrey. And you are....."

"My name is Batya, Jeffrey. My daughter is Sarah. We are grateful to you for coming to our aid. We have been praying for Jesus to deliver us from the hands of the Nazis. Sarah told me she had received a message that the Lord was sending a young man to rescue her."

"Pardon me, what did you say? She received a message from the Lord Jesus? But I didn't know Jews prayed to Jesus. I'm just a simple man and I'm afraid I'm not very knowledgeable on the intricate parts of religions other than Christianity. Tell me, how have you come to know about Jesus?"

"When we were prisoners in the Warsaw Ghetto, my daughter met with a group of Christian Jews regularly. My husband and I were not aware, you see we knew very little of Christianity and I believe my husband would have been particularly upset by that. This is why she kept her activity a secret from us. She has since told me she felt, for a very long time, that something was missing in her life. Just being a Jew and obeying the law and the prophets wasn't enough. She wanted more, you know, a real relationship with her creator. I felt the same way for much of my life, especially after some personal tragedies. I knew something wasn't right, but I didn't know what to do about it. After much study Sarah was convinced that Jesus was the very one who was missing from her life. She recognized Him as the true Messiah and she knew we, as a people, had been tragically lost all along. She asked Him into her heart, to save her, yes, but also to be her Lord. Later she introduced me to the Savior. We are both Christians now and I can tell you that I have never been happier, or more filled with joy, than I am today."

"I'm very happy to hear that, Batya. But what brought you here? I thought most Polish Jews were imprisoned in Auschwitz, Treblinka or other camps in Poland? How did you end up in Dachau?"

"Our story is a bit more complicated, Captain Shepherd. I am Ukrainian. My husband is Polish, though not from Warsaw and our daughter was born in Warsaw. You are right concerning the concentration camps, but my daughter and I were under the protection of a Nazi officer, Wilhelm Weiter, who was transferred to Dachau to act as its new commandant. He left the camp when the allied forces were drawing near. I'm sure he was afraid of being caught and prosecuted by the allies. We can only assume he went on to meet up with his wife from here."

"You mentioned your husband, Batya. Where is he now? Do you know?"

"People have told me he is dead, but I don't believe that. I feel that I would know if he had died. Our hearts are entwined. I know I would feel as if a part of my own heart was missing if he were gone. However, I don't know where he is, or how to find him. I'm sure that will happen in God's timing. I choose to trust Him. We know that for those who love God all things work together for good, for those who are called according to His purpose. I believe now that God has put us right here in this place for such a time as this, don't you?"

Just then Sarah's eyes fluttered open and the Captain found himself captivated by her fragile beauty once again. "Yes Ma'am, I believe I would have to agree with you."

"The more I see of this country, Samuel, the more I love it. I am very glad to be an American!"

"Elle and I have also discussed this, and we are glad to be Americans as well. We will always mourn our homeland and those things that were so cruelly ripped from us, but this truly is the land of promise and there is no denying that fact."

"I only wish my Batya was here to share this great land with me. She would love the wide-open spaces. I don't think she would care for the busyness of New York City. However, if we had a piece of land out here on the open prairie it would be wonderful. This part of the country is very much like the Steppes of Ukraine where she was a girl. She has spoken to me of it often, freedom as far as the eye can see and fields of golden Stipa waving in the breeze. I miss her so much, Samuel, that sometimes my heart feels like it is being torn in two. I am sure I will never know a love like that again. I suppose that is why I seem so glum sometimes. But I am trying to find happiness in other things. If I can't have my one true love, or even have the chance to leave my daughter to carry on, then I will leave the legacy of my business. That is the best I can do."

"Yes, my friend. I guess that is the best any of us can do."

"O God, we have heard with our ears, our fathers have told us, what deeds You performed in their days, in the days of old: You with Your own hand drove out the nations, but them You planted; You afflicted the peoples, but them You set free; for not by their own sword did they win the land, nor did their own arm save them, but Your right hand and Your arm, and the light of Your face, for You delighted in them."
Psalm 44 1-3

CHAPTER 20

April 30th, 1945. Dachau's prisoners were fed and rested overnight while Army medics tended to the worst injuries and illnesses among them. After arranging meals and transportation for the upcoming journey, the liberated camp was preparing to move out.

"Where will we go now, Jeffrey?"

"We will be escorting all the survivors from Dachau to a Displaced Person's Camp here in Germany."

"What will we do there?"

"I'm not sure yet. I will be right here with you. I don't plan to leave you ladies alone for a moment, until I receive orders that my men are headed back to America and I don't want you to worry, Batya."

"I'm not worried, Jeffrey. I just want to be sure that Sarah will get the medical help she needs until she feels better. We will have to figure out what we are doing from there."

"I think the UN is Attempting to repatriate as many displaced people: refugees, liberated prisoners and those who were seeking asylum, as they can. Since I'm a chaplain I hear the numbers and they are astounding. By our best estimates a number between eleven and twenty million people were uprooted from their homes by the Nazi regime. The UN Relief and Rehabilitation Administration is going to have a huge job on their hands, and they will be setting up Displaced Persons facilities in Germany, Austria and Italy. "

"Well, at least we won't have far to go then, huh?"

"You are a surprisingly optimistic person, Batya. How can you seem so unaffected by all of this?"

"Ah, Jeffrey. Someday I will have to tell you about all the things I've seen in my lifetime. The things my people have suffered and survived. As long as I know my Sarah is okay and that we will be together, then I will be fine. I know that God is still in control. This is just one more bump in the road as they say."

"I wish everyone had your resilience and your faith. You are a remarkable woman. I'm going to go find out when we are heading out."

"Mama?"

"Yes, Meyn lib? How are you feeling?"

"Better, I think. Who were you talking to?"

"That was Captain Shepherd. Jeffrey. The man who was sent to save us."

"Have I met him?"

"Yes, well, sort of. Actually, he cut you free and you fainted in his arms. He carried you to safety and out of the rain yesterday. You haven't been well my zeiskeit. I will introduce you again. Jeffrey has said he will not leave us, and I believe him. I truly believe he is the man you were told was coming to save us."

"The what?"

"The man you said was coming to save us. Don't you remember? Never mind. You will meet him soon."

When Captain Shepherd came back with word of their soon departure, he also had another important bit of news. But all that information left his mind when he saw the beautiful Sarah awake and trying to sit up. He rushed forward.

"Here, let me help you, Sarah." He placed his muscular arm around her slender back to offer support and their skin brushed briefly. They received a shock that caused them both to react in unison. Jeffrey almost fell over backward and stammered, "I'm sorry. I didn't mean to shock you. I don't know how that happened."

"I'm fine, Captain....."

"Shepherd. Captain Shepherd. But, please call me Jeffrey. Your mother and I are already old friends. We've been getting to know one another while you were resting."

"I want to thank you for coming to save us. My mother says we would likely be dead right now if not for your intervention."

"Your mother tells me you knew I was coming."

"Pardon me?"

"Yes, Sarah. Before you fainted in the courtyard you told me that you knew a man was coming to save us. Don't you remember?"

"No Mama, I don't. But who knows what was going through my mind then? I was in pain and freezing. I'm really sorry Captain Shepherd, but I don't remember."

"Sarah. You were so sure. You really don't remember?"

"I guess I don't, Mama. But here we are. It looks like the man came, so I will assume that this was indeed a message from the Lord. He is very good after all."

"Yes, my daughter. God is very good indeed."

"Then I will guess that you don't remember what you said to me either?"

"No Captain. I don't remember saying anything to you. What did I say?"

"You said, "Wiedzialem, ze po mnie przyjedziesz. Chwalcie Jezusa." At that, Sarah blushed a bright crimson red.

"Well Captain. I thank you again for coming to liberate us. God is indeed good." She looked up then, into the kindest, deep brown eyes, set in the most handsome face she had ever seen and blushed again.

"Yes Sarah. God is good all the time." Jeffrey watched as her face went red, knowing from the heat in his neck and ears that his was likely as red as hers. He didn't want to make her more uncomfortable, so he changed the subject. "I almost forgot. We will be heading out in about an hour. Arrangements have been made. We will be escorting you to the camp. We have also gotten word that Adolf Hitler was found in his command bunker. From the looks of things, he committed suicide. So, I guess his reign of terror is finished for sure."

"It's too bad we can't go back and reverse the evil he's done to so many."

"You're right, but we can at least try to set some things right. Is there any chance that the two of you will want to go back to Warsaw? Didn't you have a home there?"

"We did have a home there once, but our house was used by the Nazis as a headquarters building. It could never be the same after that. Besides, without my husband, I doubt I would be able to lay claim to the property anyway. When it was left to us there was no official deed. I suppose that was very foolish of everyone concerned. We just never expected my aunt to die so suddenly, so nothing legal was ever drawn up. I was born in Ukraine, outside of a little shtetl called Voronkov, so I have no strict family ties to Warsaw now that my aunt has died. No, we will go to the Displaced Person's camp and determine where we might go from there. My husband always wanted to emigrate to America. I wish I had listened to him when he first told me that years ago, but I was afraid of change. If I had known how much everything in our lives would transform after not making that move, I promise you I wouldn't have been so hesitant."

"I don't know that America would have been as welcoming as you might think at that time. President Roosevelt had a very closed-door policy toward emigrating Jews coming in from Poland or Germany until the war had progressed. It is quite sad, but many who have died here might have been saved if that were not the case. However, things have changed now that the world has seen the horror of the Nazi's reign and Hitler's madness. We will have to do some checking. Perhaps we can even help in that regard."

As military transport vehicles; filled to nearly bursting with Dachau's teaming masses; rolled into the recently established and U.S. managed, displaced persons camp outside Munich Germany, Captain Shepherd was appalled by what he saw. Conditions weren't much better than what these poor survivors had just left at Dachau. Hastily assembled portable buildings for administration and tents set up for new residents were the only structures visible and offered even less protection from cold and rain than the squalid buildings in Dachau provided.

Shallow ditches ran the length of the tented living areas, in which human waste and excess rain water would flow to a nearby basin; making it essential to watch where you were stepping at all times. Stations were set up where new arrivals could claim their meager rations of food, cots, clothing, blankets and other items. Batya mentally noted that circumstances weren't very much better here than in the Ghetto and wondered if things would improve as the camp became more established. She could only trust the Lord for a good outcome.

As they wandered the camp and got the lay of the land, she looked sideways at the Captain and saw that he was as upset with the situation as she felt. They registered and were assigned a tent and a voucher with which to obtain essentials.

"Listen, I promised you I wouldn't leave you until my boys had orders and I meant that. I'm not going to leave you ladies to endure these conditions alone. I will help in any way I can."

"We don't doubt that your intentions are good, Jeffrey. However, we know that you will be called away as soon as your young men receive orders from your superiors. Don't worry. We don't blame you for any of this. We will trust the Lord to see us through."

"Thank you, Batya, but I'm serious. Sarah, I promise you that I will help in any way I can." As he spoke Sarah looked into eyes she had begun to trust with her whole heart. The gentleness and compassion she saw let her know he was a man who always kept his word, within his power to do so. However, she was also familiar with the workings of government and knew that one man wouldn't be able to do much up against the administrative machine. She was prepared to endure what they must. "I know, Jeffrey. I believe you will do your very best. I know you care about us and will intervene in every way you can, but I also know how these things work. Don't worry about us. We will manage. God will provide."

"I believe that too, Sarah. I know God will provide. But as long as I'm here He can use me to provide for you, if that's okay." Jeffrey knew in his rapidly beating heart that he was falling hard for the lovely, green eyed Sarah.

Since the first moment he'd seen her, he was captivated by her beauty. But as he'd gotten to know her better, it was her sweet nature and unending compassion that won him over completely. Her voice was absolute music to his ears. Her petite size and features made him feel powerful and strong in comparison and compelled him to want to protect and look after her at all costs.

She was smart and talented, and she loved the Lord. That love shone through every aspect of her being. The three of them spent hours upon hours discussing scripture and talking about Jesus. He was feeling more and more as if God had put him in this place at this time to meet the woman with whom he would spend the rest of his life.

During the day Jeffrey tended to his duties as Chaplain and OIC of his division. Those troops were still busily cleaning up and liberating camps and villages in the region. Thankfully the fighting, at least for them, had ended.

He visited the women each evening and brought his rations to share. Batya and Sarah worked magic and did things with those food items that made them infinitely more appetizing. Whatever they did also seemed to stretch the food so that all three of them were filled. Or, perhaps it was just that Jeff wasn't very hungry when he was around the lovely Sarah.

After their meal they talked, prayed, discussed scripture and shared dreams. Jeffrey spoke about his farm and church. He missed them terribly and couldn't wait to get home. Sarah didn't know how to say so out loud, but she wished she could go there with him. It all sounded so calm and peaceful. Over those months she realized she was falling in love with the compassionate, kind eyed captain, but wasn't sure how he felt about her. So, she simply drank in every moment of his presence and dreamed of a future she knew would most likely never be.

Jacob stood on the bluffs and looked around at some of the most beautiful land he'd ever seen in his life. On his way to Offutt Air Force Base to drop off another load of military supplies, he and Samuel had stopped to stretch their legs when he noticed a small trail up into the Loess Hills from the lower Plains.

Standing at the top of the knoll he was amazed at the tranquility of the pastoral scene stretched out before him and imagined he could easily spend the rest of his life on top of that bluff, with the breeze from the prairie wafting into his face.

If only Batya were here with him. He could almost feel her hand in his and her encouraging smile urging him on to go deeper, to explore more of this beautiful territory. Pretty soon Samuel was hollering at him to quit his daydreaming and get a move on. They had more deliveries to make and he wanted to get back home to his Elle.

As the men drove away Jacob memorized the spot.

He knew someday he would own property on those beautiful Loess Hills, with views as far as the eye could see and a house nestled among the trees of the bluffs. He felt it in his bones. For now he would drive and he would save his money. With all the crews going strong he and his business was doing well. Jacob was, for all intents and purposes, a very wealthy man. More wealthy than he'd ever dreamed he might be. He could conceivably do anything he desired, go anywhere he wished. However, up to now his feeling had been that having no one to share those experiences with made it all a little pointless. What was the use of making memories alone?

All his transport crews were doing great as well. His drivers were able to embrace the American dream in all its glory. Buying homes, having children, and taking their wives on trips to places they'd never thought possible. A couple of them even bought those new television contraptions.

He'd recently had an evening at Herman's house, complete with a nice supper and an hour of "The World in Your Home" on his new television. Jacob was still amazed at the idea that pictures from a studio somewhere could go through cable wires and come out clear on the other end as something people were able to watch in their own living rooms. Though admittedly the pictures were a bit fuzzy and distorted, the technology was still amazing. What would the world come up with next? While he wasn't sure if he agreed with the head of Twentieth Century Fox, Darryl Zanuck, who said television was a fad that wouldn't last six months; he didn't think it was particularly the way he would spend many of his own evenings.

Jacob was extremely proud of the strides he'd made in his professional life. He was also proud of the difference he'd been able to make in the lives of his friends and fellow workers. He was extremely grateful for the way his new country embraced his endeavors, giving him opportunity after opportunity. The only thing that was missing was his one true love. Would he ever know that kind of love again? He didn't think so. How could anything ever compare to what he had experienced with Batya?

The day came that all three of them had dreaded for months. Jeffrey's division received orders to return home to America. Though WWII would not officially conclude until September 2nd, 1945, the fighting was over for him and for his weary men. He was excited for the troops to get home to their loved ones and grateful for every soul that was alive to see this day. However, his own heart was broken.

The thought of leaving without Sarah was tearing him apart. But orders were orders and the amount of paperwork needed to get her from here to the U.S. was mind boggling. This didn't even begin to include getting Batya there as well and he knew Sarah would never leave her mother behind. He longed to tell her how he felt about her, but he'd never officially wooed a woman before, and his imagination failed him.

On the day they said goodbye Jeffrey stood speechless. Hopeless, hands clenching and un-clenching, grasping at a dream and at nothing, dejected, crushed, tears shinning in his eyes and a look of total devastation on his face. "I, I don't know how to say goodbye, Sarah. I don't want to leave you here. Who will take care of you if I'm gone?"

Sarah's and Batya's hair had grown out significantly over these past months, from the shorn heads they'd sported when he first met them in Dachau. When Sarah turned quickly away and buried her face in her hands, trying to hide her reaction to the devastating news, her blond curls fell like a golden shawl around her shoulders. For a few moments her small body heaved silently, as she tried to compose herself, but he knew she was crying and everything in him wanted to help, wanted to reach out and wrap his arms around her.

He felt powerless, torn apart. Stepping forward and placing his large hands on her small, delicate shoulders in an attempt to comfort her, she turned and all but leapt into his strong arms. Once there, wrapped in his comforting embrace, he knew once and for all that this was exactly where she belonged. He didn't want to let go, only to hold her close for the rest of their lives. Nothing had ever felt more right. But how could he make that happen? She wasn't an American citizen after all. He didn't want to raise her hopes with empty promises that might not come to fruition.

Batya stood to the side with tears streaming from her eyes. She'd seen the relationship blossoming between her daughter and the captain, since long before either of them knew what was happening and now they would have to separate. Would they ever find each other again? Or, were they cursed to be apart in the same way that she and Jakub had been ripped from one another in this damnable war?

Voice shaking, Jeffrey spoke. "I love you, Sarah. I think I've known from the beginning that you were the only woman for me. The woman God had selected for me. Please forgive me for not saying something sooner. I've never been in love with a woman before this and I just didn't know what I should do. I didn't know if you felt the same about me."

"Oh Jeffrey, I love you too. I've known since the first time I ever looked into your eyes that you were the man I wanted to spend the rest of my life with. But I guess governments have different ideas. What do we do now? I'm not an American and your division has orders to go back to your country. Will I ever see you again?"

"I will be back for you, Sarah. I promise. I do love you and I will think of you and pray for you every day until I see you again. Trust me. I will figure this out."

"I do trust you, Jeffrey. I also trust Jesus with every single thing in my life. I will wait for you my love. I will be praying for your safety and praying that we will see one another again."

"Finally, be strong in the Lord and in the strength of His might. Put on the whole armor of God, that you may be able to stand against the schemes of the devil." Ephesians 6:10–11

CHAPTER 21

Sarah missed Jeffrey every day. However, life went on, as it is apt to do and the displaced person's camp became a sort of home, at least for now. Jeffrey had left them some extra money, which helped in obtaining food over and above the meager rations provided by the camp.

Batya and Sarah were not the type of people who could ever think to have such bounty and not share. So, their blessings became everyone's blessings. When they prepared soup, or stew, using their extra resources they used the largest kettle available and shared until every drop was passed around to those who needed it most.

While they shared soup, they also shared the Gospel. Some residents of the camp were angry over their bold evangelizing and made it quite clear they were no longer welcome to visit their tents. But others were eager to hear of the miracle which had changed these women's lives and caused them to be givers of everything they had, even in the midst of so much poverty and want. Soon there were many in the camp praising Jesus and giving their lives over to the Lord.

Jeffrey was using every available resource at his disposal to try and find an answer to their situation before leaving Germany. Many of his men, besides those few who were badly injured and still hospitalized locally for war time wounds, had already been sent home. However, since the Captain wasn't officially part of the 42nd infantry and only assigned to that combat division out of Offutt through the Chaplaincy program, he had the option of returning home separately and at his own pace. The love he had for the soldiers in his charge was the only thing that had kept him glued to their presence in the past. But if they were heading back, he rationalized, nothing said he had to go with them.

He didn't mind. There was no one waiting for him back on American soil. So, he said farewell to the young men who'd spent so much time at his side; exchanged addresses for future communication opportunities, shared lots of hugs and more than a few tears, and sent them on their way.

At this point he hadn't seen Sarah for over a month

and his heart literally hurt from the sheer absence of her company. He'd discovered, through much investigation, that if he married Sarah the 'War Bride' act, recently enacted, would see his new wife safely to America. However, that didn't answer the question of Batya. He knew Sarah would never leave her mother behind. And he didn't blame her one single bit. After all they'd been through and in the circumstances under which they now lived, he would never ask her to do anything so cruel to the one person who had been beside her all her life. He was currently attempting to contact people who might be able to help with their dilemma.

Making another trip to Offutt had become part of their normal monthly routine. Jacob eagerly took all those Midwest runs for himself so he could walk the bluffs and breathe the fresh air of the Plains and hills for which he'd fallen so head over heels in love.

Samuel was used to the predicted detour by now and always allowed a little extra time for the trip, letting Elle know he'd be home a little later than usual. He'd mentioned to Jacob that he should simply look into buying the piece of land he loved, before someone else stole it right out from under his nose. So, one late spring day, he did.

On this especially fine day he picked up his land deed and took a side trip out to view the property again. He would build a house here. He would leave Donald in charge of operations back in New York, and set up an office here, halfway across the country. Maybe at some point in the future there would be an office in California as well. It was perfect.

Sarah was beginning to wonder if Jeffrey had forgotten all about her. Every night she lay in her bed and prayed for his safety and for God to give her a chance to see him again, even if it was only to say goodbye. Had he already left Europe? Was he back on his farm? Had he gotten so busy with the people in his church that she simply slipped his mind? As these thoughts danced through her mind her heart felt heavy and then she admonished herself. Sometimes God's plans are different than our plans, she remembered, and she would wait on His mighty hand to move in this.

Batya and Sarah spent all their extra money feeding those less fortunate and now those funds were depleted. Currently subject to regular rations, like all the other residents of the camp, soups were a bit thinner these days and sharing meant there wasn't much left for them. There were others who needed the nutrition more than they did. Little ones, the very elderly, and some who were still getting well from their time in the concentration camps. If they had concern about any, it would be these.

Those opposed to their ongoing evangelical attempts scoffed. "If your Jesus is so great, will He leave you here to starve like the rest of us? Why has He not swooped down to save you from this evil place?"

Their usual response was, "Jesus loves you every bit as much as He loves us. All He asks you to do is believe. We already know He will take care of us."

Many believed and soon the camp was overflowing with those growing in faith.

Regular scripture lessons and meetings for those new Christians were so filled with the presence and evidence of the Holy Spirit that the sound of singing could be heard throughout the camp and for miles around. Praying over the sick the ladies saw great miracles happening among them. And though they took very little food for themselves, they didn't seem to feel any ill effects from the lack of provisions. It was as if God kept them strong for their work in the camp while they praised Him every day. Very simply, His Spirit was their food.

Sarah knew with every fiber of her being that if Jeffrey never came back, she would continue to share the Lord with everyone she met. She would see that the Gospel was preached to every creature and every nation. That was her calling. She also knew she would rather be sharing Jesus alongside the man she loved, and she prayed for the Lord she adored to keep him safe and bring him back to her.

Jacob was checking on the progress of his new house. Samuel nodded with obvious approval as he walked from room to room. "It's great Jacob. the windows looking out over the bluff are really something. What a view. This is going to be a place where you can really find some peace and quiet, that's for sure. I'm happy for you."

"Thanks Samuel. I'm really excited about it. I know I need to make at least one more trip back to New York, to get things settled with Donald and pack up my things, but I'm really looking forward to making this my full-time residence. Are you going to miss having me in the truck with you?"

"Are you kidding? Elle will be so happy that I don't come home in such a bad mood anymore after a trip with Mr. grouchy pants."

"Oh, go on with you."

"You know I'm kidding, Jacob. Of course I'm going to miss you. We've been through a lot together. I consider you my best friend. Besides, now I have to break in a new kid to take your place."

"I'm still going to be involved in the business, I am the owner after all. Of course, I'll still handle the government contracts since I'm not far from Offutt. That part will be easier for me than it was in the past. I may even take some flying lessons and get my pilot's license. That is something I've thought about doing for a while now. It would sure make trips back and forth to New York easier."

"That sounds like a great idea. You're close enough to the air strip on the base to make that a very sensible idea. Just don't be a stranger when you're in New York."

"That goes both ways, I hope you'll stop in and see me when you're out this way. I'm going to miss you Samuel."

"You'll not be rid of me that easily my friend. First of all, we still have a trip back to New York to make. I'm sure I'll help you to retrieve your belongings and then help you get settled in here as well. Elle would kill me if I didn't. I'll be through here at least once a month after that, so you'll probably get sick and tired of seeing me."

"No, my friend. I doubt I could ever get tired of that homely mug. Like you said, we've been through a whole lot together. I will surely never turn my back on you Samuel. When you come through there will always be a guest room with your name on it if you need a place to rest that knuckle head of yours."

"Well, let's get going. Elle wanted me to invite you for supper after we get back tomorrow night and I have to admit I miss the baby too."

"How is your little guy? Are you glad you let Elle talk you into having a baby, or are you feeling a little old to be doing this all over again?"

"You are really something, you know that? Yes, I am glad. He's great, Jacob. Such a strong little man. He perks right up and starts smiling as soon as I come through the door. He makes me feel for all the world like the most important person on earth. I don't know what I would ever do without him now. Elle and I are very happy. She's talking about trying for a girl on the next go round."

"The next go round? You're going to have two? You really have lost your mind, haven't you? I think all that grey hair on your head is damaging your brain." Jacob said laughing.

"You're one to talk about grey hair. Yours is as white as snow on top of that old noodle of yours. And, you might be right my friend, but if I go, I will die happy. There is nothing like the love of a good woman to settle a man right down............. Oh, hey, Jacob. That was pretty insensitive of me. I didn't mean....."

"No, Samuel, that's okay. I know you didn't mean anything by it. I'm glad you're so happy. You deserve it. We've all been through a lot and I would never begrudge you a happy ending. Come on, I'm anxious to get on the road and get this done."

"This is General Clark's office. We are looking for a Captain Jeffrey Shepherd."

"I'm Captain Shepherd. Can I ask what this is about?

"Yes, General Eisenhower contacted us on your behalf to see if there was anything we might be able to do about your situation. You've been trying to reach him through channels, but he is stateside and not in a position to help from there. He thought that since we are still in country, we might be able to lend assistance in your circumstances."

"Thank you for reaching out. Did Eisenhower's office relate the nature of my need?"

"Yes Sir, and we think we can help. Since the ladies in question are not German nationals and you are planning to marry....Ummm....Sarah Nowak?"

"Yes, Sarah is her name."

"Good, then after the wedding she will travel back with you under the recently enacted "War Brides" bill. However, her mother.....Ummm.....Batya Nowak? Did I pronounce that correctly?"

"Yes, Batya Nowak is her name. Will we be able to bring her back?"

"Yes, General Clark is going to vouch for her personally. He and General Eisenhower are great friends and he would like to do something for one of the young men who has been in the thick of it through this whole bloody mess. We are arranging your paperwork now. You have only to retrieve Sarah and her mother and come into General Clark's offices in Munich. We will take care of everything from there."

"Thank you so much! I am very grateful for everything. God bless you. Thank you."

"Yes Sir. Take down this contact information and call us when you've gathered the ladies. Of course, we will need to see a marriage license, so get that taken care of as soon as possible. Other than that, we will take care of everything."

"Again, thank you Ma'am. You can't imagine how happy you've made me. She will be so thrilled. I can't wait to tell her the news."

"Yes Sir. You are welcome. Thank you for your service. Have a lovely wedding under the circumstances and a happy life together. Just give this office a call when you are ready to go."

Two days later, in the middle of the night, Jeffrey knocked on the wooden post outside the tent flap of

Batya and Sarah's quarters. It took a moment before a sleepy Sarah untied the flap and peeked out into the dark of the night to see Jeffrey standing in the rain. "Jeffrey, meyn lib, come in, come in, get out of the rain. Mother, look who it is."

"Oh Jeffrey, it is you. We never doubted for a moment that God would bring you back to us. Praise Him. How are you my boy?"

"I'm great, Batya. I have some wonderful news. But, first." Getting down on one knee and pulling a small box from beneath his shirt, Jeffrey stammered his way through the most romantic thing he'd ever done in his life. "Sarah, I have been lost without you these past weeks. When I couldn't figure out how to make this happen I prayed, knowing that God was the one who brought you into my life and that He would need to be the one to unravel the way for us to be together. He took care of it all. A series of miracles happened. I already know that I can't live my life without you by my side. You are the love of my life. I hope you feel the same way about me. I would be honored if you would consent to be my wife. General Clark has made arrangements for after we are married. That is if you will, I mean, if I can convince you to be my wife. That Batya will be able to come to America with us. But I have to be able to show them a marriage certificate. Well, will you?"

Laughing, "Of course meyn lib. I couldn't think of spending my life with anyone else. If you had not come back, I would have died an old maid. I would be honored to be your wife. I love you Jeffrey. Now, let's figure out how we are to get this done."

In the morning, slogging through mud puddles from last night's rain, the trio made their way to the camp manager's office. He contacted Munich's Burgermeister and for a small fee they were informed that the marriage could take place that same day. They all agreed a civil service would do for now, but that a nicer and more Christ centered ceremony would be conducted at home in their own church. Jeffrey and Sarah agreed their marriage would not be consummated until they were married in the eyes of the Lord.

For now, they stood before the German Burgermeister and repeated their vows. No fancy dress, no frills. That would all wait until the time was right.

When they boarded the military transport plane for home, Batya and Sarah didn't look back even once. This place was not their home, it never had been and never would be. Sarah knew her home would always be wherever Jeffrey laid his head. As long as they were together, she knew they would serve God and live their lives to share the Gospel.

Batya watched them as they held hands and gazed into each other's eyes. It was easy to see they were in love and she remembered, as if it were yesterday, when she was one half of a happy couple much like this one. Her heart was filled with joy for her daughter, but it broke for the emptiness she felt not having her Jakub with her now. Would they ever find each other again? Now that she was leaving Europe, it might become even more impossible. Perhaps everyone was right. Maybe he had died that day in the Ghetto. Her heart broke thinking that could be a possibility. She would most likely never know the truth. Nevertheless, until she felt in her heart that he had been taken from her, she would pray for a reuniting with the love of her life.

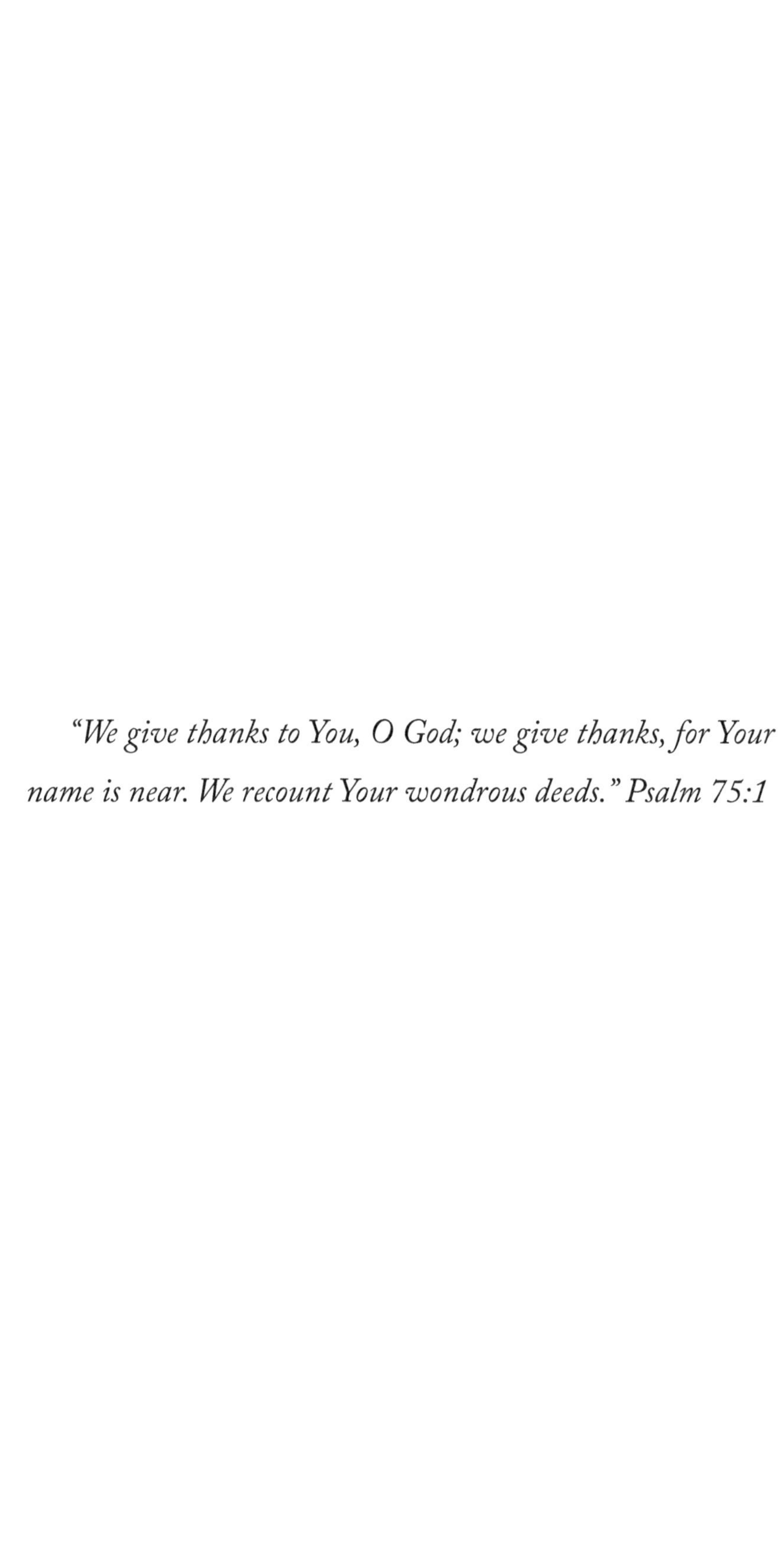

"We give thanks to You, O God; we give thanks, for Your name is near. We recount Your wondrous deeds." Psalm 75:1

CHAPTER 22

The Douglas C-47 Skytrain touched down on runway twelve at Offutt Air Field at precisely 14:20. Captain Shepherd led his new bride and mother in law down the wide cargo off ramp carrying their few belongings. He hailed a command vehicle and drove immediately to the base administration building to check in.

He reported for duty and registered his wife and mother in law with family services. Though their entry into the United States would be on a non quota basis due to the War Brides Act, they would be duly recorded as American citizens with applications for Social Security numbers authorized right away. The procedure was lengthy, and the women were exhausted by the time all the needed paperwork was completed. They made their way to the base housing facilities to check in and get settled, hoping to find a little something to eat along the way.

Home was only a little over twenty miles from the air base, but until Jeffrey was debriefed, he wouldn't be free to travel. Scheduled to be honorably discharged from the Army Chaplaincy program in one week, at his own request, there were administrative issues to address. And, considering his ample war time medals and commendations, he would be promoted to Lt. Colonel before that occurred.

Lt. Colonel Shepherd had already agreed to act as a mentor and counselor to incoming chaplains if the need arose, so he would maintain his military I.D. for easy access to the base. But he planned to live out his remaining days with his new wife, running their farm, feeding the hungry and sharing the Gospel with every creature who ventured in his path.

Batya and Sarah shared a room in the temporary base housing facility, but Mom could tell that Sarah's heart yearned to be with her new husband. The look on his face as Jeffrey wished his wife a good night, almost broke her heart. It would be good for them to be married in the eyes of the Lord so they could get on with their life together.

Jeffrey managed to save several thousand dollars of his pay during his war time years as Captain and he did something quite uncharacteristic as a result. He invested in a new white 1946 Ford Super Deluxe Tudor sedan, exactly like the one made for President Truman that same year, with which to transport his new family back to Springfield Nebraska when the time was right. He had never bought anything so extravagant in his life but thought it a fitting wedding gift for his bride.

Once she learned to drive this would be the auto she'd use to make her way around the community, as the pastor's new wife. He would depend mostly on his old truck back on the farm. He wanted her to be safe, but also thought she deserved to be properly stylish. Sarah was overwhelmed by the gift and now quite anxious to learn to drive. After the purchase Jeffrey was left with enough funds to make improvements on the farm property, which he was sure were well needed after so much time; some desperately needed improvements at the church; and a significant bit toward savings. After all, who knew what the future might hold?

Jeffrey's church had been notified he would be home from military service soon and, to top it off, bringing a new wife with him. The town of Springfield was excited and planned a hero's welcome grand enough to match anything the country offered elsewhere. A celebration, by the way, he would have altogether disapproved of. Nevertheless, four and a half years of absence from the people who'd loved him since he was a little boy, was a very long time. They would have their parade come hell or high water.

The ladies of the congregation were also busily planning another huge surprise after hearing of the new couple's recent plight. They couldn't wait to have their beloved pastor home and they were anxious to meet his new family.

Conversely, the young ladies of the town, sadly, were all prepared to despise the girl he'd married. Just for the sake of plain old jealousy. They wondered what this foreigner could possibly have to offer that they didn't, to entice such a wonderful man to marry her. Their mothers and grandmothers were having none of it and put their collective foot down on plans to make the newcomer feel wholly unwelcome. Pretty soon everyone was working together: cooking, decorating, cleaning and practicing; to prepare for the great homecoming.

Back in New York there was much more to do, preparing Jacob for his move to Nebraska, than he'd previously thought. Contracts to renew, client meetings to arrange, papers to sign, packing to finish. Jacob was anxious to be on his way, but he didn't want to leave things half done and cause problems for Donald. He trusted the man who was keeping things moving in his absence and he made sure to pay him according to his worth.

Donald was loyal. A hard characteristic to find in an employee these days. Don, as he insisted Jacob call him, had met a lovely young woman and was planning to be married soon. Jacob would likely be expected to come back for the wedding. He would remain long enough for the couple to take a week or two off for their honeymoon.

He was the only other person who knew the magnitude of work it took to keep things under control and the wheels rolling in an operation of this size. But before that happened, he wanted to get settled in at his new house. He missed the bluffs already and couldn't wait to be back home.

His flying lessons had been coming along great. He would have the required number of hours to fly solo at the end of his next lesson and his instructor already told him he was a natural born pilot. He'd already put in an order for a Stinson 108-1 from the Stinson division of the American airplane company Consolidated Vultee in Wayne, Michigan. The jaunty little aircraft could accommodate a pilot and up to three passengers, plus luggage, and would make travel back and forth from New York to Nebraska a breeze.

When they arrived at Samuel's house Elle met them at the door in her apron, wiping her hands on a tea towel. They could distinctly hear what sounded like chirping from the other room and upon entering saw that Samuel's baby son was holding himself up by the inside bars of his playpen, grinning from ear to ear. "Wow, he's too little to do that, isn't he?" Samuel exclaimed.

"Evidently not, Papa. It just started in the last couple of days. He has been anxious for you to arrive home my darling. He missed his daddy and I think he wanted to show off for you. How are you, Jacob? It's nice to see you again."

"Don't you mean, Mr. Crabby pants?" Jacob said with a laugh.

"Oh, Sam! You didn't tell him that, did you?"

"Yes, I did meyn lib. I didn't know it was a secret. Here little man. Come see your daddy." The baby giggled and laughed and wrapped his chubby arms around daddy's neck as soon as Samuel lifted him from the playpen. "My oh my. You're getting as fat as a baking piglet. What has your mother been feeding you?" Then he tickled his son, eliciting more giggles and a hearty laugh that made Jacob smile. He remembered Sarah at that age and was suddenly choked up with unchecked emotion. He excused himself and used the bathroom to wash his face and gain back the composure he'd so quickly lost.

Elle was a great cook and supper was delicious. Schnitzel with spaetzle and roasted vegetables, a good stout beer and an excellent apple strudel for dessert. After they ate Elle crooked her finger at Samuel and told him she had news. They walked into the kitchen together and Jacob heard, "What? That's wonderful. How far along are you? I can't believe it. I love you Elle."

"I love you too, Sam. I'm so pleased that you are happy about this."

"Of course I'm happy. Perhaps this time it will be your little girl."

"I don't mind either way, meyn lib. As long as it's a healthy baby. But she would be your little girl as well, wouldn't she?"

"Of course she would. I just meant, well, you know."

"Yes, meyn lib, I do know. I am just teasing. Now, go and keep Jacob company. I will be out shortly."

Samuel came out of the kitchen with a huge grin on his face. "Did you hear?"

"It would have been hard not to hear my friend. I'm very happy for you, for both of you. If you need to take some time?"

"I might take you up on that offer when the new baby comes boss man, so I can spend a bit of time helping Elle. But for now, I need to be getting in all the trips I can. I will soon have two little mouths to feed. Thank you for taking that great leap into business, Jacob. If not for you and your ambition who knows where any of us would be now."

"You're welcome my friend. But don't be silly. I couldn't have done it without all of you fine, strong men who have worked with me to build this company into what it is today. You will always have a place at B, S, & J. Someday when you get tired of being on the road, we will find something else for you to do. I am also grateful for America, our new homeland. If not for this great country, none of this would have been possible."

"I agree, Jacob. America the beautiful has been pretty

good to us, hasn't she?"

The drive home in their new car was comfortable, even exciting, but Sarah could feel her stomach doing somersaults. "Sarah, don't worry. They will love you. I promise."

"I don't know, Jeffrey. I'm a foreigner, a stranger, and I am coming into their community with nothing to offer but myself. Why would they feel the need to make me feel welcome?""Sarah! Don't be ridiculous. You take Jesus with you everywhere you go."

"Sorry mother. I know that He is always with me. I just don't know for sure what I might have to offer these people. I have married their pastor, but who am I?"

"My love, you are enough. You have the kindest and most beautiful heart of any woman I've ever known. I just wish my parents could have been alive to meet you. But you will get to know everyone, and they will all get to know you. These are good people too. They will make you feel welcomed. It will be as though you have lived in Springfield all your life. Please don't fret. As soon as we get settled in, I will teach you to drive. Then you can help get members of the congregation back and forth to appointments and the like while I am working. You will feel more useful then. Remember that you are the pastor's wife and there will be lots of people looking to you for help."

"I don't mind that at all, Jeffrey. I love being helpful."

"That's one of the many things I adore about you, Sarah. You always think of others before yourself. Like I said. Don't worry, they will all love you."

As the trio pulled into town they could hear, faintly, the sound of music in the distance. Jeffrey rolled the window down and looked confused at what he was hearing. Until he could see, just up the street in front of the church, the tiny high school band was playing. It seemed every citizen of Springfield and perhaps even several neighboring towns was there to welcome them home. Banners hung from buildings and as they got close, a flurry of confetti appeared to fall from the sky.

The town's mayor and his wife stood on the steps of the church holding flowers for the ladies and a large golden key to the town for their hero. Old Doc, the same one who delivered Jeffrey all those years ago, stood beside the mayor. Jeff turned several shades of red and Batya and Sarah, laughing at his obvious embarrassment weren't entirely sure what to do.

Jacob hadn't realized before how much work needed doing to free himself from the responsibilities of his day to day life in New York. This would take days, much longer than he'd hoped, even with Don's help. He put his nose to the grindstone and forged on. He would get his things packed up, finish all this paperwork and get his belongings on a truck right along with the next load to the air base. This would assure that the trip wouldn't be a wasted one.

He planned to take Samuel and his new recruit along. The cab would be a bit crowded on the way out to Nebraska, but the guys would have plenty of room on the way back and could even take a load back from Offutt. This would also ensure he'd have a little help moving his things into the new house before the guys left. He was pretty pleased with his plan.

Purchasing a car, once he arrived in Nebraska, would be imperative. Up till now that had not been a requirement, as he'd always had his big trucks to get him around outside the city, and of course the subway system inside the city's limits. He intended to invest in some large trucks to keep and manage in Nebraska, which would also require that he hire a couple new drivers for local runs there, but that wouldn't be a practical source of transportation for day to day use. No, a new car would be an absolute necessity.

The church's women's auxiliary group went all out. They served a lovely luncheon in the fellowship hall featuring roasted turkey and ham, replete with salads, side dishes, and desserts of all varieties. Batya and Sarah had never seen so much food in all their lives. Having lived through extremely sparse circumstances most of their lives, especially during their years in the Ghetto, Dachau and the displaced person's camp, they were not physically capable of eating the amount of food laid before them.

Batya certainly didn't want to insult any of these wonderful women who had worked so hard to make their welcome memorable, so she announced, "You have all been so very kind. Everything looks delicious. However, I'm afraid we cannot possibly do justice to all this beautiful food, so if it is agreeable to you, we would like to take several meals with us to serve as we are getting settled in on the farm. I know that Sarah and I are both very tired, but we wanted to thank you for your kindness before we leave to get some rest."

"I agree with my mother. Your welcome has been a surprise and a joy. We want to take much more time to get to know each and every one of you after we have settled in. Obviously, we will see all of you on Sunday. If any of you has a need, we will be available to serve in any capacity required to make our lives together an even bigger blessing going forward."

The church's women packed up containers of food and townspeople loaded the items into the trunk of their new car. However, before they could leave the ladies had another surprise for their beloved pastor and his new wife. "The church would like to give you a wedding day to remember. We know that you were married by a German Burgermeister in order to gain your license to come home, but we want you to have a proper ceremony before God. We hoped to do that on this coming Sunday, so that everyone in the church family would be present."

"That is very generous of you. I'm sure it would be lovely. Is this alright with you, Sarah?"

"I think that would be wonderful ladies. I am more than grateful. It will be so much work in such a small amount of time though. Are you sure you want to tackle a project like that?"

"You are absolutely right, Sarah, that there is much to do and little time to do it. With only five days until the wedding. However, we do need to measure you for a dress. Would you mind if we came out to the farm tomorrow to get that done?"

"Well now, I'm sure this will be a surprise to everyone. My mother, Batya was a renowned dress maker in Russia and then later in Poland. Tzar Nickolas' wife, the empress of Russia and her daughters wore my mother's creations."

"Oh, Sarah. You flatter me. I'm sure these ladies are wonderful seamstresses and will do a beautiful job. However, if it would be okay with you ladies, I would love to help. I've always dreamed of making my daughter's wedding dress as I did my own."

"We would be honored to sew with you, Batya. Goodness, a seamstress for the Grand Empress of Russia! What stories you must have. Shall we say tomorrow morning first thing? We will sew, and you can tell us the stories of your life in Russia and Poland."

"We would be honored to have you ladies. We will put the coffee on."

People waved and smiled. Not those make-believe smiles that sometimes plaster the faces of church people when they meet someone new, but real genuine smiles. People were still waving and smiling as they drove out of Springfield down the dirt road toward the farm.

Batya was amazed by the beauty of the somewhat hauntingly familiar countryside, as they drove slowly on dirt and gravel roads toward their new home. Then, in a flash, she realized why she was sensing such a feeling of familiarity. It was because the landscape here reminded her so much of the Steppes of Ukraine where she was born.

She felt a tear trickle down her cheek when they passed a small river snaking through the Plains and lined by trees that couldn't have survived without its sustenance in the semi arid climate. Patches of late summer wildflowers sprang up between fields filled with crops coming near to harvest. From the looks of it, lots of corn; some other low growing plant with which she was not familiar, this one taking on a golden and rust colored hue as harvest time approached; and plenty of wheat. Wheat, sporting individual, but glorious golden heads and blowing in a light breeze, like dancers moving in unison. The look of it reminded her of the tall Stipa grass growing on her beloved, childhood Steppes. It seemed through all the joy, pain and sorrow; she couldn't help but feel she had somehow come full circle.

CHAPTER 23

Jeffrey chose a beautiful cloudless day to make his way back to Offutt Air Base. With some remaining administrative issues to clear up, before his honorable discharge ceremony, now was as good a time as any to get those odds and ends accomplished.

If truth be told, he just really needed to get out of the house. Every inch of the place was quite literally crawling with happy, smiling women. Every one of those ladies was drinking coffee and snacking on tiny tea cakes; while brandishing scissors, needles, spools of thread and good intentions. So, he was feeling pretty uncomfortable and out of place. Of course, he was happy for Sarah, sure that the dress would turn out beautifully, but to stay would be impossible.

He didn't care much for crowds, or people in general, if he was honest.

Even as the thought entered his mind, he considered it odd. A pastor who didn't like crowds, or people for that matter, was a bit of a contradiction in terms, wasn't it? Well, it was important to remember, he reminded himself, that we are commanded to love. Liking is optional. He did his best. Sarah was the one who was good with people. She remembered names and certain social graces.

Utterly terrified to speak in public too, he always had been. Before presenting a weekly sermon, his hands shook so badly it was difficult to turn the pages of his Bible. He'd never shared that tidbit of information with anyone. Knowing that the Spirit of God and He alone, gave this minister the strength to deliver a message each Sunday.

As he approached the podium trembling and sweating each Sunday, he prayed for the strength to do what he must without passing out.

There was a significant part of him that hoped he would never lose that fear, as difficult as it was to deal with, for he believed it kept him in present in a deep state of awe and respect regarding whose Holy Word he spoke to the people and this went a long way toward keeping him humble.

Sarah and Batya would be well cared for by the church ladies in his absence. These same women who were currently helping with the creation of a gown, had come into the farmhouse and cleaned everything from top to bottom before the trio arrived home the day before.

He'd never seen the place so spic and span. Not in all the years he'd lived there; even clear back to when his mom was still alive. Though, with all those kids and a congregation of people to care for, she certainly had plenty of valid excuses for neglecting household chores.

Actually, who was he kidding. Busyness aside, his mother had never been the best cook or housekeeper, but that was okay. She was who she was, and she had loved him as he loved her.

When he'd entered in through the kitchen door yesterday, he was shocked speechless. He thought, at first, that perhaps they'd entered the wrong house. He looked around, suspicious at first, to validate his ownership.

Windows sparkled, floors throughout were scrubbed to a beautiful shine and everything, absolutely everything, was in its place. The whole house smelled faintly of bleach and lemon. Cobwebs that had taken up residence in the corners of every room for years, along with dust bunnies hidden under each and every piece of furniture before he left for war were miraculously gone. As a matter of fact, he and his companions couldn't see a speck of dust or dirt anywhere.

Clean sheets on the beds, washed and ironed curtains on the windows and a fresh cloth covering the kitchen table, adorned with a beautiful bouquet of fresh flowers caused him to look around again, dumbfounded. When he came to think of it, he didn't rightly remember owning a tablecloth before, so there was that.

Jeffrey, Batya and Sarah brought in all the food the ladies from the church had so lovingly packed up for them and loaded it into a clean refrigerator; which stood next to a stove that had been scrubbed so bright it might have been brand new. There was even a stack of firewood near the wood burner in the living room. He was amazed again.

Next to the flowers on the table was a chocolate cake in a glass cake stand that looked scrumptious. The three travelers looked back and forth at each other and smiled.

Jeffrey knew his wife and mother in law were grateful beyond words that they wouldn't have to tackle the mess he'd predicted they would encounter. After so much time had passed, since his departure for the European front, he had expected to be horrified upon walking in the door. He had prepared them for the worst. But here they were, and his church members had delivered the best. Perhaps people weren't so bad after all.

Helpful congregants had also taken care of the garden and fields every single day during his long absence; in order to grow more food for distribution at their weekly, county wide, open food pantries. It was true they had agreed to doing that before he left for war, but he had no idea how well they would manage that thankless job. The job he'd done alone for so many years.

He certainly had no idea that at the same time they were serving the community, they would also fill the root cellar and larder of his own home, literally to bursting, with food and supplies. Yes, these were good people after all, and he was glad to be home.

Nevertheless, he would still make himself scarce while the sewing brigade was on board and try not to feel guilty for doing it.

He took Sarah's new car, as he wasn't sure if the old truck would make the forty mile round trip without problems. He'd be sure to give the old Ford a good going over sometime this week before taking it on trips any longer than to town and back.

Smiling as he made his way to the base, he had to admit that in this new Ford sedan he felt like he was traveling in the lap of luxury. There was a very small piece of him that was almost ashamed to be driving something so expensive when there were people in Europe still starving. But Jeffrey wasn't a selfish person. He knew that of himself. So, he would enjoy today and then turn the car over to Sarah after he did a little maintenance on the farm truck.

He pulled up to a pump at the base fueling station. When he opened the door and got out, he saw a tall man fueling his cargo truck who was staring at him. "Hello there."

"Hello yourself. I didn't mean to stare. I am making a delivery to the base, but then I will be moving my belongings into a house I've built on the bluffs and I will be needing a new automobile for my personal use. I must say that I love yours. Can I ask what kind you're driving?"

"Sure thing. It's a 1946 Ford Super Deluxe Tudor sedan. The very same car that was made for President Truman. It cost a pretty penny, but I'm very pleased with it. It actually isn't my car. It's my wife's wedding gift. But my truck needs some work, so I borrowed it for the day and here I am."

"So, your wife's wedding gift? Congratulations on

your nuptials."

"Well, those won't actually take place until Sunday services. But we are getting excited. I'm actually the pastor of our church, so another will have to do the ceremony to marry us. The ladies of the church are making a dress for my wife as we speak."

"Ah, that explains why you are here."

"Is it that obvious? Crowds are not for me. But I promised her a proper wedding before the Lord and a wedding she shall have. Besides, most of it is being taken care of, so all I really have to do is stay out of the way and show up on Sunday."

Another man got out of the truck's cab from the passenger side, followed by a younger fellow. "I'm going to use the facilities. Don't leave without me."

"I'll wait Sam, but don't take forever. I want to get everything unloaded at the house."

"Sure thing. We'll be right out."

"So, you said you've built a house on the bluffs?"

"Yes. I own a trucking firm out of New York and have traveled through this part of the country many times in recent months. Once I acquired some military contracts through Offutt Air Base I was coming out here regularly.

I fell in love with a great piece of property in the Loess Hills one day so, I bought it and started to plan. I intend to set up a half-way station operation out here and then perhaps another one in California some day."

"Your wife must hate you being gone so much."

"My wife passed away several years ago. It's just me now."

"I'm so sorry for your loss. My fiancée and I live in Springfield. It's a little over twenty miles from here. Our wedding will be held at the big wooden church on the edge of town at ten in the morning on Sunday. I would love it if you could come. You don't have many neighbors on the bluffs and you'll need friends. It's no good to be alone. This would be a chance for you to meet some good people who live in the area. There will also be a lunch afterward and I have to tell you, the ladies in our congregation are great cooks. I'm sure my wife would be happy to meet you. It sounds for all the world that you have the same accent she does."

"Really? I am originally from Poland. How strange that there would be another so close, in such a sparsely populated area, with an accent from the same part of Europe. Perhaps I will come to your wedding. I would be interested in talking to your wife about what part of Poland she is from. Maybe we could spend some time exchanging stories."

"Well, she and her mother have many stories that I'm sure they would be happy to share. Probably many that I have not yet heard. My name is Jeffrey Shepherd. I hope to see you on Sunday. It was a pleasure to meet you."

"Jacob, of B, S & J Transport. And I will certainly think about it. It was a pleasure to meet you as well, Mr. Shepherd. Are you guys ready to go? I want to get this truck unloaded."

"Hold on boss. We're on our way."

After unloading Jacob's personal belongings, the three men rearranged the load they'd picked up from the base. They would rest for the night and then two of them would head back out for New York in the morning.

Jacob was up early and made a big breakfast for the guys. Bacon and eggs with potato pancakes and coffee. They ate on the deck, facing the sunrise and the wide-open spaces of the Plains. "What a view, Jacob. I could surely see waking up to this every morning. But don't just sit here in the house. Promise me you'll get out and make some friends. I don't want to drive out here and find that you've become a lonely old hermit."

"I promise, Sam. I'm thinking of making my way out to Springfield to attend Jeffrey Shepherd's wedding on Sunday."

"Is that the man you were talking to at the filling station?"

"Yes. He said his fiancée has an accent similar to mine. I'd love to talk to her and ask her some questions. It might be interesting to hear her stories."

"That sounds great, but how are you going to get there? I feel like we are leaving you stranded out here without transportation."

"I've been doing some thinking. A supplier will be coming out tomorrow, so I will be ordering more trucks. That will still happen of course, but I think my plans are heading in a different direction now, at least for my personal use."

"Well, we're going to need to get going. I'm hoping to get this load delivered and be home before the start of the weekend for once."

"Hey, that's great. I'm going to catch a ride with you, if you don't mind. I've made my decision. I'm going to buy a car. You can drop me off and be on your way."

The 1946 Ford Super Deluxe Tudor sedan he purchased was white, just like the one he'd seen at the filling station. And, it was the most comfortable car he'd ever driven. He would go to the wedding in style.

Jacob spent the next couple of days getting unpacked and settled in. He hadn't worn his good suit since the day he was sworn in as an American citizen, as the regular day to day life of an over the road trucker didn't exactly call for suits and ties. But he pulled it out and pressed it, hanging it in the closet along with a nice shirt and tie, all ready for his trip to Springfield on Sunday.

The dress was gorgeous and a true expression of love from her mother and the ladies of the church. Sarah stood in the middle of the room on a short stool so her mama could make a few last minute adjustments to her gown.

"Be still."

"Sorry Mama. You know I have a hard time standing in one place."

"If anyone knows this, I do. Even in the womb you danced a jig. But, for now you must be still, or you will have a pin stuck in your leg. You know, my Bubbe used to say, "If things are not as you wish, wish them as they are."

"What does that mean?"

"I believe it means to be happy with what you have, or the circumstances you are in. But she said many things. Many things that often made no sense to a little girl. However, for now this one means, be still."

"Do you miss her? Your Bubbe."

"Of course I do. I miss them all. I will miss them always. I actually find it much sadder now that I am a Christian."

"Why sadder now, Mama?"

"Because none of them knew Jesus. They all died, not knowing the Messiah. I suppose they'd had chances to know Him all their lives, but they didn't take hold of those chances. That makes me very sad. It also makes me take my part in the Great Commission much more seriously. We are supposed to be sharing Jesus with every creature. That means Jews also. Jews must trust the Lord for salvation just as gentiles must do. They are God's chosen people, but they are not immune from sin and they need a Savior like everyone else. I wish I could have shared the Lord with them, but I didn't know Him when I was a girl"

"There's nothing you could have done about that, Mama. It isn't your fault. You know that, don't you?"

"I suppose I do."

"What were some of your Bubbe's sayings?"

"Well, she said many things. Some very serious, and some quite silly. "Trouble is to man what rust is to iron." Would be a pretty serious one. But, "If you need a helping hand you will find one at the end of your arm." I always found quite silly. Perhaps because she said it to me so often."

"She sounds like a remarkable woman."

"She was. They were all remarkable. They worked very hard, for very little. But they loved just as hard and everything they did was for us. I wish you had known them. They could have taught you many things."

"But I have you Mama. And you have taught me many things. I do love you Mama."

"And I you my ketsele. But we have a dress to finish, so let us get on with it."

A work of art in sculpted pure white satin, with a full skirt and long fitted sleeves. Small white beads adorned the sleeves and form fitted bodice of her wedding gown. Batya had tried very hard not to make the dress too heavy.

Sarah insisted on a demure style, something befitting a new pastor's wife. No swooping back, décolleté neckline, or sheer bodice, so there was a lot of material to contend with. On her daughter's tiny frame Batya was afraid the weight of the dress would pull Sarah right down to the ground. And truthfully, at around only ninety pounds it wouldn't have taken much to do that.

Her satin booties were form fitted. She didn't want to trip over her own feet walking down the aisle. Just like her mama, she tended to be a bit of a klutz. So, she'd opted not to wear heels of any sort. This would make her appear even more petite beside her tall, handsome husband.

She'd elected to carry a lovely bouquet of yellow and white daisies, readily available along every nearby country road, with pure white satin ribbons woven throughout. Her light and airy veil would be attached to a handmade daisy headband which would weave right into her stylish up do.

Nerves frazzled, and more butterflies in her stomach than she would dare to count, oh, not about marrying Jeffrey, but about walking down the aisle of a strange church in front of people she'd only just met and without a dad to give her away, she began to pray. Sarah missed her dad whenever she thought of him, but on her wedding day his absence would be most especially felt.

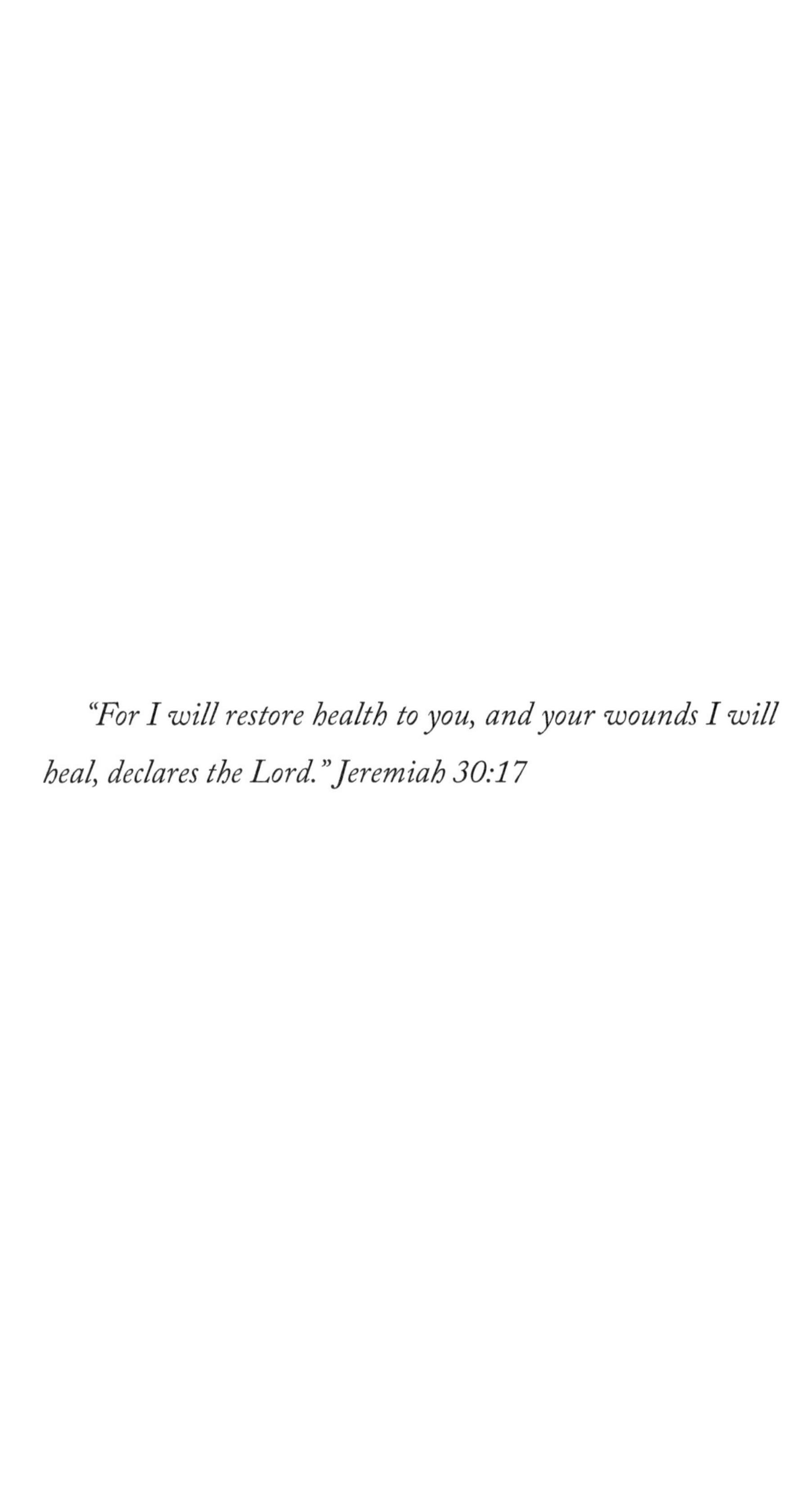

"For I will restore health to you, and your wounds I will heal, declares the Lord." Jeremiah 30:17

CHAPTER 24

Grateful he'd bought his two hundred acres before President Truman used an executive order last March to open public lands back up to homesteading; Jacob saw construction now occurring on the open plains where just weeks ago there was none. Barns, silos and farmhouses springing up all over and dotting the formerly empty landscape around the bluffs.

New farms, with new young farmers, starting a life of joy and toil; beside the faithful few who's families had been working that Nebraska soil for a hundred years. He silently wished them luck, but was glad they wouldn't be building their houses in his back yard.

Making his way to Springfield he drove with his window partially open, breathing in the crisp, fresh air. The sights of a pending fall harvest were in full view and suddenly a faint smell of burning leaves wafted in, causing him to wax nostalgic and roll his window down all the way. He supposed it didn't matter on what continent one lived. Smells of land and harvest would always be the same. What a day to be alive. He only wished his beloved

Batya could be here to share in the beauty of such a glorious day.

Mama helped her dress and slip on her booties. She was shaking like a leaf, so they held each other for quite some time. That seemed to calm her a bit. The thought of walking down the aisle alone, among all those strangers was simply taking her breath away. The only thing that kept her going was knowing that at the other end of the aisle would be her beloved Jeffrey waiting patiently to take her hand.

"Don't think about the people you haven't met yet meyn lib. Think only about the ladies who helped with the sewing. They know you and love you. See if you can pick out their faces in the crowd."

"Thank you, Mama. Perhaps that will work. I'll try."

Those kind ladies of the church and of course Mama, had done a beautiful job on her gown. It was lovely, though quite heavy, if she was honest. That was surely all her own fault due to her fashion choices. She could tell already she would be exhausted after an hour of hauling it around. But, gratefully, she'd chosen to change into something a bit more casual after the ceremony for the informal reception downstairs, so that would be helpful. Thankful she'd chosen to wear slippers instead of heels, she suspected the weight of her gown might well have toppled her from their heights. While the mental image made her giggle, she knew that would have been a disaster waiting to happen.

It was almost time. Batya hugged her daughter one last time before leaving the room. "You know I will be with you in spirit meyn lib. Don't worry, I will let you know when they are ready for you."

"I wish Papa was here."

"I know ketsele. I wish he was here too. I have prayed and prayed, but I guess it is too much to expect the Lord to bring him back to us."

"So, you really do believe he is dead Mama?"

"After so much time, meyn lib, I just don't know anymore. But, dead or alive, Europe is a long way from America. So, let us not dampen the joy of your special day with this talk zeiskeit. There is a wonderful man, who loves you very much, waiting at the altar to marry you. I will be back in a few minutes to let you know when to begin your march. Chin up and smile. One would think you were headed to a funeral instead of to your own wedding."

"Thank you, Mama. For everything. I don't just mean the dress. I mean for always being here for me. For protecting me and loving me. I will always be grateful to God for you."

"And I for you, Sarah."

Jacob walked into a packed church but didn't escape the vigilant eye of his new friend. "Well, hello! I was hoping you would make it!"

"Thank you. I was hoping you would remember me. Congratulations on your upcoming marriage. I am very excited to meet your new bride."

"Well, the ceremony hasn't happened yet, so you are just in time. Here comes her mother, so I will send her to retrieve Sarah and we will begin."

"How odd that is."

"Odd?"

"My own daughter's name was Sarah."

"That is unusual. I don't believe there are many named Sarah in this area. Batya, come here, I want you to meet my new friend, Jacob."

"Batya?"

Jacob swung around so fast he was immediately dizzy and then dropped hard to his knees when he saw his wife. Two women grabbed Batya from behind as she toppled to the floor. A little cold water and a quick fanning of the face revived her. "Jakub?"

"Batya, is this your Jacob? The husband you thought dead?" Jeffrey asked.

"Yes, Jeffrey. This is my Jakub. I can't believe my eyes." They held each other and cried, rocking back and forth in one another's arms for quite some time. "No, Jakub, we must stop, Sarah is waiting for me to let her know when to walk down the aisle. I must give her the good news that her father is alive. God has answered our prayers. We will have much to talk about later, my husband. But for now, our daughter is marrying the man she loves."

"Batya, let me. I'm her father. I would like to walk her down the aisle. This is something I dreamed of but thought I would never have the pleasure of doing."

"Of course, Jakub. She has prayed for this miracle for a very long time, as have I, and here you are."

Batya led Jakub to the back room of the church, from which a high-pitched scream of, "Papa" and then loud wailing commenced. The congregation looked puzzled and concerned, with some of the members rising as if to go help and then being urged to sit. So, while the small reunion took place in back, Jeffrey addressed the congregation and joyfully explained the unlikely, but miraculous unfolding events.

Much excitement ensued. And once the bride was ready for her march down the aisle the music began and the entire congregation exploded in applause as Sarah emerged from the back room on her father's arm, red faced and slightly disheveled, but smiling from ear to ear.

Sarah and her father walked arm in arm crying and laughing every step of the way to the altar, with Mom following close behind.

Jacob looked decidedly confused about the particular direction the ceremony was taking, but Batya told him she would explain later. He was much too filled with happiness to argue over incidentals, so it would wait.

What a day. When the ceremony was complete and the newly wedded couple was officially declared "Man and wife, joined before God and man", applause once again erupted throughout the congregation. Sarah and Jeffrey made their way back up the aisle to greet their guests and receive well wishes. Then Sarah made her way to the back room, changed into something more comfortable; and with her husband; joined her Papa and Mama for an afternoon of celebration. She was more filled with joy than she could remember on any other day in her life. She'd just married the amazing man of her dreams, and her Papa was alive!

The traditions were different and strange, but the joy was every bit as contagious. He would wait until they were alone before asking too many questions. However, he was sure he had heard the Name of Jesus mentioned many times throughout the ceremony and he'd watched his beautiful wife's face smiling and drenched in happy tears. Obviously, some things had changed.

The day progressed through a delicious lunch provided by the church ladies: casseroles, salads, and roasted meats galore. Next came the cutting of cake and throwing of the bouquet. Things were winding down and Jeffrey appeared to be anxious to leave, though not wanting to say anything purely for appearances sake.

"You two should go. This is your wedding night, and you've waited a very long time."

"But Papa is here too."

"Yes, and he shall still be here when you return from

your honeymoon."

"Actually, Batya, I thought we would go home, and let these kids have some time together. It has been a very long time since we have seen one another as well."

"Home? Do you live close by, Jakub?"

"Not so far away. I've built a home on the bluffs. I have much to tell you. Gather your things and let's be on our way. Come here Sarah. Give your Papa a hug. We will have much to talk about when we see one another again. For now, enjoy your husband."

"I love you Papa and I love you Mama." There were handshakes, hugs and congratulations all around. Church members declared that they would take care of the mess and wished both couples a good night.

"I can't believe you are here, Jakub. Yet, I don't know why I would say that. I must learn to trust more completely, because I should believe it. I have prayed for this every single day since the last time I saw you in the Ghetto. In the short time I have been a Christian, I have discovered that God is very good and that I can depend on Jesus to take care of me."

"This is what I didn't understand, Batya. It was all very confusing for me. I've never seen a Christian wedding before, but this was a Christian wedding, was it not?"

"Yes, Jakub. Sarah and I are both Christians now. She trusted Jesus while still in the Ghetto. During our time there she was meeting with a group. I came to know the Lord while we were prisoners of Commandant Weiter. Sarah and I used a Bible owned by the Commandant's wife. Jesus is truly the only reason we are still alive."

"It seems strange that you seem so happy, Batya. So far from your faith."

"That's just the thing, Jakub. I don't feel far from my faith at all. If anything, I have finally discovered my faith. I no longer question whether or not there is a God. There is absolutely a God and His Name is Jesus. My faith is in Jesus who died for me and rose again to free me from sin and death. He died for you too. But we will have all the time in the world to talk of such things my husband. Now, show me this house you have built on the bluffs."

"Yes, meyn lib. I can't wait to show you our house. Especially the bedroom. It has been a very long time." The look in his glorious green eyes left no doubt about how much she had been missed.

"I agree meyn lib, a very long time indeed." Glancing sideways at him and smiling in the way that she knew drove him crazy, Batya reached across the seat to take his hand.

"Oh Jakub, its beautiful. The view is so lovely."

"Wait until you see it in the morning. The sunrise is wonderful. I have made a habit of sitting on the deck for my coffee."

"What made you choose to build your house on these bluffs?"

"Our house, meyn lib. I remembered how you talked about the Steppes where you were born. How much you missed the place where you grew up. I don't know. I guess....."

"But you thought I was dead. Why would you build your house for a dead woman?"

"Because I love you, Batya. You are everything to me. And if I couldn't have you, then perhaps I could have something of you through your memories. Does that make sense? No, I suppose it probably doesn't."

"Actually, it does, Jakub. But how could you afford all of this? It must have cost more money than I can even imagine to do all of this."

"Well, I have many stories to tell you, as I am sure you have to tell me. However, one of my stories is that I saved my wages and bought a cargo truck. I started a transport company, which is called B, S & J Trucking, and now we own dozens of trucks that transport cargo all over the country. We are actually quite wealthy wife. I can give you anything you want."

"Oh Jakub, all I want is you, us. Don't you know that this is more than I could have ever dreamed. Yes, we both have many stories to tell and much catching up to do. May I suggest that we begin someplace more comfortable?"

Jacob laughed, picked Batya up and headed toward the back of the house.

"Good morning wife."

"Good morning to you, husband."

"I thought I would walk the property today. It looks like the church took excellent care of the place while I was gone, but I would like to check things out."

"Okay, but let me make you some breakfast first."

"I can think of better things to do than cooking."

"Oh, you can? Hmmm, pray tell, what would that be?"

Jeffrey grabbed her around the waist, and laughing, they fell back onto the mussed sheets. Breakfast could wait, at least for a little while.

"What? I don't believe it. The man from the filling station is your new son in law?"

"Yes, if I had not gone to that wedding, I might have spent the rest of my life living twenty miles from my wife and daughter and never would have known."

"Well, they say everything happens for a reason. So, are you going to introduce me to your wife? You know I've never met her, right?"

"Oh, sure. I wasn't thinking. Batya, could you come here meyn lib? There is someone I would like you to meet."

Batya entered the room. Glowing from their activities of the night before. She looked to be all of twenty-five years old, at least to her totally enamored husband. Her blond hair flowed around her shoulders, as she hadn't yet fastened it up into her usual bun. Beautiful blue eyes fairly sparkled in the light from the picture window and her smile, always lovely, was radiant. She held her hand out to Samuel.

"Well, well, well. Now it is much more clear to me why this man could not forget about you and go on with his life. Pleased to meet you, Batya. I am Samuel."

"I'm very pleased to meet you also, Samuel. Jakub and I still have much more to share about our time apart, but he has already spoken very highly of you."

"I should hope so. I am the backbone of the business after all."

"Oh, go on with you, Sam."

"No, I have to tell you, Mrs., that your husband is a very hard-working man with a vision for the future. If not for him, there would be many of us without gainful employment. His business sense has made us successful in this land of opportunity and I will be eternally grateful."

"Okay, that's quite enough, Sam. You don't need to gush. You already have the job. I have a meeting today with suppliers and Batya is going to sit in with me to get the gist of the operation. Obviously if I'd known how all of these events of late would unfold, I would not have made the appointment with these suppliers for today. But here we are. Do you have any guys with you?"

"Yes, I brought the new lad. We're going to head over to the base and unload before we pick up the return cargo."

"Why don't you bring him in then? Let us make you some dinner before you get back out on the road."

"Great. I thought you'd never ask. I'll be right back."

"I'm going to familiarize myself with the kitchen before I get dinner started. I'll let you fellows know when it's finished."

"Wow, Jacob, she is really something. I'm so happy for you."

"You know, Sam. I feel like every moment of my life has been leading to this. The one thing that is different is that she and our daughter have both become Christians. However, I can't be angry with her. I wasn't there and I wasn't practicing our religion either, at least while we were hiding out. As a matter of fact, I haven't been to temple once since I came to America. They both seem so happy. I don't know. What do you think?"

"I think you have to do what you believe is right. Elle's sister is a Christian and she's been talking to us. She even invited us to church. Perhaps we'll go. I can't really give you advice because I'm in the same situation. I suppose you should listen to her before you make up your mind. I think it's always good to listen."

"Maybe I will. So, you think you're going to go to church?"

"Yeah. I can't see what it would hurt. As I said, Elle's sister is a Christian, but she's still a Jew too. She goes to a church where everyone in the congregation is both Jew and Christian, so I suppose you can be both. We don't have to give up our traditions and holidays. She said the only difference is that as Christians we know the Messiah, the Savior. She told us that the Jews in Jesus' day were expecting Him to show up like a fancy king and when He came as a baby in a manger to a poor couple, they just weren't willing to accept that He could be the Messiah."

"Well, I guess it couldn't hurt anything to hear what Batya and Sarah have to say about things. My wife has always been pretty smart. Now that my daughter is the preacher's wife, I guess I have a church pretty close by."

"Then I guess that answers the whole thing."

"Are you men hungry? Why don't we eat?"

"Great, we're on our way."

It was a simple meal, put together from things Jakub had on hand. Tomato and rice soup, bread, cheese and fruit. But the fellows were grateful and made their delight known. Batya would become more familiar with her new kitchen, and with typical American fare. But she would always be ready to fill in with Bubbe's delicious recipes from her childhood. She couldn't wait to get back to a life of familiarity and routine.

"But you have saved us from our foes and have put to shame those who hate us. In God we have boasted continually, and we will give thanks to Your name forever." Psalm 44:7-8

CHAPTER 25

"What's going on, Jakub? Who were you talking to?"

"Donald, he called to tell me he is getting married next week. I will be flying out to New York in a couple of days. I'm needed there to keep the office running until he returns from his honeymoon."

"We."

"What?"

"We. We will be heading to New York in a couple of days. You are not going anywhere without me."

"You want to go to New York? Are you sure? You'll hate it there."

"I would hate it much more here, without you. Listen Jakub. I lost you once and I'm never losing you again. I am coming with you. Besides, you are a pilot now and I've never even been a passenger in your plane."

"You are absolutely correct. Okay, Batya. You won't like it, but you are welcome to come if you want to. I'll be there for two weeks while Don and his new bride take their honeymoon and I sure wouldn't mind the company."

"What do you say we go a day early so we don't miss the wedding? I think I should meet Donald and his new bride anyway, don't you?"

"Yes, that would be great for you to meet him. He does a great job for us."

"You've told me a lot about him. He sounds like a hard worker, very loyal. While we're there you can show me the sights. I've never been to New York and I've never seen the statue of liberty."

"That's right, you haven't. I've seen it from both the inside and out. This is beginning to sound more like a vacation than work. Well, during the day we still have a job to do, but in the evenings, I can show you the sights. I've never seen the Empire State Building either. We can see it together."

"That sounds wonderful. I can't wait to go. We can tell Sarah and Jeffrey on Sunday. We will lock the house up before we go, but we can leave them a key in case of emergency."

"It'll be like the honeymoon we never had, because your Aunt Fern was still with us after we got married."

"What fun. I will need to shop for a few things before we go. I didn't bring much from Germany when we came, and I haven't really had a chance to do much shopping since we arrived. A couple of the ladies from the church were nice enough to give me a few things, so I would have something for the wedding, but those items are too large anyway, even after some alterations."

"Yes, I would guess they probably didn't have many department stores in the displaced persons camp, did they?" Jacob's face sported a sheepish grin.

"No, they didn't. I still can't believe how far we have come in just a few short weeks. At this time last year, I wasn't sure if we would be alive to see another year. Now, here I am living in this beautiful home with my handsome husband. And we are about to take a trip to New York City. God is good all the time and I have to admit that life is simply wonderful!"

"Aw my Batya, I do love you with all my heart. You have always been beautiful meyn lib. Even after all these years you are as lovely as the day we met, inside and out. But then, when you are excited, the way your eyes sparkle, your smile, I just can't get enough of you."

"Good. I hope you will always feel that way. It is the same way I feel about you Jakub. I will love you always, until the end of time my wonderful husband."

Don's bride was sweet as the day is long and the wedding was lovely. Jakub was glad they'd come early. Batya was right. It seemed to mean a lot to Don and his new bride that they would come to see them married. They all got along famously, as if they'd known each other for years. The four quickly became fast friends. This would become more important later.

New York was great. Jakub showed Batya the location of his first job in America and then the site of his boarding house home, the place he'd stayed until he moved to the Loess Hills of Nebraska. They visited all the tourist traps and famous landmarks and ate wonderful meals in romantic restaurants. But they also tried something called a 'Hot Dog'. It wasn't made of dog at all, which was a huge relief to Batya! Instead it was a pink sausage laid out on soft bread that the gentleman, who owned the wheeled cart, called a bun. Batya tried hers with yellow mustard and was instantly hooked.

Jakub took her to his favorite Jewish Deli one day for lunch and ordered a couple of their pastrami on rye sandwiches, with sour pickles on the side, that were delicious. On their way back to the hotel they stopped at an Italian bakery and purchased a dozen Cannoli to savor with coffee in the office the following day. Jakub knew all the best places, but of course he would, since he'd lived in the city for quite some time.

Never had she seen so many people in all her life. Some friendly, but most in a hurry and just plain rude. She was practically knocked over and trampled on numerous occasions on those busy New York sidewalks and would have been if not for her husband's strong arms and intuitive protection. These occasions reminded her of their first meeting.

Thoroughly agreeing with Jakub that she would always feel much more at home in the Loess Hills of Nebraska than in the big city, she also knew that this would be an experience to remember, walking arm in arm with her husband in this exciting place. These moments would be ones she would cherish for the rest of her life.

Highlighting their trip were nightly walks in a place called Central Park. She'd never seen anything quite like it. The park was beautiful, with tree lined paths, lovely benches where one might sit and take in the fresh air or lovely scenery for a while and an atmosphere unlike anywhere else in the world. Various food carts and vendors of all sorts abounded. Even a gated menagerie. This was filled with all sorts of animals from around the world. Some familiar and some exotic and strange, the likes of which she'd never known. Throughout their stay they presented to the world like a newly married couple, laughing together in the bustling city and then rushing back to the privacy of their hotel at night.

They spent their days taking care of business and Jakub was amazed at how quickly Batya took to the administrative angle of the transportation trade. She would be invaluable in their office at home and her quickly learned skills would make it more likely that a West coast office could open in a year or less.

When they arrived back home, they were exhausted but overflowing with many wonderful memories. The next year was packed with getting an office set up in California, flying back and forth and hiring a man who proved to be an honest and loyal employee, someone they could depend on, just like Don who headed up the East coast office.

Jakub was always sure to pay his men what they were worth, and that often made all the difference in the world regarding the reliability and loyalty of his employees.

The two made a fun trip out of their time in California as well. After flying in on their private plane, they rented a car and drove through Hollywood, even seeing a few houses which belonged to famous movie stars. This proved to be an exciting adventure, filled with oohs and ahs, laughs and thrilling moments, even though neither of them had ever seen a movie picture in their entire lives.

Batya had also never been to an honest to goodness beach and was amazed at the softness of the sand under her feet and the power of the foaming ocean waves pounding the shore near where she sat. Even commenting once to Jakub that the air was filled with the smell of salt and something else, she couldn't quite describe, a smell ancient and alive that stirred her blood and made her heart beat faster.

She made a striking picture in her newly purchased swimwear, and her husband couldn't take his eyes off her. They swam first, hopping in and out of the waves, chasing, laughing and playing, and then laid on the beach letting the warmth of the sun dry them. They collected shells of all kinds and sizes, even finding one with a tiny creature living inside.

Batya took that one and set it down near a small tide pool, watching as the creature extended his front legs and pulled himself along, shell and all.

They examined seaweed and tossed stranded star fish back into the safety of the ocean depths. After a full day they were exhausted and drove to an ocean side eatery where they both tried steamed crab for the first time and deemed it delicious, dipped in warm clarified butter.

Jakub loved having his beautiful wife as his constant companion at home and on business trips. They adored one another and rarely disagreed. As time marched on, Jakub found himself more in love with his beautiful bride than ever before. Having her back in his life was more than he could have ever hoped for. Now, knowing Jesus in a real way and worshipping together, with their extended church family in Springfield, made his life complete. He was a very happy man.

To top it all off, B, S & J was recently recognized as the most trusted nationwide provider of all transportation needs. They'd added a dozen new refrigerated trucks to their fleet. This proved to be a huge draw for many customers. Over the next year the couple found that when the country needed to ship cargo of any kind, they called B, S & J.

Throughout the past year Batya had been training to obtain her pilot's license, and just last week she had taken her first solo flight. Now they would be able to share the flight time back and forth to their East and West coast offices

"No Jeffrey, I really think we should wait until they come for church on Sunday. I called Mama and asked her if they could stay for supper. I don't think she suspected a thing. "

"I can hardly believe it myself. We've waited a long time for this. You will be a wonderful mother, Sarah. You are the kindest and most patient person I know."

"Thank you, Jeffrey. I've wanted to be a mother most of my life. I was raised by the very best. I also believe you will be the most wonderful father any child could ever hope for. I can't wait to tell them the good news."

"Then why are we waiting at all? It would be so easy to tell them over the telephone."

"We are waiting, because I want to see their faces when we share our news. I want to be able to hug them, and they will want to hug us too. Please, I don't want this to just be a voice on the other end of a telephone line. It is important to me, okay?"

"Okay, I understand. I just don't know how you can keep this secret for four whole days. That means you can't tell any of the ladies at Bible study tonight, or the news might accidently get back to your mom. She would be devastated if she found out anyone knew before her."

"I know. It will be hard, but it will be worth it in the end. Now, let me finish these dishes up so we can head over to the church."

"Yes Ma'am. I'll get things together and meet you in the car. I love you wife."

"I love you too husband. Now scoot. I'll be out shortly."

Driving to Bible study Sarah slipped her small hand into her husband's larger one and he turned and smiled at her. "Are you okay?"

"I'm fine. I was just thinking about my parents. You know, it surprised me how quickly Papa adjusted to Christianity. He was always such a strict Jew."

"Oh, I don't know. He told us he hadn't practiced his faith since being captured and imprisoned in Treblinka.

As a matter of fact, he hadn't gone to temple even once when he was living in New York. I think that, at first, he was converting just to please your mother, you know, coming to church and all. But no matter how it started, once he began to hear about the power of Grace and God's love through Jesus, he was hooked."

"I would have to agree. That was the very thing that persuaded me. Jesus' love is a powerful thing. The magnitude of it, the healing strength of it, was the one thing missing in my life. Living as a Jew and living without Jesus held no answers and no power and I just couldn't stop searching until I had those answers. Then, the more I read and discovered about His sacrifices for me and His constant and abiding affection, the more I adored Him. I'm just so glad our whole family has trusted Jesus as Savior and Lord."

"Yes, I agree that it is a great comfort to know we are all on the same page. And because of this, I know that our baby will be surrounded with God's love everywhere he looks. There is no greater gift we can give this child."

"Are you so sure our child is a son?"

"No, boy or girl, I will love our baby no matter what."

"Good, because I'm pretty sure the baby is a girl."

"How could you know?"

"Just woman's intuition I guess."

"I will love her immensely, just like I love her mother!"

"Good. Now we'd better get inside. I'm sure everyone is waiting."

"More woman's intuition?"

"No, just looking at my watch."

In a tragic turn of events, the first deaths of the 1947-1949 Palestine war occurred on November 30th, 1947. Ongoing tensions erupted into civil war following the November 29th adoption of the United Nations Partition Plan for Palestine, which intended to divide what the U.N. called Palestine into an Arab state, a Jewish state, and the Special International Regime encompassing the cities of Jerusalem and Bethlehem. Never mind that God Himself had given the land to the Jewish people, in a holy covenant, thousands of years before.

Consequently, on November 30th two busses carrying Jews were ambushed. During the attack, an eight-man Arab gang from Jaffa killed five passengers and wounded many others.

"Did you see the paper?"

"Yes, Jakub. I saw it. I guessed you'd left it there for me to read."

"I did. What did you think?"

"I thought it was terrible, but nothing new. We live in a world where Jews are killed every day."

"I know it's nothing new, Batya. But it seems the tensions in Palestine are rising again."

"Jakub, what are you thinking? I know that look in your eyes."

"I don't know, Batya. I have been reading a lot about transition going on at home. Israel has recently been working on becoming an independent state."

"Jakub, I don't know why you are referring to Israel as your home. I was born in Ukraine and you were born in Poland. Neither of us has ever been anywhere near Jerusalem."

"Batya, we are Christians, but we are also Jews. I know that something is going on in that region, which is endangering our fellow Jews. Because it is, I think I would like to be a part of it. Israel is our homeland. Simply because it was given to us, the Jewish people, as a gift from God. I feel a responsibility to protect her from those who would destroy her. I have never been able to help my people in any real way, and in this I may be able to help. Please just try to keep an open mind on the subject, meyn lib."

"I will try, Jakub. But only because this sounds so very important to you."

"You are my king, O God; ordain salvation for Jacob! Through You we push down our foes; through Your name we tread down those who rise up against us. For not in my bow do I trust, nor can my sword save me. But You have saved us from our foes and have put to shame those who hate us. In God we have boasted continually, and we will give thanks to Your name forever. Psalm 44:4–8

CHAPTER 26

"Hello? Yes, Don, hold on a moment. He's right here."

"Well, hi there, Don. How is married life treating you?"

"Great, Jacob."

"Is everything okay there at the office?"

"Yes, it is. However, I'm not calling about work. I'm contacting you concerning a different matter. I don't know how connected you are to the goings on in Tel Aviv, Jacob, but I have a number of contacts there and also here in New York. People who have been watching things closely since the United Nations Partition Plan for Palestinc was adopted in November."

"I've been seeing a few things in the newspaper, Don, but I have to admit I'm not really in the loop with most of the newest information."

"Well, I'll tell you. Jews were dancing in the streets of Tel Aviv over the idea of a two-state plan. But the surrounding Arab nations appear to be readying for war, they have flatly rejected partition. Are you familiar with David Ben-Gurion?"

"Yes, well, I don't know him personally, but he's the head of the Jewish agency for Israel, isn't he?"

"Yes, you're right. He is quite knowledgeable on all of the latest there in the Middle East, and also with the new U.N. plan. He is convinced that should he declare Israel the first independent Jewish state in two thousand years, the surrounding Arab armies would attack."

By this time Batya had sat down next to her husband and was listening in on the call. She saw the desperate look in her husband's eyes and nodded the approval she knew he longed for. But even as she did so, she felt her heart grow heavy and closed her eyes tight in anticipation of what sacrifice might be asked of the man she loved.

"We're both here, Don. What can we do to help?"

"I have been talking with Al Schwimmer."

"Is that someone I should know?"

"I don't think you do, but you soon shall. When he began telling me of his plan and his need you were the first person I thought of."

"Tell me, what does he know about what is going on in the Middle East?"

"He's been talking to Ben-Gurion. They are in agreement on the fact that proclaiming Israel as an independent state is going to set off the Arabs. He knows the Jews there will need to defend themselves. With all the Arab, Muslim nations who surround them focused on wiping Israel off the face of the map; a war, without a doubt, would effectually destroy the nation. This attack by their enemies would, for all intents and purposes, be nothing short of a second Holocaust; wiping out an additional six hundred thousand Jews on top of the over six million already murdered by the Nazis. With thousands of traumatized refugees returning to their homeland from all over Europe, little money in the country's coffers with which to buy arms, and very few soldiers with any combat experience, any attempt at self defense seems an almost impossible task at this point."

"Well, what kind of background does Schwimmer have? What does he intend to do? I guess I'm not sure how I can help?"

"Schwimmer began his aerospace career at Lockheed Corporation as an engineer and received his civilian pilot's license about that same time. During World War II, he worked for TWA and assisted the U.S. Air Transport Command as a flight engineer. He plans to use his skills and contacts from the war to buy up used American warplanes. In effect he wants to build a modern army, complete with an air force superior to that of the Egyptians, if you can believe it. This isn't going to be easy. He will need plenty of financial backing and he also needs pilots. Part of my job is to call around to see if there are those who can help with dollars, but also those who are willing to put their lives on the line for a worthy cause." Batya looked into her husband's eyes and saw the urgency and desire there. So, with tears in her own eyes, she nodded again. He grabbed her and squeezed tight.

"Anything he needs, Don. Let him know he can call me directly. I will help with the finances. But I will also fly. Tell him he can count on me."

"With your permission, Boss. I will also be volunteering for service. You're going to need a gunner after all."

"Is your wife okay with that, Don? You haven't been married long and this is going to be dangerous."

"If you're asking me if she is happy about it, Jacob? No, she is not. But, just like Batya understands, she does too. I have more calls to make, but someone will be getting in contact with you very soon."

"Wait a minute, Don. Batya wants to say something."

"Go ahead, Batya. What's on your mind?"

"I just wanted to say that the business isn't going to run itself while you men are gone. So, while you fellows are building your army, I will be flying out to New York and training the women to maintain the offices there. I can handle things on this end, and I will check to see if we will still have our man in California. We can handle things just fine until all of you return."

"Great idea. That has been my biggest concern going into this whole affair. I'll put Hanna in touch with you right away."

"Good, the sooner we get things straightened out, the smoother they will run when you boys leave." Batya's world was turning upside down again, and there wasn't much she could do about it except to create a role for herself in the center of the fray.

Once the fellowship hall cleared out Sarah and Jeffrey approached Jacob and Batya. "We have news for you."

"We have news for you too."

"Please let us go first. We've been waiting for days to tell you."

"Then go right ahead. I'm sure your news is better

than ours anyway."

"What do you mean?"

"Never mind, Sarah. Go ahead. What is your news?"

"Mama, Papa, we are expecting." The room erupted in tearful congratulations and then plenty of hugs all around.

"Do you know when you're due?"

"From what the doctor could tell, my due date will be around the 15th of May."

"Then we will hope things can be wrapped up by that time."

"What things Mama?"

"I should be the one to tell her, Batya." For the next half hour Jakub did his best to explain the situation to his daughter. Sarah had all she could manage not to cry. She didn't want to make her papa feel badly about his decision. After all, what he was attempting to do was an honorable thing. But she didn't want to lose him again either, especially with his first grandchild on the way, and she knew her mama's heart was breaking. All she had to do was look into her face to see the pain there. Noticing that all the while that Papa was going on and on about what he would be taking on, and the call to action he was answering, she could see the dread in her mother's eyes.

For the next months Jacob was in and out of the house, concerned with the intricate puzzle of putting together a war machine for the Jewish nation. He worked remotely with Al Schwimmer and Don, locating and buying up dozens of rickety, surplus American warplanes; and scouring public records around the country to contact pilots with Jewish sounding names who might be willing to put their necks on the line for the sake of a new state of Israel. Although most American Jews were not Zionists, one by one those pilots signed on. Many were forced to convince their spouses, or in some cases, their mothers, why they should fly halfway around the world to fight in another war so close on the heels of WWII.

Some of those men, like George Lichter, a former U.S. Army Air Forces pilot who grew up in Newark, New Jersey remembered when he was a kid, "I didn't like being a Jew". He said that what changed his mind, and made him want to join the Zionist cause, was remembering what Hitler did to the Jews of Europe. He knew he was risking his citizenship, and possibly even jail time to assist in this crusade, but he'd decided he was going to help his fellow Jews no matter what.

A Marine, who fought in the Pacific Theater, Lou Lenart combated the anti-Semitism he'd faced as a kid by sending away for Charles Atlas's muscle-building books. He commented that, "By the time I was 15 years old, nobody was beating me up." It didn't take much persuasion for him to volunteer his talents to fly for Israel.

There were many dozens of other brave Americans that answered the call to fight alongside their Israeli brothers and sisters for a free and independent Israel.

Ben-Gurion entrusted Yigael Yadin, an Israeli archeologist, soldier and politician, with the responsibility of coming up with a plan of offense whose timing was directly related to the foreseeable evacuation of British forces. Yadin would later become the second Chief of Staff of the Israel Defense Forces and then, from 1977 - 1981, Israel's Deputy Prime Minister.

Batya took her new position very seriously. Their California office remain staffed by a man she trusted and his newly hired assistant. A pair that she and Jakub had personally vetted and trained when they opened the branch. So, she concentrated on equipping Don's wife, Hanna along with a new recruit, Matilda, to maintain efficiency in the New York offices. She also hired a secretary for her own office in Nebraska, to take calls and ensure communication when she was traveling back and forth to New York or California.

Batya would fly herself between the various offices to keep things running smoothly. She hired several new drivers, as Samuel and Herman had signed up to fight for the Zionist cause alongside Jakub and Don.

Remaining as busy as possible, so as not to spend her time moping about and missing her husband, Batya found she was at her best when tasked with numerous responsibilities. And of course, she prayed. A lot. She prayed for Jakub and for all the men involved with the creation of this new army to defend the future Israel. But she also prayed for Sarah, who was deeply worried about her father. Fearful that he would lose his life and never meet his first grandchild, the situation was causing her a great deal of stress. Batya knew that stress is not good for pregnancy.

While Jakub was off, building an army with his new comrads, Batya continued attending church in Springfield and keeping an eye on their daughter's condition. Doing the bulk of her flying and office training during the week, and making her way back home on Friday evenings, she managed an exhausting but doable schedule.

Sarah's belly grew and she radiated with a glowing aura that only a new mother to be can produce.

In the little spare time she had, Batya spent time on weekends sewing articles of clothing for her future grand baby. Missing her husband even more than she thought possible, she tried to fill her time with snippets of joyful productivity. For now, she was working on pieces in white, yellow and green, not knowing the gender of the child. But after Sarah confided in her that she was sure the baby would be a girl, she'd recently begun creating a few special articles in pink, encompassed with as much lace and as many frills as she could squeeze on to the tiny items.

Sarah and Jeffrey had chosen to name the baby, if it was a girl, Zissa; which translates, sweet one. Batya loved the name. Jeff painted the spare room yellow, with a light blue ceiling covered in fluffy clouds, and Sarah used her unique talent to add murals to the walls, complete with rainbows, trees and assorted animals. It was magical and fun, and they were sure the child would be fascinated by all the colors. Sarah's time was growing nearer.

Jacob made a quick trip home, knowing he would be leaving soon for battles yet to come. The family ate together. He hugged his daughter and patted her belly. "Papa. please be careful. I want, more than anything in the world, for your granddaughter to meet her Saba."

"I will do my very best zeiskeit. I promise you that I will be careful and mindful of all my loved ones back at home."

"And we will keep you in our prayers, Papa. We will also be in prayer for the coming new nation of Israel."

"Thank you, daughter. I love you. The three happiest times of my life were the moment your mother consent-ed to be my wife, the day you were born, and the day we were all brought together again. I am looking forward to holding your little one in my arms and nothing will keep me from that."

"Good. I will hold you to your promises. I love you

too, Papa."

After final hugs all around, Jakub and Batya headed for home. They didn't sleep, but spent the night making love. Then into the wee hours of the morning they held each other and talked quietly about joys of the past and hopes for the future.

"I know this is something you must do, Jakub. But you must also promise to come home to me. We have so much yet to do."

"I will do my best, meyn lib. You know that in your arms is where I would spend my every living and waking moment if I truly had a choice."

"I know, meyn lib. I will keep you in prayer always. Do what you must do and stay safe. I will keep things running here."

"Thank you Batya. I know I can count on you. I promise I will do everything in my power to come home to you as quickly as I am able."

Jakub held his wife in his arms for one last long moment, kissed her hard, and went on to meet his destiny.

Once Schwimmer had bought up as many junk warplanes as he could acquire quickly, with Jacob's financial assistance and the help of Don's organizational skills, his next mission would be transporting the shaky fleet from the U.S. to Tel Aviv. There was no direct route and doing so would also have required defying a strict American arms embargo to the region. It was suddenly necessary to get creative.

Those brave volunteer pilots helmed the rickety retro-fitted planes from the U.S. to Panama, on to Brazil, over to Casablanca and finally to Rome, paying off anyone who threatened to stand in their way. From Rome the rag tag crew flew on to Czechoslovakia where they had been promised a place to train and some desperately needed arms by the sympathetic Czechs.

By April 1948, the Haganah had managed to accumulate only about 20,000 rifles and Sten guns for the 35,000 soldiers who existed on paper. France had authorized Air France to transport cargo to Tel Aviv on 13 May.

On May 14th, 1948 David Ben-Gurion declared the establishment of a Jewish state in Eretz-Israel known as the State of Israel, a few hours before the official termination of the British Mandate. He then became Israel's first premier.

Later, on May 14 Syria invaded Palestine with the 1st Infantry Brigade supported by a battalion of armored cars, a company of French R 35 and R 37 tanks, an artillery battalion and other units. The Syrian president, Shukri al-Quwwatli flatly told his troops on the front, "to destroy the Zionists".

"The situation is very grave. There aren't enough rifles. There are no heavy weapons," Ben-Gurion told the Israeli Cabinet.

On 15 May, the Syrian forces turned to the eastern and southern Sea of Galilee shores and attacked Samakh the neighboring Tegart fort and the settlements of Sha'ar HaGolan, Ein Gev, but they were bogged down by resistance. Later, they attacked Samakh using tanks and aircraft, then they succeeded in conquering Samakh and occupied the abandoned Sha'ar HaGolan.

When the combined forces of Egypt, Syria, the Arab League, Lebanon, the Emirate of Transjordan, Iraq, Yemen, Jordan, the Arab Liberation Army commanded by Kauksi, and Saudi Arabia attacked, those volunteer pilots from America were still in Czechoslovakia learning to fly their makeshift planes. With the Egyptians, a force of more than ten thousand, swiftly advancing past Gaza and toward Tel Aviv, they had no time to prepare.

Very simply, the news they'd been waiting for was the catalyst that spurred them on to action. The fledgling Israeli Air Force's first official flight would necessarily also be their very first combat mission. Jacob and Don manned their craft and headed off to war.

"When I shut up the heavens so that there is no rain, or command the locust to devour the land, or send pestilence among My people, if My people who are called by My Name humble themselves, and pray and seek My face and turn from their wicked ways, then I will hear from heaven and will forgive their sin and heal their land." 2 Chronicles: 13–14

CHAPTER 27

In the distant hills the rumble of big guns could be heard and the earth pulsed and shook. Fighting had broken out between Jews and Arabs almost immediately following the British army withdrawal from the region earlier that day. Egypt had, predictably, launched an air assault against Israel that evening. However, even throughout a blackout in Tel Aviv and the fully expected Arab invasion, Jews celebrated the birth of their new nation with great joy. Especially after they received word that the United States of America had officially recognized the new Jewish state.

At the exact same time the state of Israel was fighting for her very right to exist, Sarah was laboring intensely to give birth to her daughter. The midwife who was present didn't seem overly concerned, but Sarah was becoming more exhausted by the minute and after many painful but unproductive hours it seemed no child was forthcoming.

Batya arrived home from New York late in the evening and was immediately concerned. When she saw the paleness of her daughter's face, and remembered her own difficult labor so long ago, she guessed there might be underlying problems and shooed the incompetent midwife from the room. Sarah's strength was completely spent, and still the child struggled within her to be born.

Batya took a cloth, dipped it in cool water and stroked Sarah's forehead, asking her what she might do to ease her plight. Sarah's answer frightened her. "Just let me die, Mama. I can't push anymore. Please just let me die."

"Meyn lib, please don't say such things. Mama is here now, and we will figure this out."

Sarah's labor had begun well before dawn that day, yet it was late in the evening before Jeffrey got concerned. He had no idea what was a right or wrong amount of time for a woman to labor and give birth. However, when he saw the concern on his mother in law's face his demeanor changed. Now he was gravely concerned and wanted to know what he should do. At Batya's urging he put a call in to Springfield's doctor. The same doctor who'd delivered him so many years ago. When Doc arrived, he looked Sarah over thoroughly, adopted a serious manner, and called for lots of boiling water and plenty of clean towels.

The Shepherd's Infant daughter was born, by caesarian section, at one minute after midnight on Saturday, May 15th, 1948. Zissa was beautiful, a vision, much like her mother and grandmother before her.

It seemed almost as if the baby knew her grandmother would be back in Nebraska for the weekend, and couldn't wait to meet her; or at least that was the story Batya told everyone, doctors, nurses and church members, with whom she came in contact. The fact that the baby had chosen to come into the world over the weekend, versus during the work week when her Bubbe would be flying out to New York or California, was a miracle in itself.

With a full head of curly blond hair and eyes blue as newly laid robin's eggs, she was the spitting image of Batya as a newborn infant.

At only five pounds she was a tiny thing, but already had the powerful lungs of an opera singer. Her daddy was the first to hold her, confused and unsure of himself, but she fussed, so he reluctantly yet somewhat eagerly handed her off. He would try again later.

When he kissed Zissa's soft curls and passed her to

her grandmother, placing the small squirming bundle into Batya's waiting arms, her scrunched up little face relaxed and her tightly closed eyes opened, focusing immediately on her Bubbe's perfectly matching ones. Those beautiful eyes were a carbon copy of her own and she stared intently for a moment. Her perfect, pink, pouting lips curled into a smile and she was immediately calmed, drifting off to sleep. The bond between grandmother and granddaughter was instantaneous and would go on to last a lifetime.

On the 29th of May 1948, Lenart, retired American Marine and newly initiated IDF pilot, led four junk Messerschmitts toward Egyptian lines. At that time, they represented the Israeli Air Force in its entirety. Captain Novak positioned off his left wing, with one aircraft directly behind and two others off Lenart's right, all in tight formation.

When they reached their destination Lenart said a prayer and they all dive-bombed and strafed the enemy's tanks, trucks and munitions. The bold attack by Lenart and his volunteer crew stopped the enemy attack in its tracks and likely saved the newborn country from ear-ly defeat.

Batya's time had been well spent with Hanna. She was a quick learner. In spite of their age difference, they became fast friends.

Hanna was with child. She'd thought there might be a possibility before Don left for battle but didn't want to say anything until she was sure. That surety came too late. So, here they were in a less than ideal situation.

Due to the new revelation Batya also trained extra help to be there when Hanna took time to have her baby. Thankfully the job would be one in which Hanna could bring her little one to the office once they'd received a doctor's release.

Batya found herself to be the only person Hanna could really depend on through this ordeal. With no family around, Don had been her rock and only friend before meeting Batya. Her due date was approximately six weeks beyond Sarah's delivery, which meant she could be there to help Sarah get back on her feet and then be available for the young Hanna, who would find herself alone while her husband fought the Muslim hordes. Batya was grateful for the added distractions, as she was usually most productive during times of urgency.

The ladies all longed to hear something from their men. But those men were halfway around the world and enduring who knows what. All they could do was pray for the safety of their husbands and fathers and they were already doing plenty of that.

In absolute heaven caring for her tiny granddaughter, Batya was up before dawn each morning and then retrieved the little one for mama several times during the nighttime hours, all so that Sarah could rest and regain her strength. After the baby ate Bubbe would burp her and rock her to sleep. Jeff was gaining more confidence in his role as daddy and Batya would have no qualms about leaving when the time came.

She loved the feel and the scent of the infant in her arms, reluctantly putting her back in her crib, so as not to spoil her overly much. Then, she'd wait on pins and needles for the tiniest sound, as an excuse to snatch her up again."Mother, you really must get some sleep. Jeffrey and I can handle things while you go home and rest for awhile."

"Oh Sarah, don't make me leave. The house is so lonely without your Papa and I don't want to miss a single minute of Zissa's life. They grow so quickly and learn so fast."

"Then at least go into your room and lay down for a while."

"I'm not tired, truly, Sarah. But perhaps I am being selfish. I should let you and Jeff have some time with the baby. I can go out to the kitchen and start supper."

"Fine Mama. As you will. Jeffrey has gotten so much better with her and I want him to hold her as much as possible while she's tiny, so that she'll get used to being around her Papa."

"I agree. That is a good thing. You were always very close to your Papa. It's good for little girls to know their Papa's love for them. I believe it makes for better interactions later on, don't you?"

"Yes, I do. I also believe it helps us to relate to God's love more, when we have a loving relationship with our earthly fathers. So, needless to say, this is very important to us. I do want to thank you for being here for us. I couldn't have done any of this without you. But I'm getting better every day and at some point, I'm going to be taking care of all this by myself. I will need to learn these things. All of them. I do love you Mama."

"I know you do, Sarah. I love you more than you could ever know. I'm sorry if I've overstayed my welcome."

"Don't be silly, Mama. And I do know."

"You do know what?"

"You said that you love me more than I could ever know. I might have agreed with you before I gave birth. However, now that I have Zissa in my life I have grown new love in ways and places I never thought possible. Every day I love her more, deeper and stronger if you will. Sometimes I love her so much I feel that my heart could burst right out of my chest. I never thought I could love anyone as much as I love Jeffrey, or you and Papa. But I wake up each morning and I love her even more."

"I know exactly how you feel my darling. Being a mother is a miraculous thing. I'm sure God created it so for a reason."

"I wonder what that reason might be, Mama? To love someone so much that it hurts."

"Well, for starters, it helps new mothers remain patient when baby wakes you in the night and you're more exhausted than you ever thought it possible to be. It also helps when children get a bit older and talk back or do as they please without permission. Remembering that early love keeps you from being too harsh I suppose."

"I didn't do that, did I? I mean talking back and doing as I pleased."

"No, you were actually a very well-behaved child. The world began to unravel when you were a teenager, if you will remember, so we were never really faced with much disrespect from you during those years either."

"I did go against Papa's beliefs while we were interred in the Ghetto. I spent a great deal of time with my Christian friends. I knew he would not approve, but I didn't reveal my secrets to either of you and I did it anyway."

"Since we all know how that turned out, I believe we will forgive you for that one, meyn lib. Without Christ, I don't believe any of us would have survived all the things this world has thrown at us in the past few years. I wouldn't worry about your daughter either. She has wonderful, godly parents and grandparents who love the Lord too. She will be fine. Now, I'm going to start supper. There are some nice chops in the refrigerator. I thought I would whip up some mashed potatoes and a nice salad of tasty things from the garden. I made a chocolate cake this morning and my bread will have risen nicely by now as well."

"Oh Mama, we will be so spoiled by the time you leave to go and help Hanna, I won't know what to do."

"I'm just glad I can lend a hand. Take the help while you can get it. After Hanna delivers, I will be gone for a few weeks. Though, I will try to make it home on weekends, if I can find help for her when I'm not expected to be there. I will miss you all terribly while I'm gone. I can only hope Zissa doesn't grow too quickly during my absence. I really don't want to miss a thing."

"We will miss you too, Mama. I haven't wanted to bring this up, because I know it always makes you sad, but I need to ask. Do you think Papa is okay?"

"There is no way to know, Sarah. We have no address with which to send letters, so it wouldn't do any good to write. Do you remember when we were separated from your father after our stay in the Ghetto?"

"Yes. You always told me that you would know in your soul if anything ever happened to Papa, because the two of you were connected at the heart."

"Yes, and I still feel that way. I remember after we

came to America I began to feel that perhaps he was gone, that maybe my feelings were wrong and I was living on false hope, even though I knew deep in my heart we were still connected. Later, I felt so badly that I had given up on him toward the end of that journey. When he showed up in church on the day of your wedding, I knew for sure that God was answering our prayers and I vowed to myself that I would never give up so easily again. I still feel him in my heart, Sarah, so I will not give up hope. You know, we can only pray and I do that a thousand times a day "

"I pray as well, Mama. I suppose we just have to believe the Lord will bring him through and back home to us."

"Exactly. He promised me that he would do his best to make it home, so I will count on his being a man of his word. We know that God is still on the throne. I will choose to depend on His mercy and His mercy alone."

Not so oddly, B, S & J was thriving as never before. The nation had opened up enormously to the idea of shipping items via truck, versus slower and less versatile rail services. Trucks could typically get into many areas where there was no easy access to standard rail stations; and the results were usually a speedier delivery time anywhere in the country. Adding to that positive narrative, it was helpful that the guys working for B, S & J were all hard workers and respected their bosses. Batya wouldn't allow for slackers and they were all aware she ruled with an iron fist in her husband's absence. She was a tougher boss by far than Jakub and the men knew it for a fact. But she was fair and rewarded ambition too.

Even with Jakub gone, Batya continued the company's long-standing tradition of paying the men their normal wages for a regular week's work and then supplementing that pay by providing additional bonuses for prompt and accurate deliveries. Most of the men made it a habit of cashing in on those lucrative bonuses each week, showing their owners that they were real go getters with plenty of drive.

With more supermarkets and departments stores beginning to dot the landscape, shelves would most likely have been empty without truckers filling in the gaps, and B,S & J had come on the scene at the best possible time in history to take advantage of the surge in retail sales.

Batya excelled at her job, but she also enjoyed her time with her family. Jeff's church had grown by leaps and bounds since his return home from WWll, and they were considering constructing a new church building to accommodate the larger congregation. Jeff had continued to grow food to feed the hungry in his region and had become a household name among the farmers in three states. People knew where to go if they needed help of any kind. And Sarah quickly became well loved by all.

Now the LORD *said to Abram, "Go from your country and your kindred and your father's house to the land that I will show you. And I will make of you a great nation, and I will bless you and make your name great, so that you will be a blessing. I will bless those who bless you, and him who dishonors you I will curse, and in you all the families of the earth shall be blessed." Genesis 12:1–3*

CHAPTER 28

Sources would disagree for decades about the number of arms at the Yishuv's disposal during the end of the British Mandate. According to some speculation, before the arrival of arms shipments from Czechoslovakia, there was roughly one weapon for every three fighters and even the Palmach could arm only two of every three of its active members.

Yishuv forces were well organized in 9 brigades, and their numbers grew following Israeli independence, eventually expanding to 12 brigades. Although both sides, Israeli and Arab, increased their manpower over the first few months of the war; Israeli forces grew more steadily as a result of the progressive mobilization of Israeli society and the influx of an average of 10,300 immigrants from around Europe each month. By the end of the war, the IDF had 88,033 troops, including 60,000 combat soldiers.

After the Arab invasion France allowed aircraft carrying arms from Czechoslovakia to land on French territory while in transit to Israel, and permitted two arms shipments to 'Nicaragua', which were actually ultimately intended for Israel.

Czechoslovakia also supplied vast quantities of arms to Israel during the war, including thousands of VZ 24 rifles and MG 34 and ZB 37 machine guns, millions of rounds of ammunition, and fighter aircraft, including ten Avia S-199 fighter planes.

The Haganah readied twelve cargo ships throughout various European ports to transfer the accumulated equipment, which had set sail as soon as the British blockade was lifted with the expiration of the Mandate.

Following Israeli independence, the Israelis managed to build three Sherman tanks from scrap-heap material found in abandoned British ordnance depots. These became the first three tanks of the new Israeli 8th Armored Brigade.

On Sunday evening, June 27th, Batya flew into New York city and took a car to her hotel. She was bone weary. The past five weeks taking care of baby Zissa were an experience she wouldn't have traded for anything in the world, except perhaps for the dream of having her husband home safe and sound. However, as much as she hated to admit it and as much as she missed her sweet Zissa right at this very minute, she wasn't as young as she used to be and probably wouldn't have survived another week of being up all night with the little dear without stealing away for some time to rest.

Checking into her reserved hotel suite, she requested a car for her morning commute and ordered room service. A big bowl of chicken and dumplings would hit the spot. The dumplings weren't quite as good as her own homemade ones, but she'd had them here before and they'd do in a pinch. If she closed her eyes she could almost smell and taste the ones from her own kitchen back home. Light and fluffy pillows of perfectly puffed dough, floating in just the right amount of chicken soup base with bits of tender chicken throughout, and broth just warm enough to comfort a weary traveler right through to the core.

Strange dreams woke her intermittently through the night, and a feeling of uneasiness haunted her sleep. She knew it was imperative that she pray. She just wasn't sure what she was praying for and assumed it was for the safety of Jakub. So, she dutifully asked for God's faithful intervention into the safety of the boys overseas.

Monday morning arrived too quickly, and Batya still felt weighted down with a strange sense of foreboding. She showered and dressed, then grabbed her briefcase and dashed to the elevator. Hoping she wasn't too late to catch her car to work, she dashed through the hotel lobby, almost hurtling headlong into the plate glass entry.

Thankfully the car was still waiting, so she directed the driver to the quaint little Italian bakery where Jakub had treated her to Cannoli on her first trip to New York. She needed something to lift her burdened spirits. Grabbing a dozen of the delectable treats, because she was sure Hanna would want to share, and two cups of coffee, she was off.

Eager to see her friend; having only briefly spoken with her while she cared for Zissa; she couldn't wait to catch up on what would have transpired over the past five weeks in her absence.

The feelings of anxiousness that plagued her sleep still danced around in the back of her mind, and she suddenly felt a little guilty for making a stop on the way, so she asked the driver to please drive faster.

When she arrived at her office building, she paid the

driver, grabbed her briefcase, as well as the bag of Cannoli and both coffees, expertly balancing everything as she made her way gingerly to the front door. Inching the door open and then using her foot to make the opening wide enough to squeeze through with all her paraphernalia she called out, "Hey, Hanna, it's me. You want to come grab your coffee before I spill it? I'm surprised it's lasted this long."

She heard a moan from somewhere in the back and called out again, "Hanna, is that you?"

"Batya, help me. My baby. Oh my God. Help me."

She dropped everything and then gave a yelp as steaming hot coffees crashed on the floor, burst open and splashed her legs.

It all happened so fast. There was blood. So much blood. Calling the police, who promised to dispatch an ambulance immediately, she directed her attention to Hanna. Today was actually the young woman's presumed due date, so the baby was not premature by any means. Her pregnancy had progressed beautifully, without a single problem. Nevertheless, the amount of blood she saw on the floor surrounding her friend was shocking, and she couldn't speculate on what might be the cause of so much bleeding in a perfectly healthy pregnancy.

Batya knew she wasn't a doctor herself, so she didn't want to make assumptions, but she attempted in any way she could to be a comfort. Folding her own sweater and positioning it under Hanna's head, and then stroking her arm. "Are you having contractions, Hanna?"

"Yes, and they're very close together. It happened all of a sudden. One minute I was standing and the next I was on the floor. My water broke. It felt like I was being punched, Batya, and then I think something inside of me tore. Is that possible? I can still feel the baby moving, I think, and I know I need to push, but I have no strength left. I feel as though it has all drained away." Hanna shifted and moaned, long and loud, gritting her teeth through the pain. "Please call Don's parents. They live here in the city. Their number is written in the address book that's in the zipper pouch of my bag. Promise me Batya, if something happens to me, that you will please tell Don that I love him."

"Hanna, don't talk like that. We're going to do everything we can to get through this together. Do you hear me? I've given birth before my friend, but I have never delivered a baby, so I will do my best."

"Well, this is my first time too. I'm afraid, so afraid, Batya. What should I do? Oh Lord Jesus, it hurts so bad." Moaning again, until the moan became a scream, she thrashed about in the pool of blood surrounding her.

"Just do what comes naturally, Hanna. I will help in any way that I can. Just tell me what you need."

"Hold my hand. I just want you to hold my hand. Oh Lord please save my baby."

"Yes, I'll hold your hand, but I'm also going to pray for you and your baby. Father God, help us. We need You Lord. Reach down to Your servant Hanna and deliver her. Save her Lord and save her tiny baby. Thank you, Father. In Jesus' Name and for Your glory. Amen."

For the next thirty minutes, the ridiculous amount of time it took for an ambulance to arrive, Batya held her friend's hand. Contractions were coming quickly, but the baby wasn't. With each contraction she watched as more blood gushed from between Hanna's legs, enlarging the gory puddle surrounding the young woman on the floor. At the same time she saw her friend's face grow more pale and grey as her eyes grew dim. Batya's own eyes filled with tears, but she wouldn't let Hanna see her cry. No, instead, she gazed directly into her friend's face and made promises she couldn't possibly hope to keep.

When the ambulance finally arrived, the attendants looked astounded by the amount of blood on the floor. They were in contact with the hospital, and followed directions: checking heart rate, pulse and oxygen levels, hanging a bag of saline solution and covering Hanna's face with an oxygen mask. By this time, she seemed to be barely conscious, though Batya thought she could still see movement in her belly. One of the young men looked at Batya and shook his head. Tears began to slide down her cheeks and she started to rise, slipping in the blood on the floor around her and stopping to cry out to God for just a moment. The sticky mess covered her skirt, legs, arms and hands.

She called a car and tried to clean herself up a bit before its arrival. Locking the office door, she made her way to the waiting car and directed the driver to the emergency center.

In the waiting room of the hospital she made the calls needed to keep the office running. After all, she had guys out on the road who would need instructions for pickup and delivery. She felt tremendously sad but wasn't panicking. That wasn't her style. There would be time for more raw emotion later when the emergency was done.

Glad she'd trained assistants who could pick up where Hanna left off, she called them now. Matilda would necessarily need to come to the hospital to get a key, but she had the knowledge and wherewithal to carry on sufficiently from there.

Then she called Mr. and Mrs. Maassen. They should know what was going on with their daughter in law, especially with Don away in Israel. Mr. Maassen seemed a little cool in his attitude toward news of Hanna, but Batya had no time to wonder about family dynamics at the moment. She asked them to come to the hospital to meet her.

Batya realized the amount of blood on her office floor would be a problem, so she also called a cleaning outfit to take care of the issue, and then called Matilda to warn her of the mess she would encounter when she arrived. She found it strangely comforting to realize that even in moments of extreme duress she could count on herself to remain level-headed and to meet things where they were. Even more comforting was to remember that God was still on the throne and that none of this was a surprise to Him. She knew that He was good, and that all would work out exactly the way it should.

The Haganah managed to obtain large stocks of British weapons due to the logistical complexity of the British withdrawal; and the egregious corruption of a number of local government officials; including the acquisition of a Cromwell tank.

June 29th, 1948, on the day before the last British troops left Haifa. Two British soldiers sympathetic to the Israeli cause broke in and stole two more Cromwell tanks from an arms depot in the Haifa port area, smashing them through unguarded gates and joining up with the IDF. These two tanks and others recently acquired, would form the basis of the new Israeli Armored Corps.

"Mrs. Maassen?"

"No, no, I'm Batya Novak."

"So, you're not Hanna's relative? Then I believe she must have been speaking in delirium. She was telling me she needed to call Don's mother. I thought perhaps, since the police told me you were the one that found her, that maybe you were her mother in law.”

“No, I’m her employer and her friend. I gathered, from things she’d said, that I was her only friend in the city. However, I found out just today that her husband’s parents live less than a half hour away. I’ve already called them, and they are on their way. I’m the one who found Hanna on the floor of our office and called the police. How is she? Please tell me she’s okay. And her baby. How is her baby?’

“Mrs. Novak, we weren’t able to save your friend. The placenta had torn away from the uterus, causing her to hemorrhage, and her blood loss before arriving at the hospital was simply too great. I’m terribly sorry for your loss. We did everything we could to save her. Beyond that I can’t give you any additional information without further permission from her family. Please forgive me.”

“No, no, I understand your situation. I can’t believe it. I just can’t believe it. I can’t even get in contact with her husband, since he is out of the country. She said she was fine when she came to work, and then simply collapsed. How does that happen?”

“Ma’am, I’m afraid I don’t have those answers for you. It is tragic, but women have been dying in childbirth since the beginning of time."

Batya thought that was a rather unfeeling sort of comment for a medical professional to make and began to stew on it, until she saw an older couple come through the emergency room doors.

One look told her they simply had to be Don's parents. It couldn't be anyone else. The man looked exactly like an older version of her dear office manager. She rose and quickly approached them. The woman was alternately wringing her hands and using a flowered handkerchief to dab at perspiration glistening on her rather ample face and neck. The man stopped dead in his tracks and glared at her, as if daring her to come closer.

He wore a superior look on his face and his yarmulke sat at a jaunty angle on the back of his head. This might explain his standoffish attitude toward his daughter in law when Batya spoke to him earlier.

Just like the Pharisees of Old Testament scripture he wore his Judaism like a badge on the outside instead of as a humble condition of the heart. She'd known other Jews like that in her lifetime. People who gave large sums to the temple, openly, for others to see and looked down their noses at others, considering themselves somehow better than their fellow Jews and certainly always better than non-Jews.

The Maassen's son, Donald, had converted to Christianity within the past couple of years, and it might be reasonable to assume that these folks believed Hannah was wholly to blame for the conversion. When, in fact, Don was the first to turn to Christ, even before he married his lovely bride. From there it was a decision they'd made as a couple very much together and quite energetically too, to concentrate on learning more of the Lord and going to church together.

"Hello, Mr. and Mrs. Maassen. My name is Batya Novak. My husband and I own B, S & J Transportation. I am your son's employer."

"You mean your husband is Donald's employer?"

"Actually, my husband and I are co-owners of the business. But while the men are gone in Israel, I am running all three offices and quite well I might add." She felt a little silly being drawn into his pettiness with that last remark. "Hanna was working for me while Don was busy fighting for the Zionist cause. We will call for the doctors immediately, so that they might fill you in, but I am sorry to say they have already informed me they were not able to save Hanna."

"What could have happened? All you said on the phone was that you found her in the office and that she was bleeding. How did she hurt herself?"

"Iryna, stop. You are babbling. I will handle this." Batya could tell already that she really, really didn't like this arrogant, demeaning man who was talking down to his wife right in front of her.

"Actually, from what I was told, her placenta had ripped away from the wall of her uterus and there was too much blood loss. They were unable to save her once she was brought into the emergency room."

"Placenta? Uterus? What are you talking about? She was pregnant?"

"Iryna, I told you to stop babbling. So, you are saying she was pregnant with our son's child, and no one told us? Why wouldn't Don have said something? We are his parents."

"She didn't find out until the men were already gone. By then we were unable to reach them. She told me she didn't have family in the area. I'm guessing, from your attitude here, that you made it almost impossible for her to reach out to you. How would she have shared the news

I wonder?"

"You don't understand the pain she put us through."

"The pain she put you through? You're right. I don't understand."

"The pain she caused when she forced our son to convert to Christianity."

"Actually, Mr. Maassen, Don was the first to convert. He is the one who convinced Hanna to become a Messianic Jew after they wed. He wanted them to be able to go to church as a family."

"That isn't true. You are lying."

"No, Sir. I have been Don's friend for years. Even before he married Hanna. I guess I was surprised he had parents in the area. Until Hanna told me that your phone number was in her purse, I didn't know you existed. I don't remember meeting you at their wedding."

"We were not in favor of the girl. We told him that if he continued down this path and married her without our blessing, we would not be present at the wedding."

"I see, so you were judging her even then?"

"You don't understand the position we are in. There are things expected from us in our community. Certain people we associate with and those that we don't."

"Oh, I get it now. You think yourselves superior to someone like Hanna. Well, I have news for you. This young woman, the one that you frown upon and look down on, was one of the finest young women I've ever known. She loved the Lord, was a darned hard worker, a great friend and an excellent and loving wife to your son. She also would have been a wonderful mother. It's too bad you didn't bother to get to know her better. You really missed out."

"You don't understand our Jewish culture."

"Actually, I know all about your Jewish culture. I grew up in Jewish culture, always searching for the Truth. But, I didn't find it there. My husband and I are Messianic Jews, just like your son and his wife. It just so happens that your son Don is very proud of his Jewish heritage. It also happens that he has discovered the Truth and now believes in Jesus, the Savior of the world. Once he became convinced of the divinity of the Messiah, he asked Hannah to go to church with him. They were both saved before she died. You see, Jesus died and overcame sin for all of us, even you Mr. Maassen."

"I had no idea."

"No Sir, I'm sure you didn't."

"So, what about the baby? Do you know anything more about the baby?"

"No ma'am. They wouldn't give me more information, because I'm not a family member. Let's find the doctor. I'm sure he can tell us more."

"We'll be just fine young lady. They were right, you aren't family. We'll handle it from here."

"Yes Sir. You're right. I'm not family. But, I'm the only friend your daughter in law had throughout her pregnancy, even though you folks lived right here in the same city. That is a very sad statement indeed. My numbers are on this card. If you need anything, anything at all, please don't hesitate to call."

"Thank you for your help, Batya. And, thank you for being there for Hanna when she needed you."

"You are most welcome Mrs. Maassen. Hanna meant a great deal to me. I would appreciate it if you would let me know when you will be having services. God bless you."

"We will not be having services. It isn't our responsibility to bury your friend. Come along, Iryna. Stop your incessant gabbing. Let's go find the doctor."

"Wait, sir, she is your son's wife."

"Was our son's wife. Now, thankfully, she is not."

"Then, Sir, Ma'am, please sign a release so that I might claim her body. I will bury her. You can't just leave her here."

"If you so choose, then so be it. We will get a release signed."

"Thank you."

Batya shook her head and turned to go. She never saw the couple again. She could only hope that they would do the right thing by Hanna and sign the release. She waited to speak to those in charge of the morgue to see if Mr. Maassen was a man of his word.

If only there was some way to contact Don. True he didn't know about the baby when he left, but to come back and discover he had lost both his wife and child would be a terribly devastating blow. However, there was nothing she could do about it.

Later, making her way to the morgue in the basement of the hospital down dim halls and through heavy metal doors, she signed for Hanna's body in a cold sterile room and made arrangements to receive her remains in Springfield. At least there Jeffrey could perform a proper funeral service for this young Christian woman. She would arrange to have her interred in the church's cemetery.

Batya went to the office to discover the cleaning crew had done an excellent job ridding the floors of blood and the stains which would have resulted. There was no evidence whatsoever that a young woman had lost her baby and her life on the floor of B, S & J that very morning. She checked in with Matilda, who seemed to have everything well in hand. The new recruit was picking up the routine quickly and working out well. She would check in with them regularly and be sure to compensate them properly. The girls had all her numbers in case they needed anything.

Batya collected the rest of her belongings from the hotel and boarded her plane for the trip back to Nebraska. It would be good to see Sarah, Jeff, Zissa, and all her friends at church. It felt much longer than two days since she'd last seen those loved ones.

With Jakub gone, her only real connection to life and love was this wonderful group of people. She longed to hold tiny Zissa close, feel the softness of her baby fine hair, stroke her cheeks and take in the wonderful smell of her.

All the way home in the cockpit of her plane she sang

songs of praise and worship to her Lord and tried to come up with a way to tell Don of their loss when next they met. Praise God, at least she knew that Hanna resided with the Lord.

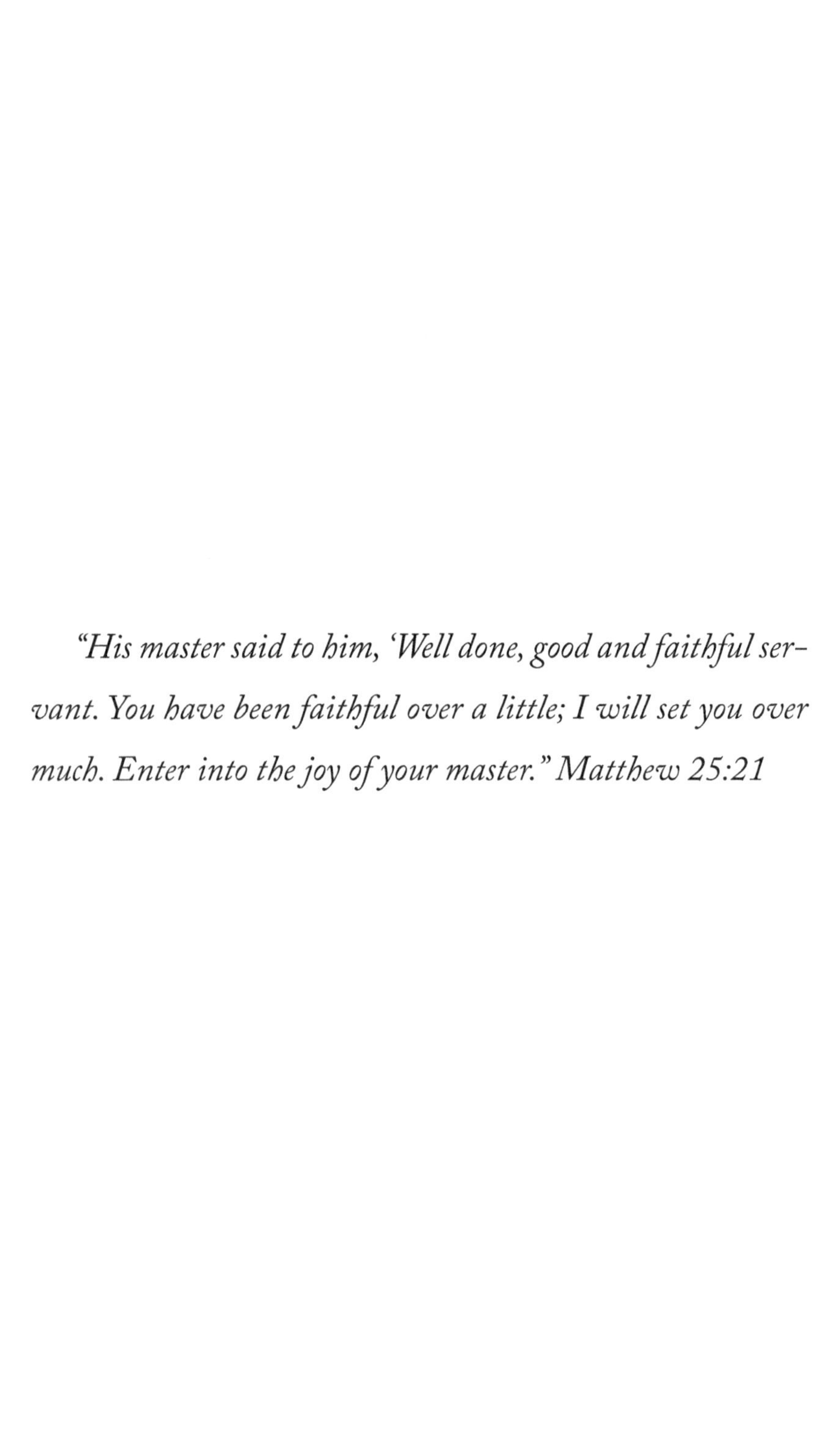

"His master said to him, 'Well done, good and faithful servant. You have been faithful over a little; I will set you over much. Enter into the joy of your master." Matthew 25:21

CHAPTER 29

After the first truce, by July 1948, the Israelis had established an air force, a navy, and a tank battalion.

Following the second truce, Czechoslovakia supplied Supermarine Spitfire fighter planes, which were smuggled to Israel via an abandoned Luftwaffe runway in Yugoslavia, with the agreement of the Yugoslav government.

Captain Novak and tail gunner Maassen took off just before dawn that warm August morning, with only a half crew of five on board.

Transporting their revamped 1937 Boeing B-17 Flying Fortress, bought with donated money raised by Schwimmer, they made their way through the cloudless skies. Jakub's co-pilot was a rookie, handpicked from the newest wave of American volunteers, that he'd met only days before the mission. Darryl was his name. But he was assured the kid knew his stuff.

They were surrounded by a squadron of Supermarine

Spitfires, escorting them over the Mediterranean until they reached the safety of Israeli air space with their smuggled aircraft.

Don was manning the essential tail gunner position, though they didn't believe they would run into much trouble on this easy delivery run, so the rest of the craft's abundant armaments were unmanned. The guys were connected by radio headphones.

Faced with one of the most beautiful sunrises any of them had ever seen they were awed by God's power and artistry even in the midst of conflict. Jakub began to pray aloud. When he was done all the men shouted, "Amen".

Don said, "That was beautiful, Boss. I wonder what Hanna is doing? I sure can't wait to get home".

"Me too my friend. Me too."

They'd just cleared the open Mediterranean and were safely in the skies over Galilee when they were suddenly surrounded by Egyptian Spitfires. A dog fight of epic proportions ensued. Surrounded by explosions and rapid machine gun fire Jakub began again to pray, suddenly wishing he'd demanded a full crew even for a so called 'simple' delivery mission.

With odds of two to one in favor of the EAF the

battle was fierce and there wasn't much the occupants of the Fortress could do without gunners for each position. Nevertheless, the IAF began to prevail. As the enemy turned tail and deserted the fight Jakub turned his head to give a thumbs up to the skeleton crew and missed seeing the rogue Spitfire coming directly at them, hell bent for glory.

The IAF, thinking they'd chased off their foe, and imagining themselves safe, had also missed their adversary worming his way back in through the escort. They'd been caught off guard. Their Egyptian opponent peppered the Flying Fortress with over a hundred rounds before Jakub could properly maneuver to safety.

Once the escort figured out what was going on, they attacked and took down the lone Spitfire, watching him arc and spin to the ground where the resulting explosion could be seen and heard for miles.

Captain Novak was having difficulty breathing. "Hey, Don, you okay back there?"

There was no response. He looked to his side to see his young co-pilot clearly dead from a wound that'd come close to removing his head. He tried to turn around far enough to see if anyone else in his crew was hurt but couldn't make the transition. Looking down he saw why. Several of the EAF rounds had made their way through his wind screen and intersected with his chest and abdomen. Which would also explain the head shot that killed his co-pilot. Oddly he didn't feel a thing. Getting his torso turned around enough to view the carnage in the rear of the plane he saw that Don and the rest of his crew were down. Judging by their various positions and the amount of blood present he guessed they were all dead but couldn't be sure. Shock began to take its toll.

Rounds from the sniper's gun had pierced the plane from front to back. He didn't have time to grieve. Sending out a May Day he was quickly surrounded by Spitfires once again. Attempting to guide him to the closest air strip, so he could put down, the squadron kept tight formation and communicated with him by radio. Jacob wasn't sure he could make it, and told the squadron commander so, but he also knew the IAF was counting on the delivery of the Fortress, so he would do his very best.

He made it to the airstrip in Tel Aviv and managed, only through apparent divine intervention, to stay conscious long enough to land the B-17. Troops entered the Fortress intent on retrieving their fellow flyers for medical aid, but all they found were bodies of the dead and the pilot, barely alive, hunched over the control panel.

Batya woke in the night, wide eyed and gasping for breath. She rose and made her way to the front room where she proceeded to call Jeff and Sarah.

"Mama, are you all right? It's the middle of the night."

"I'm sorry, Sarah, but it's your Papa. Something is wrong. I need you to pray."

"Did you hear something?"

"No, I felt it in my sleep. A tearing away. I told you I would know if your father was ever taken from me. Tonight, I feel that he is in serious danger."

"Is he dead, Mama?"

"I don't think so. At least not yet. But I believe he is badly hurt. We must lift him up in prayer. That is his only chance. We must pray and turn it over to the Lord."

"I will call the ladies from the church. They will want to help."

"Thank you, Sarah. I hope I didn't wake the baby. I'm going to come over if that's alright. I'll be quiet when I come in. I just can't be alone right now."

"Of course, Mama. I'm going to start making phone calls. I'll put some coffee on. See you soon."

Jakub woke and attempted to get his bearings. Trying to raise his head he was overcome by waves of nausea.

It appeared he was in the hospital, but where? Light green walls, sunlight streaming through the windows and clean white linens told him it was probably not an enemy base. Somehow he didn't think the Muslim hordes would treat him so kindly.

A nurse approached his room with a towel and basin. Noticing that he was awake, she smiled. "Well, Captain, it is good to see that you've decided to rejoin the living after all."

He tried to talk and choked on the tube down his throat. "Here, Sir. Don't try to speak yet. I'll get the doctor in here right away and he can remove the tube." She patted his hand and left the room.

Very soon the space was filled with white coats and scrubs. Someone removed the intubation tube, hitting his gag reflex and causing him to retch. His throat was sore. He tried to ask for water and only croaked. However, an intuitive aide brought him a cool drink. He felt a bit frantic, with way more questions than answers.

The doctor spoke. "Well, Captain Novak. We are happy that you have come back to us. We wondered if you would ever again grace us with your presence."

Croaking. "What do you mean? Where am I? What day is this?"

"Sir, you are in an Israeli hospital in Tel Aviv. The date is September 15th, 1948."

"September 15th? I've been out of it for a month?"

"I'm afraid so, Captain."

"My friend, Don Maassen?"

"I will have to let a member of the IDF speak to you, Sir. I'm afraid I don't have that information." Soon an officer joined the others in his room.

"Hello Captain Novak. I'm glad to see you back among the living. I'm Captain Adell. I've been intervening on your behalf since you arrived."

"Thank you, Captain. So, I've been here for a month. Do you know what has happened to Don Maassen? He is my friend. How about the rest of the crew on the B-17?"

"I'm very sorry for your loss, Captain, but you were the only survivor on the B-17 Fortress. I have to tell you that you are a bit of a hero around here. No one has been able to figure out how you landed that plane without the use of your legs."

"Without the use of what? My legs? What is wrong with my legs?"

"Again, I'm sorry, Captain Novak. It seems that one of the rounds of ammunition that pierced your aircraft also severed your spine. You will no longer have the use of your legs. However, we do have people here at the hospital who can help you adjust to the use of a wheelchair. You are a very lucky man. It is a miracle you are still alive."

"Yes, lucky, sure. Has anyone contacted Maassen's wife? How about my wife? Does she even know I'm alive?"

"Sir, after you were brought in, we contacted Al Schwimmer. We knew you were one of his pilot volunteers. We tried to wire both your wives, but no one was there to receive the wire at either address."

"Did anyone try to reach my daughter?"

"Sadly, Sir, none of us were privy to your daughter's address. I'm sorry."

"I would like to make arrangements to wire or call my daughter. She will know where my wife is, and my wife will know the whereabouts of Don's wife, Hanna. I must get word to them."

"Yes sir. We will take care of that right away. I will get someone in here to take down whatever message you would like to send to your wife through your daughter. I will call her myself."

"Yes Sir. Yes, she is right here. She's been staying with us, which is why there would have been no one at her address to receive a wire. Hold on, let me give her the phone."

"Yes, this is Batya Novak."

"Hello Ma'am. My name is Captain Adell."

"Hello, Captain Adell. Do you have word of my husband?"

"Yes Ma'am. I'm afraid the news is not good."

"Is he dead?"

"No ma'am, but he is badly injured."

"But, he's not dead?"

"No Ma'am. He is paralyzed. I'm afraid he will never walk again."

"Captain, as long as he is alive, we will handle the rest. Praise God he is still alive."

Arrangements were made to ship Jacob home. He played his part in the battles that ensured a free and independent Israel. Now he would face many battles of his own.

Over the next year and a half, he fought depression and feelings of worthlessness. Wishing for all the world that he'd died with his friend that day in the injured plane over Gaza. But Batya would have none of it. Almost daily she found herself spouting another of her Bubbe's sayings. This day it was, "God gave burdens, but He also gave shoulders." She prayed daily for her husband, who finally began to understand how much he was loved and that he was still a valuable part of a marriage, a family, and their business.

It all finally hit home for good the day they arrived for church and their beautiful granddaughter, two year old Zissa, fairly flew through the fellowship hall to land squarely in her Grampa's lap. The tiny, blond haired, blue eyed poppet threw her arms around his neck and said, "I love you to the moon and back, Grampa. You are my favorite." His eyes filled with tears, and he knew God had saved him for a purpose. This little angel would never lack for love.

Jesus said to him, "I am the Way, and the Truth, and The Life. No one comes to the Father except through me." John 14:6

"For by Grace you have been saved through faith. And this is not your own doing; it is the gift of God, not a result of works, so that no one may boast." Ephesians 2:8-9

"For there is no distinction between Jew and Greek; for the same Lord is Lord of all, bestowing His riches on all who call on Him. For everyone who calls on the name of the Lord will be saved." Romans 10:12-13

"Now there was a man of the Pharisees named, Nicodemus, a ruler of the Jews. This man came to Jesus by night and said to Him, Rabbi, we know that You are a teacher come from God, for no one can do these signs that You do unless God is with Him. Jesus answered him, "Truly, truly, I say to you, unless one is "born again" he cannot see the kingdom of God. Nicodemus said to Him, "How can a man be born when he is old? Can he enter a second time into his mother's womb and be born?" Jesus answered, "Truly, truly, I say to you, unless one is born of water and the Spirit, He cannot enter the kingdom of God. That which is born of the flesh is flesh, and that which is born of the Spirit is spirit. Do not marvel that I have said to you, you must be born again. The wind blows

where it wishes, and you hear its sound, but you do not know where it comes from or where it goes. So it is with everyone who is born of the Spirit." John 3:1-8

"And there is salvation in no one else, for there is no other name under heaven given among men by which we must be saved." Acts 4:12

"And when they came to him, he said to them: "You yourselves know how I lived among you the whole time from the first day that I set foot in Asia, serving the Lord with all humility and with tears and with trials that happened to me through the plots of the Jews; how I did not shrink from declaring anything that was profitable, and teaching you in public and from house to house, testifying both to Jews and to Greeks of repentance toward God and of faith in our Lord Jesus Christ. Acts 20:18-21

And I heard the voice of the Lord saying, "Whom shall I send, and who will go for us? Then I said, "Here am I! Send me." Isaiah 6:8

CHAPTER 30

Sparks seemed to fly from her blue eyes when she was angry. So much like her indomitable Bubbe. "Papa, you can't be serious. You said that last year when I graduated. You said that I should give it a year and see how I felt. I'm telling you that this is very important to me. You know I don't need your permission anymore. I'm nineteen now."

"I know Zissa. But let's be reasonable. It's so far away. You could be hurt."

"Papa, I could be hurt right here in Springfield. I've wanted to be a missionary since I was a little girl. You used to encourage me. Now you want to lock me in my room. Haven't you told me my whole life that we are supposed to be sharing the Gospel with every creature? Mom understands, why can't you?"

"Zissa, please don't disrespect your father. Yes, I understand, because this was also my dream, to be missionary to the world."

"Look at you now, Mama. You've lived in Springfield my whole life. Did you ever take Jesus to the world?"

"Zissa! I like to think that sharing Jesus with the wonderful people of Springfield, and inviting others to know Jesus right here in Nebraska, is every bit as important as sharing the Gospel in different parts of the world. Every single soul matters."

"I'm sorry, Mama. I didn't mean to make it sound like what you do isn't important. I know you and Papa do your best to be the hands and feet of the Lord wherever you go. However, the people of Israel, who are still living in darkness, are blindly searching for a Savior who landed on earth some two thousand years ago and I don't want them to miss Him, do you?"

"Of course we don't daughter. We want everyone to know the Lord. Papa, she is making perfect sense."

"There are other ways for people in Israel to hear about Jesus. Why does it have to be my daughter?"

"Papa, "How then will they call on Him in whom they have not believed? And how are they to believe in Him of whom they have never heard? And how are they to hear without someone preaching? And how are they to preach unless they are sent? As it is written, "How beautiful are the feet of those who preach the good news!" But they have not all obeyed the Gospel. For Isaiah says,

"Lord, who has believed what he has heard from us?" So faith comes from hearing, and hearing through the Word of Christ." These are words I've heard from your mouth my whole life. And now are you going to tell me that they don't apply to me, your own daughter?"

"When did you get so smart? So, it really means this much to you, Zissa?"

"Yes, Papa, it does. I know that God doesn't want to see anyone lost. Grandfather cares so much about the people of Israel that he was willing to risk his life, and lose the use of his legs, to help them. In 1948 what they needed was a pilot. In 1967 what they need is a missionary. I would like to be that missionary."

"Alright, alright. So, my daughter the missionary. You talked about a group you'd be traveling with?"

"Yes Papa. We will be leaving on Monday."

"I just hope the 22nd of May 1967 doesn't turn out to be the worst day of my life. The day I let my little girl go off into danger."

"Don't be silly, Papa."

"Jeffrey, she will be fine. Do you remember the things you were doing at nineteen years old? I do. She is strong and smart, and she knows the Word of God like the back of her hand. She loves the Lord, Papa. Have faith.”

“Well, I know we're going to be doing some double time praying, Sarah. I just hope I don't live to regret this.”

“Thank you, Papa. thank you, Mama. I promise you won't regret your decision. I will make you proud.”

“You already make us proud, Zissa, every single day. Well, I'd better make some phone calls if we're going to have a going away party on Sunday after church. There will be lots of folks upset with me if they don't get a chance to say goodbye to our missionary daughter.”

“You don't have to do that, Mama. That's a lot of work to go to at the last minute.”

“It will be fine. The weather has been beautiful, so we'll have a cookout. All the ladies can bring salads and desserts, and we'll supply the meat. Papa was going to butcher a pig soon anyway. We'll just make it a couple weeks earlier. Now, I'm going out to the office. I've got calls to make.”

“Are you okay, Papa?”

“Yeah, I'll be fine, Zissa. I'm just going to miss having you around. You've been a permanent fixture in my life for nineteen years. Who's going to help me milk the cows and the goats?”

"I'm sure some of the boys from the church would jump at the chance. I'll ask them on Sunday. Is that all you're going to miss?"

"No, of course not. But don't get me started. You don't want to see your old man blubbering, do you?"

"Oh Papa, I'm going to miss you too. Especially the fishing."

"Yeah, what about that? Who's going to be my fishing partner this summer?"

"I'm sure some of the boys from the church would jump at the chance to do that too. I'll ask around."

"It's not the same."

"I know, Papa. I won't be gone forever. Please just let me do this without feeling too guilty, alright? I love you."

"I love you too, Zissa. You'll be great. You are a natural, because you love the Lord so much. That's what the people of Israel need. Someone to share the true message of Grace with them, and I can't think of anyone better suited to doing that than you."

"Thank you, Papa. that means a lot coming from you. I will do you proud. And I will be careful."

"Good."

Papa, Mama, Grampa and Bubbe took her to the airport, for her early morning flight to Tel Aviv. Her going away party the afternoon before had alternated between joyous and sad. There were lots of well wishes from members of the congregation, and even a few small gifts. Requests for small items from the Holy land abounded, vials of oil, pieces of wood, etc. She wrote them all down, though she wasn't sure how to secure the articles.

All was silent on their drive to the air base outside Omaha. No one wanted to speak for fear that the sadness they were feeling would be instantly apparent in their voices. They were all happy for Zissa, that she was fulfilling her dreams. But they were going to miss her an awful lot.

Batya had all she could do to maintain a calm demeanor. She'd been in enough tough spots in her life to know a battle ground when she saw one. And, it seemed to her, from little reports she'd heard, that the Middle East was about to explode again. However, she kept telling herself, Zissa was a smart girl. She'd been trained well. She knew her Bible inside and out and enough martial arts to get her by. They'd all thought it a very good idea, when she was a small child, for her to take classes in taekwondo. She was always so tiny, and the ability to defend herself might come in handy one day.

At the airport Jeff pulled Grampa's wheelchair out of the car's trunk and pushed it up to the side of the vehicle. Grampa grabbed the handgrips and swung himself up and into the seat. He was always adamant about not being a burden on anyone, refusing to be fussed over. Batya was very proud of the way he had come around and the great help he was in the business and at home. No one could ever call Grampa a burden.

They entered the terminal, with Jacob carrying Zissa's bags on his lap. She checked in and her suitcases disappeared behind the counter. Her group was already gathered, so the family met and shook hands with Pastor Herman. He introduced everyone in his group, Glen, Becky, Alfred and Cindy, who would be Zissa's co-missionaries; and Zissa introduced hers. By this time she was shaking, and each of her family members felt the tremors as they hugged her goodbye.

"Aw, Zissa, weeping makes the heart grow lighter."

"Oh Bubbe. Is that another one of your own Bubbe's sayings?"

"Why yes, it is little one."

"I'm going to miss everyone so much, but I think I will miss you the most, Bubbe."

"Aw, shayna maidel, my klein ketsele. You will be in my thoughts and prayers every moment of every day until we see you again. Promise me that you will write. Once we have an address where we can write back, we will do that. And please be careful."

"I will. I love you all very much. God bless you until I see you again."

She boarded the plane. Her family stood and watched it take off, never taking their eyes off the craft as it grew smaller and smaller, until it was nothing but a tiny dot in the sky.

The mood, as they headed home, was somber.

Relations between Israel and its neighbors were not fully normalized after the 1948 Arab–Israeli War. In 1956 Israel invaded the Sinai peninsula in Egypt, with one of its objectives being the reopening of the Straits of Tiran that Egypt had blocked to Israeli shipping since

1950. Israel was eventually forced to withdraw but was guaranteed that the Straits of Tiran would remain open. A United Nations Emergency Force was deployed along the border, but there was no demilitarization agreement.

Pastor Henry and the young missionaries he traveled with had no idea the situation they were walking into when the landed in Tel Aviv. Arrangements had been made for hotels and transportation, but the group wanted to see some important sites before settling in and getting to work. All any of them could think of was that here they were, at long last, in the Holy Land!

In the months prior to June 1967, tensions became dangerously heightened. Israel reiterated its post-1956 position that the closure of the Straits of Tiran to Israeli shipping would be viewed as a declaration of war. In May Egyptian President Gamal Abdel Nasser announced that the straits would indeed be closed to Israeli vessels and then proceeded to mobilize Egyptian forces, along its border with Israel, to ensure success. On the 5th of June,

Israel launched a series of preemptive airstrikes against Egyptian airfields.

Zissa was out on the streets of Tel Aviv passing out Gospel tracts when news broke of the battles. Her group hunkered down in a nearby shelter with IDF soldiers in full battle gear. She saw an especially handsome young man across the room, and when their eyes met her face flashed crimson. She caught him looking in her direction more than once, but the soldiers were ordered back out on the streets in short order. She wasn't sure if she would ever see him again, and the thought made her sad. Much more sad than she had a right to feel per the miniscule amount of time they'd spent in the same room. She shook her head and remembered the real reason she was here in Israel.

The Egyptians were caught by surprise. The sound of explosions and gunfire rang through hills and valleys for six long days. Nearly the entire Egyptian air force was destroyed with only a small number of Israeli losses, giving the Israelis air supremacy. Simultaneously, the Israelis launched a ground offensive into the Gaza Strip and the Sinai, which again caught the Egyptians by surprise. After some initial resistance, Nasser ordered the evacuation of the Sinai. Israeli forces rushed westward in pursuit of the Egyptians, inflicting heavy losses and conquering the Sinai.

Jordan entered into a defense pact with Egypt a week before the war began; the agreement envisaged that in the event of war Jordan would not take an offensive role but would attempt to tie down Israeli forces to prevent them making territorial gains. About an hour after the Israeli air attack, the Egyptian commander of the Jordanian army was ordered by Cairo to begin attacks on Israel. In the confused situation, Jordanians were told that Egypt had repelled the Israeli air strikes. Pandemonium ensued and the Arab armies sustained heavy casualties.

Egypt and Jordan agreed to a ceasefire on June 8th, and Syria on the 9th; a ceasefire was signed with Israel on June 11th.

The Israeli success was a result of well-prepared and enacted strategy, poor leadership of the Arab states, and poor military leadership. Israel seized the Gaza Strip and the Sinai Peninsula from Egypt, the West Bank, including East Jerusalem, from Jordan and the Golan Heights from Syria. A stunning victory.

Zissa's missions group had weathered the storm. What would later be dubbed "The Six Day War" was history. It seemed all was relatively calm, for now. Back home, Jeffrey, Sarah, Jakub and Batya were concerned for her safety after hearing about the recent conflict. They insisted, through frantic letters, that she come home immediately. But Zissa wasn't done with what she felt God had called her to do. Her heart broke for what broke His. She was intent upon making a difference to those Jewish people who had, sadly and profoundly, missed the Messiah.

In the aftermath of the war, it was uncovered that Israel had crippled the Egyptian, Syrian and Jordanian militaries, having killed over 20,000 troops while losing fewer than 1,000 of its own soldiers. The tiny nation of Israel, with its population of 3,278,000; had bested the combined efforts of Egypt, Syria, Jordan and Lebanon with a total population of 48,368,000. The Arab nations were humiliated and vowed they would not rest until they'd had another opportunity to eliminate the Jews. Regardless of any signed cease fires, or attempts at peace arrangements, the combined Muslim Arab nations pledged to destroy Israel at all costs.

On June 19, 1967, the National Unity Government [of Israel] voted unanimously to return many of those fairly won spoils of war. Sinai would go back to Egypt and the Golan Heights to Syria in return for peace agreements.

Of course, the Golans would have to be demilitarized and special arrangements would be negotiated for the Straits of Tiran in the same agreements. The government also resolved to open negotiations with King Hussein of Jordan regarding the Eastern border.

The Israeli decision was supposed to be conveyed to the Arab nations by the United States of America. The U.S. was informed of the decision, but, apparently not that it was to transmit the decision. The Khartoum Arab Summit resolved that there would be "no peace, no recognition and no negotiation with Israel".

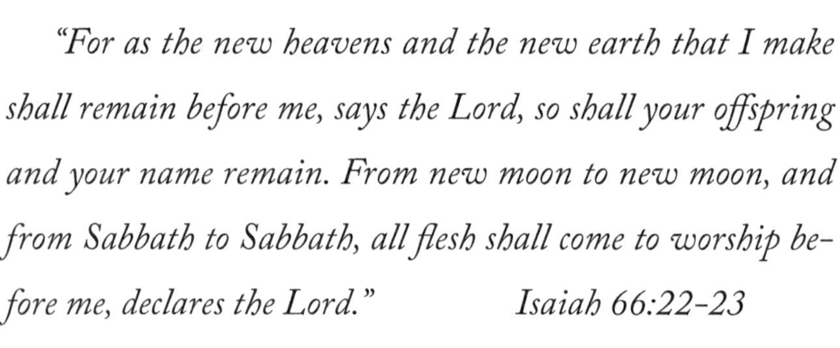

"For as the new heavens and the new earth that I make shall remain before me, says the Lord, so shall your offspring and your name remain. From new moon to new moon, and from Sabbath to Sabbath, all flesh shall come to worship before me, declares the Lord."   Isaiah 66:22-23

CHAPTER 31

Zissa and her co-missionaries were back out on the streets of Israeli cities by the end of June. Their ongoing battle was to win souls for the Kingdom of God through the mighty Name of Jesus. Their only ammunition was an abundance of love and a handful of Gospel tracts.

Many walked past them without a second glance; some argued semantics, and Zissa was even spat upon by one unpleasant fellow. But several of those who'd spent their lives searching for answers that Judaism didn't offer, stopped to listen. Zissa was knowledgeable concerning Old and New Testament scripture and shared that blessed information in a most convincing way. Soon, at the behest of Pastor Herman, she was offering sermons on the streets for any who would hear the Truth.

It was so hot on that last day of June, in 1967 that Zissa was having a hard time swallowing her own saliva through her parched throat. Water didn't seem to help, even in large quantities. The air was so dry it sucked the life-giving liquid right out of her body, in wicked away perspiration, the second it entered. It seems that perspective is everything.

What she wouldn't give, right now, for Nebraska's humid farmlands. Yes, the same humidity she'd complained about every single day of every single summer of her whole life. Rational thought was nearly impossible as the noonday sun beat relentlessly down on their heads, but she dutifully smiled and handed a Gospel tract to each and every passerby.

Positioned in the ancient city of Ashkelon that week, for their missionary outreach, she'd been able to do a little exploring the day before. Ashkelon was the oldest and largest seaport in Canaan, and part of the pentapolis (a grouping of five cities) of the Philistines, north of Gaza and south of Jaffa. She was astonished at the amount of history packed into these amazing streets and buildings. If only they were able to speak, she could only imagine the stories they would tell.

The larger missions group split in two earlier in the day to cover more territory. Zissa was posted with Becky and Cindy, on the South side, while the three fellows were way over on the other end of the city. Waves of heat caused mirages of various shapes and sizes to appear at every turn in the molten streets, which was probably the biggest reason she missed all the obvious warning signs. Their group had been cautioned about terrorist activity, linked to the PLO (Palestinian Liberation Organization) in the area, upon first arriving in Israel. However, not talking to strangers would defeat the entirety of their mission here. So, they'd spent considerable time in various parts of towns that were not considered particularly safe.

Through the undulating pockets of heat around her she saw a group of men approaching and readied herself, with her best smile, to share the Gospel. By the time the men were within ten feet of the group, and Zissa recognized the Palestinian Liberation Army camouflage they wore and the very serious looking rifles they carried, it was too late to attempt an escape.

Since its inception on May 28th, 1964 the PLO, and its essential offshoot the Palestinian Liberation Army had one goal, and only one goal. The total destruction of the nation of Israel and the "liberation of Palestine". Never mind that Israelis and their supporters worldwide knew the land in question was a covenant gift from the God of the Bible to the Israelites. The PLO believed that covenant to be a lie, and the Israeli people usurpers of Palestine's rightful land. They would achieve their goal by any and all destructive means necessary, down to the outright murder of every Jew in the occupied territory.

Paramilitary factions of the PLO employed guerilla warfare tactics from bases in Jordan, Syria, Lebanon and within Israel to attack Israeli military and civilian targets. Some ultra-militant groups are responsible for terrorist practices, including kidnappings, assassinations, bombings and the like. The men surrounding the young missionaries were obviously a part of those ultra-militant groups.

Binding, blindfolding and gagging the ladies, the PLO terrorists forced them into a nearby hidden underground passageway. Tunnels weren't a new route into Israel, especially near the Gaza strip. Like rats, enemies had been burrowing into the city for centuries. Some tunnels had been discovered over the years and summarily destroyed, but there were always others, new and improved. Some had electricity! Used to bring in cars, cows, cigarettes, gasoline and whatever else you could imagine, the passages were commonly called smuggling tunnels.

The military said weapons, Israeli uniforms, plastic handcuffs, and tranquilizers had been found in tunnels. Tools for both potential attacks and potential kidnappings.

Several civilians witnessed the abduction of the American missionaries, but felt powerless to do anything more than report the incident. A team was hastily assembled to rescue the unfortunate young ladies.

The girls were pushed, pulled and shoved through what felt like miles of underground passages; tripping, falling and being yanked back up by rough hands; slapped and clubbed until their heads were spinning, Cindy broke down sobbing uncontrollably. However, the only recognition she received for her efforts was another slap to the face. A blow so hard it resonated throughout the length of the tunnel and instantly silenced her cries.

At the end of their underground journey they were shoved headlong into a cement chamber and left on the hard floor. Determining that they were finally alone, Zissa took over. "Now, settle down girls. We've got to get free."

"What if they come back?"

"What if they do? Becky, whether they come back and find us tied, or not tied, we are still their prisoners. We must figure out where we are and see if there's a way out. I have an idea." They backed up to each other, until their fingers were touching, and untied the ropes binding their hands. Once their hands were free, they removed their blindfolds and gags.

"So, what do we do now?"

"Becky, you check over there, and Cindy over there. I'm going to check around here. Try to locate any cracks or openings, also look for anything that might be used as a weapon. Let's find out if there is any possible way of escape. There must be a way out."

"What if they catch us?"

"Cindy, stop. Do you honestly think their intentions regarding us will be any different if we sit here like sniveling cowards in the corner of the room? God is with us. I am convinced of that. And we have been given the intelligence we need to figure our way out, so let's use the brains he gave us for something besides irrational blubbering, okay?"

"Okay, Zissa. I'll try."

Searching the room proved unsuccessful. However,

through a small crack in the doorway, which was their only source of light, Zissa was able to watch some of the goings on of the men who'd kidnapped them. She didn't understand their language, but there was no mistaking the rifles they carried. She prayed, "Father God, I know that you are aware of our every breath, that you know the number of hairs on our heads, and the end from the beginning. I don't know these men's intentions toward us, but You do. I trust You Lord. Set us free from this place, Lord, to further serve You. In Jesus' Name and for Your glory. Amen."

For three days Zissa, Becky and Cindy were imprisoned in the murky, cement room. Scorpions and other creatures skittered across their feet in the dark, but God kept them, and the vermin didn't bite or sting. Zissa knew that God protected them from even that.

They could only assume they were being held for ransom, though how these men would have known who to contact was beyond them. No one brought them food or water and they grew weaker by the day. They relieved themselves in the far corner of the space, until there was nothing left to relieve, but had no way to clean themselves up. They prayed together and they slept, if you could call it that, huddled together on the hard floor.

On their fourth day of imprisonment they woke to the usual sounds of their captors going about their day, spreading their prayer rugs on the floor and praying to Allah, when suddenly, the sound of gunfire erupted in the hallways outside their cell. A cacophony of men yelling and explosions erupting that sent dust rushing through the crack in their door. The girls huddled at the back of the room, to escape the possibility of stray bullets finding them. The door burst open and they, who had been confined to the dark for days, were completely blinded by the light suddenly filling the room.

Men ran into the room and picked the girls up, cradling them in their arms, to turn and make their way back through the prison compound with their rescued lady warriors of God. The men were IDF and the girls were saved. The only remaining obstacle was the tunnel and the likelihood of booby traps there. They made their way carefully, only occasionally stopping to fight off a smattering of PLA troops sent to intercept the group. Once through the underground passage the tunnel was destroyed, taking out any possibility of further immediate use along with a few remaining PLO stragglers and the girls were taken to the nearest hospital.

Zissa woke in a bed surrounded by clean sheets and sunlight and she smiled. Turning her head, she saw a handsome young man. The one she'd noticed in the bomb shelter all those weeks ago. He was sitting in a chair near her bed. Her face flashed crimson again and he smiled at her obvious embarrassment. "I just wanted to be sure you were okay."

"I'm fine. Can I assume it is thanks to you?"

"There were six of us on the mission. Several civilians saw your abduction by PLA soldiers and called in to report. Their directions were clear enough to give us a good indication of where you were taken. We've suspected another tunnel in that area for some time now, but this incident gave it away. That passage has been completely destroyed. Well, at least for a while. I have no doubt there will be new ones."

"I don't understand why we were taken."

"The PLO kidnaps to extract ransom from the families of their victims. It's another way to fund their terror activities."

"Well, I'm sure they would have been very disappointed if they tried to extract ransom from my family. My

Papa is a pastor and my parents don't have any money."

"A pastor? Is that why you're here?"

"Truly, my parents didn't want me to come. But, I'm here to share Jesus with the Jewish people."

"I've actually been doing some Bible study myself, mostly out of curiosity. I have several friends who've converted to Christianity. I'd love to ask you some questions some time."

"I would love to answer them, at least to the best of my ability. Are you an Israeli citizen? I only ask because your English is so excellent. By the way, I don't know your name. Mine is Zissa."

"What a lovely name, Zissa. Mine is Don. I am a duel national. An American citizen, and also an Israeli national. I was born in America, but because I grew up here, I applied and became a duel citizen. I spent a great deal of time, while I was growing up, in America as well. I'm back in Israel to serve for two and a half years in the IDF. I thought every able-bodied citizen should serve, with such a limited population able to do that, so here I am doing my part."

"Well, I'm certainly glad you were serving. I owe you my life. Please, tell me a little more about yourself."

" I was originally brought to Israel by my grandparents after my mother died in childbirth; and my father was killed during the 1948-49 Arab Israeli war. The grandparents have been back in the U.S for a couple of years now. My grandfather would be angry if he knew I was studying to become a Messianic Jew, or even talking to a Christian about it at all. But, I'm nineteen now and I suppose what he doesn't know won't hurt him."

"That is fascinating. I am also nineteen. I believe I shared that my Papa is a Christian preacher, but my Mama, Grampa and Bubbe are all Messianic Jews. Bubbe was born in Ukraine, Mama and Grampa in Poland. They are all survivors of the Nazi concentration camps. My Grampa Jakub flew as a volunteer for the IAF during Israel's fight for independence. He was shot and paralyzed. He's been in a wheelchair my whole life. I've never seen him any other way."

Just then a group of people burst into the room. It was Mama, Papa, Bubbe and Grampa, with a nurse scurrying in right behind them. Where did they come from? How did they get all the way to Israel? And why were they here?

"Mama, Papa, what are you doing here?"

"Where else would we be, Zissa? We were already concerned after the six day war, but then, when we got the call from Pastor Herman about your abduction we made arrangements to fly here as soon as possible. We just found out you were safe when we landed. We wanted to come and talk to you in person to find out how you are. We are actually hoping we can change your mind. We'd like you to come home with us. This has all become very dangerous and frankly we don't think you should stay."

"Mama, you know how I feel. I'm not ready to leave this place. I feel as though God has put me here for a reason. After this latest incident, I'm convinced all the more that I need to stay here to share the Gospel."

"She's just as stubborn as her mama."

"And her papa for that matter."

The entire time Zissa was talking to her mom, Grampa was staring, rather rudely she thought, at Don who was sitting in the chair beside her bed. "Grampa, you're staring. This is Don. He is the IDF soldier who saved me from the PLO." By now, Bubbe was staring too.

"I'm so sorry. I didn't mean to stare, but you look like someone I used to know. His name was Don also. You wouldn't, by any chance, be related to Donald Maassen would you?"

"Yes sir, Donald was my father. He was killed....."

"Yes, son, I know. I am Jacob Novak. The man who was flying the plane the day your father was killed. He was a brave man and a good friend."

"Don, I'm Batya Novak. We didn't know you existed. I was with your mother the day she died. Your grandparents came to the hospital, so the doctors wouldn't give me any further information on the condition of Hanna's child. I thought you had died that day also, right along with your mother. Your grandparents didn't want the responsibility of burying your mom, so I claimed her body. She is buried in the small cemetery behind our church in Nebraska."

"I never knew any of this, Ma'am. My grandparents never spoke of my mother. Only of my father. Obviously, I'm named after him. They took me back and forth from Israel to New York, and other than for my schooling I wasn't allowed out of the house much. This is one of the many reasons I chose to serve in the IDF. I wanted a chance to be out on my own, to see and do more. I've been here in Israel on my own for a little over a year now."

"I can't believe it. Don has a son. You are the spitting

image of your father, Don."

"I can't believe I didn't know any of this Bubbe."

"Why would we have spoken of such things to you, Zissa. There was no need. Now we know and we are very happy indeed, to know that Hanna and Don have a son and he is alive."

"I should go and leave you to visit with your family."

"No, don't be silly. Even thought we just met you, Don, this feels like family. Stay. We will all get better acquainted."

By the time the family was ready to leave for the airport three days later, Don and Zissa were gazing across the room at each other in the same loving way Jakub and Batya, and then Jeffrey and Sarah, had done all those years ago. Her Bubbe smiled at the memories which filled her mind.

Zissa stayed in Israel, sharing the Gospel and answering Don's questions. He soon trusted Jesus as Savior and Lord, turning his life over to the Prince of Peace.

Don served his remaining time in the IDF and then joined Zissa's missionary efforts, sharing the Gospel with lost Jews in Israel. They eventually married and the whole family came back to Israel for the wedding. Even Don's grandparents made the trip. They didn't want to miss another opportunity.

Don and Zissa named their beautiful, blond haired, blue eyed baby girl, Hanna, after Don's mother. The name, translated, means Grace. They were truly blessed indeed.

POSTLUDE

"Now the Lord said to Abram, Go from your country and your kindred and your father's house to the land that I will show you. And I will make of you a great nation, and I will bless you and make your name great, so that you will be a blessing. I will bless those who bless you, and him who dishonors you I will curse, and in you all the families of the earth shall be blessed." Genesis12:1-3

As I researched history in order to write this book, I discovered things about my own family I'd never known. Issues involving anti-Semitism and events leading to the Holocaust, had always been of interest to me, as I knew Polish Jews were a part of our heritage on my paternal grandmother's side. However, I wasn't aware, until recently, that a number of our distant relatives died in Treblinka ll. This fact made my journey through "Steppes to the Cross", a much more personal one.

As with all my works of fiction, I have taken the characters in, "Steppes to the Cross", through a journey that leads to Christ. Because, let's face it, without Jesus there is nothing. I hope you found this tale of redemption to be one also of inspiration.

I have been asked whether I believe that Jews, who are God's chosen people, must trust Jesus as Savior and Lord to achieve heaven. Or if, as some believe, they are exempt from that gesture of faith and will automatically go to heaven upon death, due to their distinction as His chosen. I don't find any New Testament scripture to back up a claim of exemption. Quite the opposite. Once Jesus came to earth to show us that He alone is The Way, The Truth, and The Life, there is no other way.

However, just to be clear, God is not a man that He should lie. Once He has declared a people as His chosen, His word does not change. So I also believe the words of Genesis 12:1-3. If we as a people, a nation, a country, bless Israel, we as a nation and a people will reap a blessing. Conversely, if we as a nation and a people continue to curse Israel, we will reap curses upon our country.

I find it ironic that the world vilifies the country of Israel, punishing her with economic strife using Boycott, Divestment and Sanctions (BDS) and other means; accuses her of bullying other countries; and makes her out to be the bad guy in every skirmish she is engaged in with the countries surrounding her.

Have you ever looked at the numbers, to see how ridiculous those claims are?

The country of Israel. A Jewish nation of 8,900,000. Surrounded by majority Muslim nations in every direction: Lebanon, Syria, Egypt, Jordan, Palestine, Iraq, Iran, Turkey, Afghanistan, Pakistan and U.A.E.; with a combined population of 598,418,000, over a half billion people.

Let that really sink in. The combined population of Israel's enemies; people who have vowed to wipe her off the face of the earth, have denied her, over and over, the right to exist, and attack her on a whim at every opportunity; is a number more than 67 times the population of Israel.

The world media, and the U.N. have attempted, over the years, to lay the blame for conflict in the Middle East squarely at the feet of the Jewish nation. However, time and again solutions have been brought as a path to peace. An opportunity to set up a two-nation state. Each time this happens it is the Arab nations who refuse to comply, not the nation of Israel. Their enemies will simply never be happy until every last vestige of a free and independent Israel is erased from the planet.

As followers of the Lord Jesus Christ we must stand for Israel. It is our right and duty to call her legitimate. We must declare her blessed. And we must not allow the world to disavow that which the Lord has declared consecrated.

God bless God's chosen people. All of us!

GLOSSARY OF WORDS AND TERMS

* Bar Mitzvah = The end result of a boy's study, to become a young man, responsible for God's commandments. At the age of thirteen, and after appropriate study, he is declared a Bar Mitzvah. Before that age (12 for girls - Bat Mitzvah) the child's parents are responsible for his actions.

* Bedeken = Yiddish for a ceremony in which the groom looks at his bride and then veils her face; signifying that his love for her is for her inner beauty, and that they are two distinct individuals even after marriage. Many believe this tradition originates from the fact that Jacob was tricked by Laban into marrying Leah instead of Rachel by the wearing of a veil.

* Beibi = A Yiddish word, meaning: baby.

* Bubbe = A Yiddish word, meaning: Grandmother.

* Bubkes = A Yiddish word, meaning: nothing more than a hill of beans; or, amounting to goat droppings;

nothing.

* Challah = Jewish, kosher, Sabbath and holiday bread.

* Chatan = Jewish word for groom.

* Chuppah = The covering under which Jewish couples marry. It is comprised of four corners and a roof, signifying the home they intend to build together. The canopy is often made of tallits belonging to family members.

* Dankbar = A Yiddish word, meaning: thankful.

* Derfele = A Yiddish word, meaning: child.

* Dreydal = Small spinning tops. Often given as token gifts at Hanukkah celebrations.

* Eiderdown = A filled comforter or quilt.

* Eltern = A Yiddish word, meaning: parents.

* Haganah = A Hebrew word, meaning: (Hebrew: הַהֲגָנָה) The Defense. This was the main paramilitary organization of the Jewish Yishuv in Mandatory Palestine between 1920 and 1948, which later became the core of the Israel Defense Forces (IDF).

* Hanukkah (Chanukah) = Is a Jewish festival commemorating the rededication of the second Temple in Jerusalem at the time of the Maccabean Revolt against the Seleucid Empire. It is also known as the Festival of Lights. Hanukkah is observed for eight nights and days,

starting on the 25th day of Kislev according to the Hebrew calendar, which may occur at any time from late November to late December in the Gregorian calendar. The festival is observed by lighting the candles of a candelabrum with nine branches, called a menorah (or hanukkiah). One branch is typically placed above or below the others and its candle is used to light the other eight candles. this unique candle is called the 'Shamash'. Each night, one additional candle is lit by the 'Shamash' until all eight candles are lit together on the last night of the festival.

* Heymish = A Yiddish word, meaning: homey and cozy, unpretentious.

* Horah = A traditional Israeli dance.

* Judenrat = "Jewish council" A Judenrat was a World War II administrative agency imposed by Nazi Germany on Jewish communities across occupied Europe, principally within the ghettos, including those of German-occupied Poland. The Germans required Jews to form a *Judenrat* in every community across the occupied territories.

The *Judenrat* constituted a form of self-enforcing intermediary, used by the Nazi administration to control larger Jewish communities. In some ghettos, such as the Łódź, or Warsaw Ghettos, and in the Theresienstadt and Bergen-Belsen concentration camps, the Germans called the councils "Jewish Council of Elders" While the origin of the term *Judenrat* is unclear, Jewish communities themselves had established councils for self-government as early as the Middle Ages.

* Kabbalat panim = Pre wedding reception, at which the Tena'im (engagement contract) may be read.

* Kallah = Jewish word for bride.

* Kasha = Buckwheat. A grain most important to Jews in the region.

* Katubah = A Jewish prenuptial marriage contract, signed in front of two witnesses before the marriage ceremony begins.

* Ketsele = A Yiddish term of endearment, meaning: little kitten.

* Kiddush = A Yiddish word, meaning: cup for wine.

* Kiddushin/ erusin = A Hebrew word, meaning: betrothal. When the groom gives the bride a ring, or other object of value, with the intent of creating a marriage together.

* Kittel = A Yiddish word, meaning: white frock worn

by the groom under the wedding chuppah.

* Klein = A Yiddish word, meaning: small.

* Kosher = A Hebrew word, meaning: fit or proper as it relates to Jewish dietary law. Kosher foods are permitted to be eaten, and can be used as ingredients in the production of additional food items.

* Kvell = A Yiddish word, meaning: to express great pleasure and pride, such as when a grandparent is proud of a grandchild.

* Levaya = (funeral) The act of accompanying someone to their final resting place.

* Mama loshon = A Yiddish term, meaning: mother tongue.

* Mazel Tov = Congratulations!

* Menorah = Hebrew for lamp, the menorah generally refers to either a seven-branched golden candelabra that was lit every day in the Tabernacle, or the eight- flamed lamp that is lit on the eight nights of the Jewish holiday of Hanukkah.

* Mensch = A Yiddish word, meaning: a good man, a person of integrity.

* Mevushal wine = A Yiddish phrase, meaning: boiled wine. Once the kosher wine is boiled it will retain its ko-

sher state, even if served by a non-Jew.

* Meyn lib = A Yiddish term, meaning: my love.

* Mishpocha = A Yiddish word, meaning: family, extended family or a family network, which can also include close friends.

* Nissuin = The Jewish word for marriage, when the couple begins their life together.

* Nosh = A Yiddish word, meaning: to have a light snack.

* Pale = The Pale of the Settlement was an area between the Baltic and the Black Sea, originally formed in 1791 by Russia's Catherine II, concerning her extreme distaste for a certain people group, in which to contain the Jews and keep them confined to restricted areas. Later, the concentration of Jews, coupled with Tsar Alexander III's fierce hatred of the Jews (believing that they had been involved in the assassination of his father Tsar Alexander II) made them easy targets for pogroms and anti-Jewish riots by the majority population. These attacks continued until the dissolution of the settlements. The Pale was done away with in 1917, during the Russian Revolution. At its height, the Pale held around five million Jews. Within these confines the Jew could live,

but could not own land, and was allowed to farm, or follow other career paths such as merchant, or artisan.

* Palmach = A Hebrew word, meaning (Hebrew: פלמ"ח), acronym for Plugot Maḥatz (Hebrew: פלוגות מחץ), "storm troops". The Palmach was the elite fighting force of the Haganah, the underground army of the Yishuv (Jewish community) during the period of the British Mandate for Palestine. The Palmach was established on 15 May 1941.

* Pogrom = An organized massacre of a particular ethnic group, in particular that of Jews in Russia or eastern Europe.

* Privy = An outhouse, or outdoor bathroom without running water.

* Saba = A Yiddish word, meaning: grandfather.

*Sabbath = The weekly Jewish holy day, which takes place from nightfall on Friday until nightfall on Saturday.

*Schlep = A Yiddish word, meaning to drag, or lug something. To pull awkwardly, or carry with difficulty.

* Shabbat = The traditional Jewish day of worship, which, according to halakha (Jewish religious law), is observed from a few minutes before sunset on Friday evening until the appearance of three stars in the sky on

Saturday night. Shabbat is ushered in by lighting candles and reciting a blessing.

* Shamash = The ninth candle on the menorah. Typically used to light the other eight candles for the 'Festival of Lights'.

* Shashka = Midway between a full saber and a straight sword, the weapon has a slightly curved blade, and can be effective for both slashing and thrusting. This weapon is carried in a wooden scabbard which encloses part of the hilt and is worn on the soldier's side.

* Shayna maidel = A Yiddish term, meaning: pretty girl.

* Shayna punim = A Yiddish term, meaning: pretty face.

* Shepping nachas = (Scooping up nachas) A Yiddish term, meaning: the joy you feel over the accomplishments of someone close to you.

* Sheva B'rachot = The seven blessings spoken over a cup of wine, to a couple at their wedding.

* Shiva = Is the week-long mourning period in Judaism for first degree relatives. The ritual is referred to as 'sitting shiva'.

* Shtetl = A little town in the Pale of Settlement.

Usually comprised entirely, or mostly of Jews.

* Shtick = A Yiddish word, meaning: anything a person is known for - a part of who he is.

* Sonderkommando = Jewish concentration camp prisoners compelled by Nazis to act as slave labor at Nazi run death camps.

* Stipa = A tall plumed feather grass native to the steppes.

* Straw tick = A loose fabric pouch filled with straw (or for the wealthy, feathers) and used as a sort of mattress.

* Tallit = Jewish prayer shawl.

* Tena'im = A Jewish engagement contract.

* Tanakh = The Hebrew Bible.

* Tsar = Before the Russian Revolution the country was ruled by powerful monarchs called Tsars. The Tsar had total power in Russia. He commanded the army, owned most of the land and even controlled the church. Tsar Nicholas II was the last Emperor to sit on the throne.

* Tzedakah = The Jewish religious tradition of charity. A sophisticated system of volunteer Jewish social welfare organizations developed to meet the needs of the population. No province in the Pale had less than 14% of

Jews on relief, and in some provinces the numbers were as high as 22%, so this was a very important piece of the struggle to survive. Offering everything from food, to medical care, to clothing for poor students, the charitable organizations were a necessity in the poor populations.

* Velkhed = A Yiddish word, meaning: welcome.

* Voronkov = A Jewish Shtetl approximately thirty two miles SE of Kiev, on the left side of the Dneiper River.

* Yarmulke = A Yiddish word, meaning: brimless cap, usually made of cloth, worn by male Jews to fulfill the customary requirement held by Orthodox halachic authorities that the head be

covered. In non Yiddish speaking communities the yarmulke can also be called a kippa.

* Yeshiva = A learning institution where Jewish boys learn the Talmud and the Torah through daily lectures and classes called, shiurim, and with the help of study pairs called, chavrutas.

* Yichud = A special time in a special room, usually lasting ten to twenty minutes, for the newly married couple to bond and spend time together between the wed-

ding ceremony and the festivities.

* Yiddish = A language comprised by the mixing of several key languages, mainly German, Hebrew, and Slavic. It was considered the language of daily life, the 'home' language. And, it was looked down on by the Russians who heard it, but also largely not understood, thereby allowing those Jews who used it to retain some sense of individualism from their Russian neighbors.

Yishuv = A Hebrew word, meaning: (Hebrew: בושי) Literally "settlement" or Ha-Yishuv (the *Yishuv*, Hebrew: בושיה) or Ha-*Yishuv* Ha-Ivri (the Hebrew Yishuv, Hebrew: ירבעה בושיה) is the body of Jewish residents in the land of Israel (corresponding to Ottoman Syria until 1917, OETA South 1917–1920 and later Mandatory Palestine 1920–1948)

* Zeiskeit = A Yiddish word, meaning: Sweetness, or sweet one.

* Zionist = A supporter of Zionism; a person who believes in the development and protection of a Jewish nation in what is now Israel.

www.ingramcontent.com/pod-product-compliance
Lightning Source LLC
Chambersburg PA
CBHW060742210726
48292CB00012B/60